Raising the Bar

AVERY KANE

KISSINGSHARK PUBLICATIONS

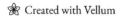

One

"Who dat?"

I stilled, my eyes drifting to Carly Crawford, and stared. It wasn't that I didn't understand the question. The context felt somehow off. "Excuse me?"

Carly, she of the light and bubbling laugh and blond hair that was almost white, giggled like an annoying twelve-year-old who had just discovered boys. "That's a thing we say in New Orleans. It's because of the Saints."

I blinked again and waited.

"I'm done talking," she said finally, a ruddy color overtaking her cheeks. "Like... *done* done, and I wish I hadn't said anything in the first place."

That had me smiling, although it took effort. "I'm familiar with the saying. I came from Michigan. We have football there."

Carly's face was blank. "You do?"

I couldn't blame her for being confused. "Yes, they're called the Lions... and they're perpetually bad. Whenever we play the Saints, we get our asses kicked."

"Oh, right." She nodded like she understood, but I knew

better. She was a nice girl, but sometimes I pictured her having a perpetual bubble machine inside her head.

I bit back a sigh and turned to survey my new kingdom. Cher. That was the name of the bar—and not after the singer. The moniker stemmed from the rich French history of the area. The Cajuns and Creoles who inhabited the neighborhoods often called me *cher*, which meant dear, and I found I liked it. I thought it was the perfect name for a bar, even though I'd gotten pushback from my new boss, Arnie Templeman. He lived in Atlanta, though, and basically allowed me to do whatever I wanted... within reason. So Cher it was. We just had to wait to see if the tourists would be as partial to the name as I am.

"Moxie."

I ran my hands over the freshly renovated bar. It wasn't new. Although when I took over the relaunch for the establishment—previously called Cajun Critters and featuring slimy crawfish shots that made my stomach threaten to revolt just thinking about them—the bar had needed a desperate overhaul. The previous owners hadn't taken care of the beautiful oak centerpiece even though it dominated the space. That meant I had to hire someone to come in and sand it, paint it, and make it the beautiful showpiece it was always meant to be. It was my crowning glory.

"Moxie."

"Did you say something?" Slowly, I turned my attention back to Carly. She was staring at me in such a way that I figured I'd missed something.

"I just said your name." Carly flashed a smile, but there was something vacant about it. "What kind of a name is Moxie anyway? That can't be your real name."

It wasn't. My real name was disturbing. Well, at least I was disturbed by it. It was also something I never spoke aloud. I figured it was like the Candyman. If I said it three times, death and destruction would follow. I picked it as a name and legally changed to it almost a year ago, I replied automatically. "It's not my birth name."

"What's your real name?"

"I don't speak of it." Never. Ever. Wasn't going to happen.

"Oh, come on." Carly unleashed the whiny, wheedling voice that had become her trademark. If I had to guess, she trotted it out when she was trying to get something from her parents. If I remembered her application correctly, they lived in Marigny and attended church regularly. Yes, she actually included that on her résumé. Carly struck me as the sort of girl who constantly manipulated those around her to get what she wanted, and if she believed regular church attendance would flip the switch in her direction, she wasn't afraid to throw it out there.

I liked her despite the realization.

That wasn't going to work on me though. No, Moxie Stone couldn't be manipulated. That was one of the things I was most proud of. "I don't tell anyone my real name." I smiled, but it was more feral than friendly. "I picked Moxie because... well... it fit me."

"If you say so." Carly didn't look impressed. She also appeared to be losing interest. "That must be a Michigan thing, kind of like when you got so excited about those mushrooms in the pasta that guy was selling on the street corner. You made all those squealing noises I didn't know you were capable of making."

I had to bite back a snarky retort. In truth, I was always biting back snarky retorts. Sometimes, I lost my cool and let it fly—I almost always regretted it—but since I was the boss at Cher, determined to make the Bourbon Street freshman contender a success, I couldn't start by pitching a snarky fit.

"Those are called morels. They're popular in Michigan."

"Do they make you see things?"

It took me a moment to realize what she was referring to. "No, they do not."

"That's a bummer." Carly continued as if she weren't treading on thin ice during a Michigan spring. "My cousin Connor did mushrooms once. I think there was a special name for them. Anyway, he got really stoned and then walked around Jackson Square telling everybody he was Andrew Jackson reincarnated. I think he thought that would impress the tourists."

"I take it people weren't impressed."

"Yeah, not so much. Since Jackson owned slaves, he's not the most popular guy these days."

"Then why did your cousin pretend to be him?"

"I think it had something to do with the statue."

I waited, confused.

"The statue in Jackson Square," she pressed. "It's Andrew Jackson. There's a plaque."

"Oh." Honestly, I hadn't been able to do as much touring in the city as I would've liked. I'd been in town for a full month, recruited after launching one of the most popular restaurants in southeastern Michigan and making a name for myself in the bar industry, but I'd been focused on my job above all else. I'd been in Jackson Square numerous times, but I'd never paid attention to the statue plaque. "Well, as long as there's a reason." I offered up a shrug and then went back to staring at the bar. "Run it down for me."

This wasn't the first time I'd said the words to Carly. She wasn't in a position of authority, but oddly enough she was thrilled to help. She said she wanted to learn the bar industry from me because I was an expert. That was her word, not mine. I was more than happy to teach her... as long as she helped me in return.

"Sure." She enthusiastically bobbed her head. "Let me grab the list."

I loved a to-do list, although I would never admit that. It made me seem too rigid. I'd learned a long time ago that people with lists made other people nervous, and in a city as laid-back as New Orleans, that wasn't a good thing.

At all.

"Here we go." Carly took a bracing breath. "We have four bartenders on the first shift. We're expecting a run because of all the free-drink tickets that have been dropped off at the hotels over the past week. We'll also have four waitresses on the floor."

I nodded as I did the math. The space wasn't overly large, but everything I'd heard about NOLA, the city that partied twenty-four seven, was that nobody enforced the capacity numbers. Technically, we were allowed to have a hundred people in the space at any given time. I was expecting to triple that number. Thankfully, the front windows opened outward and were big enough to serve as doors. That would allow people to spill out onto the street and also conveniently find their way back inside to fall in love with our ambiance and drinks all over again.

"What about the signature drinks?" I asked, turning my mind back to the business at hand. "We're sticking with the main three tonight, right?"

Carly bobbed her head. "Yup. We've got Sazerac, hurricanes of three different colors and flavors, and the Vieux Carré."

I pressed my lips together. I'd gone over the drink menu myself and settled on these specific cocktails for launch day. We were going to be swimming in people and couldn't spread ourselves too thin. There would be beer for people who didn't like hard liquor, wine for the lightweights, and signature cocktails for everybody else.

"Tell me about the music," I prompted, my busy brain a

myriad of frenzied images slipping together in a beautiful yellow, green, and purple tapestry.

"We went with Jimmy LeBlanc." Carly was all business as she ticked information off her list. "His band is the Powdered Beignets, but we've asked him not to announce that because it's lame and we left it off the fliers."

I made a face. Perhaps I was used to the music scene in Detroit—yes, there's a thriving music scene in the Motor City —but nobody would be caught dead headlining a band named the Powdered Beignets. Of course, the name was still better than the Jumbo Gumbos, who had also auditioned. I was still shuddering at that one.

"What time are they arriving?" I asked, my eyes flicking to the clock on the wall. It was almost eleven. We would open in five minutes. Then we would see if all my hard work was worth it or for naught.

"They'll be here at five o'clock," Carly replied, stilling. "Are you sure that wasn't a mistake? Shouldn't we always have live music?"

I shook my head. "Bourbon Street is full of live music, so much so that it spills into every building. It's not really a draw here unless you're going for an upscale vibe. We want to be friendly and approachable. That means one three-hour music set a night. It's better to use our budget on something other than live music in this neighborhood."

Carly didn't look convinced. "Most of the bars around here tout live music."

"Actually, only 50 percent of the bars tout live music." I knew because I'd canvassed the strip myself. I was familiar with what was working and what wasn't. "Not everybody likes live music. Some people hate it. This way, we'll appeal to both crowds."

"Oh." Carly's lips puckered out into a pretty little purse. "I didn't really think about that. You're right though. My

6

father absolutely hates live music. My mother says that's because he was shell-shocked during the war. I've never really thought about it."

I arched an eyebrow as I regarded her. "Which war?"

"One of the dinky ones in the Middle East."

Well, it was nice that she cared enough about her father to figure out which war he'd served in. Still, she was giving me an idea. "We should come up with a special drink and price for veterans," I mused.

"Oh, people love it when they think you're charitable," Carly enthused. "I mean... everybody gets thirsty, right? I know my dad gets extra thirsty when my mom won't stop yammering on and on about her prayer circle. He keeps a flask hidden in the magazine rack for when that happens."

That was a lot to take in. On one hand, it sounded like Carly's father might have a drinking problem. Part of me thought I should offer help, although I had no idea what form that help would come in. The other part had to be reminded that this was New Orleans. There was no such thing as proper drinking etiquette in a city that allowed you to wander around with open intoxicants. Speaking of that...

"Where are the takeout cups?" I was grateful to be able to change the subject and craned my neck to look at the bar. "I know I saw the delivery. Did we put them out?"

Carly bobbed her head. "Yup. All the cups have the name of the bar on them. Doesn't that make them more expensive though? Most of the other bars don't bother with that stuff."

"And we won't after the first week," I explained. "They are expensive. We want thirsty people to see the cups when patrons are walking around and ask where to find them. This is all about establishing ourselves. As a location, Bourbon Street is pretty much a guarantee of success. I want to make sure that we're one of the top bars Bourbon Street has to offer before it's all said and done."

"Because then you'll be able to move on to an even bigger space?" Carly queried.

I slid my gaze to her, curious. I sometimes forgot that she had a brain in her head. She went out of her way to look like an airhead more often than not. That was an act though. She was way more than she pretended to be. That was why I was nonchalant when I responded.

"I want to do a good job," I replied. "That's always my goal. I managed to make a name for myself in Michigan. I'm proud of that. This isn't about making a name for myself though. This is about building a stellar business for Mr. Templeman." That was a complete and total load of hooey. I didn't care about Arnie Templeman. I cared about what this could do for my career. I knew better than mentioning that in front of Carly, however. She had a mouth like a baleen whale.

"Now, tell me about the rest," I prodded, returning to the original topic. It was almost time to open, and I was ready to greet my destiny. "Lay it out for me."

"It's pretty basic." Carly was clearly getting annoyed with my intensity. Like the trooper she was—or more accurately, the business climber she wanted to be—she powered through. "Doors open. Giveaways start right away and continue throughout the entire day. We've got the influencers in place to exclaim how yummy the drinks are."

I nodded.

"Then the live music comes in a few hours from now," she continued. "We have two hours of power jazz, followed by the unveiling of the trivia system, and then we coast through until closing."

"I thought there wasn't a set closing time," Abel Miller interjected from behind the bar. He was an absolute behemoth of a man—six feet seven of rippling muscle with a kind smile and dancing eyes—and he looked ready to get this show on the road. "That's what I was told when you poached me away from Frenchman Street."

I had indeed poached him from a popular bar on Frenchman Street. Because of that, he was making double what the other bartenders were. That salary came at a price though. I'd told him—and he'd agreed—that he was to keep Cher open until business no longer warranted staying open. He would be head of the night shift crew most days. I only wanted him on the day shift for the first three days in case we ran into any unforeseen problems. He was familiar with the bar crowd in New Orleans. He could handle almost anything, which was exactly why I'd hired him.

"There's no set closing time," I confirmed. "It's all about what the business will bear. We're not in Mardi Gras season though. That's months away. I'm expecting that we'll close like a normal bar in another part of the country at least three or four days a week."

"Define 'normal.'" He threw out air quotes... and a smirk. He was charming to the extreme, and I was banking on that bringing in the customers.

"Use your best judgment," I replied. There was no way I would let him box me into a corner, given what was about to happen. "I trust you implicitly."

He snorted. "Moxie, you don't trust anyone implicitly. You're a control freak."

I took offense at that. At least I thought I did. "I'm not a control freak. I'm a trusting soul... and I trust you to help me make Cher a success."

He leaned his torpedo-like arms on the bar and regarded me with open mirth. "We're going to make this place a success together. That's why I signed on. Your tight-assed ways are going to bring the money in. That's going to make me a hot commodity."

9

Alarm rushed through me. "You signed a year-long contract."

"And I stick to my word. A year is a good period of time to prove that I can make people a lot of money. At the end of that year, you won't need me any longer. You'll be moving onward and upward too."

From his lips to the saints' ears. I smiled. "Let's make this place a success, huh?"

With determination and drive—and maybe a dash of giddy delight—I walked to the front door and swung it open. Sure, there might've been a bit of drama attached to my theatrical flair, but it wasn't out of place in NOLA. I expected at least a few faces to be lined up outside. I mean... it was opening day, for crying out loud. I found nothing but an empty sidewalk.

"What the...?" I strode out into the hot sunshine— summer in the Big Easy was essentially like being trapped in a professional wrestler's sweaty armpit—and followed the sound of raucous music to the corner. We had a prime location on Bourbon Street, lots of through traffic. The best thing about it? The bar across the street had been shut down for building code violations and was months away from reopening. We would be firmly entrenched as the bar to beat by then.

The thing is... well... the bar that had boasted boarded-up windows only hours before no longer looked abandoned. In fact, the windows were stained glass and gorgeous on one side. That would be the side facing Bourbon Street, the important side. On top of that, the draped canvas sheet that had been covering the front of the building since I had arrived in the city was gone. Behind it, a flashy new neon sign buzzed in bright pink.

Flambeaux. That's what it said. It was impossible to miss.

I stood there, confused, and then narrowed my eyes. I could hear people laughing and partying inside.

"What's going on?" Abel appeared on the sidewalk behind me. "Is that place open?"

I nodded, a sinking feeling taking over my stomach. "Apparently so."

"What do we do?" Carly was a streak of nervous energy when she landed on the pavement, hands on hips and scowl on lips. "We can't let this stand."

I was thinking the same thing. Now, how to act on that feeling was anybody's guess. I made up my mind on the spot.

"I'm going in." I marched across the street with purpose.

"Rip him a new one," Abel called out. He sounded bored as he drifted back inside Cher. "I'll wait for your report over here."

He obviously wasn't going to be a lot of help in this situation. Thankfully, I didn't need him. This was my moment. There was no way I was just going to cede my opening to these people.

No way.

No how.

Nothing doing.

Two

I went in guns blazing... and by guns, I mean my mouth was locked and loaded. I was ready to start yelling, although I had no idea who I was going to yell at, let alone why. I just knew something outrageous had happened.

The bar was bursting at the seams with people, laughs being exchanged in every corner, and the action behind the bar was even more intense than what I'd caught a glimpse of from the street.

My mouth dropped open when I realized two women were on top of the bar, both dressed in shorts that would've better fit the ambiance of a spring break beach. The tight tops they wore put on a full display of cleavage that was right out of an old Playboy mansion documentary.

"Is this a brothel?" Carly asked in a breathless tone behind me.

"I'm pretty sure it's not." I watched with indelible fury as the women tapped their hooker heels on top of the bar in time with the music while tipping bottles of spouted bourbon into the mouths of eager customers. One of the men reached up and gave the woman leaning over him a very friendly breast squeeze.

"Is that legal?" Carly whispered.

"Of course, it's legal," a male voice said from the left, causing me to jerk my attention in that direction. The individual standing there, his hair a dark-brown color that matched his eyes almost exactly, offered us a friendly smile. "Opening day, the drinks are on the house."

My heart sank, but I covered. "Opening day?" I feigned casual interest. "This is your opening day?"

"Yup." The man's expression was open and charming, his chiseled cheekbones making him look like a model rather than a bartender. His eyes started at my head and then openly roamed my body, ending at my toes before starting over again. I knew what he would see. Blond hair pulled back in a simple ponytail. Blue eyes filled with annoyance. A simple black shirt with Cher embroidered on the front. Khaki capris that could've been multi-purposed for a trip to church or a night out. Simple black flats.

"I'm Gus Kingman." He held out his hand, his gaze never leaving my face. It was as if he were completely ignoring Carly.

I stared at the proffered hand for a beat, debating, and then took it. There was no reason to turn into Medusa before I had a full understanding of what we were dealing with. Once I had a better feel for things I could let my snake-filled hair down and blast him into next week. "I didn't realize you were opening today." It was hard for me to find words. It was even harder for me not to scream then, given how loud the music was playing. How anybody could think, let alone listen, in this den of iniquity was beyond me.

"Yeah, we decided to do it on the fly." Gus's smile never waned but there was a keenness to his gaze that set my teeth on edge. "Usually, we plan these things out better, but this is

Bourbon Street, right? There's no reason to make yourself sick with lists and plans when you're on Bourbon Street."

Is that a dig at me? It felt like a dig. That, of course, was ridiculous. He didn't even know me. "You didn't have a sign," I said dumbly.

"Hmm." His expression said he was politely interested, and yet the way his eyes kept drifting to the women on the bar told me he would rather be talking to almost anybody else. "I'm sorry, I didn't hear what you said."

"You didn't have a sign," I repeated, this time louder. "There was no sign on this building this morning. Now, there's a sign."

"Wow. You pay a lot of attention to signs, huh?"

I wanted to smack him over the head with one of those bourbon bottles that kept getting waved around. Instead, I reminded myself I was a professional. My temper had gotten me into trouble a time or two in the past. That was before the miracle in Michigan though. That was before I became the go-to bar launcher in the state. That was before I branched out. Wait... what was I supposed to be focusing on again?

"I'm just saying that you didn't have a sign this morning." I sounded like a crazy person. Even I recognized it. I couldn't seem to stop myself from glaring at him though. "There was a tarp over the building. I was told that it would be months before you opened."

"Told by who? Or is it whom? I can never keep those straight." He aimed a flirty smile at a giggling woman as she brushed past him. There was more than enough room in the bar, and yet she went out of her way to press herself against his back. That was on purpose. "Hey, Sadie." He tipped an invisible hat. "I'm glad you could make it. I wasn't sure if you would stop by."

"Oh, I was here for Cher," the woman replied blankly. "That's the bar next door. This looks more fun though. I mean... look at that." She gestured toward the women pouring shots directly from the bottles. "That is so Bourbon Street."

"I thought so." Gus's smile was benign when he pointed it at me again. "Would you like a drink? I didn't catch your name, by the way."

I wasn't giving him my name. I didn't want him to have power over me. Sure, that was a ridiculous thing to think, but my mind refused to work the correct way. Seriously, had this all been planned? Did he launch his bar on the tail of my media blitz because he wanted to steal our thunder? It was the only possibility.

"Her name is Moxie," Carly volunteered out of nowhere, stealing my breath. The girl, however smart she fancied herself, could not pick up on body language. She would make a terrible spy. I suspected she wasn't done making my life difficult. She just couldn't keep her mouth shut. "She's the manager of Cher next door," she added.

"Oh, *really*?" Gus's smile told me he already knew that which is why I narrowed my eyes into dangerous slits. "That's a bummer for you, huh? I heard they recruited you all the way from Michigan. I guess you just learned the hard way that bar launches aren't one-size-fits-all."

Well, that answered *that* question. He'd most certainly done it on purpose. "I think we'll be fine." I forced out the words, even though panic, an emotion I wasn't all that familiar with, was practically licking at my soul. "We don't need gimmicks to sell ourselves. Gimmicks are for losers."

Even as I said it, I cringed. Why was I picking a fight with this man? Why was I still here? Oh, I knew why I was here. I was furious, and he made an enticing target.

Control yourself, Moxie. Picking a fight in a rival bar will end in nothing but heartache for you. Control yourself.

"I don't really think of it as a gimmick." It was hot in Flambeaux, thanks to the open windows and doors, but Gus didn't look to be sweating. He was calm, cool, and collected. I totally hated him for it, especially since I could feel the sweat trickling down my spine. "This is who we are."

"This is who you are?" I gestured toward the women on the bar. They were apparently trying to dance, but all they managed to do was swing their hips and asses at regular intervals while jiggling their boobs. It wasn't even in time with the music. Of course, the patrons—most of whom were male—didn't seem to mind.

"This is who we are," Gus agreed. He leaned to the side and peered through the open door, his gaze landing on Cher... which was empty. "Who are you again? In relation to the owner, I mean." The question was asked in a simple manner, but genuine interest seemed to be sparking in the depths of his eyes.

"I'm no one," I replied automatically. "I'm just a bar manager."

"Oh, that's not what the scuttle on the street says." Gus made a tsking sound as he wagged his finger. It was as if he were chiding a small child. "The other bar owners have been talking about you nonstop since you arrived."

That was news to me. "I've met the bar owners."

An oaf of a man cut too close to me from behind, knocking me forward. I made a grunting sound and would have smacked into one of the tables if Gus hadn't caught me.

"Sorry," the man said and moved on.

I was mortified. No one would ever call me clumsy. I wasn't exactly known for my agility either. Most of the time I was just me, just Moxie. I was professional and business oriented. This entire situation had thrown me out of my comfort zone.

"It's okay." Gus's eyes danced with amusement as he made sure I stayed on my feet. "You're obviously not used to bars in the Quarter, huh? This is tame for Bourbon Street. In a few hours, all the bars—including yours—will be bursting at the seams with people. You don't need to worry about your bar launch being a failure."

I couldn't believe he had the audacity to say it. I mean... he just laid it out there as if it were the most normal thing in the world. "Of course, the launch isn't a failure," I snapped, drawing myself up to my full height. I was hardly tall. I refused to shrink in the shadow of his charm, however. "The launch is fine."

Gus licked his lips and darted a look toward Cher again. Then his grin grew in scope. "You need a gimmick."

I frowned. "Excuse me?" Did he not just hear that I hated gimmicks?

"A gimmick," he repeated, gesturing toward the women on the bar. "Everybody loves a theme. Flambeaux's theme is going to be all things hot. That includes women... drinks... and everything else." This time when he looked me up and down, I wanted to punch him in the face. I felt lecherous intent bubbling from somewhere under the surface, and I didn't like it. I hadn't come to New Orleans for the sort of "hot" he was peddling.

"I don't need a gimmick." I was firm on that. "Gimmicks are the refuge of the weak."

His eyebrows hopped in amusement. "Is that so?"

"Yes, that's so."

"And here I thought gimmicks were the refuge of good marketers."

"Well, I don't happen to like gimmicks." That was true. I hated gimmicks with a fiery passion. Almost as much as I hated Gus and his stupid smile. That stupid lock of hair that fell down the middle of his forehead wasn't doing him any favors either. Seriously, he needed a haircut. "Gimmicks are only trendy for so long, and then you have to think of a new gimmick to keep the public's interest. If you set the proper tone from the start and wow the public with solid service and a righteous menu, then gimmicks aren't necessary."

Gus's lips quirked as he flicked his eyes to the bar. The group of men who were surrounding the dancing half-dressed bourbon suppliers had doubled just since I'd arrived. "I guess I'll have to take your word for that."

"I guess so." I forced myself to turn haughty. "Just for the record, I know what you did here."

His expression was blank. "You know what I did where?"

"Here." My finger bounced between Cher and him, back and forth, back and forth. Suddenly, I thought of my mother. She used to do the finger thing when I was a teenager, and she was arguing with me about going out. When had I inherited her finger?

"Oh, yeah?" Gus folded his arms over his chest. When he did, he pushed his biceps out in such a manner that he only expanded the male-model mystique he'd been boasting seconds before. Yup. I totally wanted to smack him. "What did I do?"

"You stole our launch."

He snorted. "I don't think you can steal a launch."

"No?" I knew better. "You let us spend on publicity for the launch. You let us take out ads in the newspaper. You let us pay for the street cleanup. Then you soft launched over top of us. I'm not an idiot."

This time when Gus looked me up and down, it was slow and measuring. "I don't think you're an idiot. I think you're making up stuff in your mind, don't get me wrong, but you're obviously not an idiot."

"I won't let this stand." I waved my mother's finger one more time, making a mental note to get that little impulse under control before I interacted with him again. "Cher is going to be a success. I'm not going to let your cheating get in the way of that."

Rather than deny the charge, he offered up a saucy salute. "I look forward to you being a success." He was far too charming. Even in the face of my wrath, he never broke character. I could not tolerate that.

"Oh, stuff it." I was furious when I pushed my way out of Flambeaux and hit the street. I could hear Carly scampering behind me to keep up.

"What are we going to do?" she demanded.

It was a fair question. Unfortunately, I had no idea. Instead, I stormed back inside Cher. There I found Abel studiously wiping things down as if he didn't have a care in the world. He wasn't panicking. Why wasn't he panicking?

"How can you not be worried?" I demanded.

Slowly, his eyes tracked to me. Amusement was reflected there. "We've been open for a grand total of ten minutes."

"Yeah, but nobody has come in."

"It's been ten minutes."

"The bar next door is packed. That guy—that Gus Kingman guy—just hijacked our opening. He's a big, fat hijacker."

Abel snorted. "So what? It's Bourbon Street. In an hour, the crowd from that place is going to dissipate, and it's going to be situation normal."

"Meaning?"

"Meaning this is Bourbon Street."

Frustration bubbled up and grabbed me by the throat. "Why does everybody keep saying that like it means something?"

"Because it's Bourbon Street," he replied. "Barhopping is the name of the game. What appeals to some won't appeal to others. If I thought this place was going to fail, I wouldn't have joined the team. You have to relax."

"Who says I'm not relaxed?"

He inclined his head toward my right hand, which was

gripped into a fist. My knuckles were white, I was so worked up. "Who are you going to throw that thing at?"

"I'm thinking Gus Kingman might make an appropriate target," I muttered.

"And who is Gus Kingman?" Abel asked after a beat. "I don't think I recognize that name."

"He's the guy who owns the bar next door," Carly volunteered. "He's really hot... but all kinds of evil. Although really hot."

I pinned her with the darkest glare in my repertoire. "You said he was hot twice."

"Well, he's hot."

Abel snickered and shook his head as he went back to wiping down the bar. I thought he was completely over the situation—and was about to meltdown thusly—and then he stilled. "Wait... did you say Kingman?"

I nodded. "Why? Do you know him?"

"I know the Kingman family. They own like thirty bars in the city. They're spread out over all the parishes. I don't know a Gus though."

"Who do you know?"

"Well, Anders and Anna Kingman own the company. They have three sons. Um... Archer, Aidan, and... oh, what's the last one?" He was talking to himself and stared at the ceiling as if trying to access a part of his brain that was somehow off-limits.

"Gus?" I suggested.

He shook his head. "No. They all have A names. It's a running joke. It will come to me."

I ran the possibilities through my head, and only one name popped to mind. "What about Augustus?"

Abel snapped his fingers and pointed. "That's it."

My eyes moved back to Flambeaux. I could see the activity through the open windows. Gus stood in the center of things, his arms folded across his chest. He was staring directly at me, as if there weren't thirty people milling about on the street between us.

"Are you saying the Kingman family is the one who opened the bar across the way?" Abel asked.

"Apparently so," I replied.

"Then we might be in trouble." Abel abandoned all pretext of not caring about our failed launch. "They're a big deal, and I happen to know they bid on this building when it was up for auction. Templeman outbid him at the last second. Maybe the Kingmans are going to make another run at getting this building."

Well, that was the last thing I wanted to consider. "They're not getting this building. We're going to save this launch."

"From your lips to the saints' ears." Abel kissed two fingers and held them aloft. "You'd better hope Baron Samedi is the saint that comes running though. That dude knows how to throw a party. You're clearly already falling behind.'"

That was exactly what I was afraid of.

Three

I prided myself on being a professional. I wanted people to look at me and say, "Wow, she's so together." My drive to win was greater than my need to be professional, however.

Because I couldn't stop myself, I spent the afternoon on the street corner watching the traffic between the bars. Flambeaux drew in a very specific clientele, the sort that enjoyed high fives, inappropriate selfies, and lewd discussions of female genitalia. As for Cher, Abel had been right. After the initial rush, the party pattern settled. Just as many people were going into Cher as they were Flambeaux. Unfortunately, the reaction to Flambeaux was much more energetic.

"Did you see that woman?" a college-aged guy asked as he brushed past me, not bothering to offer an apology for the inadvertent elbow. "She had tits like on those pornos we watched the other day... but even better. They bounced like we were on the moon or something."

I rolled my eyes until they were back on Flambeaux. I could see Gus cavorting with the customers through the opening. He didn't appear to have a care in the world. It bothered me to the extreme.

On a whim, I pulled a twenty out of my pocket and handed it to one of the young men edging around me to get inside. Surprised, the blond in the group raised an eyebrow and tentatively touched the bill. He looked confused.

"Is this for me?"

I smiled. "Yes. I need a favor though."

"Sure." It was with more than a little bit of swagger that he took position in front of me. His eyes were keen as he looked me up and down. "What do you need?" When he smiled, I could smell the cigarettes on his breath. I didn't back up.

"I'll buy your first round of drinks both here and next door if you do me a little favor over there." I inclined my head toward one of the dancing bartenders.

The blond was intrigued but suspicious. "What do you want?"

"It's a small thing."

"Just tell me what you want."

I MADE MYSELF SCARCE AFTER UNVEILING my plan, retreating to Cher so I could watch from a distance. Abel, perhaps sensing that I'd done something, landed on my right side and folded his arms across his chest. He watched without saying a word, and when one of the buxom dancers slapped the young man across the face and screeched that she wasn't a whore, he shook his head.

"That was so juvenile," Abel commented. "I mean... is that the best you can do?"

I shrugged. "I had limited time to think."

"Yeah, but it's not the woman's fault you hate the guy running that bar."

I opened my mouth to argue and then snapped it shut.

AVERY KANE

Abel arched a challenging eyebrow.

"You're right," I conceded after several seconds. I hadn't taken that into consideration. "That's why I made sure the guy will tell the bartender over there that Gus was the one who referred to her as a prostitute. I didn't want her feeling bad about herself. I mean... she looks great in those shorts. I wish I could fill them out as well as she does."

Abel let loose a snort. "I like that you're a conscientious asshole."

"That's me." I turned away from the window when I saw that Gus was fervently pleading his case to the offended bartender. He looked horrified. "Besides, he shouldn't be putting women on display like that."

"I think it can be argued that they're putting themselves on display," Abel countered.

"No. He made their employment contingent on sexualizing themselves. This is on him."

"I'm sure the tips they'll get for doing what they're doing will make up for the degradation. If not, they can dry their tears with the dollar bills being stuffed in their bras."

The way he said it made me realize he couldn't possibly understand. "The tips shouldn't have to make up for it." I blew out a sigh and focused on Cher. It was 50 percent full. It wasn't a terrible number. It wasn't great either. "I don't feel sorry for messing with him."

"No, I can see that." Abel's gaze felt heavy on my profile. "I'm guessing you've felt marginalized a time or two in your life."

I waited a beat. "What are you asking?"

"I'm not asking anything. I'm... assuming... that you've been judged more than once because of your looks. I mean... you're a beautiful woman. You're a bit of a hard case, and I wish you'd take that stick out of your ass occasionally, but I get

24

it. People don't take you seriously because of the blond hair and blue eyes... and I'm sure that butt doesn't hurt."

I slapped his arm before I realized what I was doing. "Hey!"

He laughed. "I guess we're even. You physically abused me, and I sexually harassed you. I didn't mean it in a derogatory way though. I just mean... you're pretty. People look at you and expect you to act a certain way. I get that."

I pursed my lips. Oddly enough, I believed him. He was an ox of a man, but he had a soft heart. It made me smile. "Let me guess, people take one look at you and assume you play football and throw endless touchdowns but don't get that you paint on the side."

"Pretty much," he agreed. "They see a big Black man and think I can only like one thing, be one thing. It's frustrating."

"I get that. The blond hair immediately knocks me down thirty IQ points in most people's estimation."

"Not in Arnie Templeman's estimation."

"He knows my former boss in Michigan. Apparently they went to college together, and Arnie always had a crush on Shelly. She told me that and wasn't afraid to press the advantage on my behalf."

"Because you didn't want to stay in Michigan?"

"Because she knew I needed a bigger market to achieve the goals I'm setting for myself. I want to be a success, so when I go to a different city—if that's what I ultimately decide on—my name will carry me eventually. I won't have to constantly prove myself."

"I want that for myself too. I want my own bar. Here. I want everyone to say, 'This is where the locals go.'"

My eyebrows drifted together as I regarded him. "Wait... you want a bar only locals go to? Why?"

"Because this city truly belongs to the locals. It's something you can't understand. It's like me not understanding your need to travel all over the world and make a name for yourself. It's just the thing I've always wanted."

I nodded in understanding. "I don't know that I want to travel all over the world. I just know that I want to keep building my brand. I want to be a powerhouse, and I don't want to need anyone else to accomplish my goals. I actually really like New Orleans."

"Then make it work for you." Abel squeezed my shoulder before heading back toward the bar. "There's no need to go the low route by the way. You're capable of beating him by taking the high road. He jumped your launch. There's a lot of time before the end of the race."

I smirked. "There most definitely is."

THINGS WENT BETTER THAN I THOUGHT they would, to the point where Abel started saying "I told you so" whenever he passed on drink runs. I was so busy that I lost track of watching Flambeaux—at least mostly—and focused on the customers. People loved the themed drinks. They liked the flattering lights. They loved Abel. Even the food—which was all fried, for the most part—was a big hit. Still, something was missing.

"Don't let it bother you," Abel instructed when he ushered me to the side door so I could depart for the night. He seemed to have enough energy for ten people and wasn't flagging even though he'd been working for twelve hours straight.

"You can't do this all week," I said out of nowhere. When I'd agreed to let Abel work eighteen hours a day on opening week, it hadn't felt real to me. Now though, after a full day on my feet, it felt like torture.

"I've got this," Abel reassured me. "It's only a week, and then I'll settle into my regular schedule. You don't have to worry about me."

"Who said I was worrying about you?"

He smirked. "You're a worrier by nature, Moxie. That's written all over your face."

"I happen to think I'm carefree, like a kite on a windy day."

"That could be the stupidest thing anybody has ever said."

"Aren't you going to qualify that with something? Like it's the stupidest thing you've heard today... or in the past week."

"Nope. Ever."

"Fair enough." I grabbed the box of leftover food I'd been collecting throughout the night and leveraged it on my hip. "I'll see you tomorrow."

"How are you getting home?" Abel's demeanor suddenly changed.

"Walking. I'm afraid to drive in this city. I mean... people are allowed to walk around with open intoxicants, and it's considered not only legal but normal."

He snorted. "Stick to the main streets. You don't live in a bad neighborhood, do you?"

"I live over on Clinton Street. It's a nice area."

"You're still a single woman walking around alone at night. The cops are all over Bourbon and Royal. Walk on those as much as possible. Then cut around by Jackson Square. That's monitored well too."

"I've got it. I'm tougher than I look. Remember, I came from Detroit."

"Still, be careful. You should get a whistle or something. It's safe walking around the Quarter on your own for the most part, but there are always going to be jerks." He inclined his head toward the food. "What's that for?"

I lied without batting an eyelash. "I live with a bunch of people in one of those co-op buildings with small units but a great patio."

"Oh, nice."

"They'll eat anything."

"Including cold fried food?"

"Anything," I confirmed. "I'll see you tomorrow. Good luck tonight."

"Girl, I don't need luck. I've got skill."

I'D WALKED BETWEEN CHER AND MY APARTMENT so many times I'd lost count. The French Quarter wasn't hard to navigate. I cut down St. Peter Street and counted the cross streets. Royal. Chartres. Jackson Square. The blocks in the French Quarter weren't overly large, so it only took me a few minutes.

Jackson Square was one of my favorite places in the city. Sure, I hadn't been able to visit that many places outside the French Quarter, but the Square was a definite favorite. During the day, the metal gates were open and people could wander through, taking photos in front of the Andrew Jackson statue and hanging out on the benches. On the outside of the fences, local vendors set up shops on three sides. They sold artwork, told fortunes, and put on musical displays. One of my favorite things about the Square was the guys who painted themselves in head-to-toe gold and silver and then spent hours pretending to be human statues for money. That took commitment.

At night, the metal gates were locked tight. It took me a week to figure out why. Then I walked past Pirate's Alley and saw all the benches scattered around the little alleyway. Each one, a good thirty or forty in total, had a homeless individual stretched out on them. The area was flooded with homeless people in fact. I'd asked one of my new co-op mates about it one night, and she explained that New Orleans's climate, combined with its hefty tourist population, made for an unfortunate breeding ground. The panhandlers were out of control in the city, and it made me sad whenever I crossed through the Square.

"Hey, guys." I made sure to announce my presence before stepping under the streetlights. I'd been dropping off food to the individuals bedding down at night outside the Square for almost two weeks. Most of them were mentally ill—some severely so—and some were veterans. Loud noises frightened them, something I'd learned the hard way the third night I'd visited. I'd ended up knocked on my ass when one of the men panicked. I only had myself to blame, however, and refused to make a big deal out of it.

"Dinner," I announced as I placed the food on the ground in the middle of the group.

"Nice!" Tremaine—last names weren't mentioned on the street unless you were new, or so I was told—gave me a high five as he swooped in. "What do we have?"

I left the food for him to dole out and studied the amassed faces. I'd introduced myself to all of them at some point. Bishop. Gremlin. Anthony. Benji. Whiskey. They either went by their first names only or came up with a street name.

"Sorry it's cold," I offered.

"It's fine." Tremaine waved off my apology. "You know us. We'll eat anything." He popped an onion ring into his mouth. "You bring anything else?"

I dug in the box and grabbed two smaller containers, handing one each to Bishop and Benji because they were older and needed the food. The younger guys managed to have an easier time on the street. I didn't play favorites, but I was conscientious and aware.

"I only have food." I flashed a tight smile. "You guys are on your own for the other stuff." It wasn't my place to judge, but I refused to supply them with alcohol. I wouldn't cast aspersions on them, but I couldn't add fuel to the problem either.

"How was your bar opening tonight?" Whiskey asked.

He'd grabbed one of the boxes and settled two benches down. He liked me but only from a distance.

"It went okay. I'm tired though."

"Then you should get home." Whiskey's tone was grave. "It's late for a single pretty girl like you to be on the street."

"I'm going." I smiled at each one of them in turn, lingering on Benji a moment because he seemed paler than normal. "Everybody is okay, right?"

"We're right as rain," Benji promised, his mouth full of food. "We're getting ready for the big show tonight."

"The big show?"

"We got a fifth." Gremlin beamed in such a way that I had a clear view of his missing teeth. "We're going to have fun."

"You don't want to be around for it," Whiskey said.

I definitely didn't. "I'll see you guys later." I waved and started for St. Peter, pulling up short when I made out another figure at the end of the cobblestone walkway. Someone had been tracking me, and I was just now noticing. It was someone I knew, although not well.

"Are you following me?" I demanded as Gus held out his hands in exaggerated fashion.

"Wow. Somebody thinks a lot of herself." His grin was a little too 'cat that ate the canary' for my liking. "Have you considered that I just happened to stroll by and see you with your... friends?"

"Not particularly." I squared my shoulders and moved to step around him.

"Hold up." Gus lifted a hand to stop me, although he didn't touch me. "What were you just doing over there?" He inclined his chin toward the group of hungry men.

"I had extra food at the bar. There's no sense throwing it away."

"Uh-huh." Gus licked his lips and shook his head. "I know you're new to NOLA, but you can't let them get to you. If you spend all your time worrying about those people, you're never going to sleep at night."

"*Those* people?"

"Don't." There was warning in his voice. "I wasn't trying to be mean or judgmental."

"It's extra food." I slipped past him. "I would appreciate it if you didn't follow me, for the record. I think having neighboring bars is enough interaction for you and me."

"I wasn't following you."

"Oh, right. You just happened to end up in Jackson Square at the same time as me. I totally buy that."

He pointed toward Decatur Street. "Do you see that building there?"

"The one where the brewery is located?"

He nodded. "The first floor is a brewery, a voodoo store, and a coffee shop. Above it, though, are condos. I live on the top floor."

Of course he did. That was just my luck. The building was exquisite. He had to be living in a two-million-dollar condo if he lived in that building. "Oh, well."

He snorted. "It was nice seeing you again too, Moxie. Shall we meet again tomorrow and do it all over again?"

It sounded like a challenge. "Bring it on."

Four

E ven though I told myself that I shouldn't be caught
spying on Gus, I couldn't stop myself from watching
him as he headed toward his condo. We stuck to
different sides of Decatur—he was on the river side—and I
scowled when he pulled a fob out of his pocket and waved it in
front of the scanner before pressing his thumb to a separate
pad. I had no doubt the security was top-notch.

Did I begrudge him that? Inherently, I knew I shouldn't.
As soon as I'd found out that Gus came from a wealthy family,
however, he became all the more odious to me. In my mind,
that made him entitled. He was likely used to things dropping
in his lap.

Like a bar opening he hadn't planned or paid for.

Yeah, I was still bitter about that.

Once he was inside, I put my head down and pushed
through the wall of humidity, not stopping until I arrived at
the three-story co-op I currently called home. Rather than go
through the front door, I walked to the side alley and let
myself in through the gate. We had absolutely zero security,
and yet the voices echoing from the back patio area reminded

me that we didn't need security because somebody was almost always outside.

"There she is," a voice boomed out when I hit the lighted area. Gabriel Stevens, his long hair pulled back in a stylish man bun, waved before turning back to the cards he was shuffling. "We're playing, if you're in."

"Nobody knows that euchre game you keep mentioning though," Casey Boardman drawled. His hair was cropped close to his head and dyed a bright red. He had to touch it up every two weeks, and it left a mess in the bathroom he shared with Gabriel. I'd heard them argue about it more than once.

"You guys are missing out on euchre," I replied as I grabbed a beer from the metal bucket in the middle of the patio. We weren't fancy in these parts. The bucket was old and rusty but did the job. We just needed it to hold ice and beer. "What's the word this evening?" I cracked the bottle and took a long swig.

"We're not the ones who had the big bar opening tonight," Ally Hamilton noted from her spot next to Gabriel. She had one of those pixie cuts that looked chic and beautiful under the limited twinkle lights that had been strung up in the patio area. Given the humidity in New Orleans, my long hair always looked ragged by the end of the day. Ally, however, was always fresh as a daisy.

It drove me insane.

"Yeah, how did that go?" Casey asked as he looked me up and down. He spent his time playing music on various street corners throughout the day, convinced he would eventually stumble over the right jazz bigwig and be discovered. He was a talented musician, but I was convinced he was going about things the wrong way. After our first argument on the subject, however, I learned to shut my mouth and mind my own business.

It wasn't as easy as it sounded.

"Well, it went." I flashed a smile I didn't feel.

"That bad?" Gabriel looked surprised. "All bars open with a bang here."

I made a grumbling sound under my breath. Apparently, that little tidbit was known by all but only expressed after the fact by a few. Honestly, had I known that you didn't need all the fancy trappings to launch a Bourbon Street bar, I might've reined in the budget a bit. It was far too late now.

"It went fine," I said. "I mean... we were busy throughout most of the day. We easily beat my projected revenue numbers."

"So what's the problem?"

"The problem is that the empty bar across the street—you remember the one I was telling you about, right?—well, it's not as closed as I thought it was. Turns out they were keeping all their renovations under wraps. They opened today, too, and they stole our customers right off the bat."

"I thought you said your revenue was up," Ally argued.

"It was, but the first round of customers headed inside Flambeaux because he had almost-naked women dancing on a bar and doling out free shots of whiskey."

"Oh, I'm sorry I missed that," Casey drawled, grinning. "Whiskey and naked women are my favorite combination."

"Almost naked," I corrected.

"I like those types of women too."

Gabriel chuckled. "See, this is why I'm glad to be into guys. I would be uncomfortable with that sort of bar. I'm with Moxie on this."

"Thank you." I beamed at him. I loved his face. The angles of it were so interesting. I wasn't looking for a boyfriend, but if he wasn't gay, I would totally make a play for him. There was nothing wrong with a New Orleans fling while I was here. Unfortunately, I literally had nothing to offer him that he would find interesting.

"I'm sure once the novelty of the almost-naked women wore off that it was fine," Ally offered. She worked at one of the more expensive restaurants in the Quarter. In fact, she made enough money only working two nights a week that she could pay her rent and utilities and then use the other days of the week to sell her art in Jackson Square. That was her true love. She simply couldn't make a living at it... yet. I had no doubt it would happen eventually.

"It was fine," I agreed. "I'm still mad they hopped my launch. Stupid Gus Kingman." The last part was said with a growl.

Gabriel snorted, amused. "Who is Gus Kingman?"

"Apparently his family is bar royalty in this area. His parents just gave him a bar to open, and he put zero effort into it and yet probably made a fortune today."

"Wait... Kingman?" Gabriel leaned forward. He was a mixologist at one of the popular jazz bars just off Bourbon Street. I'd tried to poach him to work for me, but he politely declined. He was happy where he was. "You don't mean Augustus Kingman, do you?"

I nodded, perplexed. "Yeah. Why? Do you know him?"

"I don't know him personally. His family, though, well... they really are royalty in this part of the city."

"I heard the Kingmans live in one of those mega mansions in the Garden District," Ally offered. "It's one of those houses over by Lafayette Cemetery that is completely fenced in with privacy hedges to keep the dregs of humanity out." Her opinion was obvious from the way she said it.

"So... they're basically awful people," I surmised. "I guessed that for myself."

"They have a certain reputation," she clarified.

"Tell me more." Any fodder I could use to fuel my Gus hate was welcome this evening. "I want to hear everything you've got."

"Remember, you asked for it." Ally wasn't shy about dishing dirt and jumped in straight away. "So, the parents are Anders and Anna. They're old money. Like... *old* money." She put so much stress on the second old that I had to hold back a laugh.

"The family started in steamboats, I believe, like in 1800 or something," she continued.

A history buff, Casey shook his head. "It wasn't that early. The first steamboat didn't even arrive in New Orleans until 1812."

Ally kept her eyes on me but jabbed a finger in his direction. "Stuff it. I was close enough."

"Whatever."

"They made a bunch of money in steamboats and then broadened their interests and went into construction stuff," Ally explained. "The family fortune was passed down from generation to generation. They branched out into textiles... and shipping... and even offshore oil rigs."

I nodded. That made sense. The oil business was huge in New Orleans. My understanding was that the workers spent two to three weeks out on the rigs, depending on their schedule, and then returned to the city to party it up for one to two weeks before doing it all over again. It was good money, and the workers were generous with tips when they hit the mainland.

"It's only been the last twenty years or so that they've delved into the hospitality industry," Ally supplied. "They own something like twenty hotels and forty restaurants just in New Orleans."

"Not strictly in the French Quarter, though, right?"

She shook her head. "No, they own good restaurants in almost every parish. There's one over in the Garden District, right by the cemetery, that has amazing food. It also has a dress code. Supposedly that restaurant is really close to their house and they eat there all the time."

"How do you know that?"

She shrugged. "People talk." She sipped her beer and then continued. "They have three sons. Archer, Aidan, and Augustus... although apparently he goes by Gus if your story is to be believed."

My eyebrows slid toward one another. "Why would I lie?"

"I didn't say you were lying."

"You inferred it."

"No."

"Yes."

"Stop fake fighting," Gabriel admonished. "If I wanted to deal with fake fighting I would spend my nights at that female mud-wrestling place over in the Ninth Ward."

"You shut it too," Ally snapped, although her eyes were filled with good humor. "I don't know a lot about the sons specifically. The oldest is Archer, which I only remember because it sounds like such a pretentious name. Augustus is the youngest. Supposedly he's a screwup."

Oh, well, now she had my full attention. "How is he a screwup?"

"He didn't go to college right out of high school."

I made a face. "That doesn't make him a screwup. A lot of people take a gap year."

Amusement flashed hard and fast in the depths of Ally's eyes. "Did you take a gap year?"

"No." There was no mirth to be found in this subject. "We didn't have a lot of money... or any extra money. I had to live at home, take on a full-time job waitressing, and take classes on the side. It took me six years to get my degree."

"See, but you wanted it." Ally was a fan of hard work, so her smile was legitimate. "You worked really hard and are still working. Those Kingman kids have never worked a day in their lives. They all went to college—from what I hear, it was the beer and beignets study plan—and then they immediately slid into posh positions in the family business when they graduated."

It wasn't hard to understand what she was saying. Still, I found myself thinking hard. "You just said Gus didn't go to college." It was hard picturing the man I met as an Augustus. Gus fit him better... not that I cared either way. "How could he slide into the family business if he didn't follow the track they'd set up?"

"He didn't," Ally replied. "That's what I'm saying. Apparently, he gallivanted all over the world on the family money, hopping from exotic locale to exotic locale. We're talking three years here of him doing nothing but partying."

That sounded about right. "And then what?"

She shrugged and sipped again. Her cheeks were ruddy, telling me this wasn't her first drink. New Orleans wasn't the sort of place where you sipped one drink the entire night and then went to bed early because you had to work the next day. That was not how things rolled in the French Quarter.

"There are rumors," she started. "They're not facts."

"Just tell me." I saw no point in playing that game. I needed to know as much as I could about Gus. If the information turned out to be wrong, so be it.

"Supposedly his mother was fine letting him run around the world and never work. He's the baby of the family, so that means he's spoiled. I was the baby of my family and know how that goes. You get less parental attention but more parental indulgence. The older kids wear the parents down until it's just easier to be all 'hey, man, whatever.'"

I laughed, as I'm sure she'd intended. "So Gus was a loser and didn't follow the family rules. Why am I not surprised?"

"Well, that's the thing." Awkwardly, she broke off and scratched her cheek. "When he was in his early twenties, he came back to New Orleans after his adventures abroad and went to school. Tulane, I believe. He took business courses and then joined the family dynasty. Unlike his brothers, though, he wasn't given a bar to manage straight out of college."

"Wait... the brothers were given their own bars when they graduated?" I tried to imagine that and came up empty. "That's one heckuva gift."

"I know, right?" Casey was beyond amused. "I got a card with ten bucks in it from my mom."

I patted his wrist. He didn't talk about his family often, but when he did, he had nothing nice to say about them. I, on the other hand, loved my mother a great deal before her death from cancer two years before. She didn't have extra money to grace me with, but there'd been no shortage of love. One of those things was vastly superior to the other.

"The whispers say the older boys were more serious than Gus," Ally offered. "They weren't considered risks. Gus had to work for his brothers before he was gifted a bar of his own. I believe this is his ultimate gift... although I had no idea the Kingmans were the ones going into the spot across from you. They kept that information on the down low."

"They really did," Gabriel agreed. He was busy studying his hands under the twinkle lights. "I got a new manicure. What do you think?" He held his fingernails up for me to study. They looked exactly the same as when I'd seen them the previous evening.

"They look nice," I lied. Really, fingernails are fingernails. "Did you do something different?"

"Matte instead of gloss on the enamel."

"Awesome." I grinned at Ally when he wasn't looking. We enjoyed his finicky side. "Go back to Gus. Do we think this is the first bar he's ever run on his own?"

"Definitely," Ally confirmed. "The family put the other

39

brothers on display. They're all known as ladies' men who jump from one woman to the next without a single thought. They don't settle down, so don't risk getting involved with him."

"Oh, right." That was the funniest thing I'd heard all night. "I hate that guy. There's absolutely zero chance I'm getting involved with him."

"That's smart, because he's the family screwup." Ally turned thoughtful. "The Kingmans aren't known to throw money away. Either they think he's ready to run his own business and do the family proud or one of those other brothers is poised to swoop in and save him."

Which one, I wondered. If one of the other brothers was the one pulling the strings, did it matter which Kingman I was really grappling with?

"Anything else?" I asked finally.

"No. I just know all those boys are charming, and they've left a trail of broken hearts in their wake. Women from every parish want to somehow be the ones to tame them. It never happens."

"It will happen eventually," Gabriel argued, finally dropping his hands. "Those Kingmans are only allowed to play until they hit thirty-five or so. Then they're expected to get married and procreate. They need more little Kingmans to keep their dynasty going."

"Just watch him," Ally said. "Gus is the one nobody talks about. That makes him a mystery."

He wasn't so mysterious to me. "I'm going to crush him." I finished off my beer and reached for another. "I just have to figure out how."

Five

Thankfully I woke without a hangover the next morning. I showered quickly, changed into comfortable capris and sandals, and then headed out. My co-op mates were either still in bed or off working—it was a toss-up because nobody had a set schedule—and I knew better than to make too much noise.

New Orleans was a city that slept as late as it wanted and made no apologies for it.

Once on Decatur, I stopped at Café Beignet long enough to grab a latte and then continued on down the street to Café du Monde for beignets. Could I have gotten the beignets at Café Beignet? Yes. Café du Monde's were better, however. Could I have gotten the coffee at Café du Monde? Also yes. However, I wasn't a chicory fan—which was sacrilegious in the Quarter—so I'd become accustomed to stopping two places for breakfast every morning.

I carried my coffee and beignets to a bench inside Jackson Square so I could watch the early morning shenanigans. Once the gates of the park opened, significant shuffling started happening. The individuals who slept on the benches outside

41

the park began moving toward Bourbon Street—they had regular routes they liked to stick to—and the vendors started lining three sides of the park.

When I'd first arrived in New Orleans, I was confused by what happened at Jackson Square every morning. People covered the metal fencing with paintings and craft projects, and over by Pirate's Alley, the tarot readers and palmistry fanatics set out tables so they could interact with the tourists. Then, on every corner of the square, musical acts set up shop. You could hear a different type of jazz no matter which direction you walked, and once you got to the Riverwalk steps on the other side of the road, it was nonstop Michael Jackson music as the impersonators took over.

It was an interesting and eclectic setup.

"Good morning."

I jumped at the new voice, whipping my eyes to the left. Inwardly I groaned when I realized Gus was the one invading my morning solitude. He had what looked to be a coffee in one hand and a cardboard container with egg-white omelet blobs poking out in the other.

"What is that?" I made a disgusted face as he popped one of the blobs into his mouth. He made sure to sit at a different bench than me, but they were close enough that I didn't have to strain to hear his answer.

"Protein, baby." He spoke with his mouth full, methodically chewing. He waited to speak again until after he'd swallowed. "They're egg-white mushroom poppers with jalapenos in them."

I was horrified. "That doesn't sound like breakfast."

He inclined his head toward my beignets. "And yet it's healthier than what you're eating. I mean... do you even know how many calories are in those things?"

I glared at him. Hard. "Are you suggesting I need to count

calories?" *Please say yes,* I fervently whispered to myself. *If you say yes, I can go off.*

I so badly wanted to go off on him.

"I would never say that." He was solemn as he shook his head. "I happen to like a woman with a bit of junk in her trunk."

I was surprised I could see given how slitted my eyes were. "What did you just say?"

"Oh, calm down," he said after a beat, waving his hand. "You're far too easy. I was just trying to get a rise out of you."

"You did a good job."

"I'm awesome like that," he agreed, popping another hunk of egg into his mouth. When he glanced between my beignets and coffee again, he frowned. "How come you have Café Beignet coffee and Café du Monde beignets?"

Ugh. Why did he have to be so observant? He was the first person who had ever noticed my morning routine. "Because."

"Because why?"

"Because."

"Yeah, I'm going to need more than that."

The look I shot him promised retribution if he didn't shut up. He didn't seem to care.

"Tell me why," he insisted.

"I like the Café du Monde beignets," I said finally.

"They're very good," he agreed. "In fact, they're the best in the Quarter... unless you're willing to head over to Frenchman Street."

"And what's over on Frenchman Street?" I didn't want to sound like a newbie, but since I already didn't like him, it didn't matter how ignorant I came off. I was soaking up the knowledge every chance I could.

"Frenchman is where the locals hang out," he replied. "The most authentic food, drinks, and music is over there.

You'll never see the locals on Bourbon Street because they prefer things when they're authentic."

For some reason, the way he said the last word grated. Was he suggesting I wasn't authentic? I really didn't like him. "I know about Frenchman Street." I sneered at him even after he brushed his hand over his cheek to signify I had powdered sugar on my face. I refused to wipe it away no matter how he looked at me. "My head bartender came from Frenchman Street. I simply thought there was a special beignet shop over there or something."

"All the beignets on Frenchman Street are good. Also, I know Abel Miller. At least I know of him. I've had my eye on him for a long time."

"Your eye on him?" I was confused. "Oh." Realization dawned. "I don't think he dates men. I mean... not that there's anything wrong with that if you have a crush on him," I added hurriedly. "Everybody loves to be crushed on. He mentioned a girlfriend when I interviewed him though. He seems pretty devoted to her." I was making that last part up but didn't want to make Gus uncomfortable.

Gus made an 'are you kidding me' face and shook his head. "Yeah, I don't want to date him. I want to hire him."

Why that came as a relief was beyond me. "Oh, well, he's mine."

"Good to know." Gus shook his head, although the way his lips curved told me he wasn't offended. That made me like him a little better, although only a smidge. There were some men who would melt down if mistaken as gay. I was glad he wasn't one of them. "Let's go back to your breakfast. Why don't you get your coffee at Café du Monde if you like the beignets so much?"

I wanted to punch him for refusing to let the topic go. "It doesn't matter."

"It does."

"No, it doesn't."

"It does or you would tell me."

Oh, I wanted to punch him so hard. "I don't like chicory," I said finally.

"And?" he prodded after a few seconds.

I shrugged. "And nothing. I just don't like it. I like a latte."

"Amateur." He sipped his coffee, turning the paper cup to make me aware it was from Café du Monde.

"We don't have chicory in Michigan," I explained. I shouldn't have to defend myself to him, but I couldn't stop myself. "I think it's one of those things you have to grow up with to love."

"And you grew up with lattes? Your mother sounds awesome."

"No. I just... like them now." I didn't know what else to say, so I shoved a beignet in my mouth, not caring in the least that I'd added powdered sugar to the other cheek, making a matching set.

"Well, at least you know what you like." He sipped his coffee again, and I could feel his eyes on me. They were like little pockets of fire burning at my soul. "How come you paid the guy to sexually harass my bartender yesterday?"

My heart skipped a beat. "I have no idea what you mean," I lied.

"Oh, don't bother." He made a tsking sound and shook his head. "He came back after loading up on drinks at your place to apologize. He thought he might be in love with the bartender—that's what eight hurricanes will do to you—and he was afraid she was holding a grudge from before."

I pursed my lips. I could lie. Anyone else in my position would do just that. I wasn't feeling all that great about what I'd done, though, so I opted to tell the truth. "I wanted you to be annoyed."

"It worked."

"In hindsight, it was a bad move. I didn't want to make your bartender feel like crap. She didn't deserve it."

"So you just wanted to make me feel like crap."

"Pretty much."

"Good to know."

We lapsed into uncomfortable silence as I munched on my beignets. He was the first to break it.

"So... can we just get along from here on out?"

He had to be joking. "No."

"No?" His eyebrows met his hairline.

"No," I repeated.

He looked more amused than aggrieved. "Why not?"

"You know why."

"Clearly I don't."

I hated that he kept smiling at me. It was as if he thought his charm was going to get him somewhere. Well, I had news for him. I'd met many a charming man over the course of my life. I knew better than to lose my mind over a flirty smile. My mother had taught me tricks to avoid falling for a charming smile... even if dimples were part of the package. I was ready to utilize all of them if need be.

"You stole my launch," I replied, seeing no reason to lie to him. "You swooped in, took the publicity I paid for, and stole it. You also perverted it while you were at it."

"Oh yeah?" He popped his last egg bite in his mouth, his gaze keen. "How did I pervert it?"

"I notice you're not denying stealing it," I muttered under my breath, shaking my head to dislodge the fury that was threatening to turn me into a Karen meme on the Internet if I wasn't careful. Sure, there was no manager to ask for, but a public meltdown where I accused him of stealing my bar opening would be just as bad.

"I want to hear how I perverted it first," he pressed.

"See, I just think you want me to talk about your

bartenders," I shot back. "You want me to use derogatory words when referring to them so you can point to me as the problem."

"That's some convoluted thinking there."

"And yet I know I'm right."

To my surprise, he smiled. "You might be right. I kind of owe you after you tried to set up one of my bartenders to be sexually harassed."

My mouth dropped open. "I did not."

"You said you did."

"No, I just wanted you to get some blowback for sexually exploiting those girls."

"Um... you can't be exploited if you're a willing participant. Do you have any idea how much those girls made in tips last night? I don't think they're upset about their lot in life."

"No?"

"No. They took home five hundred bucks each. They were thrilled." He leaned closer. "Not everybody is ashamed of showing off their body."

I glanced down at my clothes. The statement felt pointed.

"Not you," he said, as if only realizing after the fact that what he'd uttered could be construed a certain way. "I wasn't saying there's anything wrong with your body or anything. I mean... if that's what you were thinking, don't." He paused a beat. The smart thing to do would've been to shut his mouth. Apparently, he wasn't capable of that.

"Your body is nice," he added when the silence stretched on too long. "Or, well, I'm assuming it's nice. You cut a nice figure." He waved his hand vertically and shimmied it about, as if he were proving something to me. "I have no idea if you're covered in scales or anything under your clothes, but from where I'm standing, you have a nice body."

I popped my lips as I regarded him. Really, there was nothing to say at this point.

"I took it too far, didn't I?" he said after a few seconds of lip popping.

I nodded.

"I always take it too far." He was rueful. "My mother called me her foot-in-mouth child when I was younger. When I was caught breaking a rule or lying, I always compounded the problem. My brothers wouldn't take me with them when they were breaking the rules because they knew I would make things ten times worse if I could."

It was a lovely moment of introspection that made me smirk. "Is that your problem? Are you bitter about your brothers not including you in their shenanigans when you were younger?"

"Who says I have a problem?"

"You just did."

"No, I didn't say that." He crumpled up the small cardboard container his eggs had been sitting in and aimed it at the trash receptacle. I was annoyed when he managed to sink his shot, mostly because that meant he wouldn't get up and leave me to my quiet breakfast. "You like to twist people's words and actions."

"Oh, how do you figure that?"

"You keep going on and on about me stealing your launch."

"You did."

"I didn't."

"You did so!" My temper bubbled again. "You benefitted from all the publicity I paid for."

"Dude, seriously, you need to unclench." He used an utterly reasonable tone that made me want to choke him. "Take a breath."

I would die before I ever did something he wanted me to do. "Did you just tell me to unclench?"

"I believe I did."

"Well, maybe you should unclench."

"I'm not the one melting down with her Café Beignet latte and Café du Monde beignets. Don't cry in that powdered sugar, by the way. It will result in a weird substance that could come alive and kill you in the middle of the night."

"Right." I was officially at the end of my rope. "And we're back to you being charming."

"I idle at charming."

"Yes, you're completely charming... for a launch thief."

"And here we go again." He blew out a sigh. "Moxie—that's a really weird name I know you made up, by the way—I think we got off on the wrong foot." He extended his hand, as if he were greeting me for the first time. "I'm Gus Kingman."

I took it. "I'm Moxie Stone. You still stole my launch."

This time, instead of being exasperated, he laughed. "I already told you that you're wasting your time—and your employer's money, for that matter—spending on publicity for a Bourbon Street bar launch. It's not necessary."

"Then why did you steal my launch?"

"I didn't."

"You did."

"No, I didn't." This time when he shook his head, he was vehement. "I didn't even have a firm date for a launch. I was waiting for a few things to be updated in the bar. Guess what? When things were done, I opened the bar. That's all the thought that went into it."

He was angry. It practically radiated off him in solid red waves. He also looked as if he were telling the truth. I still didn't believe him.

"You stole my launch." I was apparently willing to die on this hill. "You know it, and I know it."

"Oh, whatever." He tipped back his head and downed the rest of his coffee. "You are going to give yourself an early heart attack if you don't pull it together."

"Thanks for the tip."

"I wasn't joking about you unclenching. Your bar is going to be a success simply because of its location if you step back and take a breath." If he'd left it there, I might've been able to calm myself. "I mean... your bar is not going to be as good as mine, but that was never going to happen anyway."

My eyes narrowed into slits of hate when he unloaded the last bit, so narrow in fact that I likely resembled a snake... or a really stoned pothead fighting off sleep. "Cher is going to eat Flambeaux for a midmorning snack and leave nothing but crumbs behind."

He folded his arms across his chest, amusement flitting across his features. "That came out sounding way weirder than you thought it would, didn't it?"

"No. That's what I meant."

"Uh-huh." He slowly got to his feet. "Would you care to place a wager on who has the more successful bar?"

He had to be joking. Only an idiot would make a bet on something like that. "What are the terms?" I couldn't believe I was asking that. It was too late to haul the words back into my mouth though.

"If I win, you have to do something I want."

I waited for him to expand. When he didn't, I prodded him. "I'm going to need more than that."

"Don't worry. It won't be something gross, nothing sexual or weird. It would be more akin to public humiliation. If you want specifics, I'm going to need time to think it out because I haven't come up with a specific demand yet."

"And what about if I win?"

He shrugged. "You get the same. I have to do something you want." The way he smiled told me exactly what he thought I would ask for.

"Yeah, you can't be gross when we're talking about my demands either," I said.

50

"Fair enough. Are you in?"

"We need more rules," I argued. "It's too vague. Are we talking more customers? Is it more money? What is the deciding factor when it comes to who has the more successful bar? Also, we need a time frame. Is it two weeks? Two months? I need to know."

"You need to know a lot."

"I do."

"Well... how about we both come up with a list of rules and possible rewards. Then we'll compare notes and go from there."

It would've been considered impulsive to agree when nothing had been decided, but I couldn't help myself. "You're on." I extended my hand.

He took it and gripped it tightly. "I'm looking forward to beating you." His gaze went momentarily hot. "Or something less sexually stimulating because I don't want to come across as a demented pervert because you might like that."

"Keep it up," I warned, squeezing his hand as hard as I could. "You're going to be crying by the time I'm done with you."

"Funny, but I was thinking the exact same thing about you."

Six

I took a roundabout way to work, one that had me landing at the corner of Conti and Bourbon so I could take a look at the bars stretching between that intersection and where Cher was situated. There was a lot to look at.

First up was Desire Oyster Bar, which essentially served as the in-house bar of the Royal Sonesta. I'd yet to be able to down raw oysters—people said they were an acquired taste, but I had no interest in acquiring the taste—but the cocktails I'd had in the establishment were top-notch. It was a quiet location though. It made money. It wasn't meant to be a destination trip for the evening, however.

Across the street was Huge Ass Beers (no joke). Fried food and good beer. It appealed to men more than women, although that didn't stop women from going inside. The clientele was specific, although that wasn't necessarily a bad thing, and I had to give them credit for picking a perfectly branded name for what they were offering.

Daiquiri Delight boasted Slurpee machines—at least that's how I thought of them since I was from Michigan where there was a 7-Eleven on every corner when I was growing up—with endless choices. It was famous for a singular niche and didn't try to rise above it. People loved it, though, so it was doing exactly what it was supposed to be doing.

There were pizza shops, jazz bandstands, full restaurants, and kitschy tourist stores. One right after the other. It was early in the day for people to be on Bourbon Street, but I knew in three hours, it would be packed everywhere.

So how was I supposed to make Cher stand out when there were so many other options? My launch plan, while far from a dismal failure, hadn't resulted in the sort of buzz I was looking for.

I paused outside what used to be Kitty Cat's Playroom. I'd only been in town three days when it closed. That was following a raid. Supposedly, the owner of the bar was using it to cover for his money laundering endeavors. He'd been at the airport trying to flee when they tracked him down. The dancers in the establishment had been verified as adults and citizens before things had been shut down. They had not, however, received their final paychecks. At least that was the word on the street.

"Thinking of changing professions?" a voice called out, rocking me when I recognized it before causing me to scowl.

When I turned, Gus was standing on the opposite side of the road. He had a cheeky smile on his face.

"Are you following me?" I demanded, irritation bubbling up. "I purposely took a longer route to work so I wouldn't risk running into you... again."

He snorted. "That's why I took a longer route. I guess great minds think alike, huh?"

Yeah, that was not what I was thinking at all. "Well, next time you should stick to the shorter route to get to work. I'll take the longer one."

"Is that because you need the exercise?" His grin was impish. "I already told you I like your body."

I straightened, my eyes darting around to see if anybody had heard. Then I slowly extended a finger in his direction. "You're not cute, so stop that."

"I have it on good authority that I'm adorable."

"Your mom doesn't count."

He choked on a laugh. "I like that you're fast on your feet. It's going to make this game all the more fun."

"You're not going to be laughing when you're crying in your empty bar," I warned. I told myself I was more interested in garnering business for Cher than publicly embarrassing him, but I wasn't certain it was true.

"We'll see who is crying." He offered me a salute and started down the sidewalk, toward the intersection where our bars resided. "Just for the record, you're way too cute to moonlight at that place. They've never had a very good clientele," he tossed over his shoulder.

I rolled my eyes. "Do you think you're funny?"

"Most definitely."

"Well, you're not."

"See, I think you want to laugh." He kept walking, slowing his pace when two men turned the corner on my side of the street and headed toward me. "Why don't you come over here and laugh with me, huh?" The change in his demeanor was startling.

I focused on the men I was on a collision course with. I recognized them, although only vaguely. They were homeless, opting to split their time between Jackson Square and the Riverwalk when darkness fell. They were panhandlers versus musicians. I felt no fear as I regarded them.

"Reg. Brick." I nodded my head in greeting as they passed.

"Morning, Moxie," Brick sang out. He sounded a bit slurry, as if not quite finished drinking from the previous evening. Sure, it was the next day, but if he held to form, he would find a place to sleep for a few hours and then start the party all over again. "You look pretty this morning."

"Thank you, Brick." I beamed at him and then glanced around. Reg looked even worse for wear than Brick. "Have you guys eaten this morning?"

Brick shook his head, solemn. "We were hoping to get something."

I pulled a twenty out of my pocket and handed it over. "Hit Café Beignet." I pointed toward the location across from Royal Sonesta. "Make sure you get eggs for protein. Don't spend it on whiskey."

Brick was solemn as he accepted the twenty. "No whiskey," he agreed.

"Promise." I was stern as I planted my hands on my hips. "You guys need food to sustain yourselves if you want to party again tonight."

"I promise." Brick mimed crossing his fingers across his chest. "We'll get breakfast right now."

"And then some sleep," I prodded. "Don't forget to sleep."

"I'm on it."

I watched them go, my heart pinching slightly when they turned into the Café Beignet courtyard. They would at least get some coffee, I told myself. Food was better, but anything other than whiskey would do. When I turned to resume my walk, I found Gus watching me. "What?" I demanded, my irritation returning with a vengeance.

"Why do you do that?" There was nothing playful about the question.

I knew what he was referring to. More than one person had told me not to give money to the homeless in New Orleans. I refused to listen. "What?" I purposely evaded making eye contact.

"You shouldn't give them money," Gus insisted. "They're just going to spend it on more brew."

"So?"

"So... you're wasting money. Those people are never going to change."

A pinching feeling between my shoulder blades began in earnest. That was the second time he'd used those words. "*Those* people?"

"Yes, *those* people. Do you know most of them aren't even homeless? They just pretend."

"I know that's crap," I shot back. "The only people spouting that nonsense are those who think they're somehow above the situation. Like, I don't know, maybe the high and mighty Kingman family. Do you think you're above those who struggle to get by from day to day?"

"Don't take it there," he warned in a low voice.

"It's an honest question."

"No, you're trying to box me in." His nostrils flared as he crossed the road to join me. We were half a block from the bars at this point and pretending we weren't aware of each other's presence was a waste of time.

"No, I'm being honest," I countered. "You took one look at those guys and assumed they were going to harm me, maybe steal my money or something. I saw the way you reacted. You wanted me to cross the street to you."

"I was trying to protect you."

"From two innocent guys who were doing nothing?"

Frustration creased his forehead. "How was I supposed to know they were innocent?"

"By not jumping to conclusions."

"Oh, whatever." He made a growling sound and shook his head. "Do you want to know what your problem is?"

"Why don't you enlighten me?" *This should be good,* I told myself. He was about to say something stupid.

"Your problem is that you don't see things in shades of gray. Everything is black and white to you."

56

"Excuse me?"

"It's true." He was emphatic as he bobbed his head. "You just assume I made a snap judgment—and maybe I did—but the fact that I tried to protect you despite how awful you are to me is just overlooked."

I wanted to throttle him. "I don't need protection."

"New Orleans isn't all beignets and happy drunks. There's a seedy underbelly to this city. You shouldn't be making friends with random people you meet on the street."

"Really?" All I could do at this point was shake my head. "I'm shocked that New Orleans isn't all rainbows and rum runners. Shocked, I tell you. I mean, I myself thought the world was a perfectly safe place, what with living close to Detroit and all for the bulk of my life."

It could've been a trick of the eye—the sun was fairly bright—but I was almost positive his cheeks flushed with embarrassment. "Don't worry," he growled when he'd recovered sufficiently to speak. "I won't try to protect you again."

"I don't need protection." That was true. "Those guys were harmless. They like their brew and keep to themselves."

"How can you know that?" He seemed bewildered. "You took food to those guys outside Jackson Square last night. I saw you. Is that a regular occurrence?"

Suddenly, I felt defensive. "Don't worry about it."

"No, I'm honestly curious."

"I don't care what you are." I stomped toward the front door of Cher, rummaging in my pocket for my keys as I worked overtime to avoid eye contact. "When you come up with the rules for the bet, let me know. Otherwise... mind your own business."

"Don't worry. I have no interest in your business." He made a big show of tugging on Flambeaux's door, frowning when it didn't open. "Son of a bitch!" He dug for his keys and shoved the first one he found in the lock. It didn't fit. He tried

57

again. His curses got more colorful with each failed attempt. When he finally found the right one, he was triumphant as he puffed out his chest. "Have a nice day."

"You too." I was grinning as I slid through Cher's door. "Oh, just one more thing." I poked my head out and smiled at him. "If you were a more organized individual—as I'm sure your brothers are—then you would know to have a second key ring with the business keys attached to your personal ring so you don't have to go through that on a regular basis."

If looks could kill, I would be dead. "Thanks for the tip."

"You're welcome."

I SPENT THE MORNING SLINGING DRINKS. I'd learned a thing or two in Michigan, and most of the tourist traffic was light before noon, so it wasn't difficult to keep up. By the time Abel came in, I'd settled on a plan.

"We need to figure out a promotion," I said to him as he rearranged the napkin piles I'd made. "There has to be a way to bring people in here and make sure they don't go next door."

"That would be nice," Abel readily agreed. "I think you're overthinking it though."

"And I think I'm smart." I tapped the side of my head for emphasis. "We just need to figure out which promotion will bring in the most people."

"Honey, this is Bourbon Street. People are going to come in regardless. Stop stressing about it."

That was easy for him to say. "This has to be a success. If it's a failure, I'll only have one shot after that." I hadn't meant to say it out loud. "If I fail a second time, they'll write me off."

"Oh, geez." Abel's eye roll was pronounced. "Girl, you let the weirdest crap bother you. Nobody is going to write you off. You're smart and always thinking." He tapped the side of his head for emphasis. "Sure, you're a righteous pain in the ass, but you know your stuff. Don't get freaky."

I stared at him for a long beat and then picked a random thing to argue about. "Don't call me 'honey' or 'girl.' It's misogynistic. I have a name."

"A made-up name."

I pretended I didn't hear him. "Just call me Moxie... or your majesty. If you want to give me a nickname, go with that one."

"Oh, sure. That sounds just like me." Abel blew out a sigh. "Do you want to know what you should do?"

"Absolutely." If he had an idea, I was all ears. "You should figure out where all those strippers who lost their jobs down the road went and offer them twenty bucks to serve drinks for a day. You know, have a naked day or something."

I blinked several times in rapid succession. Finally, I laughed. I was sure he'd intended for me to take it as a joke. "Good one."

He didn't even crack a smile. "I'm being serious. Naked girls are a draw."

"Yeah, that's misogynistic."

"I'm not trying to be misogynistic. I don't even really know what that means. I'm trying to get you to chill out. You want this place to be a success. Naked girls bring in the money."

"Yeah, we're not doing that. Only an idiot would do that."

"If you say so." Abel shook his head and shifted to wipe down the jukebox. It was antique, and only for the times when we didn't have live music going. I happened to think it looked fantastic in the space. Abel didn't seem to care either way. I was about to turn my back on him when he stilled directly in front of the open window and pointed across the way. "So, what were you saying?" he prodded.

I moved closer so I could see what he was looking at,

scowling when I caught sight of Gus. He stood in the middle of Flambeaux, a bottle of what looked to be absinthe in his hand—of course he would go with something expensive—and was holding court. He didn't look in our direction, instead pouring the bottle over a woman who appeared to be dressed in nothing but a fancy bra.

"What is he doing?" I squinted so I could see better, frowning when I got to the girl's midriff. There, another man —was he even old enough to drink?—was positioned at her navel and sucking the absinthe into his mouth.

"Oh, that can't be sanitary." I threw up my hands and looked to Abel for support. "We should call someone."

"Who you gonna call? And if the answer ain't the Ghost-busters, turn your cute little ass around." He twirled his finger for emphasis. "Just FYI, that's Cassie Kitty... or that was her name when she was stripping down the street. She was the most popular stripper in that place before it was raided."

I stared at him a beat, confused. "And?" I finally said.

"And your friend across the way thought ahead and nabbed the strippers."

"But... no." I shook my head, thinking about our interaction this morning. "He would've had to have the idea..." I trailed off. I knew exactly when he got the idea. It was right around the time he was asking me if I planned on shifting to another career path, if not before. He probably had one of his brothers place the call to keep me off his scent. "He is a disgusting, slimy worm." I viciously swore under my breath.

"You need to learn to vent more," Abel insisted. "You're wound too tight. You worry about stupid things. No decision has to be made right away or kept to forever. This is the Quarter—things pop up and die out within days. You need to be willing to pivot."

"There's no way I'm pivoting to *that*." I jabbed a finger at the woman acting as an absinthe shot slide. "I'll come up with something amazing. It won't be that though."

"Well, knock yourself out." Abel returned to the bar. "I don't care what you do as long as you stop tripping."

"I'm not tripping." I went back to staring out the window, my cheeks flushing with rage as the woman gyrated and caused a group of men in Flambeaux to raise their fists in triumph while screaming in delight. "Seriously, that has to be against some sort of ordinance. Do you think the health department would do something?"

"No." Abel was firm. "Mind your own business. If you start a war with that man, he has connections you don't. I guarantee, he'll be the one winning when it's all said and done."

Oh, I had no intention of letting that happen. "I'll figure something out. I just... need a little time. It will all work out."

"Yeah, you keep telling yourself that."

Seven

O ne of the things I liked best about New Orleans were the parades. They had them for anything and everything. You could even throw a parade for yourself. All you needed was a permit.

I didn't have time to secure a permit, but when I saw a parade marching down Bourbon Street that afternoon, it did give me an idea.

"Hey." I slid into the formation, ignoring dirty looks from other band members as I focused on the conductor. Wait... are they called conductors when it's a ten-person band that spends its time playing on various street corners? Oh, well. I didn't know, and I was beyond caring.

"Hello." The man leading the parade was tall—almost six feet, if I had to guess—and boasted a wide middle. He had a gregarious face and the way he bopped his head back and forth told me he loved his job. I had to appreciate that. "Do you need something?"

"That depends." I licked my lips. I'd always been assertive —that wasn't what was bothering me—but I was also a rule follower. I didn't want to get in trouble. "How firm are the authorities on the parade permits?"

The corner of his mouth quirked. "I guess that depends on what you want."

I pointed toward Cher. "That's my bar. Er, well, it's the bar I manage." Ownership wasn't important right now, I told myself. "It opened yesterday, and I'm looking for a way to make a splash."

"And you want a parade?" He looked amused.

"I want to set up a special shot bar and then add a parade to the mix," I clarified. "The thing is, if we're going to get in trouble, I don't want to risk the parade. I'll secure the permit instead and schedule it for another day if you think that's the smarter route."

"This is NOLA."

I waited for him to expand. When he didn't, I nodded. "I'm well aware."

"It's different in NOLA."

"Does that mean we won't get in trouble for not having a permit or we will? I'm still trying to figure it out."

He laughed. "I'm Clément." He held out his hand. Behind us, the band continued to play. Apparently, they didn't need him to lead to continue with the show. "Currently, we're working on a permit secured by a local conference group. They're staying at the Sonesta down the way. We could extend that permit... for the right fee."

Ah, here we go. I smiled. "How much?"

He looked me up and down, spending extra time on my capris, to the point where I would've felt uncomfortable if I wasn't so determined to win. "Five hundred bucks."

I didn't immediately balk. "For how long?"

"Um... an hour."

I wrinkled my nose. "Get real. There's no way you're making that."

His expression darkened. "You don't know. We could be making that. We're a popular group."

"Yes, and there are eight other groups doing the same thing." I opted for practicality. "Competition is the name of the game. So, while I'm willing to pay a premium for the last-minute help, I'm not going to let you hose me." *Seriously, who does he think he's dealing with?*

Clément's smile grew. "Okay, I like that you're not an idiot. I only surround myself with smart people. We'll do it for our normal rate of three hundred."

I folded my arms across my chest and regarded him with my darkest 'don't even bother running *that* on me' look. Then I didn't say a single word.

"Two hundred, and that's as low as we go," Clement said after a beat. "We'll repurpose the permit—it happens all the time and nobody asks—but we expect a round of free drinks when we're done. We're a thirsty crew."

"I'll give you two rounds of drinks," I replied. "I need thirty minutes to get the shot bar going though. Can you make that work?"

"Yup." Clement bobbed his head. "We'll take this crew down two more blocks and have a little party. When we come back, we'll be quiet until we reach this intersection. Then we'll hit it and march straight into the bar. Does that work for you?"

I grinned. It was exactly what I had in mind. "Just make sure that you come into Cher." I pointed for emphasis. "Don't go into Flambeaux."

"I've got it." Clément's smile was wry. "I don't need you to tell me how to do my job, kid."

"Moxie," I automatically corrected.

"What?" Clément's forehead wrinkled in confusion. "Did you say something?"

I held back a sigh, although just barely. "Moxie," I repeated. "That's my name."

"Oh, right." Clément honked out a loud laugh. "There's no way that's your real name. Since this is the sort of town that doesn't need real names, I guess that's fine. Don't think you're fooling nobody though."

"Whatever. Just be back in thirty minutes." I broke off to return to the bar and hesitated. "It really is my name."

"If you say so."

TWENTY-FIVE MINUTES LATER, I WAS READY. I stood on the street corner, the shot bar set up by the open windows to draw people in from the street, and watched Bourbon for signs of my parade. I knew Clément wouldn't be exactly on time, but since he struck me as a solid businessman, I figured he wouldn't be more than a few minutes late.

"Hello there," a smooth voice intoned, causing me to jerk my eyes to the left. There, a tall man with dark eyes and broad shoulders studied me with the sort of intensity that I reserved for red velvet cake and full-fat lattes.

"Hello." I kept my face placid. I wasn't in the mood to be hit on. This was a potential customer, however. I also didn't want to be rude. "Would you like a shot?" I pointed toward the shot bar.

The man glanced in the direction I indicated, offered up a tepid smile, and then shook his head. "Actually, I'm just checking out the business, trying to make a decision."

"What sort of decision?"

He gestured toward Cher and then over to Flambeaux. "Do you have an opinion?"

Was he joking? "Obviously I think the bar I work at is better." There was no sense blowing sunshine up his ass or lying. He didn't look stupid... although that wasn't always apparent on the surface. "If you want to visit that bar, however, there's nothing I can do to stop you."

"No?" His gaze was keen as he looked me up and down. "I can think of a few things. They all involve you gasping my name. That might entice me to visit your bar."

It took everything I had not to punch him in the nuts. "Are you really trying to get me to offer you sex in exchange for a drink sale?"

He laughed. "Well, when you put it like that..." He'd yet to deny the charge. "Would you be willing to have sex with me for a drink sale?"

Before I could answer, the sound of a throat clearing directly behind him drew our attention. When I craned my neck, I found Gus studying the other man with something akin to annoyance.

"Leave her alone, Archer," he warned in a low voice. "She's not going to play your perverted games."

Archer. That was the oldest Kingman sibling, if I remembered the lesson my patio mates had given me the night before correctly. I should've realized he was related to Gus. They had the same dark hair, broad shoulders, and keen eyes. They looked similar enough to have come from the same genetic experiment, except for Archer's hair, which was slicked back with enough mousse I had to wonder if it was hard like a helmet.

"And there he is." Archer forgot about me and focused on his brother, offering Gus a hearty clap. "I was wondering if you were here."

An emotion I didn't recognize flashed in the depths of Gus's eyes, but he shuttered it quickly. I was curious enough about their relationship to remain where I was standing and watch, even though Archer had clearly lost interest in me.

"Why wouldn't I be here?" Gus challenged. "I mean... it is my bar. I'm supposed to be here."

"Just because you're supposed to be here, doesn't necessarily mean you will be here," Archer argued, grinning when a third man —clearly the third Kingman brother—joined the party. This one looked more casual than Archer but more put together than Gus. He was obviously middle son Aidan, which meant that he could lean both ways on the brother spectrum when trying to fit in.

"Aidan," Archer bellowed, as if he weren't content merely having the attention of his brothers but needed everybody on the block to look in his direction. "You're late. You were supposed to meet me ten minutes ago."

Aidan barely reacted. "I was inside, checking out the setup of the bar."

"And what do you think?" Archer was clearly looking for a breakdown of Gus's business. I found the scene playing out in front of me somewhat painful, and yet I couldn't look away. It was like a train wreck... and something told me Gus was going to be the debris left behind when they were finished.

"It's okay." Aidan was noncommittal. "I mean... there's nothing special inside. He has some hot bartenders dressed in barely-there clothing, but they're not doing anything overly interesting."

I risked a glance at Gus and found him glaring. His ire wasn't directed at me. It was reserved for his brothers. Both of them.

"I told you I've got it under control," Gus snapped. "It's barely been twenty-four hours, for crying out loud. Why are you guys even here?" He paused a beat, considering, and then narrowed his eyes. "Did Dad send you?"

It was an interesting family dynamic. Gus was the baby brother, and there was clearly some angst playing out between siblings.

"We just want to make sure that you've got everything under control," Archer replied. His tone was placating, almost soothing, and yet I didn't miss the way Gus reacted to it. "This is your first big opening. We want to make sure it goes well so you can handle more openings down the road."

"Yes, we don't want it consistently falling to us as Dad rolls closer to retirement," Aidan agreed. "It's time for you to do your share."

I felt as if I were intruding and yet I didn't turn away. It felt like one of those "the enemy of my enemy is my friend" things, but I knew better than to trust Archer and Aidan. Nothing would make them happier than crushing Cher in the name of brotherly love, even if it did feel like brotherly conquest at this point. Right now, they were focused on belittling their brother, however, and I wasn't above taking advantage.

"Thanks, I think I know how this works," Gus said dryly, shaking his head. "I don't need babysitters. I've got this."

"You've got three months," Archer corrected. "That's how long you've got to make this place a success. You're already a month behind where you should be. You opened late. Thankfully, you hopped on the opening of this other place, proving you're a smart cookie, as Mom would say. That gives you a leg up."

I swear I thought steam was going to explode out of my ears, like a cartoon image I'd once seen when flipping through channels on a Saturday morning.

Gus flicked a look at me, something akin to worry kindling in the depths of his eyes. "Don't listen to him."

"It's not as if I didn't already know it," I shot back. "I appreciate the confirmation though."

"They don't know what they're talking about," Gus insisted. "Although... what are you even doing talking to them? Don't you have other things to focus on?"

I did. In fact, at that exact moment, the parade music I'd been waiting for kicked into gear. It was so loud, it caused me to jolt, and when I glanced at the street, I found Clément enticing the crowd as he put on his patented performance.

"What the...?" Confused, Gus took a step off the curb. He almost looked as if he were going to intercept Clément and demand he go somewhere else.

For his part, Clément was beyond caring. He beamed at me and offered up a saucy wink before calling out to the people on the street, who had stopped walking—and drinking —so they could focus on him. "Themed shots at Cher," he called out. "All you can drink. Party like it's Bourbon Street, folks!"

I pressed my lips together when Gus's gaze swung to me. I managed to slide to the edge of the sidewalk just in time to avoid the swath of people Clément was leading into the bar. He stopped at the door long enough to yell again, this time directing his offer of themed shots toward the clientele inside Flambeaux. Then he led the huge procession of people into my bar, emptying Flambeaux at the same time.

It was like magic. Loud, raucous, and maybe a little stinky, but magic all the same.

"You've got things under control, huh?" Archer shot Gus a dubious look. "This doesn't look as if you've got anything under control."

Gus pursed his lips—in and out, in and out—and glanced between his oldest brother and me. Finally, he offered up a shrug. "It's a work in progress."

"You're going to get sent back to the mailroom," Aidan hissed. He was intent as he stared holes into his baby brother. "How long were you in the mailroom, Augie?"

"Augie?" I blurted out the name before I could think better of it.

"Gus," the man in question insisted, pinning me with a

warning look. "Nobody calls me Augie but them." He was quiet a beat, and then his lips curved into a sneer. "They know I hate that name."

"Yes, because Gus is so much better," Archer drawled. "Seriously, dude, you have got to get it together. Dad is already convinced you can't run a bar because of... well, you know." The statement was pointed, and I was practically salivating for him to spill more. For once, however, I kept my mouth shut... although it took monumental effort.

"I'm well aware of what Dad thinks," Gus replied, his tone stilted. "I don't need to be reminded."

"You've got to do better than this," Archer stressed.

"I'll get right on it." Gus's eyes drifted to me, and they didn't move even as his brothers issued their goodbyes. Once it was just the two of us, he held out his hands. "Are you happy?"

Was he really blaming this on me? "It was a promotion," I replied. "It's not my fault your brothers decided to do a drive-by at the exact moment my promotion kicked off."

Rather than frown, Gus grinned. "It was a bold move. I have to hand it to you. You won... at least for today. I don't think a parade is going to work over the long haul, but for today, it was ingenious."

"Oh, I have plenty of ideas." That was a bald-faced lie. So far I'd come up with the parade and shot bar. Nothing else was percolating. He didn't need to know that though. "This is only the opening volley."

"Well, kudos." Gus mock clapped. "I guess I'm going to have to up my game."

My stomach constricted at the glint in his eyes. "I'm ready for whatever you're going to throw at me," I said, even though I was plagued with doubts. "This is a competition, right? One of us gets bragging rights, and to embarrass the other."

"That's right." He bobbed his head. "I should warn you, Kingmans like to win."

That earned him a smile. "I don't know how to lose."

"I guess we'll just have to wait and see, huh?"

"I guess we will."

Eight

"We're going to get slammed in about an hour," Abel announced as he strode into the back storage room, where I was fussily reorganizing the box stacks.

"Are you suddenly psychic?" I asked, looking up at him. From my spot on the floor, he looked ridiculously tall. "Also, has anybody ever told you that you look frightening from certain vantage points?"

He shook his head and made a face. "When you're sitting on the floor, everybody looks tall."

"I bet Danny DeVito doesn't look tall from this vantage point."

"I'll have you know that the screen shrinks people ten inches," Abel replied. "Danny DeVito is way taller in person."

"Are you sure that's not just some myth the pearl clutchers made up about porn?" I asked after a beat.

It took him a second to digest what I was saying, and when he did, he broke out in a wide grin. "That's funny. Also, if anybody would be making that up, it would be the male porn actors, not the pearl clutchers."

I considered it for a moment and then nodded. "I can totally see that. Go back to being slammed in an hour though. Why did you say that?"

"Because I often say what I mean... and we're totally going to be slammed in an hour."

"But... how do you know that?"

"I have a trick knee." His expression never changed. "Instead of gauging the weather, it tells me when the customers are going to come calling."

"That sounds handy." There was no way that could be a thing. Not even in New Orleans. "So, why are we going to be slammed again?"

"Good grief, girl. You're so uptight." He shook his head. "I would suggest a way you could fix that, but I don't want to be fired for sexual harassment."

I didn't have to ask what he was referring to. "First off, I'm your boss. That means I would be the one sexually harassing you." I didn't realize how inappropriate that sounded until it was already out of my mouth. "Secondly, I'm not doing that. Thirdly, I'm not here for a relationship."

"Why are you here?" He looked serious when asking the question, as if he wanted an extensive answer.

I shrugged. "Professional glory."

"Yeah, it feels like more than that, but I'm going to let it go for now because we need to prepare for the rush that's coming. I have everybody stocking the coolers in the front and wiping down the tables."

"Which brings us to the original topic of conversation." Thank the voodoo queen we'd gotten off the sexual harassment conversational train. "Why are we going to be slammed again?"

"Because thunderstorms are supposed to start rolling through in an hour. According to the weather service, they're going to be pretty steady over the next few hours. That means people will need to get off the street... well, unless they're diehards. They'll crowd into the bars when the storms hit. We'll be bursting at the seams."

"I like the idea of bursting at the seams."

"It's going to feel like a sweaty armpit in here when those seams threaten to burst. You should prepare yourself."

Even as I patted myself on the back at the notion of a full house, something occurred to me. "Okay. I'll be ready. I'm going to run out first though."

Abel's face twisted into a scowl. "You're going to run out two minutes after I told you we're going to be slammed?"

"I just need to run the extra food down to Jackson Square."

"The extra food you hoard like a little squirrel in the kitchen?"

"Yes."

"And what are you going to do when you get the food to Jackson Square?" His expression told me no answer was going to make him happy.

"I give the extra food to the homeless." I saw no reason to lie, even though I could practically feel the irritation radiating off him. "It would just be thrown in the garbage here. The guys down at the Square won't use the money they get from panhandling for food, and they're happy for what I bring. It's a win-win situation."

"Yeah, I'm not sure how we win in this situation."

"We don't have as much garbage to take out at the end of the night." It was a lame reason, but it was all I had.

"Oh, well, that makes perfect sense." He threw up his hands. "I can't believe you're going to actually risk being caught out in a storm to take those guys food."

I couldn't make him understand. I didn't have the time. Truth be told, I didn't even understand myself why I kept doing it. Now that I'd started, however, I couldn't imagine them sitting there waiting for me to swoop in and feed them. It was too much to bear. If that made me soft, well, so be it. Nobody had to know exactly how soft I really was.

"I just don't like waste," I insisted. "It will take me ten minutes to get the food down there. Then ten minutes to get back. I'll be here to help when the storm hits."

"I don't need your help. I can handle things on my own."

"So, what are you complaining about?"

He opened his mouth, what I was certain would turn out to be a snarky response on the tip of his tongue, but he ultimately didn't give me grief. "Head out. If the storm hits when you're out there, take cover in Pirate's Alley. The storms here are nothing to mess with when they're dark red on the map, and this one is dark red."

"Thanks for the advice." I managed a smile as I headed for the door. "Believe it or not, I've been through thunderstorms before. They're not unique to New Orleans. We had them in Michigan."

"Not like the storms here." He was firm. "When they roll in close to the water like this, on a hot and humid day like we've had, they can get ugly quick. If you're caught in one, don't run. Take cover and wait it out."

He seemed so serious all I could do was nod. "I've got it. Storms are bad. I'll take cover. It's not going to matter though. I'm going to take the food down and be right back."

"Oh yeah, famous last words. Those folks down there are crazy. They could snap and kill you. There's mental illness running amok down there. You realize that, right?"

"I do realize it." There was no reason to pretend I hadn't given it a great deal of thought. "I've got it under control. The sooner you stop giving me grief, the sooner I'll be back. Just... chill out. I know how to take care of myself."

"Girlfriend, I'm not sure you know how to cross the street without getting hit. I guess I'll have to take your word for it."

"I guess so."

DESPITE MY BRAVADO WITH ABEL, AFTER ONE look at the dark clouds on the horizon, I found myself increasing my pace. The air outside was like a warm washcloth, one that was so wet it had sweat dripping down my face. I ignored my discomfort and powered through, searching the area surrounding the park for familiar faces as the tourists who had gathered in the area scurried in the direction I'd come from. They were obviously heading back to their hotels. They'd registered the weather and knew it was time to take cover.

"Bishop! Gremlin!" I called out a few names but got no takers. After calling out a few more times, two familiar faces popped up... and they seemed surprised.

"What are you doing out here, Sunshine?" Whiskey asked, his voice slurring from drink. He'd obviously been amusing himself a specific way over the course of the afternoon.

I was breathless but relieved. "Here." I shoved the boxes of food into his hands. "A storm is coming. You need to take cover."

He snorted. "That's kind of funny coming from you." He lifted one of the boxes and sniffed it. "This smells good and all, but why did you bring it now?"

"Because I might not be able to bring it later."

He waited, his eyebrows impossibly high on his forehead. He only started speaking again when it became apparent I wasn't going to continue. "You know you don't have to do this every single day, right?"

"I want to. There's no need for you guys to go hungry."

I swear the man looked as if he pitied me by the time I got it out. "You're in for a world of heartbreak someday, kid." He shook his head but smiled. "You only see what you want to see."

"I see people who need food," I insisted. "I have extra. That's all this is."

"Well, thanks." He cradled the food against his chest. "The park will clear out now," he said pointedly. "You should go before the storm hits."

"Do you have someplace to go?" I asked.

"We have places we go. We'll be safe. In case you haven't noticed, though, you're the only one out here."

When I glanced around, I realized he was right. "I'll head back to the bar."

"Make sure you do that."

I watched him a beat longer, making sure he took the food with him when he left with Anthony. Once I was certain he would find shelter, I turned to head back... and came face to face with Gus. He stood in the shadow of the cathedral watching me, his expression unreadable.

"Are you following me?" I asked as the first fat droplet bounced against my cheek. I was glaring when I lifted my gaze to the sky. "It hasn't been an hour!"

"I was following you," he admitted. He almost looked dazed as he regarded me. "I thought you were going to do something to try to hurt my business during the storm."

I was incredulous. "Like what?"

"Who knows, parade queen," he shot back. "You're wily. I wanted to make sure you weren't going to be wily during the storm. I've had a bad enough day."

Since I was partially to blame for that bad day, I felt a smidgen of guilt. It didn't last. "You stole my launch and made it so I had a bad day. I guess we're even now."

"Oh, give it up with the launch!" He had to raise his voice for me to hear it over the rumble of thunder.

When I shifted my gaze to the Mississippi River, the sight

of the lightning flashing above—it was like a strobe light it was so active—was enough to have the hair on the back of my neck standing on end. "I am not going to make it back to the bar, am I?"

"Neither of us are." Gus looked resigned as he strode in my direction. "Come on." He grabbed my arm.

"Hey." I jerked away from him. "Don't get handsy."

He shot me a withering look. "Trust me, sweetheart, I don't want to get handsy with you."

"Um... all evidence to the contrary."

"I just don't want you dying on my watch." He grabbed my elbow again and herded me toward Pirate's Alley. "Come on. We have to get under something."

That sounded rather vague. "Under what? You don't mean each other, do you?"

"Oh, well, there's an interesting idea." His tone was dry as he shoved me in a corner. It was at the exact moment a huge bolt of lightning crackled close enough to make me think it had hit somewhere nearby. It was followed almost immediately by a rumble of thunder bold enough to shake the ground.

I jumped. I couldn't stop myself.

When he swung his eyes back to me, concern lurked in the depths. It was mixed with annoyance. "Now we're stuck here," he said.

It didn't take a genius to figure out that he blamed me for the turn of events. "You didn't have to follow me."

His breath was hot on my face because there was nowhere for us to go if we didn't want to get wet. And by wet, I meant soaked. The rain was coming down in a torrent. Between that and the constant lightning, he was right—for what might've been the first time ever, if I had to guess—that we were most definitely stuck.

"I thought you were going to pull something unethical."

"The parade was not unethical." I couldn't stop myself

from arguing with him. If I did, the silence would be overbearing. I wasn't the sort of person who could accept silence with someone I didn't know. It was never comfortable, despite what books and movies constantly tried to make me believe.

"The parade was actually a smart move. I wish you hadn't unveiled it in front of my brothers, but kudos." He held up his hands and mock clapped. "What you pulled yesterday was unethical though."

Ugh. Why does he have to keep bringing that up? "I apologized for that. Let it go."

"You did not apologize."

"Yes, I did."

"No, you didn't."

We were practically on top of one another. Thanks to the humidity—which the storm was surprisingly not helping with, unlike in Michigan—I was a sweaty mess. I could practically feel the little bit of makeup I'd slapped on this morning sliding down my face. I refused to look away though.

"I said I was sorry. I'm not saying it again. I won't do anything unethical. I don't have to cheat to win."

"Oh, if you say so." Gus shook his head. "I wanted to see what you were doing, which begs the question, what were you doing?"

I changed course almost immediately. "What did it look like I was doing?"

"Seriously?" His lips twitched, but he kept his frown in place. "I can't believe you just won't own up to what you were doing."

"I'm simply curious what you think I was doing. If you come up with something I'm comfortable with, I'll own up to it."

Now he smiled. "Good grief. Is that how you managed to climb to the top of the restaurant totem pole so fast in Michigan? Did you do it by flirting?"

Oh, now I was offended. "I am not flirting with you."

"I know flirting. You're totally flirting with me."

"I am not!"

His grin was full-fledged, and loath as I was to admit it, he was even more handsome with a genuine smile on his face. "You're kind of easy to irritate, huh? I think that's going to work to my advantage in this little competition we're having."

"I'm smooth as an ice cube."

"That was a really random thing to say."

"Well, that's because I'm so smooth."

We held gazes for so long I thought he might've had a stroke. His expression never changed despite the length of time we stared at each other.

"You were bringing food out to the homeless again," he said finally, his voice barely above a whisper. The storm raged on the other end of the alley, but here in our small little corner of the world, we were safe... from everything but each other.

"So what? They're hungry. I have extra food. Why does it bother you that I bring them food?"

"It doesn't bother me. I just want to know why." I flinched when his hand went toward my face. "Oh, I'm not going to hurt you." He made a growling sound as he wiped something off my cheek. "Your eyeliner is running."

I jolted at his touch, heat pulsing through me. I blamed it on the storm, which was getting so loud I could barely hear myself think.

"I don't wear eyeliner," I said out of nowhere. "It's mascara."

He shook his head. "Whatever." He paused a beat. "Did you really think I was going to hurt you?" He seemed legitimately upset at the thought.

"You just took me by surprise. The storm is loud and... I'm a little nervy."

"Yeah. They probably don't have storms like this in Michigan."

"Not exactly like this," I conceded. "Okay, nothing like this," I added after a few seconds.

His grin was back in a flash. "I'll protect you."

Oh, that was just too much. "I don't need protection. I can take care of myself."

"Which is why you're constantly coming down here and feeding the homeless. I need to know why."

I couldn't answer that. Not just wouldn't but couldn't. If I couldn't explain it to myself, I could never explain it to him... not that I wanted to. "They're hungry. I have food. That's all there is to it."

"I don't believe you."

"Well, I don't know what to tell you." I rested my head against the wall behind me. The storm showed no signs of letting up. That meant we were going to need to distract ourselves... with something other than our proximity. "So, if we're going to be stuck here, do you want to play a game?"

The question clearly caught him off guard, but he didn't back away from the suggestion. "What? Are we talking I Spy or Twister here?"

"Twister? You wish. I was thinking more like Truth or Dare."

He hesitated a beat and then shrugged. "I don't think we can do a lot of dares because if we go out in that storm, we legitimately could die."

"Then we'll just play the truth portion."

"Do you promise you'll actually tell the truth?"

"Yes."

"Are there other rules? Like... can I ask about your sexual partners?"

I was quickly losing interest in playing any sort of game with this guy. "Try not to be crass. If we're going to be competing, I simply think we should get to know each other a little better."

He considered it for a full five seconds and then nodded. "I'm amenable to those rules. Bring it on."

"Gladly."

Nine

Truth or Dare turned into a game of margins. Neither of us wanted to answer the deep stuff, although we weren't opposed to pressing the other on serious issues. Since the rain stopped us from daring one another to do anything, it was just a game of Truth. That consisted of us rapidly firing questions at one another.

"How many siblings do you have?" Gus asked.

"None. I'm an only child. Why were your brothers giving you a hard time?"

"They like it. Where are your parents?"

The question hurt my heart, for more reasons than one. "My mother died."

He stared hard into my eyes. "When?"

"About two years ago."

"I'm sorry. Where is your father?"

There was no way I was answering that. "It's not your turn. What's your favorite color?"

His eyes narrowed. "Lame."

"You still have to answer it."

"Blue." He kept his gaze focused squarely on my face.

Given our location, we had very little room to move. He had to plaster himself against one wall of the alley to avoid touching me, and I had to do the same across the way. The air between us was warm, stagnant, and heavy with animosity. "Where is your father?"

I should've known he would come back to that question. "I haven't seen him since I was a kid." It wasn't exactly a lie. It wasn't entirely the truth either.

"I'm sorry." He looked sincere.

"It's fine. Why did you hijack my launch?"

His lips quirked. "Good grief. You're obsessed with that, aren't you?"

"I'm a fan of honesty."

"Well, honestly, I didn't have a date in mind to open the bar. When it got close, I saw that you were going to open, and I figured it would be easiest to open at the same time. It wasn't personal."

That somehow made it worse. "Do you regret it?"

"No." He shot me a cocky smile. "Why do you feed the homeless?"

"Because they're hungry."

"No." He vehemently shook his head. "It's more than that. I mean... you went out in a storm."

"Before a storm."

"You still knew it was going to storm."

"So? Just because it's going to rain, that doesn't mean they're not hungry."

His eyes were piercing as they looked me up and down. "I just can't figure you out."

"Does it bother you?" I was hopeful the answer would be yes.

"It intrigues me," he said instead, causing my stomach to do a weird little dance. "Most women in this town can't throw themselves at me fast enough. They consider me local royalty."

"I hardly think owning a bunch of restaurants and bars makes you royalty."

"No, but my parents having money makes me a sought-after commodity."

I pursed my lips. "Is this a come-on?" I asked finally. "If so, I have to say, it's pretty weak. You should try something else if you want me to roll over and play nice."

This time when he smiled, it lit up his entire face. "Do you want to roll over and play nice?"

"With you? No."

"Oh, you already said it." He pushed himself away from the wall and landed directly in front of me. "It's too late to take it back." His mouth was mere inches from mine. All he had to do was lean in slightly and he would be kissing me.

Not that I wanted that. Even a little. Forget the fact that he was my archnemesis—that's totally a thing—but I had no interest in lazy rich boys who stole other people's bar launches. That didn't make him smart or charming, no matter what he thought. That made him an unethical little toad, and I didn't like him one bit.

"You're not my type," I said, doing my best to puff out my chest and create a little room. All it did was make it so we were pressed up against one another even tighter. "Also, I'm not here to date anyone."

"Who said anything about dating?" His smile was practically a dare.

"I prefer people who don't hijack launches."

"Oh, you're unbelievable." He deflated a bit and ran his hand through his hair. "If I apologize for launching the same day as you—even though you didn't own that day—will you let it go?"

"Probably not."

"Well, at least you're honest." He leaned back and stared toward Jackson Square. "It's stopped raining but still looks pretty dark out, and clouds are probably building again to the south. We should make a run for it."

"That's the first thing you've said that's made sense since I met you."

"Stick around. You might be shocked twice."

"I won't hold my breath."

WHEN HE SAID, "MAKE A RUN FOR IT." HE clearly meant it. His legs were longer than mine, so he'd outstretched me by a block within two minutes. Still, when he reached Royal Street, he stopped long enough to make sure I was still following. It would've been sweet if somebody else was checking. From him, it just felt condescending.

"I can walk back to the bar by myself," I snapped when I was within hearing distance.

"Has anyone ever told you what a joy you are?" he shot back. "No, I'm being serious. Has anybody ever looked you in the eye and said 'you're the sweetest woman I've ever met, Moxie'?"

"I'll have you know that people the world over think I'm fantastic," I huffed.

"Do any of those people question why you have such a weird name?"

"You're named after a *Cinderella* mouse," I fired back.

"At least it's a real name. Moxie is a word. It's not a name."

"It's a state of mind."

He opened his mouth again, and this time I couldn't ignore the way his lips quirked. He thought this was funny. All the arguing, the poking one another, the giving each other grief... he totally thought it was funny.

Before I could decide how I was going to annihilate him next, movement on Bourbon Street caught my attention. Both bars were still open, people taking advantage of the break in the weather to spill out onto the street, but there was a tall man standing on the corner who was set apart from the rest. He was watching us. He was dressed in a suit, a casual one accompanied by one of those skinny ties that hipsters wear when trying to pretend they're not selling out upon joining the business world. His hair was dark, as were his eyes, as they bounced between the two of us.

"Hey, there's No Fuss Gus," the man called out.

My forehead creased at the weird nickname, and when I switched my eyes to Gus, I found he looked positively sick to his stomach. "Are you okay?" I asked automatically, convinced he was about to have a delayed reaction to the storm and boot all over the sidewalk.

"Oh, now you care." Gus tried for a tight smile when he'd recovered, but it didn't reach his eyes. "I'm fine. If you don't want to get chlamydia by proximity, though, stay away from that guy."

Oh, well, now I was doubly intrigued. Whoever this guy was—and he looked important, at least in his own mind—Gus clearly didn't like him. That meant I was likely to love him. Well, at least that's what I told myself.

"Hey, Damon." Gus's tone held no warmth as he greeted the other man. "What are you doing here?"

"Oh, is that the way to greet your old childhood friend?" Damon's smile was gregarious. There was a light to his eyes that I would've found attractive if I was hunting for a boyfriend... or even a temporary distraction. Still, despite how amiable he appeared, something felt off about the situation.

I decided to watch... and learn. If Damon could get under Gus's skin, it might be a talent he could teach me. What? We're competing with one another. There's no way I'm forgetting that.

"I don't particularly remember us being friends," Gus replied.

Damon's nose wrinkled. "Um... we played lacrosse together."

"That doesn't mean we were friends." Gus had somehow turned into a pouty mess over the course of sixty seconds. He hadn't been all that fun during our time trapped in Pirate's Alley, but the guy he'd been then was much preferable to the one I found myself watching.

"This guy is such a kidder," Damon said to me, jerking his thumb toward my surly nemesis. "I'm Damon Stephens, by the way. I own the Kitty Cat Clubhouse over on St. Philip Street."

It was a weird way to frame an introduction, self-important and grating. Since he seemed to be making the statement for Gus's benefit rather than mine, however, I let it go. "Moxie Stone." I extended my hand.

"Moxie?" Damon's smile was so wide it threatened to consume his entire face, like a flesh-eating bacteria that only affected deranged clowns. "What a lovely name."

"Oh, that's not her name," Gus groused under his breath, shaking his head. "She won't say what her real name is."

"Is that true?" Damon feigned sternness as he regarded me, all the while refusing to release my hand. "Are you lying to my friend about your name? If so, I encourage that. He's a ladies' man and will do nothing but break your heart. You should break up with him."

It took me a moment to absorb everything he was saying. "Oh, we're not together." I made another attempt to pull back my hand, but Damon held tight.

"We're definitely not together," Gus agreed. "Also... stop molesting her." He reached over and pried Damon's fingers from my hand. "You don't have to put up with random guys groping you, Moxie. Next time he touches you, just kick him in the nuts. I would do it myself, but he would probably sue me."

For the first time since seeing us on the street together, Damon registered an emotion that felt legitimate. It was annoyance. His eyes darkened, his breath momentarily quickened, and then the smile was back. It happened so fast I almost wondered if I'd imagined it. "Are you going to bring that up again?"

Oh, I couldn't just let it go. "You sued him?" I wiped my sweaty palm on the front of my pants as I searched Damon's face. He acted like a nice guy. I considered myself a decent judge of character though. There was a disconnect from the Damon he showed to the world and the real man. It was possible he was faking all of it. In fact, it felt probable. Whatever he was doing here, his visit wasn't for altruistic purposes. He wanted something specific.

"My parents sued his parents," Damon clarified. "I wanted nothing to do with the entire thing. It was a terrible mistake."

"One that had you crying like a baby." Gus almost looked smug.

"You hit me in the face," Damon fired back. "With a crosse."

"You hit him with a crosse?" I was really confused. "What's a crosse?"

"It's part of the game," Gus replied darkly.

"Yeah, but what is it?" I couldn't let it go. "While we're at it, what's that little stick with a net that you play with called?"

The look Gus pinned me with could've peeled paint. "It's called a crosse."

That didn't sound right. "Um... I don't think so."

Impatience pushed his eyebrows up his forehead. "Well, it is."

"He's right," Damon offered. "It's called a crosse... and he smacked me in the face with one during a scrimmage in high school. He broke my nose and everything. It was the most

89

painful injury of my entire life. I could've died if bone fragments made it into my brain."

"And now you know why nobody wanted to hang around with him," Gus offered.

I had to bite back a smile. Gus might've been my archnemesis, but I fully understood his reaction to Damon. There was something smarmy about the guy. Sure, I was still going to figure out a way to get dirt on Gus from him. That didn't mean I was going to enjoy his company while it was going down.

"He's just saying that," Damon argued. "I was the most popular guy in school."

"The most popular guy who sued another guy because he got hit in a contact sport."

Damon made an annoyed clicking sound with his tongue. "That was my parents. You remember how they were."

"I do," Gus confirmed. "They were jerks. They still bought you the Kitty Cat Clubhouse, right? You can't hate them if they're setting you up in business."

Damon's smile turned smug. "Um... isn't that a little hypocritical?"

"My parents didn't buy this bar for me," Gus countered. "They loaned me the money to start my own bar. There's a difference."

There was a difference, however slight. The information had me looking at Gus in a new light... and wondering. I didn't voice my immediate questions though. I had to take advantage of this situation.

"Do you have funny stories about Gus when he was a kid?" I asked. "Like... was he ever caught looking in the female locker room? Or was he ever suspended from school for doing something bad? Or did he try to have an affair with a teacher and get caught?"

Gus shot me a dirty look. "Don't ask him things like that. You'll just encourage him to keep talking."

Wow. Gus really hated this guy. That boded well for me. "I'll take anything you've got."

"Oh, you're so cute." Damon pinched my cheek and gave it a jiggle, causing me to frown. "I can see what you see in her, Kingman. She's lovely. How serious are you guys?"

I jerked away from him. All semblance of amusement had fled with the pinch. "Can you not do that?"

"I told you." Gus folded his arms across his chest and gave me a serious look. "Now you have chlamydia. I hope you're happy."

There was nothing about this situation that made me happy. I decided to redirect my ire. "Gus and I aren't together," I volunteered. "We're... friendly business rivals."

"Oh, really?" Damon's smarmy smile was back. "And where do you work, honey?"

Did he just call me honey? That was all I could focus on as I scowled.

"You should run now," Gus offered. "He's never going to stop talking if you don't. He thinks he can get to me by hitting on you. He doesn't understand that's never going to work."

I was starting to grasp that myself. "Don't forget our deal," I said as I edged around Damon and pointed myself toward Cher. "We need to come up with specifics for the bet before I'm going to officially agree to anything."

"Yeah, yeah, yeah." He offered me a half-hearted wave. His full attention was focused on Damon though. He was clearly done dealing with me for the day. "Just tell me what you want, Damon. I don't have time for nonsense. I have a bar to run."

"Who says I want anything?" Damon was suddenly the picture of innocence as he held out his hands. "I just heard you'd recently opened fresh doors in the area, and I wanted to stop by and wish you well."

That was a steaming load of crap. Gus clearly knew it, too, because he was rolling his eyes. I was curious about what Damon wanted, especially because I might be able to use it to my advantage, but I knew they weren't going to get to the nitty-gritty as long as I was there to play witness. So, to hurry things along, I disappeared inside... and then immediately tracked down Carly.

"Listen at the window." I pointed toward Gus and Damon for emphasis. I could no longer hear them, but I could see their lips moving. Whatever they were talking about, neither party was happy. "I want to know what they're saying."

Carly didn't ask why. She simply saluted and headed in that direction.

Abel, who was busy behind the bar, gave me a cursory look as I joined him. "I was worried when you didn't come back."

"That storm came in a lot quicker than I was expecting. I had to take cover in Pirate's Alley."

"At least you had cover." Abel's eyes were speculative as they looked me up and down. "Were you with Gus Kingman?"

I hated the question. Not because I didn't expect him to ask it or anything but because I could sense his suspicion. "He happened to be out there. We were not together."

He didn't look convinced. "Who is the other guy?" He tipped his head toward Damon.

"Some guy he went to school with. Damon Stephens. Does the name ring any bells?"

"No, but I can ask around."

I probably should've told him not to waste his time. That wasn't the route I went. "Thanks. I figure I might be able to use him as a weapon against Gus."

"Aren't you taking this a little too seriously?"

"No, because when I win, we're going to be able to rule this intersection with an iron fist. That's the most important thing."

"If you say so."

"I *know* so."

Ten

When it came time to leave, Abel shooed me off.

"Don't fuss," he groused. "I've got this. Just pay attention when you're going home. I don't know how I feel about you walking across the Quarter alone at night."

"Maybe you're the one who should stop fussing," I fired back.

"Yeah, I'll get right on that. Text when you're safely home. If you dawdle more than twenty minutes, I'm sending my boys after you, and they won't be happy about having to go on a rescue mission when they would prefer drinking."

His boys? I filed that away to consider later. Did he have a gang? Did he simply have a group of people he liked to hang out with? Did he have brothers? Inquiring minds wanted to know. I was too tired to think about it tonight though.

Instead, I headed out, immediately crossing the street and pointing myself toward Jackson Square. The revelers on Bourbon Street were out and having a good time despite the earlier rain. It seemed to have dissipated, however, and the sky was clear. That was all the horde needed.

94

I considered the events of the day as I walked. I'd learned something about my enemy. Actually, I'd learned several somethings. He felt inferior next to his brothers. He didn't like Damon Stephens. He was also interested in how I spent my time. That could be considered both good and bad depending on how I wanted to play things.

I was halfway to Jackson Square when I heard footsteps echoing on the street. I turned quickly, halfway expecting to find someone running to intercept me. Instead, I found Gus pacing me on the other side of the road.

"Where did you come from?" I asked, scowling.

"My mommy says the stork brought me," he drawled.

"Oh, that's cute. I have some bad news for you. Babies don't come from the stork."

"Please tell me you're about to regurgitate my seventh-grade health class."

"Do you need me to?"

He nodded. "Yes. I went to a private school. It was religious. Do you want to know how they explained the miracle of birth?"

"I'm actually afraid to find out."

"They didn't explain it. They told me to ask my parents or make an appointment with the school nurse."

I choked on a laugh as I tried to picture what he was describing. "That sounds... horrible."

"Yup."

"How did you finally find out the truth?"

"I watched HBO when my parents were busy with work and fundraisers. There's this old show called *Sex and the City*. It taught me everything I know."

He never ceased to surprise me. "Who is your favorite *Sex and the City* girl?"

"I fancy myself a Samantha." He puffed out his chest as he said it, and I laughed so hard I almost tripped. "Careful now," he chided. "You don't want to fall and ruin that perfect face of yours."

I was taken aback as I recovered. "Perfect?"

"Hey, you're lacking in the personality department. That means you have to excel in another area."

"Oh, is that how it works?"

"Yup."

"And what are you lacking?"

"I'm one of those rare individuals who has it all. Looks." He flexed an arm. "Brains. Personality. I'm not lacking in a single competitive category."

"Your brothers think otherwise."

He scowled. "Do you have to bring them up?"

I held up my hands to placate him. "Sorry. You're right. It's been a pleasant ninety seconds."

"Not that you're keeping track."

"Every second with you feels like a minute."

He bobbed his head. "Oh, so you're saying time stands still when you're with me, like a magic moment. Thank you for the compliment."

"It wasn't meant as a compliment."

"That's how I heard it."

"Yes, but it wasn't meant that way."

"Perception is a funny thing," he noted. "Two people can see things in vastly different ways. That's why I find life so thrilling."

"Oh, whatever."

We lapsed into silence for half a block. He was the first to break it, although I was getting dangerously close to doing the same.

"Truth or dare?" he asked in a low voice.

Honestly, I welcomed the game. It was a way for us to converse without having to come up with our own topics. "Since it's the middle of the night, and I don't want you to dare me to do something that will get me killed, I'm going with truth."

"Where do you see yourself in five years?"

The question threw me. "I... don't... know."

"Oh, you know." He made a tsking sound with his tongue. "You're exactly the type of girl who knows where she'll be in five years."

"How come it sounds like there's an insult buried in there?"

"Because you're a naturally suspicious person. Come on. Tell me."

I huffed out a sigh. "I'm not sure what city I'll be in. I have a few ideas, like Key West... or maybe Honolulu. I do know that I'll have made enough money from my bar launches for other people to finally own my own string of bars at that point."

"Oh yeah?" He sounded intrigued more than condescending. "What kind of bar do you want to own?"

I shrugged. "All kinds. I would like to eventually go the high-class route, limited clientele and all that. I also want to go the tiki bar route. I've always had a thing for tiki bars."

"Who doesn't have a thing for tiki bars? I absolutely love a good piña colada."

"Yeah. They're my favorite too."

We lapsed into silence again. This time, I was the one who spoke first. "Truth or dare?"

"I'm going to stick to truth because I'm afraid you'll make me lick a grate or something, and I don't want to bring salmonella home, although that might be better than the last girl I invited back for shenanigans."

"Totally." I smirked to myself. He was self-deprecating, something I appreciated. He managed it without talking down about himself. He was self-assured and yet not full of himself. Given who his parents were, that shouldn't have been possible.

I had questions, although I wasn't certain I was prepared to answer his reciprocating questions tonight. I decided to go with something easy.

"Do you wish you were an only child?"

That garnered a snort from him. "Oh, so many times. I spent years wishing I was an only child. Then I realized that would be worse."

"How so?"

"If I was the only child, my parents would have nobody else to dole their sage wisdom out to. They would have exactly one child to focus on. As it is now, I'm the screwup. That means they spend more time fixating on my brothers because they still have hope for them."

I had no idea what to make of the statement. "Didn't your parents give you a bar to run?"

"Only because they're convinced I'll fail."

Huh. There was so much to unpack there. "Why do they think you'll fail?"

"Because they don't believe I've ever succeeded in my life."

Slowly, I let my eyes drift across the road until they landed on him. "You don't strike me as a failure."

"You might be surprised. Truth or dare?" He was clearly done dwelling on this subject.

"Truth," I said with a sigh as we arrived at Jackson Square. The park was closed, but I could see various figures stretched out on the benches surrounding the fence. Most were unmoving, suggesting they'd bedded down for the night. There weren't many recognizable faces present as there were on a normal night, and it left me feeling antsy.

"Why are you so interested in these people?" he asked pointedly.

We were no longer across the road from one another. We were on the quaint street that led down to Decatur. I knew better than to cut in front of the cathedral this late at night. Even if Gus were to follow, it could be dangerous.

"Because I know what it's like to feel alone in the world," I replied simply, moving away from the resting figures and toward the street. I would follow the sidewalk from there, past Gus's condo in the Jax Building, past the voodoo store and Rite Aid. In five more minutes, I would be home.

"Are you alone because you lost your mother?"

"I'm just... alone."

"What about siblings?" He looked genuinely interested. "I think I asked before, but I can't remember the answer. Is there a Poxie or Doxie out there for you to spend the holidays with?"

"I have an Uncle Mike," I replied. "I believe he lives in Alaska. I haven't seen him since I was three."

"So, that's a no."

When I risked a glance at Gus, I found sympathy creeping across his handsome features. "Oh, don't do that." I wagged a finger. "I don't need you feeling sorry for me. My life might seem pathetic in comparison to your life, but it's pretty good."

"I didn't say otherwise."

"You were thinking it."

"No, I really wasn't." He pursed his lips. "Where is your place?"

"It's not too far. You live here, right?" I inclined my head toward the Jax Building.

"I do, but I'm more interested in where you live."

"I don't think I should tell you that."

"Why?"

"Because you might be a skeevy pervert."

"Of course I am. Tonight, however, I'm just interested in making sure you get home safely. The pervert stuff will have to wait until it's not so humid."

"I'll be fine."

"And yet I'm going to walk with you."

Frustration bubbled up and grabbed me by the throat. "What if I don't want you to walk with me?"

"You'll survive."

"Listen..."

"No, you listen." He gave me a firm headshake. "I don't like the idea of you walking alone tonight. It could start storming again, and that's natural cover if somebody wants to hop out of the woodwork and grab you."

"The sky is clear."

"Here's the funny thing about weather." He leaned closer, as if he were imparting some great wisdom on me. "It changes almost constantly."

"I don't need a chaperone."

"I just want to make sure you make it home safely."

"I'll be fine."

"I know you will. I'll be with you."

I was at the end of my rope. "Can't you just do what I ask for a change?"

"Apparently not."

We lapsed into silence again. I wanted to say something when we left his building in the dust. I knew he wouldn't be dissuaded, however. He was as stubborn as me, which wasn't necessarily a good thing.

"Truth or dare?" he asked when we turned the corner onto my street.

"Dare."

He smirked. "Changing things up, are you?"

"I'm a wild woman. What can I say?"

"All right." He glanced around. "I dare you to hold my hand."

I was dumbfounded by the request. "What?" I shot him an incredulous look. "Are you kidding me?"

"Nope." He held out his hand as if it were the most normal thing in the world.

It felt somehow dangerous to me, although I couldn't explain why. "I changed my mind. Truth."

His smirk grew wider, as if he knew that would be my response. "What's your favorite movie?"

It was the most innocuous question in the world and it had me letting out a breath even as suspicion reared its ugly head. "Why?"

"Because I want to know. A person's favorite movie says something about them."

"Like what?" I was honestly curious.

"You let me figure that out. Just tell me."

I narrowed my eyes, debating. I could lie, come up with some ridiculous movie like *Titanic* or *Avatar*. Instead, I went for the truth. "*Jaws.*"

"Seriously?"

"Yeah. I saw it on the television when I was little. It freaked me out. I was afraid to go into the lake for years."

"You do know that sharks aren't in lakes, right?"

"I know. Now. I was a kid. I just assumed sharks could be anywhere. Then I saw it again when I was a teenager and realized it was actually a very good movie."

"It is a good movie. My father showed it to me when I was six to make sure I wouldn't swim too far out into the Gulf on beach days. I didn't go in the ocean for ten years, and I only broke my streak after that because my friends were making fun of me."

For some reason, that made me laugh. "Are you over your fear now?"

"Nope."

"Huh." It was kind of weird to have something in common. "Me either."

"Maybe we'll have to work on that."

Did he mean together? Did he want us to work out our irrational fears together? There was no way that was happening. "Truth or dare?"

"Truth."

"Why did you insist on walking me home?"

"Because you have a tendency to not be aware of your surroundings, and I wouldn't ever be able to sleep again if I couldn't spare the extra five minutes necessary to walk you home."

"I can take care of myself."

"So you've said, numerous times. I guess I'm just the chivalrous sort."

"And here I thought chivalry was dead."

"Nope. Not even close."

THE SOUND OF RAUCOUS LAUGHTER FILLED MY ears as we arrived at my place. I didn't have to look over the fence that led to the patio area to know that my building mates were out in the alley area having a good time.

"Well, thanks for the walk," I said as my hand landed on the gate.

"No problem." Gus tilted his head and peered into the darkness. "Do you know them?"

"If I say no, are you going to insist on walking me inside?"

"Maybe."

"They're my co-op friends," I replied. "We all live in a four-plex together. We have separate entrances but share the same patio. It's fine."

"Ah." He nodded, his eyes traveling to the place on the corner. It was run-down and empty. "This doesn't look like the safest area. Maybe you should move."

Oh, well, that just cut it. "Do you have any idea how expensive it is to live in the French Quarter?"

"I live in the Quarter too."

"Yeah, but how much did you actually pay for that palace you're probably living in?" I was annoyed, and when that happened, I couldn't control the words that came spilling out of my mouth. "I'm guessing Mommy and Daddy bought your place."

A muscle worked in Gus's jaw. "I plan on paying them back."

"Well, I don't have anyone to help me move into an expensive penthouse. The people who live here work hard, and they're wonderfully entertaining. They're also loyal."

"Oh yeah?" Gus almost looked as if he were feeling shame. "I guess I should meet them then." He swung open the gate and ushered me inside. "Let's go. I want to meet these wonderfully entertaining people."

I swallowed hard. "I... wasn't inviting you in."

"Oh, now, come on." His tone turned cajoling. "You know you want to introduce me."

I so did not. "I'm fine."

"I know."

"You don't want to hang out with us."

"On the contrary, there's nothing I want more." He raised his hand and waved. "Hello, all. I'm Gus Kingman. Do you mind if I join you?"

"The more the merrier," a male voice called out. I recognized it as belonging to Gabriel. I was going to have to kill him as soon as there were no witnesses.

"Did you hear that?" Gus beamed at me. "The more the merrier. Not everybody wants to shut me out of the fun." He cut in front of me and started down the alley. He didn't look back to see if I would follow.

I made a series of huffing noises as I scuffed my feet against the uneven cobblestones. By the time I joined the others at the patio table, Gus had a beer in his hand and was already comfortable in one of the mismatched chairs.

"We've already made introductions," Ally said, her eyes promising a tsunami of questions when we were alone. "Gus seems fun. Where have you been hiding him?"

A million pointed questions were hidden under that single innocent one. "I believe he's been hiding in a dumpster," I replied, not missing a beat. "He likes to root through the trash."

Gus snickered. "Only to find the treasure, my dear. So, what are we talking about?"

"The new bar on the corner of Bourbon and Conti," Casey replied. "We think it might be owned by a vampire. He's pale as death and supposedly doesn't eat or drink in front of the patrons."

"Awesome. I love a good vampire conspiracy theory. Hit me up."

And just like that, Gus was one of the gang. The others didn't seem to think there was anything odd about the situation. How did this even happen?

Eleven

"He's an absolute delight."

Ally was bordering on drunk when she leaned in to whisper. Well, she thought she was whispering. As with anything else she did, Ally was incapable of going small. Her voice carried... right over to the Ping-Pong table the men had gathered around to start an impromptu tournament.

"Gabriel?" I asked blandly, refusing to acknowledge the fact that Gus had clearly heard Ally's not-so-subtle gush. "I happen to love him too."

Genuine confusion etched across Ally's features. "No, not Gabriel. I mean... he's totally hot. He's gay though. You're not going to get anywhere if you try to sauce that noodle, girl."

I pressed my lips together and found something else to stare at. It was a brick wall.

"I'm totally hot," Gabriel called out from the table. "That noodle thing, though, I'm not sure it's true. There are a few women who might be able to sauce my noodle." He took a moment to consider what he'd said. I'd rarely seen him this drunk, and it bordered on amusing... despite Gus's know-it-all stare. "I don't like the noodle description," Gabriel said a few minutes later. "I don't think it fits me. It's more like I don't think there are many women who could peel my banana." His smile was smug when it landed on me. "See what I did there?"

"I do." I couldn't help picturing myself rushing from bathroom to bathroom tonight to check on all my drunk four-plex mates to make sure they didn't sleep on their backs and drown in their own puke. "You should pace yourself, though, because there's no way you would ever really let a woman peel your banana." Oh, now I was saying it. I hated this entire night.

"You don't know." Gabriel looked to Casey for confirmation. "Tell her."

"Absolutely not." Casey vehemently shook his head, almost hard enough to dislodge it from his shoulders. "You totally wouldn't let a chick peel your banana. You're just drunk and like attention. It's okay though. I get it."

"I do like attention," Gabriel confirmed for Gus's benefit. "What about you, dude? Do you land on the banana or peach side of the equation? Or both. Some people like both. I would like to be one of those people because women are more fun to hang around with, but Casey is right. It's banana or bust for me."

If Gus was bothered by the question, he didn't show it. "See, I'm only drawn to the peach... even if it is prickly." His gaze was pointed when it landed on me, causing my cheeks to heat. "I went to private school. We're talking all boys. If I could make the banana work for me, I would've found out back then. Instead, it was all fart jokes and misogynistic stories that couldn't possibly be true."

"Oh, bummer." Gabriel stumbled over to the bucket to grab another beer. He was unsteady enough that I swooped in to stop him.

"How about you call it a night, big guy?" I sent him my most alluring smile. "I can help you upstairs if you want."

"Oh, Moxie, I don't want to go upstairs." Gabriel stomped his foot as he whined. "I'm having a good time."

"Leave him be," Casey admonished. "He's grown. He can drink what he wants."

"Yeah, he can drink what he wants," Gus echoed with a grin. It made me want to punch him.

"That's easy for you to say," I shot back. "You're not the one who is going to feel like death tomorrow."

"Hey, if he feels how we all think he's going to feel tomorrow, it will be a good lesson," Casey interjected. "He doesn't need to be mothered."

I was offended. "I'm not acting like a mother."

"You always act like a mother."

Ally let loose her little-girl giggle. "It's kind of true. You are free with the orders... and scowls... and you have this little wrinkle between your eyebrows because you frown so much." Ally drew her index finger between her eyebrows to demonstrate. "My mom has that. It's totally true what they say about making a face too much, by the way. It will freeze that way if you're not careful. Just ask my mom and her line."

"I'll take that into consideration," I said drily, shooting a death glare at Gus. Honestly, this was all his fault. If he hadn't insisted on staying, we all would've gone to bed hours ago. He was the one who caused this, and he didn't even look drunk. It wasn't fair.

"Tell me what her real name is," Gus instructed Gabriel, pointing at me. "She won't tell me, and I know darned well that Moxie isn't a real name."

"Right?" Gabriel made an exaggerated face that would've made me laugh under different circumstances. "That's her name though. It's on her checks—she still writes checks for rent if you can believe that—and it's on her license. I saw it."

"None of us believed her at first," Ally explained. "We made her show us on her third night here. It's really her name."

"Nobody named her that," Gus insisted. "I mean... yeah, people name their kids stupid things like Apple... and Pilot Inspektor... but nobody named her Moxie. She has another name."

I was smug when I caught his gaze. "My name is Moxie. There's no other name I'll answer to."

"That doesn't mean you don't have another name. These guys just don't know it. I'm going to figure it out though." For the first time since he'd started pounding them back with my friends, he showed signs of being drunk and leaned to his right. He almost overcorrected when he caught himself.

"Uh-huh." It was time to push him to the gate. "Come on, Gus. I think it's time to call it a night."

"Maybe I don't want to call it a night." Even as he said it, he dropped his Ping-Pong paddle on the table and shuffled in my direction.

"While I'm walking Gus home, you guys have to put Gabriel to bed," I instructed Ally and Casey. "Throw some aspirin down his throat and fill him full of water before you do it. Be good friends tonight."

"Oh, you're no fun." Casey wrinkled his nose, but he didn't argue with me.

"I'll make sure they get to bed," Ally promised. She was as drunk as everybody else—well, except for me—but she was better at hiding it. "Are you going to take him all the way home?"

"It's like a block and a half," I replied. "It will take me five minutes."

"Okay, but... it's late. You probably shouldn't be walking home alone."

"She won't be walking alone," Gus said. "She's got me... and I know martial arts."

"You know martial arts?" I couldn't stop myself from being dubious. "What martial art do you know?"

"I'm a master at thumb wrestling."

A laugh bubbled up before I could contain it.

"Ha!" He jabbed a finger at me. "You do have a sense of humor. I knew one was buried under there."

"I do," I confirmed, nudging him toward the gate. "I laugh plenty. You're rarely funny. That's the problem."

"Oh, I'm the Kingman cutup. My father always tells me I'm a joke, so I know I'm funny... because jokes are funny."

Even though I was annoyed by the situation, I felt a pang of sadness for him. The visit from his brothers had offered me a glimpse into his life. Now this tidbit about his father. It sounded to me as if his family brought him down on a regular basis rather than bolstering him. It wasn't right.

"Screw your father." I hooked my arm through his as I led him down the walkway. "You need to develop a thicker skin. Nobody is worth constantly feeling bad about yourself."

He nodded, as if agreeing, and then started shaking his head. "It's not that easy. Dads are tough."

"Totally."

He was quiet a beat. "How come you don't talk about your dad?"

"There's nothing to talk about. He took off a long time ago. He never looked back."

"Sometimes I wish my dad would've done that."

"No, you don't."

"No, I don't," he agreed on a quiet whisper as we turned onto Decatur Street. "When are you going to tell me your real name?"

"It's Moxie."

"No. Your *real* name."

"It's Moxie."

"It's not. I'm always going to feel as if I'm racing to catch up if I don't know your real name."

The admission made him vulnerable, and it caused me to smile. "Well, then I guess you'll always be racing to catch up."

"You'd like that, wouldn't you?"

"Yup."

"That's because you're mean. Totally hot but totally mean."

My heart stuttered, and I tried to keep my voice even. "Hot, huh?"

"Yup. Oh, don't give me that look." He shook his head. "You know you're hot. You also know you're mean, and you don't deny it. That makes you even hotter."

"Are you hot for me, Gus?" I couldn't stop myself from asking the question as we approached his building.

"I shouldn't be."

"But are you?"

"I shouldn't be."

"That's not really an answer."

He shot me a wink as he started crossing the road—without looking both ways, mind you—and then he slowed his pace. Thankfully, there was no traffic on the street. "Wait a second." He looked thoughtfully between me and the direction we'd come from. "How are you going to get home?"

"I'm going to walk."

"But that's not safe." He started back in my direction, not stopping until he was directly in front of me. His chest bumped against mine as he stared into my eyes, and for one odd moment, I thought he was going to kiss me.

I sucked in a breath, did my best to keep my heart from pounding out of my chest, and adopted my most imperious expression. "Listen..."

"It's not safe for you to walk alone after dark," he said blankly. "I need to walk you home."

"I just walked you home," I reminded him, doing my best not to focus on his ridiculously kissable lips. I hadn't come to New Orleans for this. Heck, a relationship—or even a one-night stand, for that matter—wasn't on my radar. It would screw up my plans, and I'd promised my mother I would never let a man have that much control over me. It had been her dying wish. No kidding.

On top of that, he wasn't my type. This was just some weird chemical thing. Maybe I was drunker than I thought... off two beers... after four hours.

Yeah, I wasn't drunk. I couldn't use that as an excuse. Oh, screw that, I'm totally using that as an excuse.

"It's not safe," Gus insisted.

"It is." I was over this night. "You need to go home and sleep it off."

"Water and aspirin," he said automatically.

I nodded. "I'm going to head home. It's a three-minute walk. I'll be fine."

"What if you get jumped? That happens. I saw it on television."

"It does, but I'm from Detroit. It's not going to happen to me."

"Is that true? Are you magical because you're from Detroit?"

"I'm... something." I gave him a little shove. "Go home. I'll do the same. The war is back on tomorrow."

"Right. The war." He shuffled across the street, keeping his eyes on the ground until he arrived on the opposite sidewalk. When he turned back, a gleam was in his eyes. "I think you might be magical regardless."

"Maybe," I agreed. "Go to bed. I'll see you tomorrow."

"For war."

"Yup. For war." There would be nothing else between us but war, I reminded myself as I walked toward my apartment. Tonight was a fluke. That was all it was. I blamed the storm. Tomorrow was a new day, and things would be back to normal.

At least I hoped that was true. The alternative was too much to swallow.

ALLY WAS THE ONLY ONE UP WHEN I settled on the patio to drink my coffee and read the local news websites the next morning. Her hair stood on end as she stumbled through the door of her unit and shuffled across the uneven patio to join me.

"I think there might be a parade stuck inside my head," she announced as she sat down.

I shoved the box of doughnuts I'd picked up during my morning walk toward her. "You drank enough to justify a parade."

Ally wrinkled her nose as she looked at the breakfast offerings. "This is New Orleans," she pointed out after selecting a cake doughnut with chocolate and coconut. "You're supposed to get beignets as a hangover cure, not doughnuts. That's so... Michigan."

The way she said it made me laugh. "Sorry. Beignets need to be served warm, and I had no idea how late you guys would sleep."

"Have you seen the others?"

I shook my head. "I think Gabriel is going to be hating himself all day. I wouldn't be surprised if I don't see him before heading off to Cher. He was drunkety-drunk-drunk last night."

"Is that really a thing? Drunkety-drunk-drunk I mean."

"Yup. It's totally a thing."

"Is it a Michigan thing?"

"You need to let the Michigan thing go." I was adamant. "I know you think Michigan is like a different country, but it's really not."

"But it is. Michigan is like Canada lite. That's how I'm picturing it anyway."

I couldn't have this conversation again. "I need to come up with a way to put Flambeaux out of business."

Ally blinked several times in rapid succession. "Wow, it's fun out here in left field," she said finally before sipping her coffee. "You just reeled that off, didn't you? Why are you so convinced you need to put Flambeaux out of business?"

It was my turn to be confused. "Um... because it's right next door to my bar, and he stole my launch."

"Yeah, you really need to let that go." Ally was dainty as she broke apart her doughnut and shoved a hunk into her mouth. Then she proceeded to talk with her mouth full despite all that work. "This is New Orleans. It's okay for multiple bars to succeed."

"I know." I did know that. I still wanted to win. "He stole my launch though. That place has to fail for that reason alone."

"Okay, but I think you're looking at it the wrong way. If you both build up your businesses, you'll become the *must-drink* corner and that will be good for both bars. Being the only bar at that corner is actually a detriment for foot traffic."

I hadn't thought of that... and I didn't want to think about it now. "I need something to put me over the top. You're smart. You're also familiar with New Orleans. You must have an idea."

"I'm not a bar person."

I made a face and waited.

"I'm not a bar-organizer person," she clarified after a beat. "I don't know a thing about launching a bar. Just off the cuff,

I would say that you need a gimmick that is sustainable... and it can't feel like a gimmick. It has to feel organic and fun."

"That's kind of vague."

"It's all I have." She sipped her coffee again and gave me a speculative look. "You know who might have an idea, right?"

"No. Who?"

"The guy who you were making eyes at over drinks last night."

She had to be joking. "I was not making eyes at him."

"Right. I must've imagined it."

"You were drunk."

"I was, but I wasn't *that* drunk. It's okay. He was only interested in staring at you too. There's a certain spark there, no matter what you're prepared to admit."

"There wasn't a spark. We're competitors. Nothing more."

"Right. That's why you insisted on walking him home last night."

"I didn't want him to end up dead in a gutter somewhere. That's not how I want to win."

"If you say so." Her eyes danced as she stared at me over the rim of her mug. I thought she was done and was going to ask about the gimmick that didn't feel like a gimmick thing when she spoke again. "Did you kiss him?"

My face went numb, to the point where I thought I might be having a stroke. What sort of question was that? "Of course not!" I was offended. No, really. What an offensive thing to ask. Just because I walked that idiot home, that did not mean I kissed him. "I dropped him off and headed right back. It was a courtesy, nothing more."

"Okay." Ally's reaction was bland.

"I'm being serious."

"I know you are. You don't like him."

"I don't."

"You've said it multiple times now."

"And I mean it."

"Awesome." She shot me an enthusiastic thumbs-up. "Sex is off the table. We're just going to crush him and make him cry. You don't have to tell me again."

"Now you're thinking." I grabbed my third doughnut out of the box and started munching. "So, what sort of gimmick?"

"That's for you to decide. Like I said, I'm not a bar person. You're the one who needs to run your business, especially if you want to get the accolades. There's something out there that will work for you. I'm sure of it."

I was certain of it too. I just had to figure out where to look. There had to be something, but what?

Twelve

I wasn't a big fan of exercise.

However, I *was* a big fan of eating... especially in New Orleans.

That meant I had no choice but to work out. For me, that meant jogging along the riverwalk four mornings a week. Once my four-plex roommates started rising—and bitterly complaining about their hangovers—I decided that one form of torture was preferable to the other and hopped in my workout gear. Then I was out the door and heading for the river.

One of the things I found most fascinating about New Orleans was the water access. To the north was Lake Pontchartrain. To the east was Lake Borgne and the Gulf of Mexico. Then, cutting through the cool parts of the city—like the French Quarter—the Mississippi snaked around parishes until emptying into the Gulf. Essentially, there was a little something for everyone. I was a huge fan of the river, however, so that was what I was drawn to when exercising.

Mostly I stuck to the stretch in the French Quarter. Occasionally, I headed down to the Central Business District because it had a Café du Monde outlet and a fun mall. Today, however, I was in it for the sweat, so I set a brisk pace and started running.

The proximity of the river drowned out almost everything, so I could lose myself in exercise and plotting. Ally was right. I needed a gimmick that didn't feel like a gimmick if I wanted to put Cher on the map. That meant I needed something New Orleans-y that didn't feel corny or trite to the locals. I wanted to appeal to all... which was easier said than done.

"On your right," a voice called out, causing me to immediately step to my left. Runners' etiquette didn't give me a choice in the matter. I pasted a wan grin on my face as the individual who called out to alert me to his presence started to pass... and then frowned when I realized who it was.

"Shouldn't you be in bed?" I demanded of Gus as he breezed by.

"I don't know," he called back, not bothering to look in my direction. "Do you know something I don't?"

I should've let him pass me. That way, I wouldn't have to talk to him. Did I do that? Of course not. I increased my pace, not stopping until we were neck and neck. To an outsider, it would look as if we were out for a playful run together. To anybody who knew us—which were precious few people—the truth might be more easily recognizable... but only if they were really looking.

"You're supposed to be hung over," I argued as I studied his profile. He barely looked to have broken a sweat, which left me more annoyed than should've been possible given the beauty of the view. "I mean... when I left you last night, you were drunk."

"Or maybe I was just faking being drunk."

"No, you were totally bombed."

He chuckled. "I love how you refuse to give me even a

AVERY KANE

little wiggle room. I mean... why can't you just agree that I was playing drunk and let me keep my dignity?"

"Because there's no fun in that."

"Sure, there is. For me."

"Well, I only care about whether or not I'm having fun."

"Good to know."

We kept pace with one another, both of us breathing heavily by the time we reached the steamboat. I wanted to slow down, maybe even take a walking break, but I couldn't be the one to suggest that if I didn't want to give him the upper hand.

"Hey, Gus," a female voice called out, drawing my attention to a coffee kiosk. The woman waving was young, fit, fresh-faced and completely gaga over Gus in his workout shorts. Sure, fine, he looked good in them, but there was no reason to drool... and that's all this woman was missing.

"Hello, babycakes," Gus called out. He managed a wave but didn't slow his pace.

"Babycakes?" I was appalled on behalf of women everywhere. "Could you be more of a tool?"

"I could totally be more of a tool. I mean... she's got praline rolls with the coffee she's dishing out. Sweet cheeks was right there, and I refrained. I think I deserve a medal."

I could think of a few other things he deserved, like a good, swift kick in the...

"Hey, Gus," another female voice called out. This one belonged to a woman leading a yoga class about twenty feet away. Her biker shorts—aren't you supposed to wear loose-fitting clothing for yoga?—were so tight that there was absolutely nothing left to the imagination when she went into Cobra pose.

"Hey, sweetheart," Gus called out with another wave. "You're looking good."

Suspicion reared up as I followed him around a curve.

"You don't know their names." The declaration was out of my mouth before I realized I was even going to say anything.

"Of course I know their names," he scoffed. "They called out to me, for crying out loud."

"That means they know your name. You don't know their names though."

"Of course I do." He lifted his chin and flexed his arms. "Why would you even assume something like that?"

"Because you're big on names. You've been obsessed with mine since we met."

"That's because Moxie isn't a name."

"Moxie is a state of mind," I agreed. "You don't know their names, though, and to cover you just throw out bland nicknames that likely make them think that you're flirting when you couldn't care less about them."

Gus slid his eyes to me and slowed until he came to a complete stop. He swung his arms back and forth, stretching, and pinned me with an accusatory look. "Are you following me?"

It wasn't the tack I expected him to take. "Excuse me?"

"You heard me. First you show up at my place last night when I'm in no shape to fight off the advances of a determined woman, and now you're on the riverwalk, where I just so happen to work out every morning."

My fingers twitched, I was so desperate to hurt him. "First off, I've been running on the riverwalk forever."

"You've been in town for weeks. At most, you've been running on the riverwalk for weeks... something I don't believe because I would've seen you if that were the case."

"You would've seen me?"

"Yes."

"How do you know you didn't see me?"

"Because I would remember."

"Like you remember those women?" I gestured down the

riverwalk. "Babycakes and sweetheart back there. Could you pick them out of a lineup if you saw them on Royal Street in the middle of the afternoon?"

"Of course." His answer was perfunctory, but I saw the flash of doubt in his eyes. "I'm not some 'love them and leave them' lothario, just for the record. I'm a friendly guy. That doesn't mean I'm guilty of what you're suggesting."

"And what's that?"

"You know." Gus wagged his fingers. "I'm not the guy you think I am."

He almost seemed sincere. "I don't care about your girl-friends," I said as a way to let him off the hook. This was not the sort of thing I cared about. "I do care that you're spreading around some narrative about me following you home last night."

"But you did."

"I walked you home because you were drunk."

"So, in essence, you followed me to my home."

Yup. I definitely wanted to kill him. "You're a righteous pain in the ass."

His smile was blinding for a guy who should've felt like death warmed over. "Should we talk about something else?"

"Absolutely."

"Great." His smile didn't diminish. "Let's talk about how you go weak in the knees when you see me. That sounds like loads more fun."

"What is the matter with you?" It was a legitimate question. "Shouldn't you be locked up somewhere? I mean... you're obviously a narcissist."

"Oh, honey, everybody has a little narcissism in them. If they don't, they're lying when they take those tests."

He had a point. I couldn't disagree with his take. I'd come to the same conclusion myself. "I still think you should be locked up," I insisted. "You know, just for the sake of the bar world."

"You would miss me if I was gone." He poked my cheek and smirked, although his smile quickly disappeared. "About last night."

"You don't have to thank me." I was already waving my hand. "I'm not the sort of person who wants to wake up to news that the drunk guy who has been making my life hell got hit by a car because he didn't look both ways when crossing the road."

"I wasn't going to thank you."

I stilled. "No? Don't you think you should thank me?"

"No. Now who is the narcissist?"

He knew exactly how to poke me to the point of no return... and I hated it. "So, I'm thinking we should be done with this conversation." I turned to leave, but he caught my elbow before I could take a single step. "Have I mentioned I know karate? You're probably going to want to unhand me if you want to keep that arm."

"You know karate?" Laughter bubbled up, reminding me of a raucous fart when he let it go. "What sort of karate do you know?"

"There's only one sort of karate." I tried to remain haughty even though I was struggling. Why would I possibly say I know karate? The only thing I knew about karate was what I'd learned from television... and that was from old movies because it was hardly a hot topic on *The View*.

"Um... no. There are eleven types of karate."

"There are not."

"There are." He dug in his pocket and returned with his phone. "I would recite them for you, but I can't pronounce their names, and I don't want you to see me as stupid."

"I think it's too late for that, *sweetheart*."

His lips curved. "I knew you liked me. Ha!" He'd only

been navigating his phone screen for a grand total of fifteen seconds when he shoved it in my face. "I told you there were eleven types of karate."

I tried to keep my face neutral as proof that he was right danced in front of my eyes. "I know the type of karate that means I can kick your ass," I said when I couldn't think of anything else to say. I mean... why not make things worse, right? He already knew I didn't know karate.

"That could be any of the karates," Gus replied, grinning. "No, seriously, I'm a total wuss. The only people I've ever fought with are my brothers. We're all soft."

"Probably because you grew up with bodyguards."

"Yes, and if you have enough money, private schools will treat you like little kings."

"Oh, do you have a crown?" For some reason, the fact that he was so self-deprecating made me like him more. *Dammit! He's your enemy,* I reminded myself. *You can't like him, even if he sometimes comes across as adorkably delightful.*

"I have multiple crowns," he replied, not missing a beat. "I'll share them with you if you want. You can come over to my place, I'll mix a real drink for you, and we'll wear crowns while standing on the balcony and dropping water balloons on the people heading out to the riverwalk."

"You have a balcony you can drop water balloons from?"

"Yup."

"You should've told me that. That's way more impressive than the money."

His smile slipped in an instant, and I realized I'd said something wrong. "I wasn't trying to impress you when I mentioned private school," he offered in halting terms after a few seconds of awkward silence.

That wasn't the response I was expecting. "Okay."

"That's not impressive," he insisted. "That was my parents' way to protect us. They didn't think we should have to go to public school. They said we were better than that. I always wanted to go to public school though."

Why was he telling me this? I wasn't interested. Okay, I was totally interested. I didn't want to feel sorry for him though, and his expression made me feel sorry for him. So, dammit again. "Why did you want to go to public school? I would guess that your private school didn't have any fights... or overcrowded classrooms... or threats of school shooters."

Gus looked appropriately appalled. "Did you have school shooters in Detroit?"

I thought about yanking him a bit, but it was a bridge too far. "No, and I didn't live in Detroit. I know when you mention Michigan, people automatically think of Detroit. I was in a suburb, so all those stories you hear about people shooting at each other across Gratiot? Yeah, they didn't happen to me."

"What's Gratiot?" He seemed fascinated.

"It's a road."

"A bad road?"

"It depends on where you are."

"Fair enough. As for why I wanted to go to public school, believe it or not, I didn't like being singled out because my parents were rich. I wanted to do something for me."

"Did that ever happen?"

His expression turned hard. "No. My brothers were better in school than me... and sports... and getting chicks... and taking standardized tests. I trailed behind in everything."

And crap on a cracker. Now I was feeling doubly sorry for him. "I don't think that's likely true. You have more charm than them."

"How do you know that?" His smile was back.

"Because I've met them," I reminded him. "You're way more charming."

"Yes, but if you're rich enough, you can convince people that you're charming when you're really a douche."

"Is that what you do?"

"You tell me."

I wanted to give him a verbal beatdown, but I couldn't bring myself to do it. "You're more charming than them. Let's leave it at that."

"Oh, you really do love me." He knocked his hip into mine and beamed. "I think this is the start of a beautiful relationship."

"Oh, don't even." I wagged a warning finger. "I'm not falling for that. We're still mortal enemies."

"Okay, Lex Luthor." His smile didn't dissipate. "You're awful chummy with your mortal enemy. You even walked him home last night and tried to take advantage of him... sexually."

Any trace of mirth I'd been feeling up until that point disappeared in an instant. "And that's the last time I do anything nice for you. Now I wish I'd let you fall in the ditch and get hit by a trolley." I started running again, determined to leave him in the dust, but I slowed at the sight of several police officers striding down the riverwalk. They were shoulder to shoulder, intent on their conversation, and two individuals in blue scrubs walked behind them. The gurney they carried held a body with a sheet drawn over it so nobody could see who was being transported. The face was covered, signifying the individual was dead.

"Don't leave," Gus whined as he followed me. "I was joking about you sexually harassing me. I make inappropriate jokes when I feel like an idiot... and I definitely feel like an idiot after I got so drunk last night.

"I mean... I only went with you so you would be safe, and then I drank so much you felt the need to walk me home," he continued, barely taking a breath. "You were out on the streets in the middle of the night, which kind of defeats the purpose of me trying to be chivalrous."

I ignored him and kept my eyes on the gurney. My heart had sped up when I saw the sole of a shoe sticking out. They weren't the sort of shoes just anybody wore. No, they were the sort of shoes I'd seen on the homeless individuals I interacted with every morning and night.

"Who is that?" I demanded when the police officers got close enough to hear the question. Gus, mercifully, had stopped talking.

"There's no need to worry, ma'am," one of the men replied. "There's nothing to concern yourself with. The river-walk is perfectly safe."

"That's not what I asked," I snapped.

Gus, all pretense of having a good time at my expense gone, put his hand on my back. He studied my profile with overt curiosity but didn't speak.

"It's just one of the homeless guys," the second police officer replied. "He died in his sleep on one of the benches last night. There's nothing for you to worry yourself about."

They didn't realize I could worry myself over just about anything. "Who is it?"

The officers seemed baffled by the question.

"We don't know," the first officer replied. "He didn't have identification on him."

"Let me see." I took a bold step forward.

"Ma'am, stay back." The second officer raised an arm to make sure I didn't get too close to the body. I was about to take another step anyway when I felt a hand on my arm.

"Just let her see his face," Gus insisted.

I sent Gus a sharp look, surprised and maybe even a little relieved that he was coming to my defense. I wasn't good when it came to dealing with the big things in life. Heck, I wasn't good dealing with the little things in life either. I was flat out terrible when the worst happened.

"Sir, you're not part of this," the second officer said gravely.

"I'm Augustus Kingman." He reeled off the name like it was supposed to stop the police officers in their tracks. "I run this route every morning. I know some of the guys who frequent the benches. I might be able to help you."

The first police officer hesitated and then gestured toward the coroner aides behind him. "Let him see the body."

Gus remained calm as one of the men in scrubs pulled back the sheet. Gus's expression was neutral, until he slid his eyes to me. That was the moment I saw real tenderness reflected back, and it made me feel weak instead of protected. "Do you know him?" Gus asked in a low voice.

I shook my head, swallowing hard. It wasn't any of the guys I knew from my frequent stops at Jackson Square. "No."

"I'm sorry." Gus was solemn as he turned back to the police officers. "I've never seen him before."

"It's fine." The second police officer waved off the statement. "I ate at your brother's bar yesterday, the one over in the CBD by the Marriott. It was fantastic. Tell him I said so." He pressed two fingers to his lips and kissed them with gusto.

I felt mildly sick to my stomach as I watched him cavort in front of a dead body.

Gus remained at my side until the police officers and coroner's office representatives disappeared from view. "So, do you want to talk about that?" he asked finally.

"No." I was over this whole conversation. "I need to head back and get ready for work. I'm already behind."

"And you can't stand being behind, right?"

I really couldn't. "I like being prepared."

"Okay, well… I guess I'll see you at work."

"I guess you will."

Thirteen

I was still shaken when I got back to my place. The others remained on the patio hydrating and mainlining aspirin to beat back their hangovers while I headed upstairs to shower.

"Is something wrong?" Ally called to my back. She was good at reading emotions.

"It's fine." I forced a smile I didn't feel. "I'm just going to head inside and get ready for work."

"You look pale."

I felt pale. "Gus was on the riverwalk," I said out of nowhere. Why I felt the need to bring up his name was beyond me. "I got in a running competition with him, and now I feel like puking." It wasn't that much of a lie, so I didn't feel all that bad about it.

"Have you considered having a different competition with him?" Gabriel queried.

"Yeah. We're having a bar competition. I get to make him do something embarrassing if I win... and I'm so going to win."

"No, not that type of competition either." Gabriel's trademark smirk was on display. "I was thinking you could have an orgasm competition with him or something. You know, the one who gets the most orgasms wins."

My mouth dropped open. "Um... why would you say that?"

"Because we all saw you guys interacting last night, and you can't miss the heat," Casey replied.

I was appalled. No, I needed a better word than that. Horrified? Still not strong enough. "There's no heat."

"Oh, right." Gabriel let loose a belly chuckle that irritated me to no end. "You guys were trying to mount each other with your eyes last night."

"That is a despicable lie."

"Actually, I'm with Gabriel," Ally offered. "I could feel the heat too."

"You guys were drunk. The only thing you could feel was stupid because of some of the things you were saying."

"No, I'm a delightful drunk." Ally was serious. "I've been told I could drink with the best of them, maybe even do it professionally."

The sad thing was, Ally *was* a delightful drunk. She didn't get melancholy like me when I'd imbibed too much. "I don't understand what you're even saying," I insisted. "The only feelings I have toward Gus involve rampant dislike and itchy irritation. And, before you say itchy irritation isn't a thing, it so is."

"Basically, she's saying Gus is the human equivalent of a yeast infection," Ally supplied for the men in attendance.

"I wouldn't actually say that out loud, but I am implying that," I agreed. "Gus is the worst."

"What's that saying?" Casey shifted his eyes to Gabriel. "There's a thin line between love and hate. I think that's what we're dealing with now."

"Well, there's a huge gulf between hate and love," I shot back. "I don't like Gus."

"I don't think anybody is suggesting that you're ready to ride off into the sunset with him," Ally hedged. "There's a definite attraction there though."

"There is not."

"There totally is." Gabriel had a short attention span even when he was in a good mood. When he had a hangover, it was minuscule. "You might not want to admit it, but it's all right there."

"Maybe she can't see it," Casey suggested. "I have a sister like that. She denies she's into a guy, and then she suddenly turns up engaged. Then she gets bored after two months and moves on again."

"Who's getting engaged?" I sounded shrill even to my own ears, but I couldn't ratchet it down. "Nobody is getting engaged."

"You don't have to get engaged," Ally said with a grimace. "Nobody is suggesting you get engaged. I don't see any problem playing a few games with him though. I mean... he's hot."

"Totally," Gabriel intoned, bobbing his head. "So very, very hot."

I wanted to strangle them. "Nobody is playing games... other than the one where I make him cry."

"That can work in bed too," Casey said.

I ignored him. "We're rivals. That's it."

"Okay." Ally held up her hands in defeat. "If you say so."

"It's fact."

"Funny thing about facts, they can change into falsities before you even realize what's happening."

"Well, that's not going to happen here."

"Okay. It's up to you."

"It totally is."

. . .

THE BAR WAS ALREADY OPEN BUT ONLY filled to 25 percent capacity when I arrived at Cher. Abel, ever tireless, worked behind the bar as he chatted to two female tourists sucking down Hurricanes.

"You can't go into the cemeteries without a guide now," he explained. "People were leaving graffiti behind."

"But... we just want to see the cemeteries," one of the girls said, whining. "There has to be a way."

"Not unless you want to go to jail." Abel flicked his eyes to me. "You're early."

I was already feeling defensive, and I couldn't simply shut it off even if it would be the smart thing to do. "Only by thirty minutes."

"That's still early." He looked me up and down. "Late night?"

"Pretty much. My roommates decided to tie one on." I grabbed an apron from the stack behind the bar. "How late were you here?"

"Two o'clock. It's the middle of the week so people knocked off early."

"In Michigan, the law forces people to knock off at two."

"Well, we're not in Michigan." He slid me a sly look. "Haven't you figured that out yet?"

"I think the fact that you're allowed to walk around with plastic cups of alcohol, jaywalk to your heart's content, and even shop with a beer in your hand is pretty much a dead give-away. Toto, we're not in Detroit any longer."

Abel chuckled as he used the beverage gun to fill a glass of iced tea for me. We'd only been working together for a few days, and he already knew my habits. "How come your room-mates decided to go nuts last night?"

"I believe it was the individual who followed me home without invitation who spurred them on."

Abel's brow furrowed. "I don't understand. Somebody

followed you home?"

"Yes, and he's a menace."

"Did you call the cops?"

It was only then that I realized what he was picturing. "Oh, it wasn't a rapist or anything. It was Gus."

"Gus Kingman?" Abel didn't look any less concerned. "Why would he be following you?"

"He claims it's because he didn't want me to walk home alone."

Abel relaxed but only minimally. "Well, that's good."

"Then he got hammered with my roommates, so I had to walk him home."

"Seriously?"

"He kept saying it wasn't necessary, but I didn't feel right. He would've made an easy mark if somebody tried to make a move on him."

"Didn't you say he lived above the Jax Brewery?"

I nodded. "Why?"

"They have security. Nobody was going to move on him. You should've let him find his own way home."

"What if he would've gotten lost and ended up on the streetcar tracks?"

"That's his problem."

Abel was practical to a fault, something I liked about him. That seemed a bit harsh to me though. "Well, maybe next time." I grinned as I checked the liquor storage. "How was business last night?"

"Solid."

I waited for him to expand. When he didn't, I pinned him with a petulant look. "Can I get a little more than that?"

"No. It was solid. You're not going to get rich on the revenue, but it's a good start."

Four days ago, I would've been happy with the update. Now? Not so much. "Well, that's good... I guess."

"It's good."

"How did Flambeaux do last night?"

"Good."

I was starting to get sick of that word. "I want to do better than Flambeaux."

"Well, last night you pretty much did the same as Flambeaux. How many times do I have to tell you that it's not a competition? The Quarter can keep hundreds of bars afloat."

I didn't just want to float. I wanted to soar. "I want to do better than them."

"So you've told me. I think you're picking stupid things to focus on. Give it a rest."

"You give it a rest," I muttered under my breath as I turned my attention to the window that looked out on Flambeaux. The giggly young women had lost interest in Abel once we started talking business and were instead staring in the same direction. "What's going on?" I asked, moving behind them.

"Hot guy," the blonder of the two replied.

I followed her gaze, frowning when I realized Gus was holding court with a group of people... and he seemed to be holding a glass that was on fire as he entertained the masses. "What in the hell is that?"

"A hot guy," the girl repeated.

I made a face. "Not him. Why does he have a drink that's on fire?" I cast a look toward Abel, who appeared aggrieved when he moved out from behind the bar.

"Let me see," he said as he nudged between the girls and me. "Oh, that's a Flaming Dr. Pepper."

I was grossed out beyond belief. "Ugh. Dr. Pepper is nasty."

"And, oddly enough, you don't even need Dr. Pepper for

the drink. Basically, the combination of rum, amaretto, and beer mimics the flavor."

Now I was really disgusted. "And that's a good thing? Who wants a drink that tastes like pop?"

The blonder girl fixed me with a quizzical look. "What's pop?"

"She means soda," Abel volunteered helpfully. "Nobody calls it pop here, Moxie. You're going to peg yourself as an outsider right away if you're not careful."

"Well, we call it pop in Michigan."

"That's weird." The woman shook her head. "We should totally go over there though. That guy is so hot I want him to set something else on fire."

I didn't have to ask what that something was. Instead, I held out my hands and glared at Abel. "Do you know any flaming cocktail recipes?"

"Yes, but we don't want to copy them. They are called Flambeaux after all. We should come up with something else."

"Do you have any ideas?"

His grin was impish. "As a matter of fact, I do."

DRY ICE WAS SURPRISINGLY EASY TO get in the French Quarter. Abel placed one call, and a huge brick was delivered twenty minutes later.

"What do we do with this?" I asked, reaching out to touch it.

He slapped my hands away and then held up his own, which were covered in gloves. "Do you want to lose a finger?"

"Not particularly." I found I was grumpy when being scolded. "How does this work?"

"You drop the dry ice in the drink, and it looks like it's smoking."

"I thought we were avoiding fire."

"I said smoking, not flames. You're such a pain." Abel shook his head. "Trust me. This is going to work... just as soon as you update the specials board."

I was still behind on the plan, but I obediently grabbed the light-up board and wiped it down. Sometimes, I thought Abel was the one in charge... but only in really dark moments. "What drinks are we going with?" I asked when I was ready.

"Witch's Brew. Pomegranate Potion. Clementine Cauldron. Brandy Punch Bat."

I frowned as I wrote it out. "Those sound like witchy drinks."

"Yes, and in New Orleans, they'll sell like beignets and chicory." Abel promptly started mixing a drink. His hands moved so fast I couldn't see what liquor he was dropping in the shaker. When he was finished, he poured out a beautiful purple cocktail that appeared to shimmer.

"Why does it look so shiny?" I leaned over and peered into the martini glass.

"It's a baking thing I learned about years ago. You use it to make shimmering frosting or something. I stole it for drinks, and it's a big crowd pleaser."

"Okay. Now what?"

"Watch, little chatterbox." He hacked off a small cube from the dry ice block and used tongs to place it in the martini glass. Almost instantly, it began to smoke.

"Holy..." I clapped my hands, delighted. "That's amazing."

"It is. Now plant your ass on the patio and sip that thing. Let people see it."

I was caught off guard. "I'm... what?"

"We need people to see the smoke. Once they see yours, they'll want one of their own. Then we won't have to worry about advertising."

On the face of it, that made sense. I had a problem though.

"I can't drink on the job."

The look he shot me was so incredulous I worried he was about to have a stroke. "It's the French Quarter."

"I know but..."

"It's the French Quarter," he repeated before I could finish my rebuttal. "You're expected to drink on the job here."

"I don't remember that being in the job description when I got hired."

"Just do what I say." His tone was deadly. "I've got this under control as long as you don't pull a Moxie and make things difficult."

Irritation bubbled up and grabbed me by the throat. "I'm not pulling a Moxie."

"That's good because it's going to be a really long day if you do."

I MADE SURE THE DRINK WAS ON DISPLAY when I sat on the patio table, opting to be as close to the sidewalk as possible. Even though I was reticent to drink on the job—that couldn't really be a thing—I sipped anyway and grinned at the flavor. It was like an explosion of raspberry divinity.

"Um... yum." I shot Abel a thumbs-up through the open door. That was enough to have two women who were walking down the street—their necks laden with beads even though it wasn't Mardi Gras—stop directly next to me.

"What's that?" one of them asked, reverence positively dripping from her tongue.

"It's a Witch's Brew."

"Seriously?" She looked delighted. "Are you the ones serving the flaming shots too?"

I kept my expression neutral. "No. I heard those kill your taste buds. If you want to drink one of those, I would try one of these first because you're totally missing out if you don't."

"They kill taste buds?" A man who was crossing behind the woman slowed. "Is that for real?"

I had no idea if it was true. Probably not, but whatever. "It's totally true." I paused a beat and then went a step further. "They also cause temporary impotence—only five hours—but they really should declare that as a side effect before serving them, don't you think?"

"Impotence?" The guy's eyes went so wide, I thought he might pass out. "Are you kidding me?"

"I wish I was."

"Well, screw that." He changed his course in an instant and entered Cher. "I want one of those smoking things," he announced. "The ladies love them, and I love the ladies."

Abel grinned. "Absolutely. What's your favorite flavor?"

The women who had initially stopped to ask about my drink followed the man inside. Behind them, a steady line of people began migrating in our direction. Almost no one continued on to Flambeaux.

Gus, who was still outside performing with his shot, narrowed his eyes when he saw all the traffic disappearing before it got to him. "What did you do?" he demanded after a beat.

I feigned innocence. "What makes you think I did anything? I was just sitting here minding my own business with the best cocktail I've ever sipped." I held it up so the fresh batch of drinkers meandering down the sidewalk could see it. "It's called Witch's Brew, and it's magical."

"Awesome," another guy enthused as he turned to enter Cher. "I love magic."

I smirked at Gus as he frowned and shook his head. "They're delightful if you want a taste." I took another sip.

His glare was dark. "Is this how you want to play it?"

I was suddenly the picture of innocence. "I have no idea what you're talking about."

"You're full of it."

"I'm full of delicious cocktail is what I am. Don't be shy, everybody. We've got magical concoctions for anyone who wants one. Just form a line. That's right. We'll get to everybody as quickly as possible."

With that, I carried my drink back into the bar. Even though I wanted to look over my shoulder to ascertain if Gus was watching, I didn't. It was much better to leave him stewing in my wake.

Things were definitely looking up at Cher, and it was exactly what I wanted.

Fourteen

I was riding high when I stepped out the side door to take a break that afternoon. We'd been slammed for the better part of the day, and even though Flambeaux was doing good business thanks to Gus's fire shots, we were doing ten times better.

I loved winning.

Sure, I told myself that doing well was what was really important. Winning wasn't everything after all. There was joy to be found in triumph, though, and while I was okay lying to others about how good I was feeling, I had to be brutally honest with myself. I could get addicted to a feeling like this.

I ran my forearm across my forehead and exhaled heavily as the full breadth of the heat hit me. One thing I hadn't prepared myself for was the relentless heat offered up in the French Quarter on a daily basis. I was told that the weather was more comfortable in the winter months—sixties and seventies with less humidity—but that seemed like a pipe dream considering the current heat index.

I pulled out my phone and checked the weather app, shaking my head when it read ninety-eight degrees with 91 percent humidity. I didn't do well with heat. In Michigan, July and August regularly saw days go up to the nineties, but that was a temporary thing. In New Orleans it was the norm. How did people deal with this day in and day out?

"Hello," a smooth voice said from my left, drawing my attention to the sidewalk. I recognized the individual standing there right away as the owner of the Kitty Cat Clubhouse. Why he appeared to be holding ice cream topped with pralines was a mystery.

"Hello." I straightened, unsure what I was supposed to say. "It's Damon, right?"

"It is." He bobbed his head and sidled closer, his smile on full display. Up close, I couldn't stop myself from focusing on his teeth. They were so white they almost looked alien and gave his mouth a feral quality. It reminded me of an episode of *Friends* I'd caught on reruns not too long ago. In it, Ross had overwhitened his teeth to the point where they glowed in the dark. I was afraid that was the sort of situation Damon might be dealing with, and it had me stifling a giggle.

"Is something funny?"

"I find numerous things funny," I replied, shoving my phone in my pocket. "Do you need something? Did you hear about our special drinks? I can cut the line and get you one if you want. What's your flavor?"

"Oh, I'm not here for a drink." Damon's smile was rueful. "I'm just between meetings for work, and I saw you out here. You looked tired... and hot. I thought I might surprise you with a little taste of New Orleans." He shoved the ice cream, which was rapidly melting, in my face.

"Um... thanks. I guess." I took the ice cream, confused. I hadn't been outside long enough for him to catch sight of me and place an order. On top of that, as far as I could remember, there wasn't an ice cream place on this block. That meant he'd gotten the ice cream earlier and was now giving it to me. There had to be a reason. "I'm not big on ice cream," I lied, moving to hand it back.

"Everybody loves ice cream." Damon didn't reach out to take the treat back. "You have to give up your NOLA card if you don't."

"I thought that was the rule on beignets... and hurricanes... and bananas Foster. I've never heard it associated with ice cream."

Damon smirked. "We have a lot of ways for people to lose their NOLA cards."

"Well, that's nice, but I really can't eat this." I placed it on the table. "When it's hot, dairy products make me sick to my stomach." That wasn't exactly a lie. It wasn't the truth either. I happened to love ice cream. I simply wasn't in the mood to eat any, especially since it had been delivered by a guy I was naturally leery of. "Thank you for going out of your way, though."

"Oh, it's no problem." Damon waved off the thank-you. "I'm happy to be of service."

That seemed like a weird thing to say, but I didn't point that out. "Okay, well... do you need something?" He showed no signs of leaving, something I found odd. "Are you here to see Gus?"

"Oh, Gus isn't in the mood to play nice," Damon replied in breezy dismissal. "He was always high-strung when we were kids. It appears he's only gotten worse with age."

I realized this was a prime opportunity to get dirt on my nemesis. He was inside Flambeaux—I'd seen his silhouette move in front of the windows twice in the last five minutes—and that meant I had an open shot at digging deep without an audience.

"So you and Gus were lacrosse teammates but not friends at school?"

"We were friendly." Damon's smile didn't diminish but a

momentary flash in the depths of his eyes told me he was lying. Why though? "Have you ever been to private school?"

I realized he was asking me a question and forced myself to focus. "I went to public school in Michigan."

"Oh, I never would've guessed. Good for you." He shot me an enthusiastic thumbs-up that had my eyebrows lifting. "Gus and I went to three different schools together."

"He mentioned he went to an all-boys school."

"Yes, and that's not without difficulty when you're in high school," Damon readily agreed. "We had a sister school, though, and we paired with them for dances and stuff once in high school. The problem with an all-boys school is that it breeds unnecessary competition."

"I think you can find competition in any school," I countered. "I remember the boys in my high school competing over everything too. We're talking cars... girls... positions on the football team. I don't think that's unique to private schools."

"Likely not, but the competition level at a private school is much higher than at a public school because the kids competing in private schools are of an elite variety."

I stilled, confused. *Did he just say what I think?* "Are you suggesting that private school kids are somehow better than public school kids?"

"Of course not." He waved away the question, as if swatting away a gnat. "It's just that private schools are set up to provide a better education than public schools."

Did he somehow think that was better?

"Public school kids don't have the same opportunities, so they naturally fall behind," he continued, obviously oblivious to the fact that I was steaming mad at this point.

"Uh-huh." I licked my lips, preparing to tell him exactly where he could shove his bias, but he was still rambling on and on and didn't give me an opening.

"I think it's great that I didn't immediately know that you

went to public school though," he said. "It makes you an outlier, and you have no idea how fantastic that is. In fact, I'm so enamored with you and what you've managed to overcome, I was hoping we could perhaps have dinner and get to know one another better."

There was nothing smooth about the transition. Did he actually think I would want to go out with a blowhard like him, given his attitude? I wasn't certain how I was going to respond—other than with a resounding no—when another individual joined our very uncomfortable conversation.

"Damon." Gus's voice was like Freddy Krueger's finger knives running across a window. "Twice in the same week, huh? This feels like some sort of weird punishment. I would like to know who I've ticked off in the universe to earn this."

I had to bite back a laugh at the words. Gus had a flowery way of talking—including when delivering an insult—and it made me laugh.

"Oh, I'm not here for you, Kingman," Damon drawled. "You don't have to worry about that. I'm here to see your friend."

"And what friend is that?"

I was irritated with both of them. *What friend is that?* Did he not see me? Was I suddenly invisible? "I think he means me," I said drily.

Gus's expression was momentarily blank, and then his forehead wrinkled, and his nose crinkled. "I think I'm behind in the conversation."

"That's hardly the first time, huh, buddy?" Damon gave him a condescending smile and slapped his arm. "If I remember high school well—and I think I do—you were always behind then too." He shot me a conspiratorial wink. "He's not *slow* slow, but he's still slow."

For some reason, I found I was offended on Gus's behalf. The second I registered that, I became frustrated with myself.

Why was I even getting involved in this? "Perhaps I should leave you guys to... whatever it is you do when you're together." I snagged the melted ice cream from the table. If I left it out in the sun, it would do nothing but curdle and stink. "It was nice seeing you, Damon. I have to get back inside though."

Damon's hand shot out and grabbed my elbow, a move that had my cheeks burning with fury as I focused on the way his fingers dug into my flesh. "Oh, I'm here to see you, not Kingman. We were in the middle of a conversation."

Yes, a conversation that made me increasingly uncomfortable and annoyed as it progressed. "I really have to get back to work." I was insistent. "Abel will be missing me inside."

"I'm sure Abel can handle himself for a few minutes." Damon didn't lessen his grip but flicked his eyes to Gus. "Kingman, I don't suppose you can give us a few minutes, can you?"

Gus's eyebrows collided in apparent confusion. "A few minutes for what?"

"It's really none of your concern."

Gus rolled his eyes until they landed on me. "What is he even doing here?" He almost sounded accusatory.

"Don't ask me." I was frustrated as I pried Damon's fingers from my wrist. "I have no idea what he's doing here. He claims he was bringing me ice cream."

"Oh, don't say it like that." Damon had the gall to look wounded. "I did bring you ice cream. It's not my fault that you didn't eat it."

"It was melted." I paused a beat. "And ice cream is a random thing to bring someone. It's like bringing someone dish detergent or something."

Gus snorted. "Oh, a bouquet of dish detergent. That's totally something Damon would try to use as a bribe."

"Not a bribe." Damon's eyes flashed with annoyance as I

finally managed to free myself. "I'm not here to bribe her. I'm here to ask her on a date."

My heart skipped a beat—and not because the prospect excited me—but somehow, I managed to keep my expression neutral. "Excuse me?"

"I think that's her way of saying she would rather eat the dish detergent," Gus said drily.

He wasn't wrong. That didn't mean I would agree with him out loud.

"This really is between her and me, Kingman," Damon shot back. He might've prided himself on that smooth veneer he operated under, but he wasn't infallible. It slipped, and Gus seemingly was one of the people who could make it slip on a regular basis.

"Well, I made a promise to myself that when I saw parasites taking over the street, I would do something to stop it," Gus shot back. "She doesn't want to go out with you."

Even though I agreed with the sentiment, I shot him a dirty look. "I think I can answer for myself."

"Parasite?" Damon's voice ratcheted up a notch. "Did you just call me a parasite? That's rich coming from you. I mean... you're the one who had to go crawling back to your parents to siphon off the family teat after your big life adventure went bust because you couldn't make it alone."

When Damon swung his eyes to me, fire was reflected there. "Did you know that about him? He told his family he didn't need their money when he was first out of college. He said he was going to do everything on his own. He then proceeded to gallivant from country to country for years, living like a hobo while not allowing them to race in and rescue him, but eventually he had to crawl back when his parents put the kibosh on his lifestyle."

Damon looked smug. "Yeah, that's right." He was grooving into his story at this point and clearly enjoying himself. "He was living off his family's money when he was overseas—something he doesn't want other people to know about—and when his family threatened to cut him off, he was forced to come back and join the bar business. He's only working because it's that or be homeless."

Honestly, the news didn't surprise me. Sure, I hadn't known the specifics, but I figured it had been something close to that. "It's really none of my business." Believe it or not, I wasn't interested in embarrassing Gus. Well, at least not the way Damon clearly wanted to embarrass him. Other ways were okay. I just didn't want him ruining my business plan. What Damon was doing was something else entirely.

"Of course, it's your business," Damon countered. "You're in direct competition with him. He's got more money than you... and an ace in the hole because of who his parents are. You don't stand a chance."

The statement chafed. "I happen to think I'm doing pretty well."

"Of course, you are," Gus fired back. "Don't listen to him. He's an idiot. He's only here because he knows it will irritate me."

Damon was suddenly the picture of innocence. "Why would it irritate you?"

"Because your mere presence irritates me."

"Yes, but Moxie is a rival bar owner," he pointed out. "She's not your friend. You shouldn't care what we do unless..." He left the statement hanging.

I focused my full attention on Gus, curious how he would respond. Only an idiot wouldn't pick up on the innuendo Damon was throwing around in conjunction with his ill-timed hip thrusts. They obviously had the sort of relationship that was built on one-upping each other. How I played into that was a mystery.

"I think we should go out to dinner." Damon was all

smarm and charm when he turned back to me. "I haven't been able to stop thinking about you since our first meeting. I'm sure you feel the same way. We have a spark." He wiggled his fingers as if to emphasize it.

In truth, I barely remembered meeting Damon until he'd made a big show of approaching me. I hadn't thought about him even in fleeting fashion. "Oh, well..." I was trying to think of a way to let him down without hurting his feelings. I did not want this to turn into a thing. I didn't get a chance to come up with a pleasant—and yet firm —response.

"She's not going out with you," Gus fired back, his eyes burning with haughty derision. "She likens you to something she would scrape off the bottom of her boot. Tell him." He was demanding when he focused on me.

"Oh, well..."

"You don't know," Damon fired back. "We have something brewing between us. It's chemical. The air practically catches fire when we're together."

That was a gross overstatement if I'd ever heard one.

"She's not going out with you," Gus insisted. "It's not going to happen. Let it go."

"Who says you're the boss?" Damon folded his arms across his chest. "Last time I checked, Moxie was in charge of her own life. I think that means she gets to decide if she's going out with me herself."

"She's not deciding," Gus argued, causing annoyance to roll through me like a tsunami. "I'm deciding, and she's not going out with you."

"And why is that?" Damon asked.

Something stirred inside of me. "Yeah, why is that?"

Slowly, Gus tracked his eyes to me. "Because... he's horrible. He's the guy your mother warned you about."

"Actually, the guy my mother warned me about was the

dude on the corner who sold fresh fish from the Detroit River out of his trunk," I countered.

"Ha!" Damon jabbed a finger into Gus's chest. "You heard her. She totally wants to go out with me."

I balked. "Um..."

"She didn't say that." Gus slapped Damon's hand back. "She's not going out with you. I forbid it."

Well, that tore it. I had no interest in going out with Damon, but no way would I let Gus think he had any sort of sway over me. We were rivals, for crying out loud. He wasn't in control. That was never going to happen.

"I would love to have dinner with you," I said out of nowhere, surprising even myself. "I think it sounds lovely."

I internally cringed when Damon shot Gus a triumphant look. He'd clearly won. Why he was so adamant about winning was beyond me, but I'd essentially handed him a victory.

"You're not going out with him," Gus growled.

I refused to back down. I was in this now. "I'm in charge of my own life. You don't get a say." I plastered a smile on my face that I didn't feel and looked at Damon. "Just... give me a call when you want to set something up. I really do have to get back inside."

With that, I turned my back on the two men—who were still glowering at one another like toddlers fighting over the same ball—and swooped inside. My last glimpse of them involved a morose stare from Gus. It wasn't anger I saw reflected there when we snagged gazes. It was something else.

Sadness? No, that couldn't be right. I pushed the thought out of my head right away. He had nothing to be sad about. This was about losing a battle to Damon and nothing more. If Gus wanted to get his former schoolmate back, that was between them. I refused to be a pawn in that particular game.

I had my own game to win, and things were looking up.

Fifteen

I found Gus on the street corner when I exited Cher after ten o'clock.

"Hey."

"Hey." His expression was hard to read. "Ready?"

I glanced around, confused. "Ready for what? You're not going to kill me, are you?"

His gaze turned dark. "No, I'm not going to kill you. Why would you think that?"

"Because the last time I saw you, you weren't exactly what I would call a happy individual."

"Yes, well, Damon is a douche. I can't stand him. That doesn't mean I'm going to allow you to walk home by yourself."

Not this again. "I'm perfectly capable of walking myself home."

"I have no doubt. I want to walk you, though." He gestured toward the street. The revelers were still out, raucous laughter filling the air, and I had to sidestep three of them when crossing. I opted to stick to the right, and he took the left sidewalk. For some reason, I liked it that way. It made me

148

feel as if we weren't getting too close... even though I'd been starting to wonder if the lines between us were fading. Even the illusion of distance was welcome.

"Do you want to talk about it?" I asked.

At the same time, he said, "Truth or dare?"

I smirked into the darkness. "Truth."

"You don't really like Damon, do you?"

I'd been expecting the question. That somehow made it easier to answer. "I think he's... an interesting individual."

"That's not much of an answer."

"It's the best I've got."

"And you're going to go out with him?"

The question was irritating, but I pretended I wasn't bothered by it. "I will probably have dinner with him."

"And?"

"And what?"

"And what about after?"

I had trouble wrapping my head around what he was saying. "Are you asking if I'm going to sleep with him?"

"No, because Damon doesn't 'sleep' with anybody." He used air quotes so there would be no question what he was insinuating. "He has sex with people, once, and then goes on his merry way."

"So basically you're saying that you're protecting my virtue," I said drily.

"I'm saying that he'll use you, Moxie."

"Why do you care?"

"I... don't... care."

"Is it because you want to beat him?" I was honestly curious. "Is this all about your competition with him?"

"No." He was morose, his expression telling me that talk of Damon made him closed off. "Truth or dare?"

He was clearly desperate to change the topic. I wasn't about to allow that. "It's not your turn. It's mine."

"Fine."

"Truth or dare?" I asked.

"Truth."

"Why do you hate Damon so much?"

He made a groaning noise. "Ugh. I should've seen that question coming."

"You really should have."

"Can't you start with something easier? We have twelve blocks until you're home. That one can wait."

I considered pressing him and then let it go... for now. "Fine. What's the deal with your parents? I mean... is what Damon said true? Did you live on their money when you were flitting around the globe?"

"I think I liked the first question better," Gus drawled, annoyance positively permeating the street between us. "It's obvious you've formed an opinion about me. What do you think?"

It was a loaded question. "I don't know." I opted for the truth. "Sometimes I think I see a good guy inside of you. Sure, he's still trying to find his place in this world—really, who isn't?—but other times there's a sense of entitlement that floats around you like bad aftershave."

Gus snorted. "That could be the most apt thing anyone has ever said about me."

Since I expected him to be offended, I couldn't hide my surprise. "You don't have a problem with me calling you entitled?"

"I am entitled. The way I grew up made it so I had no choice but to be entitled. I've spent years trying to break the Kingman family mold, to varying degrees of success."

"And yet you're working for the family business now," I pointed out.

He hesitated and then nodded. "Yeah, well, I ran out of

options. I had plans for things that didn't involve the family business, but apparently I'm only good at one thing."

"Wearing adult diapers? Are they the ones with the special wet guard in the front?"

He choked on a laugh. "That was... a very quick response."

"Humor is my gift."

"I think you have more than one gift." It was one of the nicest things he'd ever said to me, and I wanted to say something in return... although I had no idea what, so I gawped like a fish. Instead of letting me meander, he covered quickly. "Let's just say that I did not want to end up in the family business. Unfortunately, I'm actually good at it because it's all I knew when I was growing up."

Okay, I was officially intrigued. "What do you mean?"

"We were dragged from bar to bar to watch renovations and openings," he explained. "We learned about ordering... and how to make decorations down to earth without being gaudy... and how to hire bartenders who were loyal without breaking the bank."

"And you didn't like that?" I thought back to my own childhood, to the way my mother's bitterness had filled our house with something other than the useless tchotchkes she loved so much and let loose a sigh. "I would've loved to have someone to learn from when I was starting out."

"It seems to me that you've done pretty well for yourself."

"Yeah, but you're doing better than me."

"I'm not."

"You are so. You had that awesome fire shot going for you today."

"And you totally blew it out of the water with the smoking witchy drinks. That was inspired, by the way. Even I was impressed... although I had every intention of keeping that little tidbit to myself. Apparently your witch's brew really is magical."

I couldn't stop myself from laughing. "Thanks for the compliment... I guess. I wish I could take credit for it. That was all Abel though."

"Yeah, that guy is a gem." Wistfulness momentarily invaded Gus's features. "I really wanted to get him for Flambeaux, but you had him sewn up before I even realized he was on the market."

"I'm surprised you knew he was on the market at all. And here I thought I was being so clever when poaching from Frenchman Street."

"Abel has made a name for himself in multiple corners of the city. He's going to do big things. Eventually, I wouldn't be surprised to find him owning a bar or two. He'll be good at it."

"He will be," I agreed, lapsing into silence.

"Truth or dare?" Gus asked after a full minute where the only sound was our shoes slapping against the sidewalks.

"Truth. I'm not going to do a dare with you... probably ever."

"Yes, but the truth game doesn't have the same ring to it."

"True story."

"You're not like... attracted to Damon, are you?"

The question made me incredibly uncomfortable. "Why are you so fixated on Damon?"

"You have to answer my question first." He was firm. "I'm being serious. I need to know."

I managed to swallow a sigh but only barely. "I didn't come here to find a boyfriend, so I'm guessing it will be just one dinner. He strikes me as a wiener of the highest order."

He chuckled. "A wiener? That's the perfect word for him."

"I don't disagree."

"So... why are you going out with him?"

I couldn't tell him the truth. If I explained that my hackles went up when he answered for me, and that was the only reason I said yes, it would give him too much power. "Because I'm always up for new experiences." It wasn't exactly a lie. It was fairly far from the truth, however. I'm the sort of individual who enjoys a routine. Going out with Damon was nowhere on my to-do list. I couldn't back out now though. "I wouldn't worry about it," I added out of nowhere. "He only asked me out because he thought it would irritate you. He likely won't call."

"I wouldn't be too sure about that." Gus scuffed his shoe against the ground. "You're not going to let him kiss you, are you?"

The invasive questions regarding Damon were starting to grate. "That's not the plan, but I'm totally going to make out with him in front of Flambeaux if you don't let it go."

"I thought most women liked talking about themselves."

"I think you've been hanging around with the wrong women. I would much rather talk about my favorite *Alien* movie. Oh, and I'm a big fan of the What Superhero is Best in Bed game."

Gus's lips curved into a smile. "I don't believe I've ever heard of that game. You're going to have to tell me the rules."

I gladly laid them out for him.

"I see," he said when I was done. "I don't think I'm going to be as good at this game as you are. There simply aren't as many female superheroes."

"You don't have to focus on the female superheroes," I argued. "You're allowed to speculate about the men. It doesn't call your manhood into question or anything. Geez."

"Okay." He held up his hands in a placating manner. "I was just checking the rules. Let me see." He tapped his chin, giving the matter serious thought. "I think that it would be dangerous to have sex with Superman because his sperm would shoot through a woman—or a man, for that matter; I don't want to be sexist—like a bullet. There's nothing fun about making love with someone who has an open wound thanks to super sperm."

I didn't mean to laugh, but I couldn't stop myself. "That is a very good point."

"What superhero do you think is best in bed?"

"Well, we know it's not Batman after that whole oral sex kerfuffle a few months ago."

He snickered.

"I guess I would say Mr. Fantastic. He can stretch his body parts into weird contortions. That has to be helpful, right?"

"I would certainly think so." He was quiet for a beat and then asked the obvious follow-up question. "Which superhero is the worst in bed?"

"That's easy. It's Spider-Man obviously. He would just make things so sticky."

"Sticky isn't always bad."

"With webs it totally would be. I also think Aquaman— the cartoon version, not Jason Momoa because he's clearly a sex god—would be all sorts of bad. I mean, can you even separate the dude from his seahorse? You would never get a grand gesture out of him."

Gus's forehead creased as he started across the road. At first I was confused what he was doing, and then I realized we'd reached Jackson Square and he was moving in to make sure I wasn't accosted by any of the individuals sleeping on the benches.

"I already dropped off food to them," I volunteered. "I did it two hours ago."

"I know. I saw you leave Cher with the takeout containers."

It was my turn to frown. "Are you spying on me?"

"Spying is a strong word. I saw you leave through the side door when I was working. You had the containers in your hand, and I saw the direction you were heading. I knew where you were going."

"Did you follow me?"

"No."

I studied his face for what felt like a really long time. I couldn't detect a lie there, although I didn't know him well enough to declare that with any sense of certainty. "Well, I guess that's something," I said finally.

"I kind of wanted to," he admitted.

"Why?" I was honestly curious.

"Because... you make me want to be chivalrous."

It wasn't the response I was expecting. "What?"

He laughed at my baffled snort. "Yeah, I don't get it either." He rubbed his hand over the back of his neck, seemingly weary. "Do you know what your problem is?"

It wasn't the smoothest of conversational shifts. "No, but something tells me you're about to answer your own question."

"Your problem is that you won't allow yourself to be weak."

"I'm not weak."

"Of course, you're not. You're a strong person. Everyone has weak moments, though, Moxie. You refuse to allow yourself to embrace those weak moments. That makes you brittle."

There was definitely an insult buried in there. "I'm brittle, huh?" I forced a smile I didn't feel. "I guess there are worse things."

"Not for you. Being brittle means you've closed yourself off. I think I know why—and I get it—but you should know that you're selling yourself short."

"You think you know why I'm brittle?" Irritation flooded me. "Do tell."

"It's not rocket science." His voice was soft. "Your father left when you were a kid. You haven't told me much, but you have mentioned that... begrudgingly. The fact that you don't want to talk about it means that his leaving shaped you. I'm also guessing it made you super loyal to your mother, who you also don't want to talk about."

I ignored the bit about my mother. He was right. I didn't want to talk about her. My father was another thing. "His leaving means nothing to me," I countered.

"I think you're trying to convince yourself of that as much as me. It doesn't matter though. I know... and how I know is because I'm the same way. I shut down when I don't want to talk about the things that bother me most."

"Like Damon," I surmised.

He hesitated and then nodded. "He is not a good guy. I know you don't need me telling you how to live your life, but... don't go out with him and possibly get yourself hurt to spite me. I'm not worth that."

"I'm not here to date anyone," I said when I could find my voice. The naked emotion on his face when he'd delivered the statement was enough to steal my breath. "You don't have to worry about Damon and me. If we do go out, it will just be the one time. I'll ask him questions designed to help me beat you at our little game, and that's it."

He worked his jaw, doubt flitting in the depths of his eyes, and then he sighed. "You're an adult. It's obvious you're going to do what you're going to do... which includes irritating me."

"I'm really good at irritating you," I noted as I bypassed Jackson Square and landed on the Decatur Street sidewalk. I didn't even bother asking this time if he was going to head home rather than walk me to my apartment. I already knew the answer. I was stubborn. So was he.

"You said something a few minutes ago," Gus noted when neither of us had spoken in a few minutes.

"About you wearing adult diapers? Yeah. I've known since the day I met you. It's okay. Your secret is safe with me."

He snorted. "You need to let go of the adult diapers. I'm a briefs man. No diapers in sight."

"You're a brief man, huh?" I couldn't stop myself from pushing the matter. "I'll make sure to spread the word to all the eligible women in the Quarter. I wouldn't want them to be disappointed by high expectations."

"Ha ha." He poked my side, causing me to squirm. His proximity fuzzed my head sometimes—and not in a bad way. That realization, however, made me furious at myself. It was turning into a vicious cycle. "I'm being serious. You said something I want more information about."

"You'll have to be more specific. All I remember talking about is sexy superheroes and adult diapers. You also psycho-analyzed me and my quirks, but I've decided to pretend that never happened because it bugs me."

"I would expect nothing less," he replied. "It was toward the tail end of the superhero conversation. You said Aquaman and his seahorse could never come through with a grand gesture. I need to know what that means."

I pressed my lips together, heat rushing to my cheeks. I didn't remember saying that. It must've slipped out because he couldn't have pulled that little detail out of thin air. "I... don't recall."

"You recall." He made a clucking sound with his tongue as we arrived at the gate that led to the alley behind my unit. This evening, there were no voices at the other end. That meant that my four-plex mates were either working or keeping it quiet for a change.

"I..." What was I supposed to say? It really was none of his business. Despite that, I found myself responding. "It's something my mother used to say."

"Tell me." His voice was soft.

"She was a good mother," I explained out of nowhere.

Why I felt the need to stand up for her was beyond me. "She did her best. She was just... always struggling."

"Your father didn't help financially?"

"My father fell off the map." I flicked my eyes to the dark street behind us, looking back on a childhood that seemed to have happened to someone else a lifetime ago.

"Just tell me, Moxie," Gus prodded. "Trust me with this one thing. You might find you like confiding in someone."

That was exactly what I was afraid of. Still, I did it. "My mother never got over my father leaving. He was the love of her life. For a time—we're talking a few years here—she convinced herself that he would come back.

"She made up these grand scenarios in her head," I continued, my voice flat. "She said she would make him work for her love. She wouldn't take him back right away. It was how she sustained herself.

"Eventually, she realized he was never coming back. That's when she grew depressed. She drank a bit too... although she always seemed to catch herself before she devolved into full-blown alcoholism."

Gus nodded in understanding but didn't say anything.

"One night, when I was fifteen, I came home from a school dance." The memory felt like it belonged to someone else and yet it had somehow scarred me. It was hard to wrap my head around. "She was drunk, in her closet, and looking through an old box of photos. They were actual photos, which seems weird now that we carry all our photos with us on our phones."

"It was a lifetime ago," Gus agreed.

"They were photos of her and my father at various events. She fell in love with him when he was on the stage, some local band. She always hoped he would call her on stage and dedicate a song to her. She said she wanted a grand gesture from him because that would be her proof that everything was going to work out."

"Like... a power ballad?" Gus queried.

I shrugged. "I guess. Anyway, she said she waited years for it. She even told him how much it would mean to her. She never got it though. That night she told me that if a guy didn't whip out a grand gesture at some point, then he wasn't worth my time. She also told me that putting a man before my ambitions would always be the wrong choice because the man would be the one who would never keep me warm at night."

"And do you believe that?"

"I don't know." That was the truth. "I try to stay far away from relationship drama these days. I'm focused on my career. That's what she wanted. I want it too. I don't need love because I've got myself and I know what I want to do with my life. The rest of it... well... it doesn't seem important right now."

"Are you sure about that?" His gaze was probing.

"Pretty sure," I confirmed.

He pressed his lips together, as if struggling with something internally, and then smiled. "Thank you for telling me."

My blood ran cold when he leaned in. I thought he was going to kiss me... or maybe strangle me if that was the sort of mood he was entertaining. Instead, he gave me a hard hug. It wasn't flirty or soft or even something a friend would offer. It was somehow more, although why I believed that was beyond me.

"See you at work tomorrow."

My mouth dropped open when he pressed a surprising kiss to my forehead. I enjoyed the warmth of his lips, although the sensation was gone all too quickly, and then he pulled away. "What..." I didn't know what to say, which was rare for me.

"I'll see you tomorrow." He tipped an invisible hat. "I

can't wait to see what new game you come up with for us to play."

I wanted to say something so badly and yet there was nothing. My mind was blank.

"I'm going to win tomorrow," he called over his shoulder as he departed. "You've been warned."

"We'll just see about that."

Sixteen

G us and I fell into a routine. I didn't notice it had happened until after it was already a thing.

In the mornings, three days a week, we raced on the riverwalk. Taunts flew fast and furious those days. There was comfort in the exchanges for some reason, although I couldn't explain why. The other three mornings—we took Sundays off—we somehow magically met over coffee and beignets in Jackson Square. We didn't go there together. We always ended up together though. The taunts flew fast and furious there too. Somehow, and I was loath to admit this, the taunts resembled flirty banter most days. It was something neither of us acknowledged.

During the day, we tried to one-up each other with promotions at the bars. Some days I would win. Others he would. The competition was fierce, and I found I enjoyed it. That was another thing I had trouble admitting, even to myself. I only allowed the thought to enter my mind when I couldn't sleep at night, which was becoming a regular occurrence.

At the end of our shifts, I would find him waiting on the

street corner when I left Cher. He insisted on walking me home, even though every night I argued that it wasn't necessary. We played Truth or Dare for the entirety of the walk—no dares were ever issued—and I found I knew a strange hodge-podge of facts about him in a short amount of time.

His favorite food was a crawfish boil, although his parents always frowned on it because they found sucking crawfish from their shells to be gross.

His favorite movie of all time was *The Godfather*, something he watched with his father and brothers every year. His second favorite was *Die Hard*, which only proved he was a total dude.

That meant his favorite Christmas movie was also *Die Hard*, and we'd argued at least five times about whether it was actually a Christmas movie. He maintained he won the argument. I maintained he was crazy, and I was top dog in that fight.

I discovered that his favorite musical act was the Foo Fighters, but he had eclectic taste. He also listened to the Beatles and Cyndi Lauper... and he quickly changed the subject when I accused him of liking Nickelback.

He said his favorite season in the Quarter was Halloween, insisting that he had places he wanted to take me when October rolled around because they had to be seen to be believed. He also declared Christmas season to be some sort of miracle in the city and said he was going to make me drink a Naughty But Nice Martini—whatever that was—at some point.

He also swore up and down he was going to teach me the trick to charming the voodoo ladies who constantly threw chicken feet at me whenever I crossed their paths. He'd yet to come through on that front, but I was still waiting.

Essentially, it was like we were dating... without actually touching one another. We were careful to make sure that our fingers never brushed, and our gazes didn't linger all that long. It was by unspoken agreement that we maintained at least a two-foot perimeter. I was grateful for that too.

Now, two weeks into our routine, I couldn't find him. He wasn't on our usual bench. There were no beignets—or banana pancakes, when he was feeling feisty—and there were no long legs stretched out as he basked in the shade of a low-humidity morning. Instead, there looked to be a tourist couple taking over our space... and they had at least four kids running around acting like morons.

"No, no, no." I viciously swore under my breath and glanced around. I hated change, but I could move to another bench for a single morning. The only problem was, Gus wasn't on any of the other benches. Had he stopped long enough to find the same greeting as I had and taken off to greener pastures? Or pastures that didn't feature screaming ankle biters from Duluth, at the very least.

I was disappointed, something that just made me ridiculously angry. Why should I be disappointed? He was nothing to me but a competitor. Right? *Right?*

"Hey, Moxie."

I turned at the new voice, jolting when I recognized Benji. He was one of the familiar faces in the Quarter. In fact, he was the one face I looked for every night. We only talked occasionally, mostly when I delivered the nightly leftovers, but I could've picked him out of a lineup from fifty feet away.

He had my eyes after all.

"Hi, Benji." I worked to keep my frustration in check. He was skittish to the nth degree and would disappear for days on end if any of the other park regulars got into a screaming match.

"What are you doing?" Benji's eyes darted left and right as he glanced around the park. "You're usually over there." He pointed toward my normal bench. "I always see you when I'm making my rounds in the morning."

"You do?" For some reason, I was touched by the statement.

"Yeah. You're hard to miss. You remind me of someone." He took on a far-off expression, as if he were struggling really hard to remember something.

My heart skipped a beat. "Oh yeah?"

"Yeah, I..." Before he could finish the statement, Benji shrank back, smacking into one of the fence walls in his haste to escape. There wasn't enough room for him to navigate, however, so he simply cowered.

"What's wrong?" Instantly concerned, I turned to find Gus standing behind me. He had a cup of coffee in his right hand and a cardboard container of beignets balanced in his left palm. "You're late," I said dumbly when I realized it was him.

"Good morning to you too," he drawled. "Also, if we keep accidentally meeting one another here, how could I possibly be late? It's not as if this is a date, right?"

"Of course not." That was the only appropriate answer to the question. "It's most certainly not a date."

"Just checking." He offered up a smug grimace, as if letting me know that he knew something I couldn't possibly know. Then he shot a kind smile at Benji. "I'm sorry I startled you." He extended the container of beignets without even thinking about it. "Would you like some breakfast?"

Benji's eyes were as wide as saucers, and it pinched my heart to look at him.

"It's okay," I said automatically, extending a tentative hand. It hurt when he shrank away from me. "Hey, Benji." My voice was soft when I called out to him. "You were about to tell me who I reminded you of. Do you remember?"

"What?" Benji was clearly dazed. "Do I remember who you remind me of?"

"Yes." I wanted to hear his answer. This wasn't the first time he'd said I reminded him of someone.

"Her name was Angie," Benji said out of nowhere, knocking me for a loop.

"Oh yeah?" I managed to keep my face impassive, although it took effort. "Where is Angie now?"

"I don't know. I lost her."

"You lost her?"

"In Michigan. I lost her in Michigan."

"Was she alone?"

"I... don't remember. I think there might've been a baby. It's so hard to remember though. It feels like another life. Or maybe a dream." Benji flashed a deranged smile. "It was probably a dream. There's a lot of stuff I think is real that turns out to be a dream."

I deflated a bit. "Okay, well... that's good to know."

"Yeah. You just look a little like Angie. It's in the face." He waved his hand over his face. "Like here. You don't have her coloring though."

"No, I'm sure I don't." I handed him my beignets. "Have some breakfast, huh?"

"Um... okay." He stared at the food for a few seconds. "I don't suppose you have some whiskey to go with them, do you?"

"Nope. Sorry."

"Okay. Beignets are good too." He turned and walked toward the benches on the outside of the park. "See you later, Moxie. You're not Angie's ghost. I know that."

"I'm not Angie's ghost," I agreed softly. I'd almost forgotten that Gus was with me until I turned back to him. "Oh, hey."

He flashed a smile, but it didn't touch his eyes, which were curious. "Hey." He held up his beignets. "Do you want to share?"

165

"This isn't a date," I reminded him.

"Oh, I know."

I took one of the beignets and blew out a sigh before lowering myself to the bench. The tourists were still in our usual spot, and I hated them more than I had ten minutes before. "Do you believe this?" I gestured toward the family—the kids were jumping on the benches like they were trampolines—and groaned.

"They're animals," Gus readily agreed as he settled next to me. He didn't even pretend he was going to sit one bench away this morning. Usually, he made a game of it. Apparently, he didn't have the energy today. "Do you want to tell me what that was all about?"

"What what was all about?" I was the picture of innocence. Now that Benji was gone, I realized I'd done something incredibly stupid—and in front of the worst possible person.

"Please don't do that." Gus's voice was soft. "I know that something just happened. I simply want to know what that something was."

"What makes you so certain that something just happened?" I opted to fixate on my coffee rather than his face. He looked so earnest I was afraid I would break if I met his gaze.

"Moxie." He adopted a stern tone.

"I have no idea what you're talking about," I lied.

"Don't make me pull out the Truth or Dare game. It seems beneath us at this point."

I gripped my coffee tighter. *Don't tell him. Don't tell him.* It ran like song lyrics through my head. "He's just one of the guys I feed regularly."

"I don't think that's true. Well, it's probably true, but I guess it's more apt to say I don't think that's all there is to it."

"Well, that's it." I committed to the lie. It would be easier over the long run.

"Yeah?"

"Yeah." *Please don't push me,* I fervently wished. *Please... just don't push me.*

He pushed me. "You know what's interesting?" He almost sounded as if he were talking to himself instead of me. "Three nights ago we played the game, and it was all questions about our parents. You asked me if I ever wanted to run away from home as a kid. I asked you if you ever missed having a father. Do you remember what your response was?"

"I... don't believe I do." I remembered. How could he though?

"You said that your mother—I believe her name was Angela—was both father and mother, and you didn't miss having a father. I knew that was a lie, but I didn't call you on it because... well... it's one of those lies that's not really a lie. It's okay to tell *that* lie."

"So?" My voice was weak.

"So your mother's name is Angela, and that guy said you looked like a woman he used to know named Angie. Angela could easily turn into Angie at some point."

"My mother has dark hair. It couldn't possibly be the same Angie."

"He said you had the same face." Gus was refusing to back down, and I knew it was all but over. "He said you had the same face but not the same coloring... and you have his coloring. You also said your father fancied himself a big-time musician and took off when you were a kid... and New Orleans is the place where wannabe musicians go to die."

I thought I might be sick. I'd only eaten the one beignet from his stash, but there was a very real possibility I was about to lose what little breakfast I'd consumed. "I don't know what you're saying," I gritted out.

"Moxie." He sounded exasperated. "You can trust me."

"We're competitors."

"Not like you think we are." He angled his body so I had no choice but to meet his gaze. "Is that guy your father?"

"How can you even ask that?"

"That wasn't a denial." The lines in his forehead smoothed. "That's the answer to the riddle." Now he was definitely talking to himself. "He's why you go out of your way to feed the street folks every single night."

There was no sense denying it at this point. He'd already figured it out. Instead, I turned my attention to the river, which was just visible at the top of the steps on the other side of Decatur. "His name is Benjamin—or Benji—Shepherd, but as you know, most of the guys on the street abandon their birth names."

"It's probably because they no longer feel like the people they were back then."

"Probably."

He reached over and grabbed my hand without looking. He didn't have to search for it. He seemingly knew where it was. We never touched. It was by design. He touched me today, though, and there was nothing romantic about the gesture. "When did you figure it out?"

"I was only here a week when I first saw him," I replied. "I was walking through the Square and heard him singing. It triggered something in my memory, although I didn't know what at the time. I found myself listening to the entire song. I clapped with the others, left him a few bucks, and then headed over to Cher. It was still undergoing renovations at that point."

He didn't interrupt. He just listened.

"It didn't hit me until hours later. I had a memory flash. I remembered him leaving when I was a kid. His face kind of fuzzed in my memory after a while when I was little, but after my mother died, I found an old box of photographs. I thought she'd tossed everything of his—she hated him by the end and told me on a regular basis that it was best to trust nobody but myself—but apparently, she kept the one box. It was the same man.

"Sure, living on the street changed him, but it was the same eyes and chin," I continued. "I knew... and yet I needed proof. I picked up food for them that night for the first time, and I tried to talk to him when I dropped it off. He was shy and didn't say much."

"So, you kept going back," Gus deduced.

"Yeah. I kept going back. I *keep* going back," I corrected. "Today was the first time he came close to figuring it out, although I'm pretty sure he'll never allow himself to actually see the truth."

"Do you want him to know the truth?"

"I... don't... know."

He merely nodded. "It's okay." He squeezed my hand. "You don't have to make up your mind today... or even tomorrow. You have time."

"Do I?" It was an honest question. "Two weeks ago, on the riverwalk, I thought..." I trailed off.

"You thought the body they were recovering could've been his." Gus shook his head. "I couldn't figure out why you were so upset. It all makes sense now." He gripped my hand tighter. "Geez. Why didn't you tell me this sooner?"

He had to be kidding. "Why would I?"

"Because..." He caught himself. I had no idea what he was going to say, but I recognized the moment he decided to change course. "Because I want to help you."

I was bewildered. "Help me what?"

"With whatever the plan is here."

"The plan for what?"

"Him." Gus gestured in the direction Benji had disappeared. "You don't have to tell him who you are—not ever, if you don't want to—but you must have an idea what you want to do here."

"Are you kidding? Whenever I consider talking to him, my brain fries. I don't even know what I'm doing with my own life. How am I supposed to deal with him?"

Gus studied my face, as if searching for something specific. Then he cracked a smile. "You know, you're good at pretending you've got things figured out. You convince even me sometimes. It's good to know that you're a mortal just like me though. I'm glad that you don't have everything figured out."

I shot him a dirty look. "I'm way more together than you."

"Duly noted."

"Totally."

"I get it."

"Completely," I insisted.

"Beignet?" He extended the cardboard container in my direction with his left hand. It was only then that I realized he was still holding my hand with the right, his coffee clutched between his knees.

Hesitantly, I reached out and grabbed one of the beignets. "I might not do anything," I said in a low voice. "I mean... I might just walk away."

Instead of giving me grief, calling me a terrible person, and trying to weigh me down with guilt, Gus grinned. "That's also a viable solution. I often do nothing. It's just another thing we have in common."

"You're starting to irritate me," I groused.

"I know. We have that in common too. You irritate me daily."

"Does that mean you're going to let this go?"

That question had him hesitating. "I'm going to be here when you want to talk. This is your show though."

It was the perfect answer. "Who are you, and what have

you done with the real Gus Kingman?"

He laughed. "I can't fix this for you. Nobody can, including yourself. When you want to make a move, though, I'll help."

"Great." I shoved the beignet in my mouth and started chewing.

"We can talk about it as much as you want," he promised. "Or as little as you want."

I mumbled "thanks" around the beignet.

"I just need one thing from you," he said.

Oh, here it comes. I braced myself.

"What's your real name? What does he know you as? You know, just for my own edification."

"I'm not answering that," I said when I swallowed. "Moxie is my real name."

"It's not a name."

"It's a state of mind."

"That doesn't mean you can use it as a name."

"Oh, let it go." It wasn't even nine o'clock yet, and I was exhausted.

"Since you've had a rough morning, I'm going to let it go for today. Tomorrow is a new day though."

"Hurray for that."

Gus's gaze was dark when it flicked back to the kids cavorting on our bench. "And they'll hopefully be gone. Maybe we'll luck out and the voodoo queens will get them before lunch. That would solve one of our biggest problems."

"Now that I can agree with. Voodoo queens should totally be for hire. I think that's a market that needs to be tapped into. One of us should take advantage."

"I think I'll leave that to you. I'm much too busy making my bar the best one on Bourbon Street."

I glared. "Those are fighting words."

"That's exactly what I'm counting on."

Seventeen

I felt lighter after confiding in Gus, although if someone had asked me to explain the emotions running through me, I would've come up empty. I hadn't told anyone about Benji. There was nobody to tell. Well, I could've told my four-plex mates—and they likely would've been open to talking about it—but I could never bring myself to start the conversation. Gus, however, had figured out the bulk of it himself, which proved he'd been listening during our long conversations at night.

That felt somehow miraculous.

I returned home long enough to shower, change my clothes, and grab a quick snack. Since I'd given my beignets away—and hadn't wanted to look like a total pig when scarfing down part of Gus's breakfast—I figured I needed fuel to get through the day. After that, I headed out to work.

Raucous laughter hit my ears when I arrived at the bar. It wasn't coming from Cher, however, it was emanating from across the street. I slowed my pace enough to give Flambeaux a long once-over, and what I found happening inside was enough to have me rolling my eyes.

"Belly dancers?" I complained as I walked through the front door of Cher and fixed Abel with a petulant look. "He has belly dancers over there?"

Abel's response was a simple shrug. "I don't know what to tell you, girl. He's banking on sex selling, which it does. It's not like we're hurting for business, so don't get worked up."

"Whatever." I refused to let the belly dancers—they were almost naked and gyrating their hips in such a fashion that it made me dizzy—ruin my good mood. Heck, I refused to let them dim the affection I was feeling for Gus. If he wanted to utilize belly dancers, that was for him to decide. "So, what's the plan for today?"

"I thought we would just have a normal day," Abel replied. "I mean... we can't have a gimmick every single day. We'll run out of ideas in less than a month if we do that."

"I guess. I prefer calling them promotions by the way." What he said made sense, loath as I was to admit it. "How are we doing on stock? I figured I would spend some time in the storage room making lists this afternoon."

"I did that last night with Carly. It only took us an hour."

I was understandably surprised. "You managed to run the bar by yourself all night and do inventory?" That shouldn't have been possible.

"I'm a multitasker. I told you that when you hired me."

"Yeah, but... you're making me look bad."

He snorted. "Girl, you do a lot of work, even if you don't realize it. FYI, there was a message left for you on the work number. Someone named Damon requesting a date."

I froze. I'd forgotten all about Damon's vague date request. It had been weeks ago at this point. I figured he only asked me out to get a rise out of Gus. Then, once he'd accomplished his mission, he decided to move on. I wasn't his type anyway. I'd come to that conclusion without any prodding from an outside source, including Gus, who hated Damon with such a fiery passion it almost made me laugh.

"You look as if you just got run over by a truck," Abel commented, shaking his head. "A date request should not fill you with the sort of fear that makes horror movie last girls crap their pants."

I forced myself to stand straighter. "I'm not afraid."

"You've clearly gone so long without a date you don't even know how to react."

"Oh, look who's talking," I scoffed. "I don't think you can comment on my dating life when you're not dating."

He lifted an eyebrow. "Who says I'm not dating?"

"Common sense. You work twelve hours a day—by your own choice, I might add. You don't have time to date."

He snorted in disdainful amusement. "That shows what you know. I've been out four nights this week."

"Doing what?"

"What do you think?"

I had a few ideas, but there was no way I could express them without risking a sexual harassment lawsuit. Still, I had questions. "Do you have a girlfriend I don't know about?"

"Define girlfriend."

"Person you date on a regular basis."

"Define regular basis."

Okay, now he was just being irritating. "I'm simply wondering how this works when you work such late hours."

"I can answer that for you," Carly said as she barreled into the room from one of the storage closets. "Word has spread between the barhops that Abel is on the market. Since he's hot, mixes a mean drink, and doesn't seem to be too picky, a competition has started late at night."

Oh, well, now she had my full attention. "What sort of competition?"

"The sort where the women try to outlast one another

sitting at the bar." Carly was matter-of-fact. "The last woman standing gets the spoils, if you know what I mean."

My mouth dropped open as I pictured what she was describing. "Are you being serious?"

"Yup. I've heard the competition described by two different friends now. They both wanted to play but gave up after only a few hours of competing."

"Then they weren't real competitors," Abel said with a sly smile.

All I could do was shake my head. "That is... freaking unbelievable. You can't date the customers."

"Since when is that a rule?"

"Since..." I racked my brain. "Well, it should be a rule."

"Yeah, let's go back to talking about your lack of a dating life," Abel suggested. "I mean, you're a good-looking woman... and I'm not saying that in a freaky way. You're pretty. Even when you're frowning, you're pretty, and very few people can pull that off."

I blushed under the faint praise. "Thank you."

"It's nothing to get excited about," Abel warned. "Looks rank low on the sexiness list when it's all said and done. That means you rank low."

"Excuse me?" I thought my eyebrows were going to flee from my forehead. I pictured them leaving that cartoon cloud of dust when they took off. "I'm totally sexy."

"Oh, right." Abel made a disgusted sound deep in his throat and shook his head. "Girl, your whole life is this bar. As far as I can tell, you come to work, take a break at eight o'clock every night to take leftovers to the homeless peeps in the Square, and then you go home from work, maybe have a drink or two with your roommates before going to bed at a respectable hour, and that's it. Then you get up at the crack of dawn and do it all over again. You're boring."

Oh, those were fighting words. "I am not boring... and I do way more than that."

"Name one thing." Abel folded his arms over his chest and lifted his chin in challenging fashion.

"I run three times a week," I automatically responded.

"Woo-hoo. Call the gossip pages."

I scowled. "I shop sometimes."

"Buying fudge from that place on Decatur does not count as shopping."

I was appalled. "How do you know about the fudge?"

"Because I saw you there four days ago. You went in, and they had a box waiting for you. That means you either called ahead or you're a regular. I'm guessing it's the latter."

I was over this conversation. "Let's go back to the message." I feigned sweetness. "Did Damon sound like he actually knew who he was asking for, or is it possible he believed I was simply a member of his harem and he'd stumbled across a number that he couldn't put a face to?"

"He asked for you," Abel replied. "He apologized for not calling sooner. He said he got sent out of town for work—some sort of emergency, although that's always a lie if you ask me—and then he mentioned that he lost your cell number and the only way to track you down was through work."

I gnawed on my bottom lip. "Why do you think the work emergency thing is a lie?"

"Because he works in real estate, right? That's what you said the first time he came sniffing around."

"Commercial real estate, like bar development and stuff."

"What sort of real estate emergency could he possibly have?"

It was a fair question. "Maybe I don't have to call him back. I could pretend someone else heard the messages and never forwarded it."

"Why?" Abel demanded.

"Why what?"

"Why not just go out with him?"

"Because I don't especially like him."

"Good. It's better to break your dating drought on somebody you don't like. That way, when you make a fool of yourself with those rusty flirting skills you haven't dusted off in years, it won't matter."

"My flirting skills are not rusty."

"Then call the Damon dude back and pick a restaurant. This isn't rocket science. One date won't kill you."

I needed time to think. To buy it, I decided to distract him. "Why are you so interested in my lack of dating? If you're so busy dating that you have them lining up, it seems to me that you wouldn't have time to worry about me."

"I'm not worried about you. I'm just... really sad when I think about your lack of social skills."

"I'm great when it comes to dealing with people."

"You're great when it comes to dealing with customers," he corrected. "When it comes to your social life, you're a moron."

"How do you figure?"

"Because I've seen you in action with your friend next door."

Whatever I was expecting, that wasn't it. "Excuse me?"

"You heard me. Also, I hate it when you say 'excuse me' like that should somehow shut me up. It's never going to shut me up."

"What will shut you up?" I was desperate to find out so I could put an end to this conversation.

"I mean... just give me a hint."

Abel rolled his eyes. "You have a thing going with the guy next door."

It was as if he'd stolen the oxygen from my lungs in some elaborate heist, maybe one in Vegas that involved zombies and morons. "I do not." It was an automatic answer, the only thing I could bark out.

"You do so."

"You do," Carly agreed when my eyes landed on her. "We've been talking about it for weeks now."

"You've been talking about it?" I was horrified. "Why would you possibly be talking about that when it's not really a thing?"

"But it is a thing." Carly's eyes were filled with pathological sincerity. "He waits outside for you every night to walk you home."

"No, we walk the same route home," I clarified.

"He waits for you," Abel insisted. "I've seen him. The first couple of nights he did it, you put up a fight. You don't even pretend you're not happy to see him now."

"I believe you're mistaken." My tone was icy and clipped.

"Oh, no." Abel wagged his finger. "I'm a student of the human condition. I've seen the two of you when you take off. You like spending time together."

"He's my archnemesis." I hated how shrill I sounded. Well, I also hated that I'd used a term that only an eleven-year-old boy might utter. I refused to take it back. "I only talk to him because we're competing with one another."

"Right. You keep telling yourself that." Abel was having none of it. "If you want to date the guy across the road, you need to take the edge off with this Damon dude. By your own admission, it wouldn't be a real date. Go out with him, relax a little bit, and then ask out your crush across the way."

If I thought I was frustrated before, that statement had me fuming. "You are imagining things."

"No, I'm not." Abel was matter-of-fact. "He doesn't just wait to walk you home at night. When you disappear at eight during a lull to take food to the Square, he follows you."

"No." I shook my head. "He went with me once."

"Well, he follows you now. He's always about two minutes behind you, and then he beats you back by another two minutes. I don't think he wants you to know that he's following."

"So basically you're saying he's a creepy stalker," I muttered under my breath.

"No, I'm saying that he worries about you," Abel replied, unruffled by my dark glare. "He wants to make sure that you don't run into problems when carrying out your charity endeavor."

"I'm never in any danger when I go down there," I insisted.

"Honey, I think it's admirable what you're doing, but mental illness goes along with living on the street. One of those guys could easily lose his shit, mistake you for some enemy from the past, and kill you. It's happened before."

"It won't happen to me."

"And you don't need to plead your case to me," Abel said. "I'm not the one following you... although I might be tempted if I didn't know he was already doing it. While it's sweet and kind, what you're doing is not smart. That's neither here nor there though."

I'd lost track of the conversation. "I don't even know what you're saying to me," I said finally. "How did we get from Damon calling to you uttering absolute nonsense about Gus?"

"Because I want you to succeed, Moxie. Believe it or not, despite how high-strung you are, I like you. Not everything is about work though. I get that you want to succeed. I want to succeed, too, so I think I get it better than most. There's more out there than just work though. If you like that Kingman guy, then you should make a move."

"I don't like him. He's my archnemesis." And there was that word again. What was wrong with me?

"You're a moron." Abel shook his head in disappointment. He almost looked as if he were having a conversation with himself for a beat, and then he pulled it together. "It's not my place to tell you who to date. That's your decision. I want to point out, however, that if you want to prove you don't have a thing for the Kingman guy, then dating someone else would be a nice way to go about it."

This felt like a trap. "I... don't want to date Damon. He's not my type."

"Because Gus is your type?" Carly asked hopefully. "What?" She balked when Abel gave her a dirty look. "I'm not being gushy. You told me not to be gushy when we talked to her. I'm just being me."

"Shut it." Abel lifted his hand to quiet her and kept his focus on me. "You say you don't like Gus... by the way, that's a stupid name. Wasn't that the mouse's name in *Cinderella*?"

"Yes." Carly took on a whimsical expression. "That's one of my favorite movies ever."

"Of course, it is." Abel shook his head. "You say you don't like Gus, Moxie. I happen to believe otherwise, but it's really none of my business. What is my business is seeing that you get a night or two off here and there. Why not go out with the Damon guy as one of those nights?"

"Because I don't like him." *And Gus hates him,* I silently added, internally cringing when I realized that I was proving Abel's point. I didn't like Gus. Sure, we were friendlier than before, but that didn't mean I liked him. We were making it through the days. It was easier to converse when we weren't lunging at each other's throats.

"It's easier to go out with someone you don't like," Abel said rationally. "There's no pressure. You're not going to care if he likes you or not."

"So... why go out on a date at all?"

"Because it will be like pulling off a bandage. You'll break the seal, so to speak. It will be good for you and maybe even open you up to dating someone you might actually like."

"Not Gus," I said automatically.

"Not Gus," he readily agreed.

I pressed my lips together, my eyes inadvertently crossing the road so I could look through the window and take in the belly dancers gyrating their hips in Flambeaux. Gus stood between them, mimicking their movements, clearly having a good time as he remained oblivious to the stress rolling through me.

He would hate it if I went out with Damon. He'd stopped asking if the date was actually going to happen more than a week before, seemingly content that it was one of those things that was casually mentioned before falling by the wayside.

"Maybe one date wouldn't hurt," I said finally, warily eyeing the phone Abel extended in my direction.

"Here's the number." Carly shoved a piece of paper across the bar.

Suddenly, their intense stares made me exceedingly uncomfortable. "I thought maybe I would call him later... in private."

"Or you could do it now." Abel grabbed the sheet of paper and started plugging the number into the phone.

"What are you doing?" I hissed, stomping in his direction.

"Helping you lighten up." He shoved the phone into my hand. "It's ringing."

"What?" My cheeks burned as I fumbled with the phone, pressing it to my ear as I tried to desperately think of a way out of my current predicament. I had nothing.

"Moxie." Damon's voice radiated with joy when he realized who was calling. "I'm so glad to hear from you. How does dinner tonight sound?"

"I have to work tonight," I said dumbly.

"I'll cover for you," Abel offered. "You can go."

AVERY KANE

"But..." One look at his know-it-all expression told me there was no way out of this. "Dinner sounds great." I couldn't believe I was actually saying it. "Where should I meet you?"

"I can pick you up," Damon said.

"Oh, I can walk. I like to walk."

"No, I won't have it. This is a proper date. That means I need to pick you up. I'll be there at six o'clock."

"Awesome." Really, what else was I supposed to say?

"Any special requests for dinner? You know what, I'll just surprise you."

"That sounds A-OK." A-OK? I wanted to smack myself. Who said things like that? Prairie folk. That was who. I'd proven myself to be an absolute moron, and there was no escaping my fate.

Eighteen

I spent the bulk of the afternoon trying to figure out a way to cancel my date with Damon—the one Abel forced me to make in the first place—without looking like an ass. I'd only come up with three possibilities.

I could tell him I had a work emergency, which might hold up as long as he didn't stop by to check on me.

I could tell him I had a family emergency, but if he asked anyone, he would know I didn't have a family.

I could tell him I started my period. Even though I didn't understand it, men were afraid of menstruation. That seemed like my best bet.

"What are you doing?" Carly found me on the side patio during an afternoon lull. Clouds had begun building in the sky, which suggested a storm was about to hit. That meant we would be inundated with customers taking refuge from the rain fairly quickly.

"Debating the meaning of life," I drawled as I stared at the phone.

"Come up with anything good?" Carly didn't look bothered in the least by my potential bad mood as she sat in the chair across from me.

"Yes. Men are stupid."

"Oh, everybody knows that." She let loose a haphazard wave as she laughed. "I don't know anybody who thinks men are the smarter gender."

"Men *think* they're the smarter gender," I pointed out.

"Yes, but that's because they're not the smarter gender. They can't see the truth even when it's right in front of them."

"Good point." I buried my face in my arms and refused to meet her steady gaze. "My life sucks."

"Is this about Gus?"

When I shifted my chin so I could see her face, I found her watching me with a strange mix of hope and sadness. "You guys need to let the Gus thing go. There's nothing going on between us."

"Oh, I'm not the one fixated on Gus. That's Abel."

I didn't believe her. "You've been helping Abel work against me."

"I don't like it when you phrase it like that." She fervently shook her head. "I would never work against you. You're my best friend."

What a load of hogwash. "I've met your best friend. It's that Trina girl, the one who braids weird colored feathers into her hair."

"She's a friend from high school. She's not my best friend. Who told you she was my best friend?"

"You did, and I quote, 'here's my best friend Trina. We've been inseparable since we were in grade school. We don't do anything without one another.'" I thought I mimicked her voice well, but the look she stabbed me with said otherwise.

"I think you misheard, but that's neither here nor there." Her voice took on an airy quality that told me she was about to give me an earful, whether I wanted to hear it or not. "I'm always on your side, Moxie. I should think that would be obvious now."

"Then why have you and Abel been plotting behind my back?" I wasn't afraid of confrontation, even when it revolved around a conversation I wanted to pretend hadn't happened. Besides, given my mood, it was easier for me to focus my anger on her than to work up a good menstruation story to get rid of Damon.

"Plotting is such an ugly word."

"But is it the right word?"

She held her hands palms up. "We just want you to be happy."

"Who says I'm not happy?"

"Pretty much anybody who has ever met you. The only time we see you smile is when you're messing with Gus. It's happened more than once, so we know it's not a coincidence."

"Has it ever occurred to you that I only smile because it's an easy way for me to hide the fact that I'm plotting against him?"

"No." Carly's face had zero lines, making her look impossibly young... and naive. "It's obvious you like him. I don't understand why you can't just admit it."

"Because I don't like him." *I don't,* I silently repeated for my own benefit. We were enemies... or friendly nemeses... or occasional walking buddies. Oh, and breakfast buddies... and sometimes running buddies. Who was I kidding? We were more than I wanted us to be. That didn't mean I had a thing for him.

"He's really hot," Carly persisted. "I mean... who wouldn't have a crush on him? I totally do."

"Then maybe you should ask him out." Even as I suggested it, I wanted to haul the words back into my mouth. They were a mistake, but there were no take-backsies in the bar business.

"Oh, I have asked him out," Carly said. There was no guile to be found when I stared into her eyes. "In fact, I asked him out twice just in case he was nervous and went with a knee-jerk response when he said no the first time."

"You asked Gus out?" I was floored. "When?"

"I asked him out the third day after the bars opened. He was nice but said he was busy with work. I thought maybe that was true, although deep down I knew it wasn't, and took another shot last week. Then I was more curious than hopeful because I'd seen you guys together earlier in the day."

"You saw us together?" I scoffed. "There's no way."

"Oh, that wasn't you sitting in the east corner of Jackson Square drinking coffee and eating beignets together? My bad."

I chewed on my bottom lip and refused to meet her gaze. "What did he say the second time?"

"He said that he was flattered I would want to go out with him, but he thought I was too young for him. I knew that was crap. I'm twenty-three, not twelve. I'm totally legal."

"Yes, but he's closer to thirty. He might really think you're too young. That's not necessarily a bad thing."

"Oh, please." Carly's eye roll was pronounced. "I have C-cup boobs and don't need to wear a bra. Age is just a number when you've got that going for you. The only reasons a guy would turn me down is if he's gay or interested in someone else."

She had a point, loath as I was to admit it. "And which do you think it is?"

"He's not gay. I've seen him with you. In fact, I've made a point since seeing you guys out at breakfast together to watch him during the afternoons. Whenever he gets a chance, he stops in front of that big window and looks over at us. Or rather, he looks at you. He clearly doesn't care what Abel and I are doing."

"I think you're mistaken." Even as I said it, curiosity

bubbled up. Could she be right? Could Gus be interested in more than just truth games and walks?

"And I think you're being willfully blind." Carly fixed me with the sternest look in her repertoire. "You're clearly not interested in going out with Damon. Abel thinks it's a good idea because you're wound too tight. I think Gus should be the one to unwind you. Either way, though, you need to get unwound." She pushed herself to a standing position. "We're doing this because we love you."

"And yet it feels so much like bullying," I lamented, returning my head to the table. "Did I mention my life sucks?"

"Oh, well, that sounds dramatic," a male voice said from the street. I didn't have to look up to see who was speaking. I'd recognize that voice anywhere. Gus. He'd come for a visit... and he was the last person I wanted to see. No, really. I wasn't ready to deal with him.

"Hi, Gus." Carly used her little-girl singsong voice for the greeting. "It's so funny, but we were just talking about you."

"Oh yeah?" Gus didn't look bothered by the prospect when I shifted my eyes so I could see him. I kept my cheek on the hot table rather than lift my head. I was well and truly wiped. "What were you guys saying?"

"We were just talking about how hot you are," Carly replied smoothly.

"I'm totally hot," Gus agreed, flexing his arms to show off his muscles. "In fact, I think I might be the hottest guy in the Quarter."

"No, that guy who plays the sax down at Café Beignet is way hotter," Carly replied, not missing a beat. "My friend Trina hooked up with him three nights ago, though, and she says he's hung like a pimple, so I'm guessing you've got one over on him in that department. Odds of you somehow being smaller seem long."

Amused despite myself, I studied Gus's face as he debated how to respond.

"That sounds like a terrible ailment to deal with," he said finally.

"More for Trina than him," Carly replied. "She said he didn't seem to realize he was hung like a pimple, and he kept talking about how good he was in bed. She said she got to the point where she wanted to pop that pimple because it wasn't doing any good for anyone. Too bad there's no Clearasil for bad sex partners, huh?"

Gus popped his lips, his eyes drifting between Carly and me. He seemed to be lost. "Um…"

"I have to get back inside," Carly announced out of nowhere—much to Gus's obvious relief—and she turned on her heel and headed for the door. "Take as much time as you need, Moxie. We can handle any storm rush that hits."

I waved at her back, the annoyance that I thought had abated returning. She was not good when it came to subterfuge.

"What were you guys really talking about?" Gus asked when he was certain she was gone.

"You." Lying didn't seem to be an option. Okay, not completely. "They've noticed you wait for me to walk home at night." *And think that means I want to jump your bones,* I silently added.

"So?" Gus didn't look bothered.

"They think that means something is going on between us."

"So?"

"So they think… other things." I was starting to feel uncomfortable. Well, actually, I'd passed uncomfortable long ago. This whole day was starting to make me feel as if I were an alien trapped in the body of a human.

"Like what other things?" He rested his elbows on the patio rail and grinned at me.

"The sort of things you can't do with your archnemesis."

"Yeah, you use that term a lot. I don't think it means what you think it means."

"Oh, don't Princess Bride me."

"I happen to love that movie."

"That's a chick movie."

"That's a movie for people who love movies," he countered. "It was one of my grandmother's favorites when I was growing up. We used to watch it whenever I was at her house."

"Which grandmother?" I had no idea why I was so curious, but most of Gus's stories were about his parents—who were apparently inattentive during his youth—and his brothers, who sounded like testosterone-fueled idiots.

"My mother's mother." Gus's smile disappeared. "She died when I was sixteen. She lived in a creole cottage over in Marigny. I used to love visiting her because she was part of this eccentric neighborhood collective where they did crawfish boils in the street. My mother hated visiting and wouldn't shut her mouth, but I knew she was missing out on something special."

I was confused. "And what? Did she drop you at your grandmother's house all the time as punishment or something?"

"No. I went over there voluntarily." He hesitated and then sighed. "My grandfather left her when their kids were young. He had all the money and only gave her a small settlement. My mother thought it was somehow a failing on my grandmother's part that she didn't get more. It was a whole big thing."

"No offense, but your parents sound like assholes."

He let loose a low chuckle. "They kind of are. They're also oblivious to the plight of the everyday man. I made it my mission to be different from them. I'm not sure I succeeded."

My initial reaction was that he'd indeed succeeded. I didn't say that though. "Well, I know what archnemesis means. We're in competition in case you've forgotten."

"Oh, I haven't forgotten." The smile he slid me was sly. "In fact, the reason I decided to come over here when my bar is twice is busy as your bar is because I thought we could take the competition to a different level this evening."

I scowled. "Belly dancers are not hygienic."

He pretended I hadn't spoken. "They're opening a new place over on Royal and doing a huge crawfish boil. It's supposed to be a proper crawfish boil and everything. I thought... um... maybe we could take our dinner break together this time and head over. I promise to argue with you the entire way, if that makes you feel like it's a working dinner."

I was caught off guard. Was he inviting me out on a date? "Um..."

"It's nothing big," he said hurriedly. "I just really love a crawfish boil, and I'm betting you've never been to an authentic one."

To buy myself time, I shook my head. "I've had crawfish boil. It's good."

"Not like this. They're supposed to be doing it up right." He was insistent, which somehow made me uneasy.

"I can't tonight."

"Why?" He straightened. "What are you planning?"

"I'm not *planning* anything. I just have... um... plans."

"You have plans?" He looked doubtful. "If you're worried about your nightly food run to the Square, I can help you with that. We'll hit the Square first and then loop around for the crawfish boil."

"It's not that." Honestly, if I could've found a hole to crawl into and die, I totally would've done it. "It's something else. Something personal."

"Really?" His expression was hard to read. "Is it something to do with... Benji?" He almost said "your father." I recognized the moment he made the choice not to push things. I was grateful he seemed determined to hold to his word and keep my secret.

I was also annoyed.

I opened my mouth to shut him down, but Abel picked that moment to slide through the side door. He didn't look surprised to see Gus, offering up a "hey, man, how's it going" head bob before focusing on me.

"The storms will be here any second," he said. "They look big. We're going to need your help. They should be gone in plenty of time for your date, though, so you have nothing to worry about."

My mouth dropped open. I couldn't believe he'd outed me that way—and so casually to boot. There was no way he hadn't done it on purpose.

"Date?" Gus's eyebrows collided as he absorbed the word. "Since when are you dating the guys in the Square?"

I tried to think of a convincing lie—and fast. I wasn't quick enough on my feet though.

"No, she's actually going out on a date," Abel volunteered, practically stealing the oxygen from my lungs when he pinned me with a "This is your fault" expression. "Some dude named Damon called wanting to take her out, and I insisted that she needed to take him up on it if she didn't want to die an old maid."

He insisted? Why was he taking credit for my decision, unless... ? Slowly, I slid my eyes to Gus. His cheeks had turned a mottled shade of red, and he looked as if he were ready to explode.

"It's not a big deal," I said automatically, hoping beyond hope that I wasn't coming across as apologetic. I didn't owe Gus anything.

So why are you so worried what he's feeling, a small voice asked from inside my busy brain.

"You're going out with Damon?" Gus's voice had lost all traces of warmth, and I was looking for that hole to hide in again.

"I..."

"It's just dinner," Abel explained on my behalf. "She doesn't even like him. It's best she gets this first date out of her system because she's going to be an absolute idiot on it. You can catch her on the flip side." He slapped Gus's arm hard enough to have him rocking backward off the curb.

"It's definitely not a big deal," I agreed, searching for the right words to... do something—anything, really—to make this conversation more tolerable.

"Right. It's not a big deal." Gus's expression was cold as he stepped to the middle of the street, ignoring the car that was trying to cross Bourbon and retreating toward Flambeaux.

"Gus..." I didn't know what to say to him. I certainly didn't owe him an apology. *Then why do you feel as if you do?* That infernal inner voice that never quieted refused to leave me alone. I couldn't explain what I was feeling.

"Have fun on your date." Gus whirled so his back was to me. His feet looked heavy as he stomped them against the ground. "Don't say I didn't warn you about Damon though."

"Well, that last statement felt like a threat, didn't it?" Abel commented once Gus had disappeared inside.

I was beyond annoyed with my magical bartender. "Why did you do that?"

"You'll thank me. Eventually."

"No, I won't. That was... so uncalled for."

"And why is that?" Abel crossed his arms and fixed me with a serious stare. "Why should Kingman care that you're going on a date with someone else? I mean... there's nothing going on between the two of you, right? This is really none of his business."

"It's none of *your* business either," I reminded him.

He snorted. "Honey, you really have to get yourself untwisted. You're making a mess of things. When you do manage to get your head out of your ass, you're going to realize I just did you a favor."

It didn't feel like a favor. "I'm mad at you," I said finally. "This is all your fault."

"I can live with that." He held out an arm to usher me inside just as the first fat droplet hit my face. "Come on. We're going to be busy for the next two hours. You can curse my name while delivering drinks."

That sounded like more fun than I'd been having over the last hour to me. "Fine. I'm still mad though." I cast a final look toward Flambeaux. I couldn't make out Gus inside. He'd seemingly disappeared.

"It's going to be okay, Moxie," Abel said as I crossed in front of him. "You'll see. In the end, I just did you a kindness."

I wasn't in the mood to take his word for it.

Nineteen

I didn't bother to change my clothes for the date. I didn't even like Damon, and that wasn't an exaggeration. Besides, it was New Orleans. Unless he was taking me to one of the rare restaurants with a dress code, I had nothing to worry about.

"You're wearing that?" Abel gave me a dark look as I left the storage room. I'd applied a bit of powder and lip gloss, ran a brush through my hair, and was calling it good enough. Apparently, Abel thought differently.

"What's wrong with my outfit?" I glanced down at my khaki capris and simple Nike comfort slides. "I think I look fine."

"You're wearing a shirt with the name of the bar emblazoned on it."

Yes, well, there was that. "It's fine. It's going to be a really short date."

"Here's hoping he's not short," a woman sitting at the bar said as she raised her glass in a toast.

I merely blinked.

"You know," she continued when nobody responded.

194

"Down there." She pointed toward Abel's crotch and then grinned at him. "I'm betting you're not short down there."

Abel returned her smile, although there was a feral glint to it. "I think you've had enough for one night. I'll get your tab."

"Oh, I'm not done yet." She managed a pretty pout. "I think I'm going to stay for the long haul this evening."

"And I think you're done." Abel moved to the register so he could call up the tab but kept his eyes on me. "Don't you have another shirt?"

"At home."

"So have him pick you up at home."

"And then he'll know where I live."

"Why is that a problem?"

"Because, the way Gus makes it sound, this guy is going to have eight hands. I'm fine with my shirt."

Abel stilled. "Wait... are you saying that there's something wrong with this guy?"

"Gus thinks there is."

"And what do you think?"

Abel looked concerned enough that I decided to take pity on him. "I think that Damon is full of himself and only wants to take me out because he believes it will annoy Gus, although why that is escapes me."

"Yeah, you just make yourself sound stupid when you say things like that," Abel said. "I'm being serious. If there's something wrong with this guy, then maybe you should cancel."

Oh, he had to be kidding me. "I didn't want to make this date in the first place. You forced me."

"Yes, well, maybe I was wrong."

I threw up my hands. "Oh, maybe you were wrong." I wanted to throttle him. "Now that it's too late and he's probably walking through the front door right now, you think you were wrong."

He was blasé. "Stranger things have happened." His eyes

went to a spot over my shoulder, his lips quirking. "I think your date is here, Moxie."

I turned quickly, expecting to find some drunk tourist about to rub himself all over my back. Instead, I found Damon, dressed in an expensive black suit and carrying a bouquet of flowers. The grin on his face was all smarm and no charm.

"Hello, Moxie," he drawled as he swept toward me like the biggest tool from Tooltopia. "I'm so glad we're finally doing this." He aimed his mouth for my lips, but I shifted at the last second, so he caught my jaw. "Whoops." He wiped the wet from my face. "Sorry about that."

"It's fine," I said automatically as I accepted the flowers. Honestly, this date was already painful, and we still had hours to go. "Are those for me?" I took the flowers before he could respond and eyed them. They clearly weren't from a grocery store. He'd spent a lot of money on the bouquet. "They're lovely."

"Just like you." He beamed at me in such a way I wanted to punch him.

"They're beautiful." I handed them off to Abel. "Could you put them in some water for me? They'll wilt if I leave them out too long."

"No problem." Abel took the flowers without a hint of hesitation. His attention was for Damon instead of me. "Where are you taking her?"

"Oh, I thought I would take her over to the Garden District," Damon replied. "There are a bevy of wonderful restaurants over there, and it's always nice to get a break from the grime of the French Quarter."

Sure, New Orleans wasn't technically my home, but annoyance reared up at his dismissive tone. "I happen to like the French Quarter."

"And everybody knows the best food in the city is in the

Quarter," Abel agreed. "I think you should stay over here for dinner."

Damon blinked several times in rapid succession. "Excuse me?" He said it as if he were actually having trouble under-standing what Abel was saying.

"Stay. Over. Here." Abel replied, enunciating in a drawn-out manner that had me biting the inside of my cheek to keep from laughing.

"But... why?" Damon glanced between Abel and me. "Am I missing something?"

I was a little confused myself. "Oh, well..."

"I need Moxie close," Abel replied before I could come up with anything witty—or even serviceable—to say. "You made the date without giving us much notice. I might need her to come in and help if something goes haywire this evening. She is the boss."

"Yes, but she works so hard," Damon countered. "Doesn't she deserve a night off?"

Abel wrinkled his nose, and I could clearly see the debate raging in the depths of his eyes. "Okay, I'm just going to lay this out for you because you're either being purposely obtuse or you're too slow to survive over the long haul. I don't want you taking her out of the Quarter."

Damon let loose a low chuckle, one that clearly showed off his nerves. "I'm not sure I understand."

"You don't have to understand." Abel was firm. "If she needs help, I need to be able to get to her."

"And why would she need help?"

"Because you're clearly a tool." Abel might've been blunt to the point of impolite, but I genuinely liked his style. "I don't think this date is going to go late, but it doesn't matter because she's going to be close if she needs it to end early."

"I don't believe I've done anything to warrant your vitri-ol," Damon said stiffly.

"Keep it that way." Abel moved his stern gaze to me. "If you need me, you know where to find me. Keep her away from Frenchman Street, and if you even think of taking her to that underground vampire bar, I'm totally going to hunt you down." The warning in his stance was firm, but he managed a deranged smile that felt out of place. "So, I believe that's it. You two kids have a fun evening."

I took a moment to stare down at my shirt, picking at an invisible ball of lint, and then I fixed Damon with a smile. "Are you ready?"

He looked torn, as if a war between his fight-or-flight response was raging. Finally, he held out his hand. "I think we're going to have a great time tonight."

Yup. Abel was right. He was either purposely being stupid or he had no ability to read a room. Either way, I was stuck. I would have dinner with him and then flee as soon as possible. If I had to fake an emergency call from work, Abel had just given me the opening. I wouldn't hesitate to take it.

"I think I like food," I said as I evaded his hand and moved to the side door. My eyes sought—and immediately found— Gus across the road. He stood inside the open window, his gaze dark, and watched Damon and I step onto the sidewalk.

I opened my mouth when I saw Gus. Nothing came out. What was I supposed to say? We weren't a couple. I didn't owe him an apology. I wasn't doing anything wrong.

So why did I feel so guilty?

"Ready?" Damon's smile was bright. It wasn't pointed at me though. No, he'd also noticed Gus, and he seemed much more interested in my rival—was he still my rival?— than me. Damon crossed the street toward Flambeaux, and I had no choice but to go with him. "How's it going, Kingman?"

Gus straightened. "Life is good," he said as a giggling woman appeared at his back. She was clearly drunk and in the mood to get touchy-feely with him because her hand automatically landed on his chest.

"Oh, you do work out, don't you?" she cooed as she moved her hand to the other side of his chest. "You're... neat."

"Aw, you're moving up in the world, Kingman," Damon called out. "You're so... neat."

"Shut up, Damon," Gus growled. "I don't need your take on the situation."

"That's good because I'm leaving." He added the next part in his smarmiest voice. "On a date. You know Moxie, right?"

Gus's eyes were almost black when they locked with mine. "I thought I did. Turns out I was wrong. Have fun on your date." His voice was listless as he turned to face the inside of Flambeaux. He didn't look back.

I had to force myself to do the same. I had no idea what was happening. Whatever it was, though, I was locked into a course for the night. There was no getting out of it.

THE DATE STARTED OFF BADLY ENOUGH that you would've thought it couldn't get worse. It did.

The next bit of trouble hit when we arrived at one of the few restaurants Damon deemed "good enough" to eat at. Apparently, he had a delicate stomach—or maybe he was just a delicate jerkwad, who knows—and he had to be careful when choosing a restaurant. That meant Angelo's Italian Eatery, a restaurant I'd yet to visit because it looked far too fancy.

Since we didn't have a reservation, we had to wait for a table to become available, which Damon likened to something that would only happen in a third world country. He complained nonstop for the entire twenty minutes we waited.

And when we were finally seated? He proceeded to send back both glasses of water—even though I was happily drinking from mine—because he claimed there were spots on the glasses. He sent back all the silverware too. He was so loud when requesting new napkins, ones that had been properly pressed, that multiple sets of eyes swung toward us in disdain.

Honestly, I didn't blame those people for thinking we were jerks. I thought we were jerks, too, and I wasn't even the one making the complaints.

"Ah. That's better." Damon beamed at me over the rim of his fresh water glass. "There's nothing worse than poor service. Am I right?"

That was not the word I would use to describe what we were dealing with. "You're... something." I forced a smile even though the corners of my lips felt as if they were weighed down by anvils. "Just out of curiosity, aren't you afraid to eat whatever they bring you?"

Damon merely blinked. "I've eaten here before. The sauce is serviceable. It's not bad enough you need to be frightened of it."

"Yeah, that's not what I was talking about." I shook my head. "I'm talking about the fact that they're probably back there licking your food right now."

His eyebrows started drifting toward one another. "I don't believe I understand what you're saying."

"You made a big scene." I'd already started down this conversational road. I figured I might as well commit to it. "Restaurant workers don't like being treated how you've been treating these guys. They'll retaliate by doing something to your food. Licking it would probably be the nicest option at this point."

He sat straighter in his chair. "That's not a thing."

"Oh, it's a thing." I had news for him. "Sure, this is a nicer restaurant than most, but that doesn't mean the workers are okay with being ridiculed. I worked in a restaurant when I was a teenager, and there was this horrible guy who came in and used to act just like you, and we used to rub the buns of his sandwiches in our armpits."

It was probably the worst thing I could've said. Damon paled two full shades, and for a moment, I thought he might fall out of his chair. "That is not a thing," he repeated.

I doubted he believed it. He might've lived in a blessed la-la land about this sort of thing before I brought it up, but now there was no way he could possibly get it out of his mind. I decided to change the subject.

"So, you went to a private school with Gus, right?" I smiled at the server when she delivered my wine. I wasn't much of a wine drinker—I much preferred beer or a mixed drink—but that was the only option at Angelo's. Apparently, beer was a four-letter word in this particular establishment.

"I went to three private schools with him," Damon corrected. "Elementary, middle, and high school."

"But... they were all under the same private school banner, right?"

"Yes, but they were different schools."

Ugh. I couldn't stand this guy. Talking to him was like trying to make conversation with fancy china. He might look okay, but he lacked character and thought way too much of himself.

"What was Gus like in school?" I had no idea why I was so determined to keep the conversation revolving around another man, but I couldn't seem to control myself.

"He was... difficult." If Damon was bothered about my insistence on talking about Gus, he didn't show it.

"Difficult how?"

"He was... a special boy." The way Damon said it was not flattering. "He liked to think of himself as the protector of the downtrodden."

"I don't know what that means," I hedged.

"He was very delicate." Damon's smile was so wide, it

threatened to engulf his face. He wasn't green, but he suddenly reminded me of the Grinch. "He liked to spend time in the library, read books, and he was only interested in playing lacrosse and basketball. He refused to play soccer or football."

"And that's somehow bad?"

"It wasn't normal. He simply liked to be different to be different."

"Or maybe he just liked to read," I suggested.

"Yes, because teenage boys like to spend all their time reading." Damon's eye roll was pronounced, but he uttered the admonishment in a 'you're so cute' way. That only served to make things worse. "Kingman figured out early that he could stand out from the crowd by acting like a geek. He took full advantage of it."

There was something he wasn't saying. "You had a sister school, right? Did you and Gus ever pursue the same girls?"

"Of course not."

"Never?" He was lying, and he wasn't very good at it.

"We didn't have the same taste. He would occasionally go after the girls I liked just to irritate me, but I refused to lower myself to his level and do the same to him."

Yup. He was definitely full of it. "It's weird that you keep going out of your way to stop by Flambeaux when you obviously hate him so much," I noted.

"I don't *hate* him," Damon scoffed. "We were friendly rivals in school." He leaned closer, as if imparting some great wisdom on me. "If you want to know the truth, I believe he developed an aversion to sports because he hated losing to me. He never came right out and said it, but I knew."

I very much doubted Damon knew half the stuff he pretended. "Uh-huh."

"The real problem was that thing with the school nurse, although I'm certain he's already related that tale to you."

"He never mentioned a school nurse."

"Of course, he did." Damon gave me a "Don't be ridiculous" wave. "That's his favorite story as far as I can tell. More than one person has repeated it back to me, even though it's not remotely true. Like I would waste time on the school nurse."

I wasn't completely caught up on the story, and yet it wasn't too hard to follow. "You made a move on the school nurse when you were in high school?"

"Of course not." Damon looked outraged. "That was the rumor she started. She actually had my parents called to the school and said I was sexually harassing her, if you can believe that. Like I would want some old, dried-up hag."

My stomach did a little heave. Damon was clearly even more of a tool than I initially realized... and that was saying something.

"I showed her though." He puffed out his chest, his expression far off, as if reliving some great moment from his childhood. "My parents donated a new library to that school, and that was before she started telling her lies. Who did she think they would believe?"

"I don't... um..." My discomfort was a tsunami, and I felt mildly sick to my stomach.

"There's a lesson in all of this," Damon continued as if he hadn't registered the change in my demeanor. "Don't play with the big dogs if you're the runt of an inferior litter." His eyes gleamed with evil intent.

I couldn't take another second of this. "I think I'm going to excuse myself and go to the bathroom." I gripped my small purse tightly, hoping he wouldn't notice I was carrying it. I couldn't leave it behind if I planned to run.

Oh yeah, I totally planned to run.

"Of course." Damon's smile turned indulgent. "I'll get you a new glass of wine while I'm waiting. That one looks to be... well, a strange color. It's pink or something."

"I believe that's the lights bouncing off the wine."

"Well, they'll have to fix it. I hate that color."

"Yes, well... have fun with that." I turned in the direction of the lobby. I had no idea where the bathroom was actually located. I just knew I had to get out of there.

"When you get back, we'll talk about you," Damon called to my back. "I'm dying to know about your relationship with Kingman."

Of course that was what he wanted. I never should have doubted it. That was his intent from the start, and he'd never even tried to cover. I simply refused to see what was right in front of me.

Man, I couldn't wait to rip Abel a new one. It was rare that I got to be a bitch for a good reason. It was finally happening, and I felt vindicated... and maybe a little dirty. I should've listened to that inner voice that told me going out with Damon was a mistake.

Ah, well, I wouldn't make that mistake again.

Ever.

Twenty

I could've returned to Cher. It would've been the responsible thing to do. It was still early after all. Abel might need help with the evening rush.

That would be the first place Damon looked when he realized I'd ghosted him, however, and I had no interest in running into him again this evening. Or ever.

Instead, I pointed myself toward home. The idea of a relaxing bath and book held so much appeal, I could barely contain myself. By the time I reached Jackson Square, I realized the one thing I'd forgotten. Dinner for those who bedded down on the benches at night.

I froze in place, debating. I could run back to Cher long enough to grab the extra food—it was likely the cook kept it out of habit—and hope I didn't run into Damon. I could also order pizzas and have them delivered, although I didn't have a lot of money in my accounts and covering that would be iffy.

I was still standing there, thinking and chewing on my bottom lip, when I realized nobody had staked a claim to their benches. In fact, all the benches on the east side of the park were completely empty. That never happened. Most of the benches were taken every night.

I eased out so I could get a better look at the area to the north of the park, and when I did, I found an amazing sight.

"We have pizza for everybody," Gus announced as the regular loiterers surrounded him. "We have the regular stuff, vegetarian stuff, gluten-free stuff, and even two boxes of vegan pizza... although I'm guessing that will be the last to go."

"The dogs will eat it," Gremlin called out. He was double fisting pizza and didn't look bothered in the least that he might come across as a glutton.

"Good point," Gus said, ripping several sheets of paper towels from the roll he'd positioned on a bench. "There's plenty for everybody. There's no need to inhale it."

Gremlin took the paper towel and offered up a sheepish smile. "It's habit, man."

"I get it." Gus's tone wasn't condescending. "I also have breadsticks, wings, and huge chocolate chip cookies. Again, there's enough for everybody, so let's try sharing."

I'd started gravitating toward him without even realizing it. I couldn't believe the feast he'd managed to procure, and it clearly wasn't for my benefit. It wasn't some move designed to impress me. For all he knew, I was just starting my dinner with Damon. This was something I would've likely never found out about, which meant he'd done it for them.

My heart threatened to burst.

"Hey, Moxie," Bishop called out, causing me to snap up my chin and blink back tears.

Gus swiveled his head in my direction, surprise flashing bright. "What are you doing here?"

I took a moment to collect myself. If I wasn't careful, I would start crying... and maybe I would never stop. That would be hell on my street cred. "I was just about to ask you the same thing."

He ran his tongue over his teeth, clearly debating, and then he shrugged. "I brought dinner."

"He told us how you were sad about not being able to come yourself," Bishop explained. He had pizza sauce smeared on his cheek, although he didn't seem to mind. "It's cool you arranged this."

What? "I..." Bewildered, I flicked my eyes back to Gus.

"It's okay," he said softly. "I told them that you were upset about missing your usual visit."

I *was* upset about that. I was upset about a lot of things. "Gus did this," I blurted, refusing to take credit for something I hadn't arranged. "This is all him."

"It's awesome, so we're thanking you both," Anthony said, his mouth full of food.

"It *is* awesome," I agreed. My eyes burned from the effort not to cry. "It's very, very awesome."

Gus was tentative as he drifted toward me. "How was your date?" he asked when he was within five feet.

The laugh that escaped made me sound like it was erupting from a crazy person. "It's not even eight o'clock," I said when I'd regained my faculties. "How do you think it went?"

"I'm guessing it didn't go well."

"No, not even a little."

"Where is he?" Gus glanced up and down the street behind me. "You didn't bring him here, did you?"

"As far as I know, he's still sitting at a table at Angelo's waiting for the food to be delivered. He thinks I'm still in the bathroom... or maybe he's finally catching on that I'm no longer there. I'm quite sure he hasn't figured it out yet though."

Gus's lips quirked. "You ghosted him?"

I held out my hands. "Honestly, I didn't want to go out

with him in the first place. That was Abel. He thought I needed to liven things up."

"I think Abel had a specific plan in mind," Gus countered. "Something tells me he changed his mind after Damon showed up though."

"Why do you say that?"

"Because the second you were gone, he came storming over to Flambeaux. He wanted to know the skinny on Damon. That was his word, not mine by the way. Skinny. I've always thought that was a weird saying."

He wasn't the only one. "Yeah. I think he originally thought Damon was harmless. He realized right away he wasn't and threatened Damon. That's why I'm hopeful, when he realizes I skipped out on him, that Damon decides to go home instead of looking for me. The bar is the first place he will go."

"I'm kind of hoping he does go to the bar," Gus countered. "I think if he says the wrong thing to Abel, that could result in the end of Damon. Who doesn't want that?"

I laughed as I shook my head. "I don't want him dead... just dead to me."

Gus bobbed his head. "Yes, well, we don't have to want all the same things in life." He glanced over his shoulder at the happy feast happening behind him, and his eyes were soft when they locked with mine again. "Are you hungry?"

I was, but there was no way I would invade the happy meal going down in Jackson Square. "I was actually thinking I would take a walk on the riverwalk."

"Oh." Gus momentarily looked disappointed. "Well... do you want company?" Vulnerability tinged his features, and he had trouble meeting my gaze.

"That sounds great." I didn't even have to think about my answer. It was automatic. "Let's do it." I extended my hand, surprising even myself with the gesture.

Gus didn't question me about what I was doing. Instead, he linked his fingers with mine and tugged me toward the east. "We're going for a walk, guys. Please clean up the boxes when you're done."

Gremlin offered up a hilarious salute. "You can count on us, boss man."

"Thank you." Gus smiled. "I'll make sure Moxie gets home safely tonight. You guys make sure you're tucked in before midnight and there's no mess. If you leave the boxes out, it will draw rats, and then there will be trouble."

"No rats, man," Gremlin promised. "We've got this. You two... do you."

"Have fun," Anthony added. "Don't do anything perverted on the riverwalk though. The cops will arrest you for sure, even if you're not one of us."

"Thanks for the tip." Gus gripped my hand tightly as we started toward the stairs. Decatur Street had limited traffic, but the timing of the lights meant we had no problem crossing. "So," he prodded once we were at the top of the stairs.

"So," I echoed, unsure what he wanted me to say.

"Do you want to tell me about it?"

The breeze from the river hit me full on, and I sucked in a breath. I loved few things more than the scent of the air coming in off the river. It was somehow magical, warm, and cooling at the same time. It was like being transported to a different place.

"There's not much to tell," I said when I'd had my fill of the breeze. "We don't have anything in common."

"You and Damon, you mean."

Technically, I could've said the same thing about Gus, I realized. Our backgrounds were completely incongruent, and he had different goals than me. Despite that, we had more in common than I would've been comfortable admitting weeks before. Now it wasn't as much of a hardship.

"Of course, I was talking about Damon," I said as I swung our joined hands. I thought it would be odd to do something so out of the ordinary for us. Turned out, it felt normal. No, worse, it felt right. Crap. I had a lot of emotions I was going to have to grapple with after this night. They wouldn't all be pleasant either.

Ah, well, that was a problem for Future Moxie. For tonight, after the date from hell that had barely been a date, I figured I deserved some enjoyment.

"I was just checking," Gus said as we walked toward the west. It seemed the direction to go since both of our homes were in that area. "Did he... do something... to you?"

I didn't have to ask what had him so worried. "No. The date was... very brief. He's obsessed with you. You know that, right?"

"I figured."

"Why didn't you say anything?"

Gus made a protesting sound with his tongue. "I tried."

"You just painted him as a douche."

"He is."

"You left out the part where he's obsessed with you."

"I don't know that I would use that word." Gus suddenly looked uncomfortable. "We had a... tempestuous—I guess that's the best word to use—um... relationship back in the day. If you believe my brothers, I reacted badly to Damon my first day of kindergarten. I don't really remember what happened, but I know we got in a fistfight and our parents were called in. Since we both came from rich families, absolutely nothing happened."

"So no punishment?" I wasn't surprised. "You guys were in kindergarten. They couldn't have known that you would hate each other forever following one fistfight."

"No," he agreed with a hollow chuckle. "It was my first lesson in money talk though."

"As in money talks?"

"Yup. I punched Damon hard enough to give him a black eye. My parents bought new gymnastics mats for the school. I wasn't even admonished for the most part."

"Well..." I didn't know what to say. I'd never met anyone who was still angry about a kindergarten fight.

"It got worse," Gus volunteered. Now that I'd gotten him talking, there was apparently no stopping him. "We fought all the time. We hated each other. We each had our own gang to fight with, and if you think I'm proud of that, I'm not. My gang consisted of the sons of people who worked for my father. They were all instructed that they *had* to be my friends. Want had nothing to do with it."

My heart went out to him. All this time I'd been picturing him as a rich, entitled brat. Perhaps his life wasn't as easy as I envisioned. "I'm sorry." It was all I could say.

He waved his free hand and shook his head. "I'm the one who is sorry. For years, I thought what was happening at that school was normal. As I got older, though, I realized that wasn't the case. I didn't want to fit the mold of those schools. I wanted to be my own man. It was just... really difficult."

"I'm sure it was." There was one more question I had to ask. "What happened with the school nurse?"

Gus froze, his eyes momentarily widening. Then he sucked in a breath to settle himself. "He told you about that? Damon?" He was incredulous.

"He assumed you had told me." I chose my words carefully. It seemed as if we were at a dangerous crossroads. "He seemed to think you were going to spin the story in a specific way where he looked bad."

"He is bad in that story no matter how you look at it." Gus's voice ratcheted up a notch.

"I figured that out myself." I moved my free hand to his chest to calm him. "Relax. I'm not saying he's innocent. I'm the one who left him in a restaurant by himself—with two entrees heading his way, mind you. I think that's proof enough that he's not my cup of tea."

Gus let out a hollow laugh, dragging his hand through his hair and sighing. Briefly, he pressed his eyes shut. "I'm just surprised he told you. An agreement was struck that nobody would talk about it."

"He just assumed I knew for some reason. I still don't know what the story entails though."

"He groped the nurse. I saw him. She slapped him. Hard. Then she reported him to the office. That was one of my last lessons about money talking. That poor woman was fired even though Damon was to blame.

"I told the truth," he continued, his eyes clear as they locked with mine. "I told the superintendent exactly what I saw. Do you know what he did?"

"He fired the nurse," I supplied.

"Yes, and that was the breaking point for me. I knew in that moment that I didn't want my parents' lives. I didn't want any of this."

"So... you headed abroad," I surmised. "You decided to find something else for yourself."

"Yes, but I failed at that too."

"You probably shouldn't have done it on their money," I suggested.

He managed a rueful smile. "That would've been smart. At that point in my life, I had no idea what it meant to hold down a job. I should've done it all on my own. I didn't though. I just... let them fund a lifestyle that I hadn't earned, and that made me exactly what I hated."

"You're here now," I pointed out.

"I am."

"It's okay to be a work in progress. I clearly am."

He smiled and shifted, his body moving in front of mine.

His expression was hard to read. Emotions moved back and forth in his eyes as he brushed my hair from my face. Being this close to him had my breath clogging. The fresh air I'd been absorbing seconds before disappeared in an instant. In this moment, on this riverwalk, we were the only two people in the world... and I wasn't sure I could breathe.

"I wasn't just angry earlier," he admitted. "I was... *really* angry."

"I wasn't all that happy about the situation either," I said when I'd found my voice.

"No, but... I was angry for different reasons. The first is that I should've known Damon wouldn't just let it go. The second he realized I was interested in you, there was no way he was just going to retreat to the background and let me live my life."

My heart stuttered. "You're interested in me?"

His eyes lit with amusement. "Are you kidding me?"

"No. I... um..." There were no words to be found.

"Geez, Moxie." He rolled his eyes. "I've been walking you home for weeks. I've been stopping in three times a day when we're both at the bars because if I visit more than that, I will look desperate. Less than that and I will look disinterested."

I bit my lip. "I just thought that was part of the game."

"What do you think the winner is going to get?" he asked. "No, I'm being serious. What is it you want?"

"I... don't... know." That was the truth. I had no idea what I wanted. I had no idea what he wanted. Suddenly, the life that had seemed so settled twenty-four hours ago had been thrown into turmoil.

"It's okay not to know." His voice was soft, husky, and full of naked lust. It had my stomach constricting and my nipples pinching. There might've been some below the belt stuff happening as well, although I chose not to focus on that. "Just... give it some thought."

He leaned in.

My mind was working so slowly, like being trapped in molasses, I didn't realize what he was going to do until his lips were already pressed to mine. They were warm, full, and altogether delicious. He'd clearly had a Hurricane sometime before he delivered the pizza. When mixed with the wine I so disliked, life suddenly tasted sweeter.

As far as kisses go, there was nothing to compare it to. It started out relatively chaste, a first date kiss, but it turned dirty fast. His hand tangled in my hair as I wrapped my arms around his neck, my body being pulled flush against his.

Our tongues tangoed and our breath started coming out in raspy gasps. Nobody reached under a shirt. Nobody grabbed a butt, although I did consider it. The only thing that happened was the kiss, and yet when we finally separated— who pulled away first? I had no idea—everything had changed.

"That was…" I was back to having no words.

"Something to think about," Gus replied as he took a deep breath. His eyes were so dark they almost looked black. "Are you thinking about it?" he asked after a beat.

I nodded.

"What do you think?"

"I think I might pass out," I admitted. "I don't want that to happen because I'll hit my head. Then an ambulance will have to be called, you'll freak out because that's your way, and I'll have to call Abel to sort things out, and I'm still mad at him."

He burst out laughing, his smile so wide it threatened to swallow his entire face. "We can't have that." His voice was barely a whisper as he brushed his fingers over my cheek. "I should walk you home."

"I can walk myself. It's still early."

"Yes, but we have things to think about... and I'm not quite ready to say my goodbyes for the night yet."

"I think you just want to see if you can get a repeat of what just happened."

"Are you against it?"

"No. I just want you to be honest."

"Okay, if that's the case, then I definitely want a repeat."

It was hard for me to admit, but I couldn't stop myself. "I do too."

"Then I guess it's settled."

I nodded. "Yeah. Can we pick up some food on the way? I never did get my overpriced pasta."

"Absolutely. There's a great gumbo place on the corner."

"I love gumbo."

"Somehow I knew you were going to say that."

Twenty-One

The walk back to my place should've been quick. It didn't exactly work out that way. New Orleans was a city of small blocks, and whenever we reached an intersection, Gus twirled me so my back was to a wall, and he could easily move in for a kiss.

It was ridiculous, the sort of thing that drunk college students would do. I didn't stop him though. I was a willing participant.

At one point, several drunk guys leaving the brewery stopped long enough to cheer him on. Gus offered up a haphazard wave, but he never took his eyes off me.

Then we moved down another block.

"What's your favorite book?" he asked between kisses.

The question threw me. "I... don't... know."

His gaze was stern. "Everybody knows what their favorite book is. Come on."

"I guess it's *Lord of the Rings*."

He made a 'you've got to be shitting me' face. "There's no way *Lord of the Rings* is your favorite book."

"But it is," I protested. "I read it after seeing the movies. I

216

know it's supposed to be the other way around, but the book always looked so big when I was in the library as a kid."

"Right."

"It's a great book!"

"It *is* a great book. There's no way that's your favorite book though. Come on. Give me another book."

"I like *The Shining* too. What? I love horror books. There's nothing better than burrowing under the covers and reading a scary book."

"I like the idea of burrowing under the covers," he said absently.

I stiffened. "Um..."

"Don't." He shook his head. "I'm not trying to get you into bed tonight. There's no reason to get worked up about that. It's not happening." He straightened and tugged down his T-shirt. "I'm a gentleman, for crying out loud."

His cheeky response had me grinning. "You're definitely... something."

"Yeah." He leaned in for another kiss. This one softer, almost achingly sweet. When he pulled back, his face was flushed. "You fuzz up my brain."

"That could be the nicest thing anyone has ever said to me."

"Then you've been hanging out with the wrong people."

"Damon?"

"You definitely shouldn't be hanging out with him. He's a complete and total tool."

"I don't disagree. I'm just glad I never told him where I lived. I don't want him to show up out of nowhere and demand an explanation for ghosting him."

"That's probably for the best," he agreed, his cheek coming to rest against mine. It was a warm night, the humidity causing our skin to glisten and stick together. His breath was warm on the ridge of my ear and yet it sent a chill down my spine. "I like being the only one who knows where you live."

I closed my eyes, relishing the warmth of his toned body against mine. We might've been acting like teenagers, but there was something so right about the way his body felt when pressed against mine that I couldn't be bothered to care. "He does know where I work though." That was a sobering thought, I realized.

"Abel will take care of him." Gus didn't seem bothered. "It's possible he'll be so embarrassed he won't bother showing up."

Given my limited interaction with Damon, that seemed unlikely. I didn't want to spend the rest of our time together talking about his childhood nemesis, however. "Why did you want to know my favorite book?"

"I don't know. It just popped into my head."

"That's a weird thing to have pop into your head."

"I don't disagree."

"What's your favorite book?"

"Whichever one has the hero getting the girl."

I pressed my lips together to keep from laughing. "So you're a contemporary romance guy. Is that what you're saying?"

"I think of myself as a romantic comedy guy."

"I can see that. You definitely fit that mold."

He stroked his hand through my hair. The humidity had made it twice as big as it should've been. He didn't seem to care. "If this were a romance novel, what would we do next?"

The earnestness in his eyes caused my heart to clog. "I... don't... know. What do you want to do next?"

"I have so many ideas."

"And what do those ideas entail?"

He pulled back far enough to look me up and down, and then he smiled. "I think I'll continue walking you home."

"And then what?"

"And then I'll kiss you some more."

"And then what?"

He shrugged. "I guess we'll see where the city takes us."

It was the exact right thing to say, and for once, I didn't wonder if he were simply saying it to ease my suspicions regarding his intentions. "I guess it's good we live in a magical city."

"It most definitely is."

I WOKE THE NEXT MORNING FEELING hungover. I'd only had one glass of wine over dinner, and I hadn't even finished it. Gus's kisses were enough to leave me feeling inebriated, however, and when we separated by the gate outside my unit, we spent a good twenty minutes saying good-bye. That was likely why my lips looked swollen the next morning.

"Hey." I slid into the chair across from Ally, a mug of coffee in my hand. I was freshly showered, as was she, and still absorbing the swerve my life had taken the previous evening.

"Hello." Ally's expression was hard to read as she looked up from the magazine she was flipping through. "What time did you get home last night?"

That was a good question. "I have no idea." That was the truth. I hadn't even bothered to check the clock before tumbling into bed and passing out.

"I think you must've gotten in late because we were out in the courtyard until about one or so," she said. "You're usually home well before then. We were a little worried."

"I was fine." I smiled into my coffee as I sipped it. "You had no reason to worry."

"Is that because of your date?"

I froze, my mug pressed to my lips. I was understandably

confused. "What do you mean?" I asked finally, slowly lowering my mug to the table. "What do you know?"

"I know that I called Cher last night when you weren't home by midnight," she replied, mischief sparking in the depths of her eyes.

"Why didn't you call me?" I demanded.

"I did. You didn't pick up."

"What?" I rummaged in my pocket for my phone. I'd unplugged it without looking at the screen after my shower. Sure enough, I had eight missed calls. Two were from Ally, two were from Gabriel, two were from Casey—apparently they'd taken turns—and two were from Cher, which meant Abel had gotten in on the action at some point. "Oh." I pressed my lips together, uncertain what to say.

"Abel said you had a date," Ally pressed. She wasn't the type of individual to let something go until she'd found the answers she was looking for.

"I did have a date." I lowered my phone to the table and debated how I wanted to respond. "It was with this guy I met. Damon."

"Yes, Abel told me that too. Apparently, he doesn't like him."

"Well, since Abel was the one who forced me into that date, I don't really care who he does and doesn't like."

"He told me that too." Ally absently tapped her fingers on the table. "He said that he maneuvered you into a position where you had no choice but to go out with this Damon guy. Then he felt bad about it after the fact because he's convinced there's something wrong with him."

"Oh, there's definitely something wrong with Damon," I agreed. "He's a complete and total jackass."

"And you stayed out with him until after one?" Ally looked dubious. "That doesn't sound like you."

"Oh, I wasn't with Damon. I snuck out of the restaurant

right after we ordered because he was such a tool. By the way, if he shows up here, tell him I moved."

"If he shows up here, I'm going to introduce him to Gabriel and Casey and let them handle the situation," Ally said drily. "I'm glad to know you weren't out with him. It does bring up another question though."

I didn't volunteer any information. I knew it would drive her crazy. I wasn't ready though. I needed more time to think.

Apparently, Ally didn't care what I needed. "Who were you out with, Moxie?"

I pursed my lips and turned my attention down the alley. "You know, I was thinking, we should really take a day and clean this place. It's lovely out here at night, when we can't see the garbage, but if we give the patio a spruce, it will be so much better."

"Moxie." Ally's voice was low and full of warning, earning a sigh from me.

"I happened to run into Gus when I was walking home," I replied.

"I see." She leaned back in her chair and sipped her coffee. I had no doubt she was hiding a smile behind that Kiss My Sass mug. "Did you guys go out to dinner with one another?"

"No, we did not." That was true. Mostly. "He happened to be dishing out pizza to all the people in Jackson Square when I saw him."

"Of course, he was." Ally let loose a very unladylike snort. "I guess he knows the way to your heart, huh?"

For some reason, the words bothered me. "He didn't know I would be there. He knew about the date. There's no way he could've figured out what time I would be passing by. In fact, if he was trying to arrange it so I would see him, he would've aimed for at least an hour—more likely two—later."

"I see." Her smile only widened. "So what did you and Gus do?"

Well, that was a loaded question. I wasn't certain I was ready to answer it. "Um... we went for a walk on the riverwalk." That wasn't technically a lie. It was pretty far from the truth though. We'd done so much more than that.

"Oh yeah?" Ally's tone was light, as if we were having a simple conversation. Just two girls gabbing over coffee. Could anything be more innocent? "You guys walked on the riverwalk until one o'clock? Isn't that dangerous?"

"We were fine." I refused to meet her gaze.

"Uh-huh."

"We didn't even see anybody when we were walking."

"That is so odd in such a big city."

"I guess we just lucked out."

"Hmm. Do you know what's interesting?" She sipped her coffee again, and the light in her eyes told me I wasn't going to like whatever came out of her mouth next.

"I find many things interesting."

"So do I. Like, I have this friend. Sven. He works at that art gallery over on Royal. You know the one, right? I've taken you there."

"I know it." The entire art gallery was filled with boobs. No, seriously. It was boobs in every color of the rainbow. Every size you could imagine. Not only did the artist just paint boobs, he also sold them for like a grand each. It was a total racket.

"Well, Sven happened to be out on Decatur Street last night," she continued, her eyes on me as my heart dropped. "He said that he was leaving the Jax Brewery around midnight or so and saw a couple making out on the other side of the road."

"It's New Orleans," I said blandly. "I'm sure people make out here all the time. Sven should find something to do other than stare at people on the street."

"I'm sure people make out here all the time too. The thing

is, he said this couple caught his interest because they kept pressing each other against the buildings. They would stop, make out as if their lives depended on it, and then walk a few feet before starting again. He said they made quite the scene with all the heavy panting and moaning."

"There was no moaning," I snapped, realizing far too late that she'd caught me. "I mean—"

"Oh, don't bother." She shook her head and let loose a tinny laugh. "Sven knows you. He recognized you. Did you really still have on your Cher uniform top? Because, knowing what I know now, that seems like a really weird thing."

"I... don't know what you mean." I wanted to be mortified. I couldn't quite muster the energy though.

"Well, I assumed you were wearing the Cher top because you'd just gotten off from work. You walk back with Gus every night."

"Not *every* night."

"People have seen you. Stop denying it." Ally's tone was chiding. "When Sven told me the story—he likes to video chat as a way to wake people up—I assumed this was something that had been going on for a while. I was going to give you a hard time about holding out on me."

"It's something new," I hedged.

"Something new that happened right after he ordered pizza for the Jackson Square crew."

I made a grumbling sound under my breath. "I guess you could say that."

"What would you say?"

"I would say that... it just sort of happened." And there it was. The truth. I'd acknowledged what she already knew... and I only felt mildly exposed.

Her grin was lightning quick. "So, let me get this straight. You were supposed to go out with a guy who might have dirt on Gus. You ended up ditching him because he was a tool."

"The king of the tools," I confirmed.

She continued as if I hadn't spoken. "Then you ran into Gus, who was feeding the homeless, and you went for a walk with one another on the riverwalk. That somehow turned into you two making out all the way down Decatur Street, and now you look like you're hungover and your lips are swollen. Have I missed anything?"

"I believe that's it," I said primly.

"Awesome." Ally abandoned her coffee and rubbed her hands together. "So, what kind of kisser is he?"

My cheeks colored in embarrassment... and maybe a little pleasure. It was so nice to have someone to talk to, someone I trusted, someone I could be myself with. "It was pretty nice. The thing is... I don't know what I should do now."

"I have a few suggestions."

I jabbed a warning finger in her direction. "I think I can imagine your suggestions. We're not there yet. We just stopped hating each other."

"Oh, honey, you never hated one another." The look she shot me was pitying. "That wasn't hate. It was foreplay."

"Oh, no." I was adamant. "I hated him. He stole my opening."

"He charmed you from the start. You might not have wanted to be charmed, but he managed it. He always knew what he was doing."

I wanted to deny it outright, but she had me thinking. "Do you really believe that's true?"

"I think he took one look at you and decided he was smitten. He's played you really well. He's engaged you on a competitive level and gotten to know you through games. I mean... it's been fairly interesting to watch."

"I still don't know what to do now."

"Maybe try purposely flirting with him instead of accidentally turning him on with insults."

That was an idea. "I guess it couldn't hurt to flirt with him."

"Definitely not. Have fun with it. You can still be mean to him if the situation warrants it. Try being nice to him too. You might find you like it."

Hey, it was worth a shot.

I HUMMED TO MYSELF AS I GRABBED a coffee from Café Beignet. Gus had warned me the previous evening that he wouldn't be able to meet for our regular breakfast shenanigans. Apparently, his parents were due at Flambeaux for the first time, and he had things to set up for their visit. I didn't blame him for being nervous.

I cut through Jackson Square, making sure to check the area on the far end of the park to confirm all the pizza boxes had made it into the trash receptacles. I was gratified to find there wasn't a single piece of garbage on the ground. Everything had been tidied up—and nicely.

I waved to a few familiar faces as the local vendors started setting up their tables. There was an entire row of tarot card readers—gregarious women with infectious laughs who always made me smile—and I made a mental note, not for the first time, to stop and get a reading one day. I scanned the crowd, looking for Benji. He'd been present for the pizza party the previous night—I'd seen him from afar—but he didn't seem to be around this morning. I wasn't exactly alarmed, but a break in a routine for these guys was unheard of.

"Hey, Gremlin," I called out as I approached one of the individuals I knew best. "Have you seen Benji this morning?"

Gremlin blinked several times and then shook his head. "No. I don't remember him being around when we woke up. Sorry."

"It's okay." I flashed a smile, reminding myself that Benji

was an adult and not beholden to anyone. Why did I even care? He'd left me. He'd left my mother. I shouldn't care.

"I can tell him you're looking for him if I see him," Gremlin offered.

"That's okay," I said. "It's not important. I'll see you guys tonight."

He offered up a mock salute. "I'm looking forward to it. Bring your boyfriend with you when you come. He's not too bad... for a dude."

Boyfriend? Ugh. "I'll tell him you said that."

"I'm pretty sure he already knows. He's one of those guys who always feels good about himself."

I thought about the way Gus's features twisted when he mentioned a visit from his parents. "Not always, but close enough. I'll swing by when I can."

"Have a good day," Gremlin sang out.

"You too. Have an absolutely wonderful day."

Twenty-Two

I was excited for work, a fact I registered but tried not to dwell on. If I spent too much time thinking about it, the internal flogging would begin... and nobody wanted that.

Abel was waiting for me behind the bar when I wandered into Cher, and the look he graced me with wasn't full of warm fuzzies.

"I see you're alive," he said drily.

Guilt rolled through me. He'd been worried when I left with Damon the previous evening. I should've taken that into account. "I'm sorry. I ended up sneaking out before our food was even delivered. I... didn't think about calling you."

"Oh, I know you snuck out." Abel's chuckle was low. "Your date stopped by for a chat about forty minutes after you left. He was not happy."

I cringed. "He didn't hurt you, did he?" Why that was my first assumption, I couldn't say. Abel could crush Damon just by looking at him. Still, Damon wasn't coasting on clouds of mental stability, as far as I could tell.

"Girl, please." Abel rolled his eyes. "He tried barreling in here and demanding your cell phone number. I politely explained that I wasn't giving it to him. Then he went after a few waitresses, which is when I stopped being polite."

I stilled. "You didn't kill him and hide the body in the dumpster, did you?"

"First off, if you kill someone, you never leave the body someplace it can be traced back to you. If he was dead, I would've tossed him in the dumpster at that new strip place."

That didn't make me feel better. "Abel—"

"It's fine." He waved off my concern. "I explained it was corporate policy that personal numbers were not given out. He then demanded that I call you on the house phone so he could talk to you. I declined that request as well."

I wasn't used to him talking in such a prim and proper manner, and it drew a smile. "How mad was he?"

"He was spitting mad. I guess it took him thirty minutes to realize you weren't coming back. He made a waitress at the restaurant look for you in the restroom, and when informed that you weren't in there and had likely left in a hurry, he said that simply wasn't possible. That's what he kept repeating over and over again. 'It's simply not possible.' I wanted to smack the shit out of him."

I snorted. "Well, at least he knows." Even as I said it, a niggling worry worked through my squirmy stomach. "You don't think he'll come back, do you? I don't want him causing a scene here. I mean... this is my place of business."

"I wouldn't worry about that. This is the Quarter. Bar fights go with the territory. People will enjoy it."

"Yeah, but—"

"If he lays a hand on you, I will break him in half."

I stared at him for several seconds, debating whether he was serious, and then smiled. "I didn't know you cared."

"You're not as bad as I originally thought you were going to be." Honesty was reflected in his eyes. "You're still high-strung, but you're also funny, although you probably don't even realize you're being funny when it happens."

"Oh, I know I'm funny." I shot him a haughty look that was designed to be over-the-top. "I could headline my own comedy tour if I wanted."

"You're humble too."

"Totally."

Abel hesitated a moment, running the rag he'd been using to wipe down the bar when I came inside through his hands. He looked like he had questions. Ultimately, he just shook his head. "I'll keep an eye out for the douche canoe. You do you today."

It was an odd thing to say. "What does that mean?"

"It means that you're a little shiny for my liking. That either means you got laid or you laid the groundwork to get laid."

I tried to keep my gaze even, but it was difficult given the way my cheeks were heating. "I have no idea what you're talking about."

He snorted. "You're a horrible liar."

"It's just a normal day," I insisted.

"Oh, whatever. Just... don't worry about Captain Tool. I'll handle him if he comes back."

I was more than happy to cede that duty to him. It felt like my responsibility, however. "Maybe he won't show up. A good night's sleep will likely have him rethinking it. I mean... he doesn't want to be embarrassed in public."

"Girl, I don't think he realizes he is being embarrassed. That's the problem with guys like him."

It was an interesting observation. "Let's just treat it like a normal day. If he shows up, we'll handle it together."

"Sounds like a plan to me."

. . .

I TRIED TO FOCUS ON WORK—NO, REALLY—but it was hard to keep my gaze from drifting to Flambeaux. At one point I distracted myself with washing a window that would be filthy again in five minutes flat but just so happened to afford me a clear view of our rival bar, and that was when I saw a huge stretch limo—the thing was almost a full block long, I swear—pulling up.

I kept wiping the window with my paper towel and watched as a tall man, dark hair graying at the temples, climbed out of the limo. He held open the door until a petite blond woman stepped out. They were dressed in expensive suits—the sort of clothing you never saw on Bourbon Street unless there was some sort of mafia deal going down—and they seemed out of place.

"What are you looking at?" Carly appeared next to me, her lips quirking when she caught sight of the limo. "Oh, that's just ostentatious."

"Right?" I found I was annoyed, although I had no reason to feel that way. "Who goes barhopping in a limo?"

"Bachelorette party peeps. Well, and bachelor party peeps. It happens all the time."

"Okay, but that's meant to be over-the-top and fun. This doesn't look like any wedding party I've ever seen."

"Definitely not." Carly's face was scrunched up in concentration. "Why do they look so familiar?"

"You recognize them?"

She shook her head. "No, but... wait a second." She snapped her fingers, as if having an epiphany, and took off toward the bar. I watched, curious, and when she came back, she was beyond excited. "Now I know why I recognized them. They were in the newspaper this morning."

"What?" I took the newspaper she handed me and studied the front page. Sure enough, the people currently standing on the sidewalk staring into Flambeaux were indeed the individuals on display in the prominent news article. I frowned when I read the headline.

"Those are Gus's parents," Carly explained. She was practically giddy. "Those people are richer than rich. That's why they're in the limo. They really are ostentatious."

I lifted my eyes and stared at the man a bit harder. "Anders and Anna Kingman," I mused to myself.

"Yeah. It's all As in that family. That's ostentatious, too, if you ask me."

I couldn't disagree. "This article says they're spearheading an attempt to clean up Jackson Square." My throat was tight. "They want to move out all the homeless people to increase the tourism."

"Yeah. I read that." Carly's face was blank. "It's not a bad idea. I always get nervous whenever I'm in that area because they're all over you the second you appear. They're like gnats."

I frowned. "They're still people."

"Yes, but they're people that hurt the city. They make the tourists uncomfortable. It's only a matter of time before the city does another sweep."

"Sweep?" I had no idea what she was talking about. "What's a sweep?"

"When they go in and roust all the homeless people and drive them away from the city."

She was speaking English, and yet it didn't compute. "Where do they take them?"

She shrugged. "Elsewhere. It usually takes them days to complete one full sweep."

"But..." My heart started hammering. I didn't like this one bit. "What happens to the people they sweep up?"

"I don't know. I think they're taken to shelters or something."

"And what if they don't want to stay in a shelter?"

"I don't know." Carly increased the distance between us,

clearly uncomfortable with my newfound intensity. "I'm not an expert on the subject."

I clenched the paper towel tighter, my mind working a mile a minute, and then I nodded. "Okay, um, I'll be right back." I handed her the filthy cleaning towel and plunged through the door. There was no hesitation when I crossed the street—I barely checked for traffic—and I barreled through the door of Flambeaux without taking a breath.

Anna and Anders were inside at this point. They'd headed directly to the bar and looked to be conversing with Gus. I wasn't an expert on Gus's expressions—not really anyway—but it didn't take an empath to figure out he wasn't thrilled with the visit. He went through the motions, though, smiling at his mother and shaking his father's hand while I got close enough to overhear their conversation.

"It's nice to see you." He leaned over the bar and pressed a stiff kiss to his mother's cheek. "I can't say I'm not surprised that you picked today to come for a visit."

"We want to check in on our investment," Anders said in a booming voice. He was clearly the type of guy who liked to command a room. "I've been hearing interesting things from your brothers."

"Right." Gus licked his lips, discomfort practically rolling off him in waves. "Well, look around. It is your investment, as you mentioned."

"It looks good." Anders flashed a smile. "It's definitely a good location. I still don't know how you managed to sweep in and get it when I didn't even know the building was up for sale, but kudos to you."

"I know people in the business." Gus appeared to be in pain when he glanced up. It was as if he had some sort of radar, and he immediately found me. Out of nowhere, he smiled. "I like sticking close to the competition."

I'd headed to Flambeaux with every intention of giving his

parents a hard time. If Carly was right about the plan for Jackson Square—a project the Kingmans were spearheading—I wanted to give them a piece of my mind. Gus wasn't responsible though. This was his parents' doing, and it wasn't my place to ruin whatever they had going on over here. I took a step in the direction I'd come from, intent on escaping.

"Speaking of my fellow business associates, here's one now," Gus said, calling out to me. The smile he flashed me was rich and flirty. "Mom, Dad, this is Moxie Stone. She manages Cher."

Anders turned first, and his gaze was appraising. He looked me over head to toe, and back up, and then smiled. Nothing about the expression was friendly. "You're the girl from Michigan." He took a decisive step forward and extended his hand. "You're supposed to be some sort of miracle worker."

Under different circumstances, I would've loved to have my accomplishments brought up in front of a rival bar owner. Gus was more than that now. "I don't know if I would call myself a miracle worker," I hedged.

"She's pretty good," Gus said, sending me a wink behind his parents' backs. His mother turned at that exact moment and caught the wink. Her lips quirked in response, but she didn't say anything. Instead, she demurred to her husband.

"The people I've talked to say you're quite determined," Anders said. "I was dismissive when I heard you were coming from Michigan—I mean, that's not what I would call a fun state—but it seems you have a handle on things."

I bristled, even though I told myself it was a waste of time. "Michigan has a lot of great bars."

"Really?" Anders didn't look convinced. "I've never heard of any."

"Well, I guess that's your loss." I was annoyed... and sympathetic at the same time. Gus was trying so hard to break from the shadow of his parents and yet he couldn't do it as long as he was on the payroll. He had to stay on the payroll until he earned enough money to branch out himself. It was a vicious cycle.

"Are you visiting for a specific purpose?" Anna asked out of nowhere. Her voice was softer than her husband's, and she seemed much more interested in her son as a man than as an entrepreneur.

"I was just going to tell Gus that we're running a watermelon Hurricane special today," I said dumbly. "We usually coordinate drink specials so we don't serve the same thing. That lets the customers have a better idea which bar tickles their fancy on any given day." That was an absolute lie, but I couldn't think of anything better to say.

"You share cocktail specials?" Anders's forehead creased as he turned back to his son. "That's... weird."

"It's a cooperative thing," Gus lied smoothly. "It's working out well for us. The other day, I did fire shots, and Moxie did dry ice drinks. People freaking loved it."

"Oh, well... if it's working." Anders's smile was pleasant enough, but disinterest lurked in the depths of his eyes. He didn't care about me. I had to wonder if he cared about his son as anything other than a moneymaking machine.

"Thanks for the update," Gus said, drawing my eyes to him. There was an apology in their depths even though his parents' attitude wasn't his fault. "I'll stop by later and coordinate the appetizer menu." He was giving me an out, a chance to escape.

I took it. "I'm looking forward to it." I kept my voice brisk. "I'll see you later." I didn't glance over my shoulder as I left, even though I desperately wanted one more look at Gus. He had to handle this battle on his own. There was another one I wanted to involve him in later, but I couldn't ruin his parents' first visit to Flambeaux. It wasn't fair.

My concerns regarding the Jackson Square sweep would have to wait... for now.

"HEY."

Gus was all smiles when he found me at the bar in Cher two hours later. His hair was messy, to the point where it looked like it had survived multiple frustrated swipes. His grin was real, though, and it had something stirring inside of me. What, though? Lust? Amusement? Yearning? All of the above? I just couldn't be sure.

"I'm sorry I interrupted your meeting with your parents," I offered. "I didn't realize they were already there when I stopped by."

"It's fine. I was glad to see you." He looked sincere. "I'm sorry I missed breakfast this morning."

"It was rough mainlining caffeine without you, but somehow I managed."

"I'm still sorry. I just... needed to make sure things were ready for them. They're... difficult."

That seemed like a ridiculously underwhelming word given what I'd seen of his parents. "I can see that." I wanted to bring up the newspaper article but compounding his frustrations from earlier seemed somehow wrong. It could wait for our walk home tonight, I told myself. It would be better to give him some time to relax. "How did things go?"

His shrug was noncommittal. "As well as can be expected."

"Is that saying anything?"

"It is what it is." Frustration momentarily clouded his features. "I love my parents," he started. "I just don't know if I like them, if that makes any sense."

"It does." I felt sorry for him. Sure, my father had abandoned me, but my mother had been my biggest champion. She'd instilled fear in me when it came to men—something I was starting to regret—but she was always there for me, telling me what a good job I was doing and propping me up. He had none of that. His parents didn't praise him. They didn't encourage him. They compared him to his brothers and fostered an unrealistic competitive environment. It had to be frustrating. "Will you be walking home around ten o'clock this evening?"

Gus's grin was back, the one that made him look impossibly young and mischievous. "Yes. Why? Do you know someone who will be walking home at the same time?"

"Maybe." I tried not to smile in return... and failed. "I guess I'll see you then."

"You definitely will." He leaned close to whisper, making sure I was the only one who could hear him despite the music and milling people. "I'm thinking maybe we can take our time when going across the Quarter this evening. I have some shady alcoves I want to show you."

My cheeks were on fire. "I guess that sounds okay." I caught Abel looking at me and quickly averted my gaze. "I'll see you then."

"You definitely will." He didn't kiss me. He knew better. Instead, he saluted Abel and headed toward the door. "It's going to be a beautiful day, people. Let's enjoy it."

I took a full two minutes to collect myself before risking a glance at Abel. He looked amused. "What?" I demanded. "I'm not doing anything."

He snorted. "Did I say anything?"

"No, but you have a look."

"Yeah, and there's a reason for it."

"Nothing is going on," I insisted.

"I don't know who you're trying to convince when you say that, but it's not going to work on me."

Sadly, I already knew that was true. Crap. What was I getting myself into here?

Twenty-Three

I focused on work for the bulk of the day. Carly and I did some brainstorming on what might bring people in. Abel unloaded the order sheets on me, occasionally barking out items to add from behind the bar as I filled them out. The humidity grew to be oppressive by early afternoon, and I knew that a storm was coming. The sky was dark enough that I recognized I wouldn't be able to make it to Jackson Square to drop off a round of dinner before it hit.

"We could make a run for it and try," Gus offered as he sidled closer to me. I hadn't even noticed he'd crossed the street to join me as I held out my hands and waited for the rain to come.

"I was thinking that," I admitted. "But we'll get trapped out there if we try."

"You say that like it's a bad thing." His grin was flirty. "I happened to enjoy it the last time we were trapped."

"Oh, really?" I didn't believe him. "That's not how I remember it."

"That's because you were too busy trying to convince

yourself that you hated me to see what was right in front of you."

"And what was that?"

"Raw animal magnetism."

"You did kind of smell like a wet dog."

"Ha, ha." He poked my side and then sobered. "Those guys know how to take care of themselves during a storm. They've been around the block a few times. They haven't survived this long by being stupid."

"I know. I just don't like to think of them going hungry."

"Well, hopefully the storms will be finished by the time we head out tonight. We'll take them food then."

"Right." Worry niggled at the back of my brain. "Benji wasn't out there when I was making my rounds this morning."

"No?" Gus pursed his lips. "Well, we'll check again tonight. It's not as if those guys keep to a schedule, Moxie. They go where they want when they want."

"You make it sound like they've got absolute freedom."

"Don't they?"

I vehemently shook my head. "No, they're trapped by circumstances they can't control. I know a lot of those guys ended up out there because they made poor decisions, but it's not exactly easy to climb out of a situation like that and create a new life."

"You're assuming they want to create a new life."

"Who would want to live like that?"

"You would be surprised." He squeezed my arm and tilted his head, as if debating. "I have a question for you."

"Yes, I find you attractive. No, I will never admit that to another living soul because it might make me look bad after all the trash talking I did. I'm too vain to admit when I'm wrong."

He snorted. "Well, that wasn't what I was going to ask about. It's good to know though."

"What were you going to ask? If you want to circle around to favorite horror movies again, I'm never going to agree that the third *Halloween* was a good movie. It didn't even have Michael Myers in it."

"That movie is so misunderstood," Gus lamented. "My question has nothing to do with horror movies."

"Okay, then I guess you can lay it on me."

"I know you're worried about Benji." He licked his lips, clearly choosing his words carefully. "Have you considered alternative solutions for his problem?"

"Like getting him a job?"

"I would hope a job would be part of the scenario eventually. He needs to get clean first."

"Yeah, but how can I force that on him? He doesn't even know who I am."

"He could know. You could tell him."

"No." I didn't want that. "I... can't deal with that. I'm not ready."

"Okay. That's okay." He squeezed my wrist. "What about rehab? We could get him in a program. You don't have to tell him who you are until you're ready. Heck, if you never want to tell him, that's okay too."

"How am I going to pay for that?" I made a good living, but it was expensive to live in the French Quarter. I had some money put away in savings, what little my mother had left when she passed and what I'd made in Michigan before heading south. It was nowhere near enough to pay for the type of residential program he was suggesting.

"I could help."

"No. Absolutely not."

"Why not?"

"Because... we... you..."

He folded his arms across his chest and waited.

"Oh, don't give me that look." My annoyance was on full display. "I can't take money from you, Gus. We're not... we can't... I can't..."

"We're not there yet," he surmised.

"I don't know that we'll ever be there." I opted for honesty. "I don't even know what we're doing."

"I believe we're dating."

"Oh yeah?" I arched an eyebrow. "When have we ever been out on a date?"

"What do you think our morning breakfasts are?"

"A happy meeting of the minds."

He snorted. "We might not have been dating conventionally, if that's even still a thing, but we were most certainly dating. I guarantee I know you better than almost anybody."

"That's some bold talk there."

He laughed. "I'm willing to do this however you want to do it. If you want to take it slow, that's fine. If you want to come home with me tonight, that's better than fine."

My cheeks heated. "Oh, um..."

"Or I can just walk you home like I normally do," he reassured me. "Don't overthink it. That's always your problem. You overthink things until you make something out of nothing."

"I'm pretty sure that's an insult."

"Then you're not listening." He was firm. "If you're not ready to admit we're dating, I can deal with that. We'll work up to it. If you don't want me to give you money for your dad's rehab, I get it. I can loan it to you though. You don't have to wait until you save it up. I mean... the longer he's on the street, the more likely it is that he'll succumb to his own demons—or that something else will happen."

What he said made sense. I didn't know if I could wrap my head around it though. "I need time to think about that." I was suddenly uncomfortable. "I just... I can't think about it right now."

"Fair enough." He held up his hands in a placating manner. "I'm here when you want to talk." His eyes flicked up to the sky and back to me. "The rain is here. I need to head back." He hesitated and then smiled. "Try to get off thirty minutes early tonight, huh? That will give us time to drop off the food and then take another walk."

A smile washed over my face, unbidden. "I know what that's code for. You're not being sneaky."

"I'm not trying to be." He pressed his fingers to his lips and then blew a kiss at me. "See you in a couple of hours."

"I'm looking forward to it," I murmured under my breath.

AS I'D COME TO EXPECT, THE BAR WAS slammed within minutes of the sky opening up. I busied myself with waiting on customers, stocking coolers, and being an all-around utility player for the next two hours. The crowd was just beginning to dissipate—along with the rain—when a familiar visitor stepped through the door.

My heart immediately plummeted. "Oh no."

Abel, who was busy wiping down the counter, looked up sharply. I didn't miss the growling sound that escaped his throat when he caught sight of Damon. "I guess it was too much to ask that he fall through a storm grate and drown during the storm, huh?"

I had to bite back a laugh. "I guess." I found I was suddenly nervous. "Am I supposed to apologize for ghosting him last night?"

"Are you sorry for ghosting him last night?"

"No."

"Then screw him. The second he comes over here, lift that

leg and kick him in the nuts. You're little. His ego is huge. He won't even see it coming."

"Yeah, that seems a little rude without provocation."

"So? That dude is a tool. You don't owe him anything. The only reason you went out with him in the first place is because I backed you into a corner."

"Yeah, about that..." I trailed off, leaving an opening for him.

"I'm not sorry about that either." He was stern as he fixed me with a look. "You were being stupid. By maneuvering you into going out on a date that you didn't want to be part of, it moved things along that you do want to be a part of."

"What are you talking about?" I asked blankly, doing my best not to make eye contact with Damon no matter how hard he stared.

"You know exactly what I'm talking about."

"I really don't."

"Kingman?"

My heart skipped a beat. What did he know? "I... don't... know what you're talking about." Oh, well, that was believable. Oh, wait, it wasn't.

"Please, people saw you on Decatur last night. Even if you're not a totally recognizable face yet, he is. You guys took your tongues for a walk after hours last evening, and everybody knows about it."

I. Was. Horrified.

"Don't look at me like that," Abel warned. "I did what I did. I'm not sorry. As for that guy, I'll handle him if you don't want to deal with his... well, I'm sure it's going to be whiny whatever he does. I created the problem, and I clean up my own messes."

It was an interesting offer and one I wanted to take him up on. Instead, I heaved out a sigh. "No. You're not the one who excused yourself to go to the bathroom and never came back. That's on me."

Abel's lips quirked into a smirk. "I am mildly curious how long he sat there expecting you to come back."

"I can ask him if you want."

"Only if you can slide it into the conversation without looking too obvious."

"I'll keep that in mind." On a sigh—the sort that teenage girls have perfected over the ages—I walked out from behind the bar and pointed myself toward Damon. "Hey." I attempted a smile and came up with a grimace. "Fancy meeting you here."

"Did you think I would still be at Angelo's?" Damon's tone was icy to the extreme.

"I don't know. I guess anything is possible." It was time to put on my big girl panties and handle this problem once and for all. "Listen, I'm sorry I left the way I did—"

"Are you?" Damon folded his arms across his chest, puffing himself out like a furious cat. "You don't look sorry."

"Well, I am. It was rude for me to take off that way."

He waited for me to continue. When I didn't, he pinned me with a furious look. "That's all you're going to say?"

"I don't know what else to say. I'm sorry I inconvenienced you. Please forward me the dinner bill, and I'll gladly cover it." That was all I had. I was ready to put the nightmare that was Damon Stephens behind me.

Apparently, he had other plans. "I can't believe you're not even going to bother making up an excuse. I thought for sure you would whip out some story about a sick parent... or maybe a sibling getting arrested. You're not even going to try, though, are you?"

"I don't particularly enjoy lying."

"Nobody enjoys lying. You do it so you don't appear rude."

"Well, that's not who I am. None of those things happened. I simply wasn't having a good time and decided I should leave."

"You weren't having a good time?"

"No."

"I took you to one of the fanciest restaurants in the Quarter."

Was he seriously going this route? I couldn't believe it. Well, that's not true. I could believe it. I wasn't happy about it, but I could believe it. "Is that supposed to impress me?"

"I was going to take you to a fancier place over in the Garden District, but your bodyguard took away that option. It's not my fault he's such a... goon."

Incredulous, I glanced over my shoulder to gauge Abel's reaction. He'd moved to the side of the bar closest to where I was speaking to Damon, and he looked positively furious. "Um..."

"You should go," Abel suggested. His tone matched Damon's perfectly. Since Abel was practically twice his size, he was a lot more intimidating.

"I'm here to talk to Moxie," Damon snapped. "I'm not here to talk to you."

"Well, I believe Moxie is done talking to you." Abel pushed himself away from the bar and headed for the opening. Each step he took had my heart pounding harder. Was he really going to pick a fight with Damon Freaking Stephens? That would not end well if it got back to the boss.

"Stop right there." Damon extended his hand, palm up, and fixed Abel with a warning look. "If you take another step, I'll have no choice but to teach you a lesson."

Abel cocked an eyebrow. "Is this the part where you tell me you know karate?"

"Of course not." Damon's lips curled into an unattractive sneer. "Karate is for amateurs. I know Brazilian jiu-jitsu."

"Is there a difference?"

"Well, Anton, Brazilian jiu-jitsu is a mixture of martial arts and combat. It involves ground fighting and submission holds while focusing on skill versus girth."

I pressed my lips together and shifted my eyes to Abel. "His name is Abel," I said in a low voice. Why I felt the need to interject myself into the conversation at this point was beyond me.

"So, do you think you can take me down with your... what did you call it again?" Abel looked like a stealthy cat—a big one you can only find at a zoo—as he slowly stalked toward Damon.

"With BJJ, I can take down a man twice my size," Damon insisted.

"BJJ, huh?" Abel shot me an amused look. "Do you spend a lot of time doing BJs in addition to making women uncomfortable?"

"BJJ."

"I said what I said."

Damon huffed out a breath. "I'm not afraid of you. I've been trained, and I'm a lethal weapon."

"Uh-huh."

Part of me wanted to watch Abel wipe the floor with him. It would be cathartic... and so very funny. The other part had a warning alarm beeping in the back of my brain. If Abel put his hands on Damon, we would all be in trouble.

I opened my mouth to stop him, knowing that I might not be capable, and then another body joined the fray.

Gus slid in through Cher's side door, his eyes bouncing between faces before they settled on Damon. I had no idea if he was here to help or hurt the cause, but I was utterly terrified.

"Hey, Damon," Gus said. "Fancy meeting you here."

Damon's eyes were dark slits of fury when they landed on Gus. "Do you think you're funny?"

"I happen to have it on very good authority that I'm downright hilarious," Gus replied. "Is that important for this conversation?"

"That... *man*... is threatening me." Damon extended a wobbly finger toward Abel. "Call the police. He said he would strike me."

Suddenly my tongue came unglued. "He didn't say that!"

Gus shot me a quelling look and then turned back to Damon. "Do you really want me to call the police?"

"Of course, I do." Damon tugged on his shirt to straighten it. "I'm a Stephens. That means I don't put up with threats from people who... don't understand what class is. I want the police here right now."

"Sure." Gus appeared amenable to the prospect, which had my temper flaring. "Just be forewarned, once the police get here, I'm going to be forced to tell them about the way I caught you groping Moxie last night when you tried to take her out on a date."

Okay, now things were definitely getting out of control. I opened my mouth to tell Gus that hadn't happened, but the sharp look he shot me had me snapping my mouth shut.

Damon was incredulous. "Excuse me? That didn't happen at all."

"And Abel didn't threaten you," Gus shot back.

"So you're saying you'll lie to the police, are you?" The way Damon kept rocking his head back and forth reminded me of a chicken. "You just threatened me in front of witnesses, Kingman. You're so stupid. They'll tell the police what happened, and you're going to be in a lot of trouble."

"Oh yeah?" Gus didn't appear worried in the least. He looked around at the people in the bar who were witnessing our confrontation. "How many people heard me tell Damon here that I was going to lie to get him in trouble?"

Not a single hand went up.

Gus's evil smile was a thing of beauty. "And how many people heard Damon admit to trying to cause trouble for your favorite bartender even though Abel didn't earn it?"

Every person in the restaurant shot a hand in the air.

"I think that's your answer, Damon," Gus said. "I also think that your business here is done. There's no need for you to come around anymore. Moxie has no interest in talking to you. Abel definitely has no use for you. And me, well, I wouldn't piss on you if one of those gas lamps on the corners exploded and caught that ridiculous thing on your head on fire."

I couldn't help myself. I peered closer to Damon's full head of luscious hair. "Is that a rug?" The question escaped before I could think better of it.

"It's my hair!" Damon screeched. He lobbed eye daggers at us as he moved toward the exit. He might hate to lose, but he clearly knew he was beat. "This isn't over."

"It's over," Gus shot back. "If you come back here again, I'll have to start telling that story about how you got caught pouring honey on your private parts when we were in school and then stuck your dick in an ant pile to get off."

Damon's face turned so red, I thought he might explode. "That never happened!"

"Who here thinks that happened?" I asked, raising my hand.

Everybody in the bar automatically raised their hands in kind.

"This isn't over," Damon hissed one more time as he slipped outside. "I'm totally going to make you pay for this, Kingman."

Gus was blasé. "Bring it on."

Twenty-Four

G us was waiting for me when I left Cher. I was no longer surprised to see him. Sure, we'd made plans to meet tonight—which was different from how things normally played out—but somehow, over the course of the weeks we'd spent sparring with one another, his presence had become expected. It was the realization that I would have been disappointed if he hadn't been there when I exited that rattled me.

"What's with the face?" Gus asked as he waited for me to cross to him. "Are you upset about Damon? Don't be. He has no real power. If he shows up again and causes a scene, I'll handle him."

My legs felt like jelly as I erased the distance between us. I could feel his eyes on my face—that was concern lining his features as much as happiness to see me—but I didn't meet his gaze. "I'm not worried about Damon," I said when I was in front of him. "He's a petulant toddler on a playground demanding he get all the turns on the slide."

Gus smirked. "I believe he actually did that when we were in grade school."

"I don't doubt it." On a whim, I rested my hand on his chest, familiarizing myself with the steady heartbeat.

"What's with this face?" Gus looked pained as he placed his finger beneath my chin and tipped it up. I had no choice but to look at him. "Are you trying to kill me?"

I shook my head. "No. I'm... starting to figure things out."

"Oh yeah?" He cocked an eyebrow. "What are you figuring out?"

I licked my lips, debating, and then sighed. "I might have feelings for you." There was no reason to lie. He knew. They all knew. Apparently I was the only one who didn't know, which made me an idiot. Looking back all the signs were there.

"*Might*?"

I smirked. Of course, that was the word that was going to trip him up. "I looked forward to seeing you," I said out of nowhere. "When I would look through the window to see what you were doing, I told myself it was because I wanted to know if you were running a promotion that could hurt us. That wasn't it though."

"No, that wasn't it," he agreed. Amusement lit his face, making him look impossibly handsome. "Are you really telling me that you're just figuring this out now?"

"I thought we were enemies who played games."

"Geez." He shook his head. "Abel was right." That last part was likely not said for my benefit, but it had me lifting my chin anyway.

"What?"

"Abel. He told me last week that I was going to have to make a move because you weren't ever going to open yourself to the point where we could make a move together. He said it was going to have to be me, and I laughed it off. He was right though."

I felt as if I were falling through a window. "Abel told you to ask me out?"

"What?" Gus snapped his eyes back to me and shook his head. "No. We were talking about how awkward you are when you flirt. I thought you realized you were flirting and that the game was heating up. Abel explained that you had no idea you were flirting... and it turns out he was right. *Dammit!* That means I owe him a hundred bucks. I hate losing bets."

My mouth dropped open. "You thought I was flirting with you?"

The amusement was back. "You were flirting with me."

"I didn't know I was flirting with you."

"It's not my fault you're slow." He brushed my hair away from my face and attempted a serious expression. He failed miserably because the smile that crept over his face was the stuff of sweaty legends. "Let's walk." He held out his hand for me.

"I have to grab the stuff I put aside to take to the Square tonight," I replied dumbly. "They'll be hungry."

"No, they won't." Gus shook his head. "I had subs delivered down there an hour ago."

He never ceased to amaze me. "You did?"

"Of course, I did. I'm invested now." He rested his hand on my shoulder, his eyes probing. *Invested.* That was the word he used. He wasn't invested in feeding the homeless, though, at least as a primary goal. He was invested in me. "I need you to trust me, Moxie. That's the real barrier we can't quite overcome."

Someone sighed. It was me. "This is all coming as a surprise to me," I said finally. "I don't know what to make of it."

"Then we'll talk it out together." He held up his hand again. "It's time to take a walk with me." He was offering me more than a walk. I had to meet him halfway.

I didn't respond with words. Instead, I threaded my fingers through his, my eyes never leaving his face.

"You're still absorbing," he noted as he gave me a gentle tug to start crossing the street. "I think we should walk while you're absorbing."

"Where are we going to walk?" I asked dumbly.

"Where do you want to go?"

I used to have an answer to that question. I wanted to go to wherever I could make a name for myself as a bar promoter. I wanted to be someone important, the sort of person who didn't get left by a father who was shirking his responsibilities. I wanted to be someone who lived large, who wasn't being held back by a frightened mother. Now I wasn't so sure.

"Let's go to the river," I said automatically.

"Sure." Gus was amiable as we fell into step together. "Can I ask you a question?" he asked when we'd walked a block.

"No Truth or Dare?"

"I think we're beyond that."

I happened to agree. "Then sure. Ask away."

"What have you seen since you've been here?"

I wasn't sure what he was asking. "Two nights ago, I saw a glass trailer being hauled behind a pickup truck. Inside there was a stripper pole and a good twelve women dancing around it for a bachelorette party. Only half of them were wearing bras... or tops."

He burst out laughing. "That is not the answer I was expecting."

"What answer were you expecting?"

"I was going to invite you on a date this weekend. I thought I could take you over to the Garden District, show you my favorite cemetery, take you to dinner at Commander's Palace. I even thought we could ride the streetcars. It's a bit touristy, but I love this city. I kind of want to see it through your eyes, and I've only ever been in the French Quarter with you."

"Oh." I felt as if my heart were growing bigger. "We could probably do that. I'll have to check with Abel though."

"I've already done that."

"Of course, you have." I cracked a smile. "Are you going to show me your city?"

"I'm going to spend time with you," he replied. "Time away from work... and competing jobs... and your father... and my parents."

"And Damon," I added.

"Definitely Damon," he agreed. "I think that's what we both need, a chance to get to know one another without you believing we hate one another."

I turned sheepish. "I didn't hate you."

He slanted his eyes toward me, clearly unconvinced. "You didn't hate me," he conceded after a beat. "You thought you hated me though."

"Yes, well, my heart isn't always smart."

He grinned. "Your heart is unique. That's one of the things I like best about you. You give of yourself without thinking and yet you still want to win. There are very few people who can pull that off and still be likable."

"And I'm one of them?"

"You are... more than I ever could've imagined." He dragged me through the crowd of people bedding down for the night when we reached Jackson Square. Several of them waved and called out, but the wrappers being collected for the trash confirmed the story about the subs. He had indeed come through... again.

"It's going to storm," he noted just as a rumble of thunder rocked the ground.

I jerked my head over my shoulder to check on the people stretching out on benches and wasn't surprised to find them getting to their feet. Benji wasn't with them again tonight. I was starting to get worried... and yet the only thing I could focus on was Gus.

"They'll find cover," Gus said, his lips brushing my ear when he spoke. I hadn't realized how close he'd gotten until a shiver ran down my spine. "They know how to survive on the street."

They did.

"They know how to live," he added.

I nodded. "Yeah." Did I know how to live? When I turned, a fierceness gripped my heart as I regarded him. "What do you want more than anything in this world?" The question was barely a whisper.

His eyes lit with wicked delight. "See, I don't think I should answer that. You're not ready."

He was wrong there. "Try me." I grabbed the front of his shirt and went in for a torrid kiss. This time I was the one pushing him into an alcove.

He let me guide him, his eyes momentarily searching mine. He must've been okay with what he found when he studied me because he embraced the kiss with a lot of enthusiasm. And tongue. There was a lot of tongue too.

When we'd first kissed, the exchange had almost been chaste. Sure, it had spiraled into something else pretty quickly. Nothing about this kiss was chaste. No, things were unbelievably dirty... just how I wanted them.

His head rattled against one of the storm shutters affixed to the wall, but he didn't complain. Instead, he moved his hands from my waist to my ass in record time and squeezed. "I knew it," he gasped between kisses.

"You knew what?" I was confused, and the limited light filtering into the alcove made it impossible to see his features.

"I knew that all that running you do in the mornings was going to lead to something fantastic." He gave me another squeeze and then nipped in to kiss me. "Now I want more of...

that." He caught my lower lip between his and made a growling sound. "I want a lot more of that."

He wasn't the only one. I plastered myself against him, not caring in the least that the humidity was making sweaty fools of us both. Somewhere behind us, near the Square, I could hear catcalls. Were they directed at us? Someone else passing by? I no longer cared. At this point, there was nothing that could drag me from this alcove... and especially this man.

"We're going to need to talk tomorrow," Gus warned, his eyes glinting, thanks to one of the gas-powered streetlights. The natural flame gave him a dangerous look. "I don't want you getting weird... or freaking out... or thinking this is some passing thing. I want a real plan."

I was taken aback. "You're not a planner."

"No, but you are. That's how I know you'll stick to the plan."

I stared hard into his eyes, debating. He wasn't part of my plan. He knew that, which was why he wanted me to adjust the plan so there was room for him. Could I? Being rigid had gotten me places I never dreamed. Could it get me him? The idea sent a shudder down my spine.

"Look at me, Moxie," he said in a low voice as he gripped me tightly against him, his hands never leaving my ass as he squeezed. "I'm not asking you for forever right now. We need to spend time together, out in the open and not playing games. I'm asking you not to make your decision about us until we've had that time."

It was a simple request, I realized. He needed reassurance too. I had qualms about his family and things from his past that had been hinted at, but I didn't yet know about. He likely had the same qualms about me. Trust was earned, not freely given. We would both have to earn it.

"Fine." I kept my voice low. "I won't make any decisions right away... unless you're bad in bed."

He made a snorting sound.

"I'm being serious," I insisted. "I haven't dreamed about you a hundred times to have it go badly. No pressure though." I sent him an impish grin.

"A hundred times, huh?" His fingers trailed down my cheek, and for some reason, that simple gesture felt desperately intimate.

"No pressure," I repeated.

He grinned. "I have you beat. I dreamed about you two hundred times."

I wasn't certain if he could see my eye roll, but he'd been around me enough to know exactly how I was reacting. "It's not a competition."

"Of course not. I've already won." He nipped in for a small kiss. It wasn't sexy, and yet goose pimples broke out on my arms. "No weirdness in the morning," he warned. "We're jumping ahead a little bit. I thought it would take longer for you to accept you had feelings for me when it was pointed out to you."

I was beyond confused. "Excuse me?"

"You're not the only one who can enact a plan." He scooped his hand over my hair and rested his forehead against mine, his eyes shut as he hummed a song I recognized from somewhere in the Quarter.

"What's that?"

"Hmm?" He sighed as he opened his eyes. "Have I ever mentioned that I love parade music?"

I shook my head. "No. Is that what you were humming?"

He nodded. "When I was a kid, I loved the French Quarter. Like... absolutely loved it. I would beg my parents to bring me here every weekend. They weren't big fans. They liked to keep me isolated in Uptown because they thought it was less likely I would run into bad influences there. And Marigny and Bywater? Forget it. They were strictly forbidden."

AVERY KANE

I had no idea where he was going with this.

"I would sneak away though," he continued with a smile, his thumb moving back and forth across my cheek. "I would use my streetcar pass and come down here when I was supposed to be doing something for school. My whole goal was to see a parade. I loved the pomp and circumstance, even though my parents would roll their eyes whenever I brought up parade music."

"And that's what you're thinking about now?" I was beyond confused.

"That's what I'm thinking about now," he confirmed, grinding himself against me. "Did you know that you can throw your own parade? It's like creating a reward for yourself."

My lips curved into a smile. "Is that what this is? Are you creating a reward for yourself?"

"We're creating a reward together." This time when he pressed his lips to mine, the heat was back. "I need to spend some quality time with you," he gritted out.

I couldn't stop myself from laughing. "Is that what we're calling it now?"

He shrugged. "I don't care what we call it. If you're not ready though..." He trailed off, as if regrouping. His tone was firm when he spoke again. "I need you to want me. If you're not ready, though, we have time. I can wait. I just want to be able to spend time with you."

I studied his face for hints that he was lying—or perhaps forcing himself to say something he didn't believe. I found nothing but earnest devotion. I made up my mind on the spot. "I don't need time. I know what I want."

"Is it me?"

I nodded. "Yeah... even though I convinced myself it could never be you."

He swooped in for another kiss. "Does that mean you're

finally ready to see my place?" He inclined his head toward the building to our right. It was only then that I realized we were in front of the Jax building.

I bit my bottom lip and nodded. Nerves crashed through me, and yet I knew I was ready.

"I need you to say it," he said quietly. "I need to be sure. I cannot take it if you look me in the eye tomorrow and tell me it was a mistake."

"I'm sure," I promised. He was beautiful up close. Heck, he was beautiful from far away too. That smile was so achingly sweet, it caused my heart to swell. "I won't regret you, Gus."

"Good, because I think I might burst soon." He gave me one more kiss and then grabbed my hand. He didn't bother fixing his hair before starting across the road. "Come on. Let's get off the street."

That reminded me of something. "Did you know that people saw us last night and nobody was surprised by what they saw?"

He snorted. "I knew people had seen us. I've had it brought up six or seven times. I was wondering if anyone would be brave enough to bring it up to you." He stopped at a door with a security panel and fumbled for his wallet. "I have to grab my key card. I forgot."

I was amused when I realized his fingers were shaking. Apparently, he was as nervous as I was. "Here." I took his wallet from him and deftly pulled out the key card that had been giving him all the trouble. I kept my gaze locked with his as I waved the card in front of the light. "I guess I'm not the only one who is in danger of freaking out, huh?"

His smile was back in an instant. "Do you want to freak out together?"

"I've had worse offers."

He swept open the door. "Come on, baby. I think it's time to make our own parade."

Twenty-Five

I hadn't grown up poor. Sure, there were times when my mother had to tighten our belts to get through a month, but only once did I remember finding my mother crying because she was having trouble with the bills. That was a rough stretch. I was nine and couldn't yet contribute to the household finances. She worked out a deal with a neighbor to watch me so she could balance two jobs. That lasted for almost a year. When she was finished and we were no longer teetering on the edge, she explained how it would never happen again. She'd taught me how to balance a checkbook when I was thirteen and about budgeting when I was fourteen. I never got in financial trouble because of that.

The world Gus lived in was like something out of a fairy tale. Even though I'd never yearned for great riches—other than the ordinary daydreaming, of course—the opulence of the Jax building had my eyes going wide.

"Hello, Mr. Kingman," a deep voice boomed when we were on the other side of the door, causing me to freeze in my place.

"Hey, Jordan," Gus replied easily, keeping a firm grip on

my hand as I focused on the huge individual sitting behind a desk in the lobby. He had several monitors going, and it was pretty easy to figure out that he was security. That meant Gus lived in a building with twenty-four-hour security, which meant the digs were probably even more fantastic than I had envisioned.

"Moxie, this is Jordan Dorn. He's on security here a few nights a week."

"Moxie, huh?" Jordan's expression was hard to read as he looked me up and down.

Instantly I smoothed my hand over my waist and realized I was still wearing my Cher apron. I'd forgotten to take it off.

Gus calmly captured my free hand. "She'll probably be stopping in on a regular basis from here on out." His tone was authoritative. "I know you guys have paperwork if I want to get her a key card. Can you leave a note for the day shift so they deliver the paperwork tomorrow?"

"Absolutely." Jordan bobbed his head. "You know there's a fee if you have to cancel a card, right?"

I wasn't quite sure what he was asking. Gus clearly didn't like it because he made a face. "I won't be canceling the key card." He nudged me toward the elevator. "Don't worry about it, okay?"

Jordan nodded, but I didn't miss the way his gaze swept over me. He clearly didn't think I belonged there.

I waited until we were going up in the elevator to speak. "What's the deal with the keycards?"

"It's nothing for you to worry about." Gus looked annoyed, but not with me.

"I just want to understand."

He blew out a sigh. "This building has many fine offerings. I love the location. There's nothing better than heading out to the riverwalk every morning and not having to go out of my way to get there. I love how close it is to Jackson Square. I actually like the security because this is a town where drunks run rampant."

"But?" I hedged.

"But there's a certain mindset that goes along with high HOA fees that I'm not always comfortable with. Not all the units here are... opulent. I guess that's the word I would use. Most of the people who have units in this building don't live here full time."

I tried to wrap my head around that. "I don't understand."

"It's a winter place for some. It's a weekend place for others. I would guess that only a quarter of the tenants live here year-round. Also, short-term rentals are banned. That means the building is pretty quiet."

"That sounds safe."

He snorted and shook his head. "It's actually more lonely than anything else. I don't know my neighbors. The security guys, while nice, have a job to do. They're supposed to keep outsiders from getting inside."

"And that would be me."

"That would be anyone who can't afford twenty-four-hour security."

"So... me."

He shook his head as the elevator dinged to alert us that we'd reached our destination. "Trust me, Moxie. What you've got going on with your friends is so much better. That feels like a home even though you're renting. This is... something else."

The hallway was quiet as he led me to the far end. He had to wave the same key card to get inside, and when I saw where he was living, the place he was basically making apologies for, my mouth went dry.

"This is..." I couldn't find the appropriate words.

"Sterile," he provided.

"I was going to say really cool." I shot him a lopsided grin and headed straight for the windows. They were ornate, with slatted blinds setting off thick glass. One entire wall of the condo was lined with windows. "You have a view of the Mississippi."

"Yup. I happen to love the view."

"Do you have a balcony?"

"More of a terrace patio."

"Can I see it?"

He laughed and nodded, pressing his hand to my back as he led me to a door. Calling it a patio felt somehow disingenuous. It was walled in, keeping a small pool and fanciful hot tub hidden from prying eyes.

"This is incredible." I shook my head as I looked around. "You can see half the Quarter from here. You have the river on one side and Jackson Square on the other. It's... amazing. It's beautiful."

"I think other things are more beautiful."

When I turned to face him, I found him watching me with intense eyes. "You know I'm going to want to get into that hot tub eventually, right?" I challenged.

He nodded. "We can get in now if you want."

"I think it can wait." This time I was the one to reach out and grab his hand. "Give me a tour."

"Sure. Any particular room you want to start with?"

"Your bedroom sounds fun."

He sucked in a breath, his eyes drifting back to me. "You don't have to if you're not ready."

"I thought we already talked about this."

"We did, but you can change your mind."

"What if I don't want to change my mind?"

"Then I'll be a happy man."

"So... show me your bedroom."

He stood next to the door and stared directly into my eyes.

His lips were mere inches from mine, but he didn't lean in. Instead, he traced his fingers over my face and studied me hard. I wondered if he was preparing for a test.

"The first time I wanted to kiss you was that day we took shelter in Pirate's Alley," he said out of nowhere. "We were so close. I swear I could feel your heart beating. My heart matched the rhythm, and it was... exciting. Do you know when the last time I felt excited over simply being in the same place with someone was?"

"On one of your trips?"

"No. Those trips, at least the most recent ones, were all for business. I wasn't dating anyone on those trips."

"Really? I heard the Kingman brothers were notorious in these parts. Someone said you guys have left a trail of broken hearts ten miles deep in your wake."

"Someone said that? Who is this someone?"

I decided to play coy. "I have no idea."

"You're full of it." He broke into a grin. "I'm guessing it was your roommates. I guess I'm going to have to put in some effort to charm them, huh?"

"They're not technically my roommates."

"Close enough." His lips were so close to mine I could practically feel the friction. "I know you felt something that day in Pirate's Alley. I need to know what."

I licked my lips, enjoying the way his eyes lit up when he registered the action. "I felt annoyed." I opted to tell the truth. "I wasn't annoyed with you. Well, not totally." I smiled at the memory. "You were full of yourself, and that was most definitely annoying. I was annoyed with myself, though, because you made my heart race... and my breath was all gaspy... and I really wanted to fist my hands in your hair and smother you with my mouth."

He laughed at my description. "You hid your feelings well."

"I didn't want to have feelings for you, Gus. I was pretty certain it was a mistake I didn't need."

"Do you still feel that way?"

"Now I feel afraid." I grabbed his wrist and pressed my fingers to his pulse point. His heart was racing in tandem with mine. Again. They always matched one another. "I think you're afraid too."

"I am." He rested his forehead against mine, seemingly happy for the contact and yet content to keep dragging things out. "In this town, people bow to the Kingman name. It was something I registered a long time ago. It was something understood. It's also something that my brothers and parents feed off."

"But not you."

"I was raised to think that was important. That's not me though. I want someone to like me—or dislike me, for that matter—because of who I am, not who I was born to become in the eyes of the elitists in this town."

And that was when the truth finally became clear. "You want to be your own man."

"Yup, and you want to be your own woman."

"Yeah."

"We can have something together and still be ourselves. I need you to understand that going in. I don't want you to think you can only have your job because that's not true. You can have everything that you want. I don't expect you to choose me over anything."

While a nice sentiment, it fell short. "See, that's where you're wrong, Gus." I pressed my hand to his cheek and smiled when I realized he was doing the same thing, only from the other side. "It's not choosing someone over something else. It's choosing someone in tandem with something else. It's okay to want more than one thing."

"Do you want more than one thing?"

"Do you?"

He stared hard into my eyes. "You just can't be the first one to admit something, can you?" He let out a small laugh. "It's fine. I'll be the first. Just remember, I'm always going to bring this up. This is the competition I won."

I frowned. "I don't know what you mean."

"I want multiple things, Moxie." He was earnest as he regarded me. "I want you. I want to make a name for myself that's separate from my family. I thought I had to go to another country to do that, but I was wrong. I can do it here. I don't just want one thing. I want *all* things, and you're a very big part of that."

My heart squeezed.

"Now it's your turn to tell me what you want," he prodded.

"I want multiple things too," I admitted. "I want to make something of myself, something my mother would be proud of. More than acknowledgement, though, I want to be happy in my own skin. I don't think I ever have been. For the first time in—well, ever—I want to be happy with a person too. I didn't even know I wanted it until I realized I was already halfway there."

His grin lit up his entire features. "That was a really good answer."

"I'm not always good with words," I admitted.

"I think you're better than you think you are." He traced his thumb over my bottom lip. "We still have things to discuss. I want to come up with a plan that works for both of us. I think I might explode if I don't get to kiss you again though."

"Oh, that might be the most romantic thing anybody has ever said to me," I teased.

"I can do better. I just need to take the edge off." He leaned in and pressed his lips to mine, tentative at first then more insistent. Within seconds, the kiss had turned so hot it was as if bubbling lava were pouring from him to me.

Somehow—and part of me thought I would always wonder about this—all of the oxygen disappeared from the room. We gasped into each other's mouths, my hands fisting in his shirt as his hands found my butt again.

"Bed," he growled as he dragged me through the penthouse. "No more waiting."

I laughed at his urgency, delighting in the need that he was more than happy to put on display. I didn't bother looking around his bedroom when he kicked in the door. There would be plenty of time for a proper tour later. Instead, I focused on him, on the way he kept his eyes open as we kissed and the little sighs he made as our tongues started to tangle.

I expected him to be smooth in the bedroom—he was a Kingman after all and likely had tons of practice—but the first thing he did when trying to strip off his jeans was trip because he'd forgotten to take off his shoes.

"Son of a bitch," he growled when he landed on the hardwood floor. He seemed surprised at the predicament he found himself in, the bottom of his jeans wrestling with the sneakers he should've discarded first.

I bent over at the waist and broke into raucous laughter. I couldn't help myself. He was always different from what I expected. Instead of ego, I found generosity. Instead of haughty laughter, I found warm chuckles. Instead of superiority, there was delightful self-deprecation. He was the whole package.

"Would you like some help?" I asked when I'd recovered.

"I'm stuck," he complained, fruitlessly pulling on the ends of the jeans. "This is my punishment or something. There can be no other explanation."

I plopped down on the floor with him. He hadn't bothered with hitting the lights, but I could still make out his features thanks to the ambient illumination shining in from the street. "Here." I tugged on his left shoe, yanking it off with little problem. I had to grapple with his right shoe because it was buried in the denim but finally managed it.

Once he was free, I looked to him expectantly. I thought for sure he would tackle me he was so excited. Instead, I found something else reflected back at me from his eyes. It was something I wasn't expecting... and couldn't identify.

"What?" Suddenly I was self-conscious and reached up to order my hair. I had no doubt it was a mess because his hands had been in and out of it multiple times over the last hour.

"You're beautiful," he replied. "You're just... really beautiful."

My heart rolled for a different reason. "I kind of like you too," I teased, trying to get things back on track. "You're pretty handsome when you're not being full of yourself."

He grinned and snagged me around the waist, pulling me to him as he stood. I was breathless when he somehow managed to swing me up in his arms and stand at the same time.

"Do you work out?" I deadpanned.

He angled his head so his mouth was directly above mine. "I guess you're about to find out." He hesitated and then barreled forward. "No regrets, right?" He seemed to need one more bout of reassurance.

"No regrets," I confirmed, cupping his face. His skin was ridiculously soft, and I found I wanted to rub myself all over him, burrow inside that warmth and live there. "Gus," I said after a full sixty seconds of staring into his eyes.

"Hmm." He almost looked as if he were in a trance.

"I think the time for talking is over."

"I was just coming to that conclusion myself," he agreed. "Are you ready to play a new game?"

"No. It's the same game. We're just finally getting to the dares."

He barked out a laugh. "Now there's an idea. I dare you to let me take you to a new place, Moxie."

"Sure. Let's see what you've got."

Twenty-Six

The night came to me in bits and pieces as I began to stir.

Gus's mouth on my neck... and breasts... and other places. The little words he whispered. The way his fingertips glided over my collarbone on their way down. He was good, better than I'd imagined. I thought money would've made him lazy in the sex department. I was never so happy to be wrong.

"Hey," he murmured in my ear when he realized I was awake, his lips brushing against the sensitive ridge. He'd spooned behind me when falling asleep and apparently hadn't moved for the entire night. His body was warm against mine, rigid and yet soft at the same time. It felt magical.

Then I felt something else.

"Again?"

He barked out a laugh as he shifted to hold me tighter. "I can't help it. Mornings do that to me."

"We did it three times last night."

"Three glorious times," he agreed. His lips were busy

against my neck. "If you give me a few seconds, we can hit number four. I prefer even numbers."

That sounded like a load of crap if I'd ever heard it. "Oh, really?"

"Yes, really."

"Well... I'm thinking not." I rolled so I was facing him, taking a moment to absorb his messy hair and amused eyes. His features were softer in the morning somehow, which shouldn't be possible. The grit on his cheeks felt like sand-paper under my fingertips... and yet I couldn't stop rubbing his jawline.

"Are you done with me already?" The question was asked in jest, but legitimate fear was in his eyes.

"No. I have big plans for you. I happen to like odd numbers though. I was thinking we could take a break, grab some breakfast, and then hit it twice more before I have to head home and get changed for work." The realization that the world hadn't stopped turning during our time together had me glancing at the clock. "Or maybe we'll only be able to fit in once if I want to be on time."

His lips quirked. "So... you don't regret last night?" There was hope in his eyes.

"I don't regret it." I didn't say it because he needed to hear it. I said it because it was the truth. "Last night was pretty good."

"Pretty good?" He cocked a challenging eyebrow.

"Pretty good," I confirmed.

"I'll have you know that last night was perfect," he coun-tered. "Abso-freaking-lutely perfect. I used all my best moves."

I practically choked on my laughter. "Are you saying you have no moves left? Maybe I do have to rethink this. I thought you would be wowing me for days."

"I'm going to wow you forever."

I stilled. Had he meant to say that? If he had, what did he

mean by it? *Crap!* Was I suddenly going to start driving myself crazy with questions? I was a woman who liked a plan. I liked lists. I couldn't ask his intentions after the first night. Nobody knew their intentions after the first night.

"Moxie." His voice was soft, making me realize he'd nuzzled his nose against my cheek. "Are you freaking out now?"

What answer did he want? "Maybe a little," I conceded.

"Is it because I said the word 'forever' without context?"

I hesitated. "Um..."

"Yeah." He was all business when he rolled to his back. Sneaky as he was, he had his arm under my body when he did it and brought me along for the ride, not stopping until I was on top of him.

There was no mirror to check my reflection. I knew I likely looked wrecked. I hadn't bothered to remove my makeup the night before. Thankfully, the New Orleans heat usually had my makeup sweating away to nothing by three o'clock most days although I might have a bit of raccoon eyes to worry about. Gus's gaze was so intense I realized he didn't care about the way I looked. He only wanted to make things better for me.

"I'm not going to pressure you because I think that will set us back," he said in that soft way of his. He was loud when he wanted to be, but when he wanted to make a point, he always softened things up. It was appealing, although I wondered if he even realized that. "I know you like to work things out in your head, but I do want to be with you. That means for more than one night."

I was rueful when I lifted my eyes to his. "I might be a bit of a freak sometimes."

"*No.*" He dragged out the word in sarcastic fashion then grinned. "I never would've guessed."

"This wasn't in my plan." I opted for honesty. "I wanted to hate you when we first met."

"Even though I was nothing but charming."

"Yes, a charming launch stealer."

"Ugh." The groaning sound he let loose reverberated through the room as he shifted beneath me. We'd both fallen asleep naked, which meant there was no barrier between us as he held me tight. "You have got to let that go."

"Just as soon as you admit you planned your launch in an effort to steal mine." Technically he'd already admitted it. I wanted to hear him say it again.

"It was a coincidence."

"Whatever." I forced myself to remain upbeat even though it was my natural reaction to pout. "So, what were we talking about anyway?"

"How my raw animal magnetism can break down the walls of even the prickliest of women."

My eyes narrowed. "I am not prickly."

He gyrated his hips, rubbing himself against me. "I am. I'm also ready to discuss our breakfast plans—and everything else—whenever you finish what you feel you need to say about our future. That doesn't appear to be happening though."

He was right. I was meandering. "I can't remember what I was going to say."

"I believe it was something about how you didn't want a boyfriend and now you have one."

There was a dare in his tone and words. "I didn't want a boyfriend," I conceded. "I'm not sure how this is going to work."

A muscle operated in his jaw, but he remained quiet.

"I want to try to figure out how to work it though," I said finally. This time I said it for him... and maybe for myself too. "It's going to be weird."

His grin was lightning quick upon my admission. "It's

really not," he promised, his fingers trailing up my spine. "We both have jobs to do. We already spend every morning together. We also walk home together every night. We see each other regularly throughout the day. The only thing that will change is where we sleep."

When thinking about it like that, I realized he was right. "We were dating before I even realized it," I blurted.

He laughed so hard I thought he would choke on his tongue. "You're not wrong," he said when he'd recovered. "Unfortunately, I got none of the perks of us dating until last night. You wouldn't even hold my hand. It was so insulting."

"But..."

"No." He shook his head and pressed his finger to my lips. "We don't need to define it. We just need to enjoy it. Do you think you can do that?"

"Probably," I conceded after a few seconds.

"Probably?"

"I have questions."

"Oh, here we go." He wiggled himself against me again, showing no signs that he was going to roll me over and engage in an encore presentation despite his frisky nature. "Lay them on me."

Well, since he was open to the conversation and all, I really had no choice but to do just that. "Are we going to sleep together every night?"

"I don't know that we need hard and fast rules. I have no interest in sleeping apart from you, but if you need space, then you just have to tell me."

For some reason, simply hearing him lay it out like that filled me with relief. "I don't need space."

"Good to know."

"If you're a butthead, I might need space though."

"Also good to know."

I chewed on my bottom lip. "Just out of curiosity, will we

always be spending the night here?" It seemed like the easiest route since he lived alone. It also gave him all the power. I was eager to gauge his reaction.

"No." He immediately shook his head. "I like your friends. I have no doubt they'll start hating me if I keep you away from them. I figure we can play it by ear. My environment is much more sterile. I expect to spend the night at your place though."

"It's nowhere near as nice as this place."

"I think you're calling me a snob."

"No, I just... I mean, I don't even have a bed frame. My bed is a mattress on the floor. I also rent... and the walls are kind of paper thin."

"That's okay. Knowing your friends are listening to us have sex will make me feel manly, especially when you say, 'Oh, Gus, nobody has ever satisfied me the way you do.' For the record, I expect to record you saying that and send it to Damon in a voice memo."

My eyes went wide.

"And I'm joking," he said quickly. "I would never record you. I might, however, beat the crap out of Damon if he ever shows up again."

"What are the odds of that? Also, for the record, if you'd told me we were dating before I had dinner with him, I likely wouldn't have gone out with him in the first place."

"I shouldn't have to tell you that we're dating. I wanted you to come to that realization on your own."

"I guess I can see that." I rested my head on his chest, my fingers tracing the sparse hair he had going there. "Do you manscape?"

I could feel him contorting to get a look at my face. "Is that really what you want to ask?"

I shrugged. "I think it's a fair question. We're getting to know one another, right?"

"I guess. I might manscape a little."

"Define might?"

"Let's talk about something else. You mentioned breakfast. I know we normally hit Jackson Square so we can verbally copulate in public there, but how would you feel about getting food delivered this morning and actually copulating here instead?"

"I guess I could be convinced. I'm going to need a good breakfast though. I feel weak after last night. You sexed all my energy out of me."

"A huge NOLA breakfast it is." He lightly patted my bottom. "How about you make a list of questions you have while I'm ordering, huh? If we time it right, we might be able to get through them by the time we're finished eating."

Oddly, it was comforting that he knew me as well as he did. "Good idea. I'm going to need a piece of paper."

"Somehow I knew you would say that."

WHEN GUS SAID HE WAS ORDERING FOOD, apparently he meant it. He had to go downstairs long enough to retrieve our breakfast, which allowed me to climb into a pair of his boxer shorts and a T-shirt, and I was already rooting through his refrigerator when he walked back into the penthouse.

"You have like eight types of beer in here and no juice," I pointed out as a I straightened, pulling up short when I got a look at his face. "What's wrong?"

He shook his head. "Baby, you need to learn to read a face. I wasn't making a 'what's wrong' one. I was making a 'geez, I totally need to get you naked again' one. We'll work on that though."

He moved closer to me and pressed a kiss to my forehead. The sigh he let loose said he'd been dying to do it, which seemed odd because we'd been apart for a grand total of five minutes. He leaned in close, and I was certain he was going to give me a different type of kiss, the type that meant I wouldn't be getting my breakfast. Instead, he whispered. "Open the other side of the refrigerator."

The anticipation that had been pooling in my stomach died in an instant. "What?"

He laughed. "You're adorable in the morning. Sure, you're a tad slow, but that happens to do it for me. I guess we lucked out there." He inclined his head toward the right-side handle. "Open the other door."

I did as he instructed, my eyes lighting up when I saw the cornucopia of juices laid out. "Just out of curiosity, do you actually drink this juice, or is it for mixers?"

"A man needs to leave some secrets for second-date discovery."

I nodded. "True story. Which one do you want?"

"I thought I would make coffee."

"You need juice too. It's healthy."

"Oh, really? I'm not much of a juice drinker."

"You need stamina for after breakfast." I had no idea why I was being so insistent. I just wanted to win an argument, however minor.

He seemed to realize that, too, because he nodded. "I'll take the grapefruit."

"Awesome." I grabbed a bottle of grapefruit for him and tomato for me.

"Your breath is going to smell if you drink that tomato juice," he complained as he carried the food into the living room. He didn't even give the kitchen table a second glance.

"I happen to like tomato juice," I said as I followed him. "You'll survive."

"Tomato juice is only good for Bloody Marys."

"I guess that answers the question about the juice," I

drawled as I got comfortable next to him. "Where did you get the takeout from?"

"Oceana."

"I've never eaten there. Is it good?"

He grinned. "Breakfast at Oceana is a Bourbon Street necessity. They have this bowl—it's like a big freaking pasta bowl—and they serve biscuits and gravy in it. It's like a big pasta bowl of soupy biscuits and gravy. It's perfection."

"How do you know I like biscuits and gravy?" I happened to love biscuits and gravy. I also liked being difficult. Since we were in his home and he seemed to know things I didn't, I wanted to regain a modicum of control.

"Oh, see, I knew better than ordering for you even when you said you would eat anything." His eyes twinkled. "I got omelets. Eggs and hash browns. There's sides of bacon and sausage links in there. They were out of the patty sausage this morning, even though that's my favorite. There are pancakes, waffles, and French toast in there. That's on top of the biscuits and gravy. If you can't find something to eat, then there's something wrong with you."

He had a point. "I want the omelet."

"Fine."

"And the sausage links."

He made a flirty face. "I think I can make that work. I'm a bacon man myself."

"I want to try the bowl of biscuits and gravy too."

"We can share those." He leaned in, his nose touching mine. "How much do you think we can eat without making ourselves sick?" His voice was breathy.

"I have no idea. I guess we're going to find out."

"Yeah. What does the winner get?" He studied me as confusion took over. "You like to make competitions out of things. What does the winner get in this case?"

"Oh, um..." I popped my lips. "The winner gets to be the boss when we head back to the bedroom."

"Oh, see, that's the best thing you could've possibly said." He gave me a deep kiss. "That right there is the sort of competition I love. We both win when those are the sorts of games we play."

"Yeah."

We dug in, and the only sounds for a good ten minutes were the yummy noises we made as we inhaled the huge amount of food he'd had delivered. I didn't consider myself a dainty eater, but I went at the biscuits and gravy as if I were a *Lord of the Rings* dwarf on holiday, which had Gus laughing so hard he fell into the pillows that decorated his couch. I joined him, lost to a magical interlude, but the moment couldn't last. That was when the sound of twin throats clearing had me jerking my head toward the door. My mouth went slack when I realized Archer and Aidan had gained entry to the penthouse... and they were watching us.

"What are you doing here?" Gus demanded when he realized his brothers had invaded his space... and without knocking. "I told you to give those keys back. I must've been crazy when I gave them to you in the first place."

"You gave them to us in case you needed someone to water your plants if you decided to take off again," Archer drawled. His gaze was entirely for me, and it made me distinctly uncomfortable. "Who is your friend?"

I expected Gus to turn weird in front of his brothers. In fact, I figured the magic of the moment was going to be completely forgotten now that real life had come crashing down on us. We were from two different worlds after all. How was this supposed to work?

"This is Moxie," Gus replied, not missing a beat. "You've met her. She's the manager of Cher."

"Ah, the bar right across the road from Flambeaux." Archer looked me up and down. "I remember you."

"You're the girl Gus won't stop talking about," Aidan teased as he moved around the couch to survey the extra food. "Are you feeding an army we don't know about?"

"We wanted choices," Gus said. "You can eat the extra."

"Oceana?" Aidan looked hopeful. "Mom is on a gluten-free kick again. I would love an Oceana breakfast."

"Then maybe you should move out of our parents' house," Gus suggested. He shot me an apologetic smile. "Archer and Aidan show up here on a regular basis to hide from our parents. I apologize in advance for them being the kings of the tools. They can't help themselves."

That was a lot of information to digest in a short amount of time. "Wait... are you saying your brothers still live with your parents?" That was the thing that stuck out most.

"Yup. They're total losers."

"Says the guy who let Mom and Dad buy him a penthouse," Archer scoffed. He'd already grabbed one of the uneaten boxes of food and was making himself comfortable.

"Oh, see, that's where you're wrong." Gus wagged his finger. "I took a loan from Mom and Dad for the down payment on this place. I pay my mortgage each month. On top of that, I pay money to them for what I owe. I'm not quite the deadbeat you guys are."

"Hey, they have cooks and maids," Aidan said. "I don't want to move out on my own. Then I'll have to do my own laundry."

The conversation was surreal. It was something else too. It was enlightening. I'd thought there was something odd about Gus's relationship with his brothers—and there was—but there was something normal about it too. They were different people in front of their parents. For some reason, it made me like them more. It also gave me endless fodder to mess with them.

"So, I want to know what Gus has said about me," I said as I returned to my endless bowl of biscuits and gravy. "You guys knew who I was. That means he's been talking."

"Oh, he's been mooning over you for weeks," Aidan confirmed. "It was pathetic."

"Totally," Archer agreed. "If you share information on what he's been up to, though, we'll share information with you."

"Yeah, that's not going to happen." Gus was insistent. "She's my girlfriend. You're going to tell her nothing."

Archer's eyes gleamed with amusement. "Yeah, you're going to have a rough morning, little brother. You'd better buckle up and suck it up."

Ah, finally, I was going to get something I wanted for a change. Information was key, and I finally had access to the good stuff.

Twenty-Seven

Aidan and Archer weren't as horrible as I had envisioned. They were entitled, but I wasn't sure there was a possibility of them turning out any other way given how they'd been raised. My brief interaction with them before wasn't indicative of who they really were.

"So... you lived in Michigan?" Archer shoveled food in his mouth and gave me a long once-over. "Have you ever been caught in a gang shooting?"

I didn't bother to hide my annoyance at the question. "Michigan is more than Detroit."

"Sure. Sure." He bobbed his head. "That means you were in the Upper Peninsula, right?" He sounded knowledgeable. Unfortunately, that only made the statement all the more moronic.

"No, I grew up in Oakland County. That's a suburb of Detroit."

"So you have seen a gang shooting. Interesting." Archer flicked his eyes to Gus. "You're going to want to be careful with this one, Augie. She's likely to be packing heat. If she catches your eye wandering, she'll shoot it out of your head."

Augie? I flicked my eyes to Gus.

"Don't ever call me that," he warned, as if reading my mind. "I hate that name."

"That's why he calls you that," I surmised. "Well played, Archie."

Archer's expression turned dark. "Did he tell you to call me that?"

I snorted. "No. It simply made sense given what you called him." Now it was Aidan's turn for my studied gaze. "I would call you Aidie, but that doesn't make sense as an insult. It's not annoying enough." Something occurred to me. "They called you Aida, right?"

Aidan groaned. "She's smarter than you by a long shot, Gus," he complained. "You'd better run now."

Rather than agree, Gus offered up a shrug. "I kind of like that she's smart."

"Yeah, but her name is Moxie," Archer pointed out. "That can't be a real name. You know what that means."

All three men nodded knowingly, making the fact that they looked so similar jarring.

"What does that mean?" I asked, playing the game.

"It means you're hiding a terrible name," Aidan replied. "Let me guess... is it Sloane?"

That was so not what I was expecting. "No... and why would you think that?"

"I dated a girl named Sloane." He took on a far-off expression. "She had seven toes on one foot and swore it wasn't because her parents were actually first cousins."

"Ah, Sloane Butterfield," Archer said knowingly. "Her parents *were* cousins, but nobody was supposed to comment on it. She had a brother, Sly, and his lips wouldn't move in tandem." As if to bolster what he was talking about, he grabbed his top lip and pinched it with his fingers and tried to talk. "The beignets are particularly lovely this morning," he slurred.

I didn't want to laugh—making fun of people for obnoxious reasons rather than in good fun was never an acceptable thing, in my book—but I couldn't stop myself. "That is... appalling. Were their parents really first cousins?"

"Oh yeah." Archer let go of his lip. "Everybody knew about it. Everybody whispered about it. Nobody could bring it up to them though."

"People said Sly had a third nipple, but he was excused from gym class for four years straight," Aidan said. "We never got to see if it was true."

I looked at Gus to see if they were telling the truth and found him nodding.

"You guys grew up in a very strange world, didn't you?" I asked.

Gus shrugged. "It was normal to us, which makes it all the sadder. You can't tell me that your life was all cool cats and color-coordinated Converse. I mean... you've got 'hipster' written all over you. You like weird stuff, though, which tells me you were a geek in school."

My cheeks flushed hot. "I was not a geek."

Archer and Aidan bobbed their heads in unison.

"She was a total geek," Aidan confirmed. "She doesn't want to acknowledge it, but there's no denying it. I bet that's why she was never shot when those gangs started popping caps in one another across Eight Mile."

I frowned at the reference. "How do you know about Eight Mile?"

"It was a movie."

"Oh, right." I choked on a laugh. "Just for the record, Detroit isn't as bad as you're picturing. There are rough neighborhoods—don't get me wrong—but there are rough neighborhoods here too. I've been warned away from the Seventh Ward and St. Claude more times than I can count."

"And it's smart for you to stay away from those areas," Gus agreed. "Basically, you're telling us that all our pop culture references on Detroit are false, huh? That's rather disappointing."

"Oh, not all of them," I countered. "There are parts of Detroit that are great though. They've revitalized part of the downtown area, thanks to the casinos and all the sports stadiums. The suburbs are cool too. Macomb is all about the lake activity, and Oakland is all about the bars."

"And you ran a bar in this Oakland County?" Archer prodded.

I nodded. "Ferndale. It was... fun. I loved it a lot."

"And yet you ended up here."

It wasn't a question and yet I felt the need to respond. "I wanted to move on to a bigger market. After my mother died... well, there wasn't much keeping me in Michigan. What little family I have left I'm not close to. They live on the west side of the state. The opportunity to come here popped up. I've always wanted to see New Orleans, so I jumped at the chance... and here I am."

"Are you going to stay?"

I should've expected the question. It made me feel uncomfortable all the same. "I don't... um..." I had trouble meeting Gus's speculative gaze.

"We're still figuring things out," Gus replied. "I have every intention of keeping her here. It's not like there aren't plenty of bars for her to focus her magic on. She needs to be brought to an idea kicking and screaming though. For now, we're just operating neighboring bars."

"Well, it's kind of cute." Aidan had a dimple when he smiled. It made him look more accessible. "I think it's good

Gus finally found a woman who won't take his shit. He needs some direction even if he doesn't want to admit it."

Gus scowled. "Let's not go there."

"Oh, poor Augie." Archer grabbed his brother's cheek and gave it a good jiggle before Gus could slap his hand away.

"You guys have pretty much overstayed your welcome," Gus noted pointedly when he'd finally managed to escape his brother's grip. "It's not that I'm not happy to see you—although, for the record, I'm not—but what are you doing here? If Mom wants to demand my attendance at another garden party, I'm going to have to respectfully decline."

"Actually, she's got a party hitting Sunday," Archer replied. "That's not why we're here though. We've already told her we're going to have Ebola that day."

"Yes, she wants us to have a speedy recovery but is not bothered by our lack of interest in tea," Aidan drawled.

The brotherly repartee was kind of cute... although I would never admit that out loud.

"If you're not here to badger me into a party, why are you here?" Gus asked. He'd finished off his breakfast and was collecting the empty takeout containers. I moved to stand and help, but he put a hand on my knee to still me. "I've got it. Relax. You'll have plenty of time for cleanup at work today."

"Aw, how sweet," Archer crooned. "Augie has a girlfriend he actually waits on. I can't wait to use this against you later."

Gus's glare was hard and quick. "Tell me what you want or get out."

That was the first time I realized that Archer did indeed have an ulterior motive for the visit. The quick dart of his eyes toward Aidan told me there was something serious brewing. I was instantly alert.

"I don't want to ruin your morning," Archer hedged, his smile completely disappearing as he glanced at me.

"I can go," I said, automatically standing.

"No." Gus hurried back into the room after dumping the containers in the trash. "I want you here."

"Yes, the little puppy wants to hump your leg again," Aidan teased.

Gus ignored him. "You don't have to go, Moxie. You still have time before you have to go home and change for work." He almost seemed desperate for me to stay.

"Your brothers have something they want to tell you and don't want to do it in front of me," I noted. "I don't want to be a bother."

"You're most definitely not a bother." He pinned Archer with a serious look. "Tell her she's not a bother."

"You're not a bother," Archer said. "Not even a little. It's just... um... there is a problem." He licked his lips and adjusted his tall frame in the chair. "It's Damon Stephens, Gus. He stopped in to see Dad yesterday."

My stomach constricted. This wouldn't be good.

Gus let loose a snorting sound. "Is that all? I don't care about Damon. He's a complete and total tool."

"Yeah, and that's why we have a problem." Archer was all business now. "He requested a meeting on the books with Dad. He had his mother in tow with him."

"Edna?" Gus's expression grew even darker. "I was kind of hoping she would be dead by now."

"Evil never dies," Archer replied. "That's why Damon took her with him to meet with Dad. I happened to be in the office when they showed up even though it was after the workday had ended." He looked unbelievably uncomfortable. "Gus, Damon is coming after you."

Gus carefully blanked his face. "Meaning what?"

"Meaning something happened that put his panties in a twist, and he tapped his mom to get retribution. They're threatening Dad with a lawsuit."

Niggling worry grabbed the back of my brain and

squeezed, but I didn't say a single word. I couldn't. I had nothing to offer but squeals of worry, and that wasn't going to help anyone.

"Just tell me," Gus insisted. "Don't drag it out."

"I eavesdropped a little," Archer admitted. "Damon blew up a couple times during the meeting. He's accusing you of breaking the NDA from high school."

I didn't know what that meant. When I focused on Gus, I noticed all the color was draining from his face. "Is this over the nurse at the school?" I asked automatically.

"Oh, Gus." Archer made a growling noise deep in his throat. "You *did* break the NDA. Do you know how bad that is? Edna is going to sue. She says you're spreading bad stories about her son around the Quarter. The case might be more than a decade old, but there's no statute of limitations on it. Dad warned you when this all went down."

"You mean when Damon essentially tried to rape a school nurse and I was the one who got in trouble for it," Gus growled.

"He denies he touched her. The nurse now denies it too."

"The nurse was paid off."

"That's neither here nor there. Damon says that you've been spreading lies in the Quarter, and it's hurting his business. He wants Dad to do something about it... and that something includes taking your bar and giving it to Damon as a form of settlement."

I felt sick to my stomach. "No." I pushed myself to a standing position on shaky legs. "No, no, no. I'm sure it's Damon who's lying. Gus didn't tell me about the nurse. Damon did."

"Moxie, it's going to be okay," Gus said automatically. "There's nothing to worry about. Damon can threaten me all he wants. He can't prove anything."

"He's only going after you because of me," I insisted. "This is because I ghosted him at dinner the other night."

"Wait... what?" Archer angled his head so he could look at me. "What does this have to do with you?"

"Nothing," Gus replied automatically.

"Everything," I countered. "Damon asked me out. I had no interest in going out with him but... well... your brother was irritating me. He forbade me to go out with Damon. Of course, that meant I had no choice but to go out with him."

"Of course." Archer rolled his eyes. "Are you seriously telling me this is all because you stole Damon's woman, Gus? What the hell?"

"I was never his woman, and that's a completely sexist thing to say," I complained. "I went out to one dinner with him. We didn't even make it to appetizers. We ordered, and that was enough for me to realize he was unbearable. I excused myself to go to the bathroom, and then I left the restaurant."

"Did you tell him before you left?"

"No."

"Oh, well... that's either hilarious or really sad." Archer blew out a sigh. "You need to tell Dad about this, Gus. He needs to know why Damon is moving on him. Right now, he's just furious that you let a high school grudge come back to bite us in the ass. I think he's really considering giving Damon your bar."

"Shit." Gus dragged a hand through his hair and turned to the windows. He looked shaken. "I should've realized how this would go down. This is... not good."

"You should've stayed away from Damon," Aidan insisted. "None of your interactions ever turn out well."

"No, they don't," Gus agreed. "He's the one who turned up out of the blue though. He's the one who went after Moxie."

"This is just a pissing match," Archer agreed. "He recognized you had feelings for her and moved in to teach you a lesson. He's got the upper hand right now. You need to do something to stop this before it gets out of hand. We're talking serious damage control."

"I'll call Dad," Gus conceded. "I'll tell him everything, even if I know it will end with a yelling match."

"You do have a tendency to lose your head over women," Archer agreed, shooting me an apologetic smile. "No offense."

"None taken." My response was stiff. Really, what else was it supposed to be?

"Moxie, don't let this get you down," Gus instructed. "I'm going to talk to my dad and fix this. You have my word."

I forced a smile I didn't feel. "Sure. You have everything under control." I stood and pointed myself at the bedroom. "I need to get dressed and head home. It's time to get ready for work."

"You have two hours before you have to leave," Gus complained. "We were... going to spend time together."

"Is that what they're calling it now, bro?" Archer demanded. He didn't look as if he were leaving anytime soon.

"Shut up." Gus chased me toward the bedroom. "I can get rid of them. Don't go."

"It's okay," I reassured him even though I felt pretty far from okay. "You need to work this out with them and your father. I'm just in the way."

He grabbed my hand and pressed it to the spot over his heart. "You're not in my way. I promise. That's not what this is."

"I've caused issues."

"This isn't your fault. It's between Damon and me. It's *always* been between him and me."

"And yet I'm at the center of it." I had no idea if I was smiling or grimacing at this point. "You need to fix things with your father... and I have work. We'll talk later."

He didn't look thrilled at the prospect. "Moxie, please don't use this as a reason to shut me out."

"I won't." I didn't mean it. I was already shutting down. "I'll see you in a couple hours. Things will be fixed by then. I'm sure of it."

ALLY WAS ON THE PATIO BREAKING IN a new pair of heels when I got home. The look on her face when she saw me was straight out of a soap opera.

"Where have you been?"

"It doesn't matter. I'm here now. Is something wrong?"

"Um... yeah. There are rumors swirling everywhere."

"Rumors?" I had no time for French Quarter gossip. I had a business to run and a mistake to somehow clear up... although I had no idea how. "I'm pretty sure I'm not gossip worthy."

"Maybe not, but you're at the center of the gossip. People are saying that the Kingmans are in negotiations to buy Cher... and give it to Damon."

"That's ludicrous," I scoffed. "Damon is going after Flambeaux. I was just with Gus and his brothers. That's what they said."

"Maybe they didn't want you to know."

My heart sank a little bit. "I... don't... think..." The mistrust I'd been harboring for the Kingmans and their methods came back with a vengeance. "How would I find out if that's true?"

She blew out a sigh, seemingly resigned. "I know a guy. He's got his finger on the pulse of the bar scene in the Quarter. He owns a magazine. If anybody knows, or knows where to point us, it's him."

"Can you get us in to see him?"

"Let me place a call."

Twenty-Eight

I showered and changed. By the time I was finished, Ally had set up a meeting with a woman referred to us by her magazine friend. Ally knew this individual as well, which turned out to be a lucky break. The woman worked at one of the jazz bars, a small space that boasted strong drinks and loud music. It was called Trombone Time. It wasn't yet open, but Amanda Dawson was stocking the bar and let us in.

"You guys want something while we're talking?" she asked. She was in her forties, trim, and had a no-nonsense air about her.

"I think we're okay," Ally replied as she sat on one of the stools. "Thank you for seeing us on such short notice."

"Oh, it's no bother." Amanda offered up a hand wave. "I love dishing dirt on the Kingmans."

"Do you know them?" I felt out of place in the bar for some reason, as if I couldn't figure out what to do with my hands.

"I know them," Amanda replied, her expression impossible to read. "I had an affair with Anders Kingman for ten years."

If I'd had a drink, this is about the time I would've choked on it. "What?"

She nodded. "I worked for him for almost twelve years. We... grew close. I was with him when he bought at least ten bars in four different parishes."

"And you had an affair with him?" I darted a look toward Ally, but she refused to meet my gaze.

"Yup. I was an idiot. He charmed me for months. Then we went on a business trip up to Baton Rouge so he could talk to some financial people. It was just us. We got drunk at the hotel bar, one thing led to another..." She trailed off, her eyes drifting toward the window.

"Afterward, I was willing to pretend it never happened," she continued. "He said he'd been hiding feelings for me for a long time. It was stupid, but I believed him. We embarked on an affair. All the while, he kept telling me that his wife was cold and he was just trying to arrange his businesses so she couldn't take them from him in a divorce."

I pursed my lips. "I'm guessing that wasn't the case," I said finally.

"Nope. It took me ten years—and catching him with his new secretary after my 'promotion'—to figure it out." She used air quotes and scowled. "When I called him on it, he denied it. Then he blocked me from calling him, had the head of Human Resources call me into a meeting, and I was fired with two weeks' severance. That's how I ended up here."

I felt sick to my stomach. "Well, that's lovely."

"Here is good," she said. "It's a great bar. It's not where I saw myself at this age though."

"Moxie has had some dealings with Gus Kingman," Ally started. "He opened a bar directly across the road from her."

"Augustus?" Amanda arched an eyebrow. "He's considered the black sheep of the family."

I had no idea if that was a good or bad thing at this point. "Meaning?"

"Meaning he doesn't follow the family mold. He was in trouble in school. Anders talked about it all the time. How Aidan and Archer followed the rules, did what they were supposed to do, and never questioned authority. At first I took that to mean that Augustus was rotten to the core."

My heart sank.

"But then I realized it meant he was the only one who actually thought for himself and didn't follow the family edicts like the sheep they expected him to be," she said.

I allowed a small bit of hope to seep in. "Seriously?"

"Augustus refused to do what they wanted. He couldn't be controlled. Come to find out, the fights he got into when at school, they were because he was trying to do the right thing. Some nurse got fired, and he refused to let it go, said the kid who got her fired was the problem. It caused waves in their social group."

"Damon Stephens," I volunteered. "He's been sniffing around lately."

"I heard at work last night that the Kingmans were going to give Damon a bar to shut him up," Ally volunteered. "It was all anybody was talking about. Apparently, this Damon guy is the worst of the worst."

"I don't know much about him, but if he's the kid that Augustus fought with in school, Anders let a few things slip when drinking one night," Amanda said. "Apparently the kid had a thing for sexually harassing young girls and women. Anders said he thought he was a predator. He was secretly proud of Augustus for standing up for the nurse... although it caused some sort of rift in Anna's social group, and she didn't like it one bit."

I thought about Gus, the easy way he handled people, the

big smile on his face whenever he was having a good time. He was an authentic person. I had no doubt about that. Unfortunately for him, he was surrounded by inauthentic people, and eventually that would leave a mark.

"Have you heard anything about the Kingmans paying off Damon Stephens?" Ally asked. "Because I heard that he was making noise about Gus breaking an NDA and the family was going to have to shut him up somehow."

"It was the NDA about the nurse," I said. "Gus mentioned it, although he didn't go into a lot of details. Damon assumed that Gus had said something to me. He brought it up when we went to dinner. I didn't confirm or deny it. I just... left. I shouldn't have done what I did. That's what set him off."

"And what did you do?" Amanda queried.

"She ghosted him," Ally said with a laugh. She was enjoying herself way too much. "She said she had to go to the bathroom after ordering their entrees and breezed right out of the restaurant. Then she was seen up and down Decatur Street with her lips pressed against Gus's lips... and now here we are."

"Now here we are," I echoed.

"Tell me what's going on," Amanda prodded. "I can't help you if I don't know what the deal is."

I instinctively trusted her, so I told her. I didn't embellish or go into detail about my night with Gus. I just hit the basics. When I was finished, she let loose a sigh.

"I don't understand why the Kingmans would buy your bar just to give it to Damon," she said after a few seconds of contemplation. "It makes no sense."

"Unless that was the price," I said. "I mean... I don't own Cher. I manage it. The owner is Arnie Templeman. He doesn't even live in New Orleans. He lives in New York City. He owns a huge mountain of bars and restaurants. I thought getting in on the ground floor with him would be a good thing. I figured I could work my way into another market."

"I've met Arnie," Amanda offered. "He had a few dealings with Anders. They hated each other." She smiled at the memory. "Arnie was a real ballbuster, and Anders hates anyone who doesn't kowtow to his whims... which is probably why he and his wife have had separate bedrooms for fifteen years."

That was a detail I didn't need to know. "I wonder if Arnie feels the same way about Anders as he does about him," I mused.

"Oh, definitely. There's no way Arnie will sell a bar to the Kingman family. He doesn't like the way they do business. I don't think that's what's happening."

"So why is that the rumor going around?" Ally asked, her eyebrows threatening to collide as she mulled over our problem.

"I'm guessing Damon started the rumor," Amanda supplied. "I mean... he is a real shit, right? If word has gotten out that Gus stole his date the very night he was supposed to be getting cozy with her, he's the type to be mortified. He's likely causing problems for a reason."

"It's Gus." The realization hit me like a punch. "Damon wants to rattle Gus. He wants Gus focused on helping me save Cher, but it's Flambeaux on the chopping block." The more I talked, the more certain I became. "The Kingmans are going to give Damon Gus's bar."

Amanda's smile was rueful. "Now that right there I can see happening. Damon might want to talk big, spread a story, but it's Gus he wants to hurt. No offense because you're a pretty girl, but it's not you that he's after. It's always been Gus."

I pushed myself to my feet. "I have to warn Gus."

Amanda made a tsking sound with her tongue. "Girl, if I were you, I would stay out of it. You're a small fish trying to swim upstream. Those Kingmans will eat you alive if they can. That's what they do."

"I don't care." I meant it. My job was important to me. The notion of hurting Gus was unbearable though. "I have to warn him. I can't stop his parents from giving away that bar, selling it out from under him. I can let him get ahead of this though."

"And what if he blames you for his misfortune?"

I swallowed hard. It was a possibility. "Then I guess I'll have to live with it. If I'd just gotten rid of Damon that first day, this never would've happened. I kept him around, though, thinking he would have dirt on Gus."

"Turns out Gus has dirt on him, and it's the type of dirt that could get him in trouble over the long haul."

"That's why I have to warn him." I'd already made up my mind and was heading toward the door, not even waiting for Ally, who wasn't giving chase. "This is my fault. Gus shouldn't have to pay. The very least I can do is warn him."

"Well... good luck with that." Amanda tipped the brim of an invisible hat as I pulled open the door. "I guess if you're going to risk getting involved with a Kingman, Augustus is the only acceptable one."

"I don't really think I have a choice any longer. I am involved." With that, I disappeared through the door. I knew exactly where to point myself.

FLAMBEAUX'S DOORS WERE SHUT WHEN I arrived, causing my heart to skip a beat. Had it already happened? Had Gus lost what he'd worked so hard to build? I stood in the middle of the street, my hands gripped into fists at my sides, and glared at the building.

What was I supposed to do?

"He's in there," a male voice said from someplace behind me, causing me to jolt.

When I turned, I found Abel watching me. He had a bag slung over his shoulder and a curious look on his face. "Who?" I asked dumbly, hating myself for even playing the game.

"Gus's parents showed up twenty minutes ago. They had the dumbass with them in their limousine."

My heart sank. I knew who the dumbass was without asking. "I did this. This is all because of me."

"What is?"

"They're going to take Gus's bar away and give it to Damon. He's pitching a fit, accusing Gus of doing something he didn't do. I have to fix this."

"Or you could stay out of it."

"I can't. Did you not hear the part where this is because of me?"

Abel let loose a sigh. "This must be because you're from Michigan. Here in NOLA, people mind their own business."

That was a dirty lie. "I've heard you on the phone. You stick your nose in everybody's business. You won't let your sister date that dude from the band."

"He's a tool."

"You won't let your mother go to dinner with the pastor."

"He's a religious tool."

I almost laughed. Almost. I couldn't allow myself to leap the final hurdle to absurd giggles. "You threatened Damon to keep me safe."

He let loose an exasperated sigh. "I guess you're saying part of this is on me."

"No. I'm not. It's all on me."

"No, it's really not." He planted his hand on my shoulder and prodded me toward Flambeaux. "Come on. If we're going to make fools of ourselves, we should probably get it over with."

My heart hammered so hard I thought it might punch right out of my chest. I felt as if I were marching to my death.

I didn't knock before sliding through Flambeaux's open front door. It seemed unnecessary. A shudder ran down my spine when I heard the raised voices inside, however, and I almost turned around and ran. I'm not sure I wouldn't have done just that if Abel hadn't been with me.

Gus was facing his parents and in the middle of a rant when we moved into the main bar area.

"You're not giving him my bar," Gus snapped. "It's not going to happen."

"It's already done," Damon interjected in a sniveling voice. "All of this, this place you love so much, well now you're standing on my property."

"No, I'm not." Gus glared at Damon and vigorously shook his head. "I'm the owner on the deed. It's me." He thumped his chest. "I made sure of that when I went into business with my father. He can't do anything without me agreeing to it."

"That's true in theory," Anders hedged. His back was to me, and I wanted to punch him in the head given the things I knew. That wasn't important today though. Today was about saving Gus.

"You own the bar," Anders continued. "If you don't sign it over to Damon, however, I can pull funding. That means you'll be on the hook for the lease... with no backup from me."

Gus worked his jaw. "The lease is high. I won't make enough to cover it for at least six months. You know that. We've gone through the business proposal together on this place six times. It's going to be a moneymaker. It's not there yet though."

"It will be a moneymaker for me," Damon said with a high-pitched laugh. He reminded me of the Joker, although somewhat more unhinged. "I guess I'll be the one to reap the rewards when this place moves into the black." He leaned closer to Gus, so close I was surprised Gus didn't pop him in the nose. "Or maybe I'll just shut the doors and call it a day."

"Why are you even doing this?" Gus demanded of his father. His face was red enough that I worried he would explode all over Damon. So far, he was keeping his temper in check... although I had no doubt that wouldn't last very long. "Why are you here with... *him*?"

When Anders didn't answer, I cleared my throat. The look of surprise on Gus's face when he saw me had my heart threatening to shred. "I'm sorry to interrupt." I took a step forward, my voice softer than was normal for me.

"Who are you?" Anders demanded as he looked me up and down.

"Moxie Stone. I saw you when you visited a few weeks ago."

Anders looked confused. "Moxie? Is that a name?"

"It's a lifestyle," I said automatically.

Those three little words were enough to jar Anders's memory. "We met you before. You manage Arnie's place across the street."

I bobbed my head. "I do. I'm here about this place though." I sucked in a calming breath. "And I'm here about him." I inclined my head toward Damon. "This is all my fault."

Anna leaned in closer to her husband. She'd been so quiet I'd almost forgotten she was present. "I'm confused," she said in a low voice. "Who is she again?"

"She's no one of importance," Damon said on a sneer.

I seriously wanted to smack him around, and I wasn't a violent person unless I saw someone abusing an animal. I was mellow... at least mostly. "I'm the reason this is happening."

This time my voice was stronger when I declared it. "This is all because of me. You can't hold this against Gus."

"Moxie, no." Gus shook his head. "Don't take this on yourself. It's my fault."

"But it's not." Whether it was smart or not, I decided to lay everything out for all interested parties. "I knew when Damon started sniffing around that he was trouble. At the time, I thought he might have dirt on Gus." I shot the man in question a rueful smile. "I was still mad you stole my launch."

Gus scrubbed his hands over his face. "It doesn't matter." He looked frustrated, likely with me. "Just... don't."

"I can't let your parents do this to you." I was firm as I faced Anders and Anna Kingman. "I agreed to go out with Damon even though I didn't like him. I was trying to prove to myself I didn't have feelings for your son. We didn't even make it to the appetizers before I knew it was a mistake, so I snuck out of the restaurant. Damon's ego took a bruising, and now he wants to make Gus pay."

"That's not what's going on here," Damon insisted when Anders's gaze slowly swung to him. "I don't even remember going out with this girl. I think she's making it up. I mean... her name is Moxie. That's clearly a drug name."

I pretended I didn't hear him. "You can't take Gus's bar from him. He's been working so hard. Damon just wants to beat Gus. He wants it so badly he can't see straight. Your son is ten times the man Damon is. That's what's really bothering him."

"What's really bothering me is that Gus broke the NDA," Damon fired back, his lizard eyes on Anders. "My parents told you what would happen if he ever opened his big, fat mouth."

"Gus didn't tell me about the nurse you sexually harassed," I blurted. "Stop thinking he did." The only reason I knew I'd said the wrong thing was because Gus squeezed his eyes shut. It was only after the fact that reality washed over me.

"If Gus didn't tell you, then how do you know?" Anders asked stiffly.

I wanted to cut off my own tongue. I had such a big mouth. Instead, I did the only thing I could think to do. I told the truth.

"Damon bragged about it over dinner," I replied. "That's the reason I left the restaurant." Even I was surprised at how easily it fell from my mouth. "He did it to himself."

"She's lying!" Damon sounded like a screaming toddler as he lost his shit. "She's making that up. I would never say that."

Anders's expression turned grave. "Would you be willing to sign an affidavit saying that?" he asked.

I nodded. "Yes." It was akin to lying under oath. I didn't stop myself from doing the right thing for Gus though. "I totally would."

"No, she wouldn't," Gus said in a low voice, extending a finger in my direction. "Moxie, you don't understand what you're agreeing to do."

"It's fine." I meant it. "Damon is the one who set this in motion. He's the one who has to pay the consequences."

"I'll sue you both!" Damon hissed. "You're making a mockery of my name. I will ruin you."

Anders hesitated and then he squared his shoulders. "I'm going to request my lawyer have a meeting with your lawyer, Damon. They'll come to an agreement on this."

"The agreement needs to be that Gus keeps his bar," I insisted. "That's the only agreement that will work for me."

Anders took a deep breath, as if debating, and then nodded. "I'll see what I can work out."

"That's all I ask. And, by the way, there's nothing serious going on between me and Gus." I turned to leave and smacked into Abel's wide chest. I'd forgotten he was with me. One look at his face told me he wasn't done. "Don't make things worse," I hissed.

Abel pretended he didn't hear me. "Hey, little maggot," he called out, drawing Damon's furious gaze toward him. "You and I are going to have business of our own before it's all said and done. I can't wait to finish it out."

Damon visibly blanched. "I hate all of you."

"Oh, dude, the feeling is mutual."

Twenty-Nine

Abel followed me outside, ever the stalwart wingman.

"I could still go back inside and beat him bloody," he offered when I didn't speak for a full thirty seconds.

I let loose a hollow laugh. It bordered on a sob. "I don't think that will be necessary. The Kingmans will take care of Damon. He's not smart enough to get one over on them."

"And yet you felt the need to run to their rescue."

"Not *their* rescue." My voice was soft.

"I can't help but feel part of this is my fault." Abel planted his hands on his hips and gave me a serious look. "I should've let you handle your own personal life. I didn't... and now we're in a bad spot."

I didn't know how to respond, so I opted to remain quiet. When I heard the door open behind me, I cringed. Raised voices could be heard inside Flambeaux. It sounded like Anders and Damon were about to throw down. Gus wasn't a part of the argument though. No, he'd followed me out.

"Abel." I could make out Gus's silhouette in the window as I wasn't looking in his direction. He nodded toward my protective bartender. "I don't suppose I could have a talk with Moxie, could I?"

Abel nodded. "Yeah, but she's in her head now. You should probably know that. Anything you say will be wasted."

"She does that, doesn't she?" Gus's smile appeared wan in the reflection. "I don't think she can help it."

"Life shapes us," Abel noted. "Her life was built on a dude who left her for something better. Now she lives her life trying to be something special so no one will ever leave her again. Why else do you think she changed her name to Moxie of all things?"

I'd told Abel about my connection to Benji after Gus had guessed he was my father and now regretted confiding in him. The psychoanalysis was just a bridge too far. "I happen to like my name!" My voice came out a lot shriller than I intended.

Abel and Gus chuckled in unison.

"I'll take it from here," Gus said. "Thanks for offering her backup though."

"That's my job." Abel tipped an invisible hat and started across the street. He stopped before crossing. "Girl, I don't want to tell you your business."

"But you will," I surmised.

He didn't acknowledge the statement. "Try listening with your ears, and maybe your heart, instead of that busy brain of yours."

"No good ever comes of that," I said hollowly.

"Actually, it's the opposite. I think you're too messed up to see that right now." Abel let loose a sigh and then switched his gaze to Gus. "When you screw this up—and you will because you're not much better at this than her—I'll be around to fix it."

"Thanks." Gus looked as if he really meant it. "I'll keep that in mind."

"You do that."

Once Abel was gone and it was just the two of us, with the only noise coming from inside Flambeaux because it was too early for tourists to start drinking, we did nothing but stare at one another.

Say something. Those two words played over and over again in my head. I didn't say anything, however. That left him to do the talking.

"You didn't need to do that," he said finally. He looked to be choosing his words carefully. "You didn't need to take the blame."

"It was my fault," I said. "I'm the one who left him sitting like an idiot in an expensive Italian restaurant and fled like a coward."

"See, that's one of my favorite things you've ever done." He attempted a jocular wink and gave up halfway through. "Moxie, I need to know what you're thinking."

"I'm not sure I'm thinking anything." That was true. I was numb.

"Well, let me tell you what I think you're thinking."

I bobbed my head. "Sure. That sounds fun." My voice was vacant, but no matter how hard I tried to engage, I couldn't.

"You're thinking that this is all too much," Gus said. "The idea that I'm a Kingman and you're the manager of a rival bar has you wondering how you got here. You were just supposed to set up shop for six months, make a name for yourself, and then move to a bigger market. All of that has changed now."

"Maybe it doesn't have to change," I suggested. "Maybe this was a warning to right my course before things get too out of hand."

"Don't you think things have already spiraled out of control? I mean... your control. That's what this is really about. Your constant need for control is what fuels you."

I pressed my lips together and didn't respond.

"It doesn't have to be the only thing in your life," he said in a soft voice. "You can break from the plan. You can set a different course. You can... do whatever you want. You're just that amazing. Nothing can stop you."

The words were everything I wanted to hear and yet they rang hollow. "I don't want to be one of those girls, Gus."

"Which girls?"

"The ones who can't keep their eye on the prize because of a man. I can't just sacrifice everything I've been working toward because I found a guy who..." I trailed off. I couldn't say the next part out loud.

"A guy who what?"

"Don't make me say it."

"I need you to say it." He was firm. "I can't just watch you walk away. I didn't work so hard to get past those defenses you brandish like sharp swords to have it blow up in my face within twenty-four hours. That is too freaking much. Even I am not so destructive that I could've managed that."

"You're everything most women would want," I said. "You're everything I might want... someday."

"Someday. Meaning not today."

"I shouldn't want you." My voice cracked. "I just... should absolutely not want you. You're not in the plan."

"Plans change, Moxie."

"What if this one shouldn't?" My hands were shaking so I clasped them together to keep from falling apart. If I started to cry, he would feel the need to soothe me. If he did that, it would be over. All the resolve I'd worked so hard to build would disappear in an instant.

Somehow—and I was still trying to figure out how this had happened—he'd stolen my heart. I didn't even know I'd left it unprotected. How did that even happen?

The look on his face was almost enough to shatter me and my resolve. "I can't just let you do this, and yet I feel as if there's a wall going up between us. If I try to push against that wall too hard, it's going to topple over and crush us both."

"So, you agree we should go back to how we were, right?" I was almost hopeful. Could we go back to sparring and walking back from the bars together at night? Would that be enough for both of us?

"No, I don't agree with that." Gently, he lifted his fingers and brushed my hair away from my face. "The thing is, I'm dealing with a mess in there." He jerked his thumb toward Flambeaux. "It's not going to be sorted out in a couple hours. There will be meetings with lawyers, threats from Damon, and lectures from my father. He's warned me not to engage with Damon so many times I've lost count. I never seem to be able to stop myself from messing with him though."

"Maybe that's why you wanted to be with me," I suggested. "Maybe you just wanted to mess with Damon, like he wanted to mess with you, and now that it's over you'll realize that I was never what you really wanted."

"No, that's not going to happen. You're so far inside your head you can't see that right now though. Abel was right about that. Nothing I say to you is going to make this better."

"Probably because it can't get better. We don't belong together." An invisible knife stabbed me in the heart when I said it. "Our worlds are too different."

"I think our worlds are remarkably similar," Gus countered. "You're in a place where I can't reach you right now, though, and I can't give you the attention you deserve because my father is about to come out here and lecture me on a multitude of different things."

"Like messing with Damon."

"Yup." He bobbed his head. "And falling for the girl who runs the bar next door. He's going to totally hate that move."

I considered mentioning what Amanda had told me about the affair but immediately discarded the notion. That was none of my business. Besides, Gus was a cagey guy. He likely already knew.

"I should go," I said automatically. I found it hard to meet his heartbroken stare because there were too many emotions—the sort I didn't want to acknowledge—flitting through his eyes.

"To work?" he asked. "Are you going to work your shift tonight?"

That was the original plan. Now, though, I couldn't imagine forcing myself to go through the motions, especially knowing he would be there to walk me home when it came time to leave. "I think I'm going to take a sick day, maybe head home and go to bed. I have a headache." *And my heart hurts so much, I'm convinced I need a new one,* I silently added.

Rather than argue, Gus nodded. "Maybe that's best. I'll be seeing you."

"Sure." I turned to leave. "We run bars across the road from one another. It's impossible for us not to see each other."

"That's not what I mean."

"I really need to go." I hung my head as I started across the street. All I could think was that I needed to get away from this place, from him.

"This isn't over, Moxie," he called to my back. "I'm not retreating. I'm just... giving you the time I think you need."

"My head is a mess," I agreed.

"Yeah. It will be okay though. Try having a little faith."

Faith was something I was in short supply of. I didn't expect that to change anytime soon.

I DIDN'T GO HOME. SURE, THAT WAS the original plan. It didn't happen, and instead I found myself grabbing a hurricane from one of the slushie places and plodding toward Jackson Square. That was my favorite place in New Orleans after all. I would feel better once I got there. The hole that had taken up residence in my chest would be gone as soon as I reached my destination because something else would fill it.

The park was bustling with activity when I arrived. I sucked on my straw and watched the tourists meander around. Some posed for photos in front of the Andrew Jackson statue. Others perused the items on sale around the outside of the park. Me? I plopped down on one of the benches and did my best to pretend I wasn't in danger of curling up into a ball and crying for the next twenty-four hours.

I didn't even know what was wrong with me. Gus and I had barely dated for crying out loud. We'd spent one night together.

You're fooling yourself. That was what the voice inside my head said. *You were actually dating all this time, and you didn't even realize it.*

I was bitter about that. Oh, so bitter. Gus had known. He'd recognized we were dating. He hadn't bothered to tell me. Why?

Because he knew you would run away, you idiot, my internal monologue hissed. Gus knew that I was afraid to let him get close. That was why he skated under the radar while I did... what? What had I thought I was doing that entire time?

Winning. That was the only answer. I thought I was winning, and he wasn't even playing the same game. I was lobbing volleys over the tennis net, and he was slapping the puck past the goalie. He'd totally and completely figured me out. And me? I floated along without recognizing that I was in danger of losing my heart. Well, thankfully I'd nipped this potential relationship in the bud. I was no longer in danger of losing my heart. I was... so, so too late.

I placed the hurricane on the bench next to me and dropped my head into my hands. Tears threatened to spill out, but I fought them. I couldn't allow myself to cry. Not in public— and not over a man. My mother had made sure I knew what a mistake that would be.

"Hey, Moxie," a voice said, drawing my attention to the right.

I plastered a smile on my face that likely looked so deranged that it would scare small children. "Hey, Gremlin." I hadn't seen him in days, I realized. "Where have you been?"

"There's a festival down in Crescent Park," he replied, his gaze on the tourists rather than me. I'd interacted with him enough to suspect he was autistic, at least on the spectrum somehow. He wasn't big on making eye contact, so I didn't force him.

"You like festivals, do you?"

"I like the people who go to festivals," Gremlin replied. "When people go to festivals, they're happy. When they're happy, they like to give me money. I like money."

I nodded. "Money gets you food."

"And other things."

"Yeah." There was no need to talk about the other things. I'd discovered early on that trying to *fix* their problems never worked. If they weren't open to the process, then they would never accept a helping hand. The only way to make things better was for them to want to make things better. Very few of them ever reached that point. "Was Benji with you?" I thought about my father, the man who had made my mother bitter and in turn made me unbreakable. "I haven't seen him in a few days."

"Benji?" Gremlin shook his head. "No, he's gone. They took him to the hospital, and he never came back. He's dead. God rest his soul." Gremlin made the sign of the cross.

My heart, which was already in a precarious position, stuttered. "What do you mean he's dead?"

"He's dead," Gremlin repeated. He turned his head in my direction but didn't meet my watery gaze. "The hospital people came for him a couple of nights ago. They took him in the ambulance. He didn't come back, so that means he's dead."

That couldn't be right. "Isn't it possible he's still in the hospital?" I tried to remember if there was a hospital close by. I could go there and find him.

"No." Gremlin shook his head. "No way. He doesn't have money. They won't keep him there with no money. They send us back once we can walk again. It happens all the time. If he was let loose, he would've come back here. He's totally dead."

I really wished he would stop saying that. "You don't know that," I persisted. "He could be... somewhere else. Maybe he's in a long-term care facility or something."

"Nope. He's dead." Listless, Gremlin pushed himself to his feet. "I need to make my rounds. I'll see you later."

If I thought I was numb before, Gremlin's bomb had rendered me completely empty. I reached for my hurricane slushie, which was almost all liquid and no ice at this point and downed it. The heavy alcohol content did nothing to reach the coldness permeating my heart.

Benji was gone. I'd never truly had him anyway. Gus wanted me to tell him who I was, make an attempt at getting to know him, but Benji had left this world before I could make up my mind. Was it the same way with Gus? Would I let him go without a fight like I had Benji?

The fiery part of my personality wanted to say no. It wanted to march right back to Flambeaux and stake my claim, declare this wasn't over and that we had a fighting chance. The realistic part of me, however, the part my mother made sure to build up as my foundation, knew better.

Gus was already gone. He might not be able to recognize that, but I did.

We weren't right for each other. These feelings weren't real. We were two ships passing in the night.

I finished the hurricane and tossed the empty cup into a trash receptacle, closing my eyes to fight back the nausea threatening to have me doubled over with my head between my legs.

Gus was a mistake I never should've made. My mother warned me about men. Why didn't I listen to her? Now I was in pain, and it was completely unnecessary.

Well, that was okay. It was a lesson learned, right?

I would never make that mistake again.

Thirty

I would like to say I was depressed. At least that was an emotion I could grapple with. That wasn't what I was feeling though.

Er, well, at least that wasn't only what I was feeling. Something else was there, something I couldn't put a name to, and it was making me a hermit.

My co-op mates were at work when I got home, something I was glad about, and that allowed me to trudge up the stairs and hit my bedroom. I passed out quickly, embracing the refuge of sleep, and when I woke again, I could hear voices out in the courtyard.

Slowly, disheveled and numb, I made my way to the window to look out. All three of them were there, having cocktails and discussing their day. My unit was shrouded in darkness, so they couldn't see me watching them. Part of me wanted to join them. They would be sympathetic to what happened. They would bestow kind words and love on me. They would also listen if I needed to rant. I didn't go out to them. Instead, I returned to my bed and pulled the covers over my head.

I must've drifted off, because the next thing I knew I was being woken by voices... and they were a lot closer than the patio.

"Maybe she's sick," a male voice suggested. I recognized it as belonging to Gabriel. "She could have the plague or something."

Ally let loose a scoffing noise. "The plague?"

"Stranger things have happened."

"She doesn't have the plague." Ally was firm. "That's not what's ailing her."

"Okay, wise one, what's got her in bed before midnight if it's not a sickness?" Gabriel demanded. He sounded agitated.

"Oh, it's a sickness. It's not catching though." Ally pulled down the covers hiding my face and stroked her hand over my hair. "I know you're awake," she said even as I screwed my eyes shut. "I also know you're heartsick."

I made a grab for the covers... and missed. "I'm not heartsick. Don't be ridiculous."

"Gus called," Ally countered.

I went rigid. "What did he say? Not that I care or anything. I'm just... curious."

Ally snorted. "Right. You're just curious."

I considered picking a fight with her—I was in that sort of mood—but I didn't have the energy. "What did he say?"

"He said that he's worried about you." Ally kept stroking my hair, reminding me of my mother the first time I came home from middle school crying because Billy Hopkins told the other boys I walked like a duck and that was why he didn't like me. "He gave me a brief rundown of what happened with his parents."

"Did he say if they're letting him keep Flambeaux?"

"He didn't. I don't think he cares about the bar."

That was the most ridiculous thing I'd ever heard. "Of

course, he cares. That's his first solo project. He wants it to be a success."

"I'm sure he does." Ally's tone was light. "The Kingmans can't be easy to deal with. I mean... they're the Kingmans. That's quite the shadow to live in."

"They're going to be riding him hard from here on out," I mused.

"Yeah, probably. Like I said, though, I don't think he cares about that."

"Of course, he does. That bar is the most important thing in his life."

"See, I don't think that's true." Ally shifted so she was next to me on the bed, her head resting against the wall because I didn't have a headboard. "I think the most important thing in his life right now is you."

"Don't even." I couldn't listen to the words escaping her mouth, no matter how well-intentioned. "We didn't even really date."

"No, you just made out all over the French Quarter," Casey drawled, smirking when I glared at him. "News travels fast when you have loose lips, missy." He plopped down on the other side of the bed, essentially wedging me between Ally and himself. That left Gabriel to crawl onto the bottom of the bed.

"Moxie, I'm not good when it comes to coddling people who are having emotional breakdowns," Ally offered. "On top of that, I don't think you really want to be coddled. You might think you do, but that's not the truth."

"I just want to sleep." I meant it.

"You don't want that either. You want the hurt in your heart to go away."

"That's not going to happen." I decided to lay it all out there for them. "Gus needs to focus on work. I put him in a precarious position. We can't be together. It's too much."

"Are you concerned because you put Gus in a precarious position or because it's too much?" Casey queried.

"What's the difference?" I was legitimately confused.

"There's a lot of difference." Casey plucked my hand up so he could study it. "Do you want to know what I think?"

"No, but I think you're going to tell me anyway."

He didn't miss a beat before continuing. "I think you fell head over heels for Gus Kingman, and it scared you. There wasn't a lot of time for you to wrap your head around what you were feeling—something Gus recognized—and you were more than happy to push him away because it makes things easier for you."

"Yeah, I don't think that."

He ignored my sarcasm. "I think Ally is right. Your heart hurts because you miss Gus. You let yourself believe there was something other than work for a split second, and then when things got tough, you did what you always do and walked away."

Well, that tore it. I forced myself to a sitting position. My hair was wild. I could feel it sticking up at odd angles. I didn't care though. "You don't even know me."

Casey snorted. "Please. We know you."

"And we love you," Gabriel added.

"You don't always make it easy to love you," Casey interjected. "You actively push people away. I think what's really bothering you is that you assumed Gus was keeping his distance when, all the while, he was sneaking in under your radar. The realization that you genuinely feel something for him was enough to push you over the edge."

"We barely dated," I repeated. "We spent one night together."

"Technically you spent one night getting swollen lips with him and another night getting something else that was swollen from him," Gabriel countered on a cheeky grin. "You also spent weeks walking home with him every night. Those might not have technically been dates, but they were pretty close."

I didn't want to admit he was right. "I can't take this." I was at the end of my rope. "I just... want to sleep."

"Sleep isn't going to fix this situation." Ally turned stern. "You have got to silence that inner voice you have going and do what your heart wants for a change. That voice you hear in your head is your mother's voice. She's using her hurt to ruin your future, and I don't think that's what she intended to do. That's what she accomplished though."

"My mother... just wanted me to keep my eye on the prize." Even as I said it, a lump formed in my throat. "She didn't want me to let a man derail my life."

"Do you think that's what Kingman is doing?" Gabriel queried. He looked legitimately curious. "Do you think he's trying to derail your life?"

"Well... we did make that bet."

"Oh, geez." Ally shook her head. "*You* made that bet. He agreed to it because it kept him close to you. If you can't see that he was interested in more than a bet right from the start, I don't know what to tell you."

I looked back over the time we'd spent together, getting sicker to my stomach with each passing second. She was right... and I hated that she was right. "I just... don't think I'm built for a relationship."

"That's the fear talking," Ally insisted. "You're built for more than you realize. You're not your mother."

I wanted to tell her about Benji disappearing from Jackson Square. It was an added blow I couldn't quite absorb. I didn't though. It would add absolutely nothing to the conversation. Instead, I gave in to the defeat. "I'm really tired."

"Okay." Ally blew out a sigh and patted my hand. "I'm going to let you feel sorry for yourself tonight—mostly because I don't know what else to do—but that's it. I'm not going to coddle you a second longer. Tomorrow, once you've gotten all of this morose nonsense out of your system, we're going to make a plan to get Gus back."

"I don't want him back." I practically choked on the words as I buried my face in the pillow. "I'm fine."

"Oh, even you don't believe that any longer," Casey noted. "I think we're finally making progress."

"Totally," Ally agreed as she stood. "Keep feeling sorry for yourself. After tonight, it's no longer allowed. We'll leave you to your maudlin thoughts for now though."

"That's all I ask."

I WOKE FEELING DRAGGY. I TOOK A cold shower, whipped my hair back in a simple bun, and headed to work sans makeup. It was early, but I figured busying myself with organizing a storage room at Cher was better than facing the firing squad that had invaded my bedroom the previous evening.

I cut through Jackson Square because that was part of my routine, and a knife slid through my heart when there was no sign of Benji. Was it possible that he was really gone? Had he died without even knowing who I was? It was one thing to purposely keep him from the information until I was ready to share it. It was quite another to have the choice taken from me.

I blew out a sigh and adjusted my trajectory. I was tired, and that meant I needed coffee. I'd blown by Café Beignet in my haste to bypass the Square. That meant I would have to settle for chicory if I wanted some liquid energy to get through the day.

All thoughts of forcing myself to drink the chicory flew out of my head when I turned to find Gus sitting on our normal bench. My breath clogged in my throat, and I thought

I might pass out. Then I collected myself... and prepared to run.

Apparently, he was ready for that course of action.

"I have a sugar-free vanilla latte with almond milk," he called out before I could take a single step in the opposite direction. "I have a double order of beignets too."

I stilled. He sounded so... normal. How could that be? Why wasn't he as upset as I was? Maybe he wasn't in mourning. Ally had used that word the previous evening, and it had stuck in my head. I wasn't depressed. I was mourning. Gus didn't seem to be struggling in the same way. That was enough to fire my outrage.

"You look good," I noted as I stalked to the spot in front of him and looked him up and down. "Sleep well?"

He shook his head, catching me off guard. "Nope. I slept twenty minutes here and there. Finally, I gave up and walked the riverwalk."

"Oh."

"Oh." He smirked as he handed me the latte. "You look like you need the caffeine."

My hand immediately flew to my hair to smooth it.

"You still look beautiful," he reassured me.

I took the latte, frowning when our fingers brushed and the energy I'd come to associate with him zinged through me. This thing wasn't going away. I'd gone to bed the previous evening, determined to get Gus Kingman out of my system. I'd failed.

"Sit down, Moxie," Gus instructed. His tone told me he wasn't messing around.

"I'm not sure I should," I hedged.

Gus didn't respond, other than to hold up the cardboard container with the beignets.

I frowned. "That's bribery," I noted. I could smell the powdered-sugar goodness. "I don't think I'm bribable."

"Sit down, baby." This time his voice was softer. "I need to talk to you."

It was the vulnerability in his voice that did it for me. I plopped down on the bench next to him and plucked one of the beignets out of the container. "What?" I knew I sounded petulant. I seemingly couldn't stop myself from going that route.

"First off, our lawyer says that Damon has no case. He can't win, even if he tries to litigate, so that's done."

"But... isn't your mother friends with Damon's mother?"

"Yes, but my father isn't friends with Damon's father. That's the important distinction. My father has always put his needs in front of everybody else's."

I thought about what Amanda had told me about the affair and swallowed hard. I wanted to talk to him, soothe his obviously frayed feelings. Instead, I shoved the entire beignet in my mouth and proceeded to chew.

Gus slid his eyes to me, amusement obvious. "Oh, if I wasn't already in love with you, I swear this would be the moment it would happen." He leaned forward with his napkin to dab at the powdered sugar on my face as my heart threatened to leap out of my chest.

The beignet wasn't completely chewed, so when I tried to speak, I choked.

"Geez." Gus thumped my back until I spit out the beignet. "Don't die on me now," he instructed. His eyes were fierce when they locked with mine. "What part threw you? I think I know, but I'd like to hear it from you."

I was bewildered... and near tears. This time I didn't think the tears were due to sadness though. "You can't love me."

"Why not?"

"Because... we don't even really know each other."

"Oh, no? I think I know more about you than anybody else. I know your favorite movie... your favorite ice cream

319

flavor... and book. I know that you think about what you're supposed to say more than any other person I know. I also know that you're terrified of letting me in.

"Here's the thing though," he continued as he shifted off his bench and knelt in front of me. "I don't care about any of that. I mean... I care. I want to know what you're thinking. I'm not going to let your fear ruin us though. I love you too much."

I pressed my eyes shut. He'd said it again.

"Tell me what you're thinking," he said after I'd gone quiet for a full sixty seconds. "I can't make things better until I know what problem to tackle first."

"You can't love me." I was more insistent this time when I opened my eyes. "It's not possible. I'm... too high maintenance."

His smirk was instantaneous. "You're just high mainte-nance enough," he countered. "I happen to like that you don't take any crap. You're... perfectly you. I happen to think that's what I need in my life."

"Me?"

"Yes. I want you to be perfectly you in my life."

"But... we haven't really dated." I was stuck on that. I couldn't let it go.

"Then we'll date." His smile was impish. "I'll take you out right now. Where do you want to go?" He surveyed the restau-rants surrounding the Square. "Oh, the Stanley has really great omelets. How do you feel about a crawfish omelet with extra mushrooms?"

"I love mushrooms." My response was automatic.

"I know. You love mushrooms... and pickled beets... and you absolutely adore dipping pickles in tomato juice, even though it grosses out most people. Do you know how I know that?"

"I told you."

He bobbed his head. "Yup. You told me all of it." Now he reached over and gripped my hands. "I listened when you talked because the thing I wanted most in this world was to know you better. Do you know what else? You listened when I talked too. I know you did. I could see you taking it all in."

"Yeah, but I took it all in because I thought I was going to use it against you for the bet."

"Is that what you really thought?" He didn't look convinced. "If you really don't care about me, then I'll have to accept that. I don't believe it, but I'm not going to push you to be in a relationship when you don't want it. You just have to say the word."

I studied his face, the beauty of it. The lines of his cheekbones were sharp. The look in his eyes was soft. The curve of his lips was wide. All of those things combined to make a face that I couldn't imagine not waking up to again. "I..."

He waited, although I could tell it was torture for him.

What was I supposed to do here? What would my mother do? Even as I asked myself that question, I recognized the folly in it. My mother was gone. I'd loved her, but she wasn't perfect. In death, I'd canonized her, taken her pain upon myself. I was free of that now.

At least, well, I could be free if I wanted to be.

"I... love you too." Even I was surprised when the words escaped. I hadn't known I was going to say them until they were already out.

Joy flashed in the depths of Gus's eyes, but he tempered it quickly. "Are you sure? I mean... I don't want to push the issue when I know your feelings are still raw, but I need you to be sure."

For some reason, that was enough to solidify my resolve. "I'm sure. I can't guarantee that I won't need to be bolstered again at some point though. This is a whole new thing for me."

Gus cupped my chin, blowing out a sigh as he swooped in for a kiss. It wasn't hot like the ones we'd shared on Decatur Street—both times. It wasn't soft like the wind either. It was firm. His lips were implacable. It seemed somehow fitting that he kissed me that way at the same time I realized there was no shaking the love I'd been feeling for him... even though I still couldn't fathom how it had managed to happen.

The kiss turned needy after a few seconds, and I found myself gasping as I finally pulled back to suck in gaping mouthfuls of oxygen. The smile he graced me with was smug.

"Oh, you're full of yourself." I shoved his shoulder, hating that I immediately wanted to pull him back so I could do it all over again. "That was just a kiss. We still have things to work out."

He nodded without hesitation. "We do. I need you to promise you're going to work with me instead of against me for a change. It's exhausting being the only one trying."

My heart gave a little stutter. "I didn't know I was supposed to be trying."

"I know." He bobbed his head. "It's okay. You can try now. We can work through this together. And, when it's time to move on up the bar food chain, I was thinking we might do that together as well."

The offer had my eyes going wide. "What? You want to run a bar together?"

He shook his head. "I want to own a bar together, at least to start." He brushed a flyaway strand of hair out of my face and grinned. "Believe it or not, I think you have a knack for this... Mabel."

For the second time in as many minutes, I couldn't breathe. This time it was for an entirely different reason. "You... how... when...?" How could he know my real name? How had he figured it out? There was a reason I hated that name. My mother had named me after my father's mother.

The name had never fit me, and after my father abandoned my mother, I could tell she detested it whenever she had to utter the name. That was why it had been so easy to change it... something I had done legally—and permanently.

Gus's eyes lit with delight as he regarded me. "Your father told me."

Even though I was basking in the moment—it wasn't quite a grand gesture, but it was close enough—the words delivered a bruising blow to my sternum. I leaned back. "When?"

"About three days ago... when I met him in the park, had a long talk with him, and told him I knew his daughter." Gus had turned serious. "I didn't tell him it was you. He knew though. I think he always knew."

"He's gone, Gus." My voice cracked even though I fought desperately to hold it together. "The others, they say he died. An ambulance picked him up, and he never showed back up again. They said that's a sign that he's dead."

"Or it's a sign that, after he was transported to the hospital for dehydration, I talked him into going to rehab." Genuine apology shone from Gus's eyes. "I'm sorry, baby. I didn't realize you would freak out. I wanted to surprise you with the news... after he'd made it a full week and I wasn't quite as terrified that he would bolt back to the street."

Without realizing what I was going to do, I gripped the front of his shirt. "What? How?"

"He has a lot of regret," Gus explained. "He feels bad for leaving you. He's not brave enough to approach you though. Well, at least not yet. I told him that the best way to prove he was sorry was to try rehab. If he can make it through the initial cold-turkey period, we'll see if we can get him in a residential living program."

He hesitated a beat and then continued. "I don't want to make promises because I can't keep them in this case. I think you need to know him, though, and I want you to have the things you need. So, we're going to try. You and me, that is. We're going to try and make this work, put genuine effort in, and not run away from each other."

I couldn't form words. All I could do was nod.

"Good." He gave me another kiss, this one quick and to the point. "While we're working on us, your father is going to be working on himself. I wish I could give you guarantees that things will get better for him. I can't though. I just... don't know."

That was enough to loosen my tongue. "No, you've done way more for him than anyone else would have. I don't know how I can repay you."

"I can think of a few ways." He arched an eyebrow and grinned. Then he sobered. "You don't need to repay me. I wanted to do something for us. It wasn't just for you. All you need to do to repay me is unclench a bit."

Color flooded my cheeks, and I blew out a sigh. "I'll do my best. If I backslide, you might need to remind me."

"I think I can do that." He leaned in and pressed his forehead to mine, a sigh escaping as he sucked in a breath. "This is nice, huh?"

I nodded. "Yeah, but those beignets are getting cold. So is my coffee."

He snorted so hard I thought he might choke. When he retrieved the beignets and his coffee, he settled on the bench next to me. Like... right next to me. There was no space between us for the first time ever.

"We can still have our coffee dates in the morning, right?"

He nodded as he picked through the beignets. "Absolutely. They're my favorite part of the day."

"And our walks home?"

"Yup. Those are my favorite part of the day too."

I was amused. "What's your least favorite part of the day?"

"When you go home, and I have to crawl into bed alone."

"I guess we can work on that too."

"Oh, I like that idea." He bit into a beignet and methodically chewed. "There's one other thing."

"What?" I was curious when I lifted my eyes again.

He smirked as he brushed the powdered sugar off my face. "You didn't think you were getting out of this conversation without a grand gesture, did you?"

Confused, my eyebrows drew together. "What do you mean?"

The question was barely out of my mouth before the drums and trombones started. Startled, I looked up to find on the walkway the same bandleader who I'd hired to draw business to Cher that first week.

I didn't recognize the music. It was bouncy and jaunty, which was all I cared about. The band had eight musicians, and we drew a crowd quickly. Clement waved when he saw me, high-stepping as he turned in circles. Around us, people clapped to signify their love of the show.

"There's more," Gus offered when I turned to say something to him.

My gaze drifted back to the band, and sure enough, three familiar faces made their way to the center of the group. Ally, Gabriel, and Casey. They were all dancing while holding signs. There was one word on each sign.

I.

Love.

You.

My throat clogged, and it took a full thirty seconds for me to dart my eyes to Gus, who was leaning back on the bench and watching the show with smug satisfaction.

"I'm good," he said to my unexpressed delight.

I nodded. "I have a question." I was surprised he heard me over the din of the parade, but he slid his eyes to me, tacit agreement that I should ask. "If you'd won the bet, what were you going to make me do?"

"Publicly admit you loved me, of course."

I shot him a look. "We made that bet at the start."

"And yet I always knew I was going to love you. Funny how that worked out, huh?"

My heart, I was embarrassed to admit, melted. "I still won the bet." It was all I could think to say.

"Baby, we both won." He slid his arm around my shoulders and tugged me to his side. "Now, let's eat these beignets and watch the show."

"And what do we do after that?"

"Whatever you want."

I smiled. It was the exact right thing to say.

Epilogue

ONE YEAR LATER

"Open the door," Gus ordered. He had a po'boy in one hand and an onion ring in the other. "Come on. There's no need to drag it out."

My eyes were narrow when I glanced over my shoulder. "We're not supposed to open the doors for another fifteen minutes," I reminded him.

"It's New Orleans. The city doesn't run on a clock." He took a bite of his po'boy, not bothering to wipe his mouth despite the sauce congealing in the corners. "In fact, if you set up a test to see how many locals could tell time, I bet it's less than 50 percent. If you ask how many of them care what time it is, that number goes to zero, baby."

I hated that he was even cute with food all over his face. "Gus?"

"Yes, dear?" His tone was full of amusement.

"We can't open the doors until you finish your lunch."

"That's not a rule."

"Of course, it is. I'm going to need your help when the first rush hits." We'd opened our own bar, or would, in the next few minutes. Like... it was completely our own. Moxie's

Cantina. Gus had picked the name and refused to budge on it. I wanted to go with something trendier, but he refused. This was our bar after all. He said that trends weren't necessary... and he was probably right.

"Mox, what have we talked about?"

Oh, I hated it when he used that tone. I answered anyway. "That I'm the love of your life," I fired back without thinking.

His eyes lit with delight. "We *have* talked about that, and it's true. That's not what I was referring to though."

I let loose a ragged sigh. "That it's Bourbon Street and it doesn't matter how we launch," I replied grudgingly.

"That's right." He shoved the rest of his po'boy into his mouth and moved toward me, ramming the onion ring into my mouth before I could start arguing. "No." He gave me a kiss. I could freaking taste the shrimp on his breath. "It's okay," he whispered as he ran his fingers through my hair. "We're going to do great."

I jerked away from him and immediately looked at my reflection in the antique mirror on the wall. I'd found it at a flea market in Louis Armstrong Park almost six months before. That was the day Gus and I had finally found a location for our bar. He'd handled the lease—I was still tied to Cher by contract and couldn't work on our bar until I'd finished out that contract—and I'd happily started planning for the day we could work on something that was truly ours.

"You're beautiful," he insisted as he moved in behind me, grinning at our reflections. He looked calm, per usual, and my cheeks were flushed with angst. That was also a normal thing. It was different when I was launching my own bar. It felt as if there were more riding on it.

"Of course, I'm beautiful." I did my best to appear stoic. The knowing look in his eyes told me I wasn't pulling it off. "I'm just... excited."

"I know you are." He kissed the tip of my nose. "We're

going to be fine though." He turned to move back to the bar. "By the way, I have something I want to show you. I need to find it though."

"What?" I didn't mean to sound irritable, but that was how the question came out. "Since when are you shopping for things for the bar?"

"I like to shop," he countered as he disappeared behind the counter. "I'm just not as good at it as you."

That was the truth. "Have you talked to your parents?" I asked, hoping to distract myself from the doors that would be thrown open in the next few minutes. I glanced at the clock on the wall. We still had twelve minutes to go. It was going to be a torturous wait.

"I have, and they're thrilled with how Flambeaux is doing," Gus replied. He was bent over and seemingly looking for something in one of the coolers. "They asked if I wanted to come back and run it—after all, I'm the reason it's doing so well in the first place—but I politely declined."

My eyes were shrewd when they landed on him. "You did tell them we were opening today, right?"

"I just need to find the thing."

I couldn't see his face, but I could hear the deflection in his voice. "Gus," I warned in the growliest voice I had at my disposal.

He poked his head above the bar. "Yes, my love."

I wanted to hurt him... and then maybe kiss him to make him feel better after the fact. "You told your parents we were opening the bar today, right?" It would be just like him to avoid the entire problem. When Anders and Anna heard we were opening a bar together, they were less than thrilled. They thought it was a mistake to go into business together when we hadn't been dating long. Gus politely—although not all that politely now that I thought back on it—told them to mind their own business. He wasn't asking them for money to fund the business. We did that ourselves. Looking around the bar, I had to say, we'd done a good job.

"I told them," Gus reassured me. "I just might've told them not to come around until tonight."

"Why?"

"Because it's NOLA. People don't start drinking in earnest until after noon."

"I think that's a lie, but okay. As long as you told them." Pushing him on issues with his parents was never a good idea. It was always better to let him work things out on his own. "Can I open the door yet?"

"Not yet. I have to find the thing first." Gus went back to rummaging beneath the counter. "What about your dad? Did you tell him we were opening today?"

I was expecting the question. Despite that, my acid reflux kicked in. "Yeah." I glanced at my shoes. They were comfortable saddles, which in hindsight likely wasn't a good idea when dealing with drunks. I should've gone for sneakers.

"How is he?" Gus's voice was soft, and I knew he was looking at me.

I opted not to meet his gaze. "The counselor at the halfway house says he's doing really well."

"That's not what I asked."

I tried to keep my expression blasé as I turned to face him. "He's not doing well. He's chafing under the rules. He doesn't like having a curfew. He says the drug tests aren't fair. He also says that there's no dignity in having to do a breathalyzer every night before going to bed."

"We talked about this, Mox. He's going to do what he's going to do. You can't force him to stay there."

I was well aware of Gus's opinion on the subject. My father had been in and out of three residential homes since Gus had paid for his initial rehab. Inevitably, he escaped back to the street every time. Then we found him, talked him into trying again, and he would struggle through several days before disappearing and starting the cycle over again.

"I know we talked about it," I said. "It just... feels like this is our last shot. I don't think we can force him to try again after this. He won't do it."

"Probably not," Gus agreed. "I don't know what else we can do though."

Not every ending was happy, I reminded myself. Good had come out of the situation despite everything. My father and I had been able to talk about a lot of things, make amends. He was never going to be the man I wanted him to be. but we were in each other's lives. I had to let the rest of it go.

"What about your brothers?" I asked, changing the subject. "Are they coming?"

"They will be here," Gus confirmed. "I believe they're both bringing dates."

"Good dates?"

"Nope. They're Uptown socialites. I believe one of them actually wears a hoop skirt."

"You're making that up." I drifted closer to him. "Can I open the door yet?"

"Not yet." He pinned me with a dark look and then moved to the drawer at the far end of the bar. "Nobody is going to be out there for ten minutes. You're the one who told me that not five minutes ago."

"Eight," I corrected.

"Baby, people aren't lining up out there. They'll drift in when they drift in. You know that as well as I do."

My head knew that. My heart was convinced I could change the laws of New Orleans. I'd yet to be able to manage it, but that didn't mean I was going to give up trying. "Fine. Entertain me."

"That's the plan. I... ha!" Gus sounded triumphant. "Found it."

"Awesome." I expected him to bring me new matchbooks. He'd been obsessed for months with perfecting a logo for matchbooks, although why I couldn't say. Instead, he slipped something velvety in my hand when I extended it toward him. My eyes were on an offending smudge I'd just discovered on the bar, and I didn't pay attention to what I was holding. "I need a rag."

When Gus didn't respond, I flicked my eyes to him. "Did you hear me?"

He folded his arms across his chest. "I just gave you a gift."

"Oh, right." I looked down, ready to praise his matchbook to the high heavens, and realized I was looking at a jewelry box instead. "What... is... this?" My heart skipped a beat. Okay, my heart skipped ten beats. I couldn't keep track, though, because it had immediately sped up when it resumed beating.

"Open it," Gus suggested.

I licked my lips. "Um..."

"If you're wondering if that's what you think it is, it is," he said.

"Gus." Suddenly, I felt sick. "We talked about this." He'd mentioned getting engaged three months in. I'd shut him down. It was too soon. Then he proceeded to mention it three months later. I told him we weren't ready, that we had to focus on the bar first. When he hadn't mentioned it again, I thought he'd given up on the idea.

Obviously not.

"Yes, much like we talked about opening the new bar and how you weren't going to be uptight about it. You went back on that, so I went back on this."

"But..." I was at a loss. I was supposed to say something here. What though? My brain was no longer working. "You were just supposed to mention it again," I said when I'd regained my faculties enough to form words. "You weren't supposed to do this."

"Yeah, well, just bringing it up wasn't getting me anywhere," he explained. "You're a woman who needs to be dragged kicking and screaming to the finish line. Asking you when it's a good time to propose was no longer working for me. I decided to accelerate things."

"But... we're opening the bar today."

"Yup. I figure it's good timing. You'll be freaking out about customers. That means you won't be able to freak out about being engaged. Personally, I think I'm an evil genius. I expect to be rewarded thusly when we get home tonight."

Home. The house we'd purchased together. He'd sold his penthouse—it didn't fit either of us—and we'd purchased a creole cottage on Ursulines Avenue. It was only two-thousand square feet, but it boasted an adorable courtyard and guest-house. We had both loved it on first visit, almost as much as we loved each other. Also, by buying it together, we were on even footing. That benefitted both of us.

"Gus..." What was I supposed to say here?

"Open the box, Mabel," he ordered.

The use of my old name—a name he was strictly forbidden from using—was enough to snap me back to reality. "I'm not marrying you if you call me Mabel. You promised."

"Open the box," he demanded.

We held each other's gaze for an uncomfortable length of time, and I finally blew out a sigh. I expected a huge diamond when I looked inside. Instead, he'd gone a different route. He'd opted for an emerald-cut amethyst—my birthstone—in a platinum setting. The design was a bit bohemian, just like me.

"Gus." My heart melted.

"I love you," he said from somewhere close, making me realize he'd moved out from behind the bar when I'd been distracted. When I found him, he was kneeling before me. How did he even manage that without me seeing?

"I love you too." I'd never meant anything more. "I don't know if we're ready for this though."

"Baby, of course we're ready. I've known from the moment I told you I loved you that you were it for me. You've known it too... even if that stubborn streak you refuse to shake won't acknowledge it.

"We belong together," he continued. "I want you to be my wife."

"What if I'm bad at it?" The ring had my full attention. The fact that he'd known the exact right thing to buy somehow floored me. He always knew. It was beyond frustrating.

"You can't be bad at it. You're already perfect at it. I mean... you're already my wife in my heart."

Tears flooded my eyes, unbidden. "I'm just afraid."

"I know. You don't have to be though. Just like everything else, we're going to do this together."

"Yeah."

"Yeah." He wrapped his fingers around my wrist to draw my attention to him. "You're always going to be the love of my life. I need you to marry me though. I need this to be permanent in your heart, just like it is in mine."

Was he kidding me? "You've been permanent in my heart since the moment I met you... even though I worked really hard to keep you out."

"I know." His grin was lightning quick. "Is that a yes?"

I nodded. I was crying now and couldn't form words for a different reason.

"Awesome." He swooped to his feet and pressed his lips to mine, sucking the oxygen out of my lungs with his intensity as he lifted his hand toward the door. It was only then that I realized he had the lock remote with him.

"What are—?" He swallowed the rest of my question with another kiss, and then the doors burst open.

Music immediately filled my ears, and I jerked my eyes in that direction as Clement and his band rolled through the door. Behind him, Anders and Anna stood and watched the festivities. They looked more bemused than excited, but it was still nice they'd managed to come early. His brothers were also with the group, as well as my former apartment mates and the other friends we'd made up and down Bourbon Street.

"You planned this," I realized, shaking my head. "You've been planning this from the beginning."

"Pretty much," Gus agreed as he slipped the ring on my finger, smiling when he saw the way the stone glinted under the mood lighting. "Like I said, Mox, you need to be dragged kicking and screaming. I figured weighing you down with work and personal stuff on the same day was the right way to go."

"You know I'm going to melt down tonight, right?" I opted to be practical. "I won't be able to help myself."

"I know." His smile was benign. "I'll be there for that. I'll be there for it all."

A tear slid down my cheek. "How do you always know the right thing to say?"

"I'm the perfect man."

"Other than that ego," I muttered.

"Details, baby." He leaned in for another kiss, this one more sensuous than the first. "Oh, and we're having an engagement party after six o'clock tonight," he added when he pulled back.

"Where?" I was confused. We couldn't leave our bar on opening night.

"Here, of course. What better way to draw in a crowd than to wow them with an engagement?"

I was dumbstruck. "I thought you said no gimmicks." My tone was accusatory.

"It's not a gimmick. I just hijacked my own proposal. I happen to think it's smart."

He wasn't wrong. "Will there be cake?"

"Of course... and a new signature drink named after you. Abel designed it as an engagement gift."

Abel. I jerked my eyes to the people congratulating us and found him watching. He was the one who had talked me down from more than one meltdown over the past six months. It wouldn't have been right not to have him here.

Thank you, I mouthed to him across the sea of people.

He nodded in acknowledgement. "Thank you," he called out. "Did I mention I'm the new manager of Cher?"

No, but I'd been the one who recommended him for the position. It wasn't exactly a surprise. "I think you finally found your spot."

He winked at me. "You too."